A Tale of Ashes

Ann Dayleview

A TALE OF ASHES

Book One

Onyx Fire Press

Onyx Fire Press, LLC

ISBN: 978-1-7363705-1-3

Printed in the United States of America

Design by Jessica Pierce

For Felipe,

Who sees wonder in all my stories

CHAPTER I

Freddie

Freddie knew this story would likely get her into trouble, but that's what made it worth covering. Dust tickled her nose as she leaned over the dash of her ancient Toyota, her ears primed for the pulsing beats of a nightclub. Raul sank into the creaking pleather, and Freddie rolled her eyes. Easing off the gas, her knuckles turned white on the steering wheel as they rolled toward three shabby rowhomes and a small army of protesters.

"This is it?" she said.

A two-hour drive from the nearest Fairy border, it was supposed to be Easton's best and most authentic fae club. The perfect setting for an illegal blood sale, a magic trafficking ring, or even a brawl she could spin into a story to land an internship with the *New Wall Inquirer* and secure her entrance into the upper school. But this couldn't be right. She eyed the crowd outside the rowhomes; perhaps the protest could be her back up story.

"Yeah, this is it." Raul leaned forward and sucked in a breath. "Sure you still wanna go? We can turn back. There's a party at my frat and—"

Freddie held up a hand. "This is the only night Pelrin isn't around to keep tabs on me, and I need this story. I'm going with or without you."

With her ever-present ex across the border at a briefing on Fairy's civil war, this was her one chance to celebrate sweet, sweet freedom and finally catch a scoop.

Raul groaned. "Haven't you heard the news? Humans are going missing—all of them students. Like us. Well, like you."

"Not like you, Chupa?" Freddie said, the sides of her eyes crinkling as his flashed yellow in the passing streetlights.

"I told you, that's not short for chupacabra. It means...well, it means something different. Besides, you're avoiding the point. It's not red fae, like me, who are disappearing."

Freddie brushed a curl from her face. "It was only a few people in the South. Easton hasn't been impacted. I'm fine. This is the most boring place in the country. Besides, the police, and the school, have taken precautions." Still, she bit her lip. According to the news, the kidnapper, or 'nappers, were moving north...toward Pennsylvania.

"All they did was put up some fliers and send out that email telling us to stay in groups. Freya—"

"Could be anywhere. She's just one person, Raul. She'll turn up." Freddie risked a glance at her friend—for his sake, at least, she really hoped so. "I could always drop you back off at the house..."

Raul shook his head. "Nah, Pelrin would kill me if I let you go alone."

Freddie grumbled as she neared the club; the shouts of the protesters grew louder, and she could just make out the anti-fae slurs and racist slogans on their signs. Perfect. Her blood heated. She'd make them all infamous. A pinch-faced redhead stood at the crowd's front, shouting into a megaphone. Freddie's body went rigid, recognizing the girl—Mallory Sheppard.

If people had opposites, Mallory would have been Freddie's. Where Mallory was milk-pale with ruler-straight hair and a boney stature, Freddie's skin resembled the color of a chai latte—heavy on the chai. She had coily, black hair that bushed out and down her shoulders and hips her grandmother would lovingly describe as "child-bearing wonders." Their differences continued beyond appearance to their politics, choice in fashion, and choice in friends. Even their rooms were on opposite ends of the same dorm.

"Humans first! Refugees go home!" Mallory shouted into the megaphone.

Freddie grit her teeth and slammed on the brake, making Raul grunt. A faun in a red vest inched around the protesters to tap on the window with a yellow card. Freddie rolled it down, forcing back the rage boiling in her chest.

"Sorry about the commotion, folks." He tensed. His eyes skimmed over her all-too-human appearance. Freddie forced a smile as she pried open a bobby pin with her teeth to re-pin a stray curl back into her high bun. Raul leaned forward and took the ticket, allowing the light from the solitary streetlamp to make his eyes flash yellow—hinting at his fae heritage. The valet's shoulders relaxed. "I'll need your keys," he said.

Freddie's hand jerked, and she yelped. Where the plastic nub at the end of the pin had been, sharp metal now gleamed. She stuck her thumb in her mouth and the metallic tang of blood sent tingles down her tongue. "Sorry," she muttered and fumbled for her keys.

Turning a pale shade of green, the man clopped back a few feet on his goat legs. Frowning, Freddie tossed him her keys and carefully tucked the pin back into her hair, avoiding the keen metal. She stepped out of the car and tugged down her metallic blue skirt. It was a far cry from her usual uniform of blue jeans and red hoodie. Bracing herself for the October chill, Freddie shrugged out of her hoodie and tossed it into the back seat. She stared at the crumpled lump, dreading the evening of pulling down her skirt and readjusting her top. But it wasn't like she could wrap the hoodie around her waist, and paying for the club's coat check was way out of budget. She closed the door and waved to the valet as he drove to the crowded lot.

"Go home, werewolf!" Mallory pointed at Raul.

"I am home, human," Raul said. "I was born here."

A girl on Mallory's left giggled. "Red fae snuck over here from Fairy just like the rest of the fae leeches," she said. "We've had enough of you people claiming you've lived here as long as us. It's called the *Human* Realm for a reason."

3

Raul growled, and Freddie put a hand on his shoulder.

"Send them home!" Mallory chanted; the rest of the crowd took up her cry.

"With birth control!" the giggler said. *She just had to add the double dose of racism.* Raul shot them a dark glare while Freddie trailed half a step behind him toward the center house.

"Stop taking our jobs!" a boy shouted as he passed.

"My parents are business owners. They create jobs, puto!" Raul barked.

"Doubt it," Mallory muttered.

Freddie stopped and turned on her heel to face her rival. "Camping out here 'cause they won't let you in, Mal?" She folded her arms and took a step closer.

"Shut up, you whiney sympathizer." Mallory tossed her fiery braid over her shoulder. "I wouldn't be caught dead inside there. And it's Mallory."

"That sounds like jealousy. You'd better be careful, *Mal*. Red hair and now a greenish tinge, people might start thinking you're a leprechaun." Freddie winked and hurried up the stairs after Raul.

Mallory shrieked curses at her back. The rest of the protesters fell awkwardly silent now that their leader had lost her composure. Taking one last look at the fuming redhead, Freddie snapped a pic with her phone and chased Raul up the remaining steps.

Pulsing bass rose from the porch planks as they approached the middle unit. A bulky man in a too-tight tee stood at the door, his arms crossed over his chest. When he tilted his head to look the two of them over, he revealed a pair of massive horns hiding beneath a broad-brimmed hat. The horns — coupled with the thick silver hoop in his nose — marked him as a minotaur, a magicless brown fae like the faun valet.

"Looks like they're scattering. You guys got IDs?" he said in a heavy rumble.

Freddie had an ID, it just didn't say she was eighteen — only that she was old enough to drive but a year too young to have fun.

Glancing back at the crowd, she shrugged. "I think I forgot

mine in the car. Please don't make me go back and get it." Freddie used the same look on the minotaur as she'd used on Raul to get here—her eyes wide and her lip slightly puckered.

From behind her, Raul sighed. "Are you serious?"

The minotaur scratched his chin. "You *were* pretty bomb back there. I wish we had more folk like you in Fairy."

Freddie grinned. "I want to be a foreign correspondent, so fingers crossed I will be one of those people. Where or how you were born doesn't matter."

"True, true. I'll tell you what, I'll let it slide, but don't forget next time, and no drinking. Okay?" Giving her a pointed look, the brown fae handed her a white wristband.

Raul forked over his ID and the twenty-dollar cover charge for them both. The bouncer gave him a white wristband, too.

"I don't know why you want to be a journalist," Raul said as they entered what once must have been the house's foyer. "You were clearly born to be an actress." He hauled open a wooden door at the end of the small space.

Freddie shrugged and followed him in.

They walked down a flight of concrete stairs into a room doused in bright blue lights; white lounge furniture gleamed around a tightly packed dance floor. The air vibrated with the familiar beats of one of the latest pop remixes. Freddie's eyes widened as she took in the scene before her. At first glance, it appeared like any other club in the Human Realm: colored strobe lights, a sun-glassed DJ, a long glossy bar, but then...

A pale-faced man looked up from the counter. His eyes glowed blood red as they caught the light. *Vampire.* A group of harpies argued loudly from a booth in the corner. Unlike Raul or the bouncer outside, a large amount of magic-wielding green fae mingled throughout the club. Freddie spotted a couple undines, a group of leprechauns, and even several fairies with translucent wings flit across the dancefloor. There were even a few humans, like Freddie, whose eyes didn't glow in the dim light.

No one was disguised or wearing a glamour. It was almost as exciting as being in Fairy, minus the war of course. She took another picture and secured her phone in her wristlet. *I am so out of my realm.*

"Welcome to Illusion, Freddie," Raul shouted over the pulsing beats. "Be careful about the drinks. Remember, it's a fae club and Pelrin would literally kill me if you got drunk and..." He saw her expression and trailed off.

"I know. I can't even get anything." Freddie held up her wristband. Besides, she'd visited the Summer Court plenty of times when she and Pelrin were dating. She was fairly sure she knew which mixers had stronger or magical effects on humans. Raul probably had less experience with fae drinks than she did.

"Be safe, okay? Just don't go too far," he said.

She rolled her eyes. There were plenty of other humans here without babysitters.

Sweat and body heat washed over her as she bounced her way to the middle of the dance floor. Spicy cologne stung her nose, and she whirled around. A blue-skinned young man decorated with glittering gold jewelry surveyed her.

"I hardly expected to see another genie here," he said in an accent she couldn't quite place.

"I'm not a genie." She laughed. Her non-glowing, brown eyes and perfectly ordinary form marked her as human.

"But you must be. I wished you would dance with me, and here we are."

Freddie smirked and twirled closer to the green fae. Soft mist drifted over the floor from a dry ice machine in the corner. A pair of wings, thin as cellophane, brushed against her side as a fairy couple squeezed their way closer to the DJ. The genie spun her out, and Freddie's eyes fell on a handsome fae leaning against the wall. Blue flames twisted and coiled their way down his arms like writhing snakes. He turned. Brushing a stray lock of wavy black hair from his face, he fixed his glowing, amber eyes on Freddie. She shuddered as the genie pulled her close again.

"Are you all right, beautiful?" The gold hoop in his ear glinted as the crowd shifted, blocking the other fae from view.

"Fine," she said.

The song faded into the next. Freddie's eyes wandered again,

6

searching for her next dance partner. At the far end of the sea of bodies, Raul danced with a girl whose long, red hair swept her back. Had Mallory found her way inside? The girl turned, and her emerald eyes glowed bright in the low light. Definitely not Mallory, then. Even from across the room, Freddie could see the dreamy expression on Raul's face. Flowering vines curled around the green-eyed girl's arms and legs, steadily inching their way toward Raul.

"For the love of God," Freddie muttered under her breath. The wood nymph had Raul completely under her spell. If Freddie wanted to save him from getting pranked into making a complete fool of himself, she had to act now.

"'Scuse me." Freddie shimmied away from the genie and through the sea of bodies toward Raul. She creeped her fingers along his waist, tickling his sides. He jerked and spun around. For a moment, he looked from Freddie to the nymph in a wide-eyed haze. The nymph doubled over laughing, tears glittering in her bright eyes. Raul's brow creased.

"Fuck you, Fred!" he shouted over the music. "I knew what I was doing."

"I'm sure."

The nymph cast Freddie a mischievous look. "Don't worry, I wasn't going to do anything to him. Just playing." She giggled.

A dark flush bloomed across Raul's face, but Freddie couldn't help from joining in with the nymph's laughter. He glared at them before slumping off to the bar. Before Freddie could follow, the nymph grabbed her hand.

"It's nice to have a girl's night sometimes. Doncha think?" She pouted her lips, her eyes flashing.

"Sometimes," Freddie said. Her thoughts drifted back to her article as she danced alongside the green fae. There was nothing other than ordinary club happenings here. The story would have to center around the protest. "Did you see those people outside?"

The nymph pulled her lips tight. Her movements became stiff and nearly as unfluid as Freddie's human ones. "Those people have no idea what it's like in Fairy. Someone should toss them over the wall and see how they fare."

"Tell me about it," Freddie said, hoping she actually would.

"My family was lucky enough to escape Autumn before it fell to the Dark Fae Army. It took them years to save up enough money to qualify for my visa."

"Sorry. I'm glad you're here now, though."

The nymph's words would be a great quote. All she needed to do was research a bit more about the visa process, and she'd have at least a halfway decent article she could send to the editor. Giving the young woman a half-smile, Freddie grasped her hand and swayed to the music. As they danced, the nymph's aura pulled at her, enticing her to let go of her inhibitions. She shook her head and continued moving to the flutes and electronic beats of the fusion music. Only those with weak minds would fall under a wood nymph's spell.

As the night wore on, the wonder of the fae club wore off, and Freddie's feet screamed for attention. Pausing to catch her breath, she again met the bright amber gaze of the fae from earlier. He looked to be her age or perhaps a couple years older, though with fae it was hard to tell—he could be well over a hundred. Dark, shoulder-length hair fell over his olive-toned face as his flames flared up, and he turned quickly away. *What kind of fae is he?*

"Let's get a drink." The nymph cut into Freddie's thoughts.

"Ok, sure." Freddie limped behind her. What she wouldn't give for fae stamina. The other girl propped her boobs up on the bar. An auburn-haired vampire appeared before her. He looked down and grinned.

"Two Embraces," she said, holding out two fingers.

Freddie shook her head. "Oh, I can't—"

Before Freddie could hold up her wrist band, the nymph said, "Don't worry, babe. They're free." She gave the bartender a wink, and he licked a gleaming fang. Freddie's gaze followed him as he glided off to the other end of the counter.

She bit the inside of her cheek. The prospect of tasting something new was tempting, but it went against the countless lessons her teachers, her parents, and Pelrin had drilled into her.

Beware of fae food and drink; the word "beware" echoed in her head. Nothing with yarrow, belladonna, agrimony, or angel trumpet. All top shelf mixers, she noted, and he hadn't reached for any of those. Instead, rose hips, refined peppermint oil, mullein syrup, and something purple called moon wine were added into a crystal shaker. The last one was probably what made it alcoholic.

Freddie straightened and pulled her lips into a thin line. She didn't need her ex or anyone else telling her what she could and could not drink. There were other humans here, and they were fine. Besides, even if she did get drunk, Raul would look out for her. In a blink, the vampire set down two shot glasses. The liquid inside faded from a bright fuchsia on the top to a deep purple on the bottom.

"May our night be fruitful," the nymph said, holding up her drink.

"Indeed." Freddie couldn't keep her voice from wavering as she held up her own glass. *Screw it.*

They clinked glasses, and she tipped hers back. Deep scents of fresh cut roses and apricot blossoms assaulted her nose while the tastes of rich, dark chocolate copulated with a salty oyster-like flavor on her tongue. Freddie coughed and set the glass down, grimacing. At least she hadn't spent money on that. She put a hand to her head as a dull buzzing sensation swarmed her mind. An intense wave of heat shot up through her toes, causing her to stumble back.

When she looked up, the nymph was climbing over the bar to wrap herself around the vampire. The green-eyed girl paused for a moment to look over her shoulder and wink at Freddie before shoving her chosen victim into a passionate kiss.

The warmth racing through Freddie's veins intensified. All thoughts of her article swam away like mermaids from a speed boat. A dull ache blossomed across her chest — her heart pounded like a wild animal's. She needed...something. Scanning the crowd, her eyes landed on the flaming fae. He ran a hand through his hair and stared out at the dancers with a hunter's concentration. Her feet, acting of their own accord, moved closer to him. Freddie couldn't help but notice his broad, muscular shoulders and the seductive fullness of his lips. Before she knew what she was doing, her arms were wrapped around his neck. He jerked, stiffening beneath her grasp. Her lips met his. His eyes widened. The pounding ache in her chest soothed as her mouth crushed against his. His lips moved slow and uncertain while his arms hung limp at his sides. She sucked in a breath, pulling him closer. He smelled like the sky just before a rainstorm.

His fingertips brushed against her cheek just as a strong hand jerked her back. The world spun as she was lifted into the air and tossed over someone's shoulder. For a moment she thought she would vomit, but they were moving before her stomach and head were able to reach a decision. There was a bang as the door to the outside flung open. Cool wind brushed against her bare back. Freddie's toes touched down on the pavement where the protesters had been. *Where were her shoes?* Raul's strangely pale face stared at her, his mouth opening and closing wordlessly.

"Can I help you, sir?" a voice squeaked.

Raul turned and growled. The faun valet cringed.

"Get the car!" Raul barked. He shoved the ticket into the faun's chest. The skinny creature clopped off in the direction of the parking lot.

Freddie swayed into Raul's hard-muscled body and breathed in his scent of Old Spice and frat house beer. A screech of tires signaled the arrival of her Corolla. She held her hand outstretched for the keys, but Raul brushed it away. He snatched the keys from the valet as Freddie stumbled around to the passenger's side and tumbled into the seat. Raul slammed on the gas and sped out of the parking lot. Frowning, Freddie was not sure her elderly car could handle such a pace.

"Que carajos estabas pensando?!" he shouted. "I thought I said no drinking!"

"It was just one, and it was with a girl." Freddie's head pulsed. Outside, the streetlights made pretty streaks as they flew past. Freddie hiccupped, a chalky sweetness filling her mouth.

"Yeah, a girl who apparently didn't know you were human

10

and stupid enough to... to..." He was shaking, his face still ghostly white.

"I'm fine. All I did was make out with that hottie." She hiccupped again.

"He was not just some hottie."

Raul swerved onto Main Street. A crowd of drunken upper schoolers stumbled into the street in front of the car, forcing him to slow down. The dashboard clock read eleven forty-eight, a little over two hours before the bars closed.

"He was at least a seven." He'd looked more like a twelve, but factoring in her current state of inebriation, she reasoned seven was probably more accurate.

"He's not a good guy, Fred. You leave him alone!"

Pelrin must really hate this guy if Raul was this upset.

"I'm gonna be a—hic—journalist, you know. I can track down just about anyone."

"I mean it, you can't go after him."

She grinned. "Challenge accepted."

11

CHAPTER 2

Aiden

Aiden's stomach sank as he headed back to the Winter Palace, the ghost of the kiss burning his lips. It wasn't real. The taste of moon wine had been unmistakable, but something inside him ached for her actions to have been genuine. He shook his head to rid it of such nonsense thoughts.

Snow crunching beneath his boots, Aiden made his way toward the three towers of glimmering lights. A gust of wind tore across the frigid wasteland that was the utmost point of Winter. He let out a cloudy breath as the cold bit into his cheeks like spring nettles. Wrapping his hands around his shoulders, Aiden drew his thin leather jacket tight to his body.

It was lucky, for the girl at least, their Majesties had let him recruit alone tonight. The others would probably have wanted to hunt her down, just to see the terror in her eyes when they tore her to pieces. He shuddered as another blast of wind pierced his thin layers.

"Freezing frosts." The sound of Aiden's voice was lost in the windswept tundra, drowned out by the moans and howls of the drekavacs.

Who was she? The thought nagged at the back of his mind. A human at a fae club was only a slight oddity — there were always others — but she had been the only one who'd ever dared approach him. The ripples of magic that rolled off him, even when his flames were out, always made those with lesser magics wary — unless of course they sought to use his power for their own purposes. Perhaps, if his parents were still alive, they could teach him how to dim his aura and appear as other fae...at least in terms of magic. Then humans wouldn't fear him, but he didn't, shouldn't, care about humans, or about who she was. Just some magicked human he'd likely never see again.

A long bridge of ice arched across a black crevasse — bottomless and lined with jagged shards of ice. The bridge's intricately crafted shapes mimicked curling vines in icy hues of blue and white, standing in stark contrast against the barren expanse. And just beyond, the sharp spires of the palace loomed like icicles perched on their end, each stabbing up at the green-streaked sky.

A tug on his jacket snapped him out of his thoughts of the strange girl and the even stranger kiss. He spun, blue flames alight on his arms. A drekavac boy stared up at him with milky blue eyes. He appeared human, but for his soulless eyes, nearly hairless body, and jerky movements. As brown fae, the boy had no magic of his own and was cursed to wander these desolate Winter plains.

"Food, sir?" The words grinded from the boy's mouth like rough stones. Aiden recoiled and surveyed the small creature. A yellowed tunic hung to the boy's knees — his bare feet curled against the snow. Ice crusted on the few wisps of hair dangling to his shoulders.

Shaking his head, Aiden carefully nudged him out of the way. Shards of Aiden's own shattered childhood reflected back at him through the drekavac's cloudy stare. Once, he would have taken pity on the boy, perhaps even snuck him into the warm palace kitchens. Now he couldn't stand even the sight of the tiny figure huddled against the cold.

The boy howled as Aiden continued across the ice bridge. The creature's voice added to the cacophony of moans rising up from the desolate landscape.

Cold stabbed through the soles of his feet like thorns as he drew near the ornately-carved ice doors. A giant with three bearded heads stood guard. Strapped to his back was a wooden shield and a broadsword the height of Aiden's body. A shackle choked the man's ankle, its chain leading off into the shadows of the castle's translucent walls.

"What, not wending in tonight, dog?" Triglav's middle head spat. All three sets of lips curled in disgust. Aiden didn't react. People at court often called him 'dog' and worse.

The once-powerful lord of Winter had betrayed his people to their majesties. Now he had no more power than the lazy swamp dragons the Summer fae kept chained in their yards. Still, Aiden wished he could magically transport himself directly inside the palace and avoid having to deal with the three-headed man.

He squared his shoulders. Even with the heavy weight of exhaustion upon him, he was more than a match for the three-headed giant. "The wards are up. No one is wending."

"Their Majesties didn't make an exception for you?" Triglav grinned.

"Security is more important tonight."

The middle head sniffed, and the man stood aside. Aiden pushed past him and stepped through the ice-crusted gates.

Inside the palace it was as warm and luxurious as the outside was cold and barren. He shook the snow from his dark hair and allowed himself a moment to savor the warmth of the entrance hall. Archways carved in geometric patterns and inlaid with sapphires and diamonds surrounded the open space. Cool blue light glowed from the walls themselves — imbued by the magic of the Winter fae who'd crafted them eons ago.

Drums, fiddles, and flutes made up a raucous rhythm which echoed out from the throne room. Aiden followed the music through the palace taking note of the white-haired frost fairies and red-capped elves darting out of his way as he passed. Only five years ago, these green fae had been free citizens of the Winter Realm. Now they were bound, as he was, in service to their majesties.

The sounds of drunken chatter grew louder. Aiden stepped into a massive ballroom, avoiding the stomping feet of the various brown fae swooping wildly past in an off-beat dance.

One warped, glass pane surrounded the far wall, letting the moon and starlight pour through its rippled veil to cast a ghostly glow onto the frost-covered walls. Overhead hung a chandelier of hundreds of glimmering bubbles. Each bubble contained a shrunken fairy. Some of the captives pounded on the glass while others sat still, resting their chins on their hands and looking out over the dancers below.

Aiden tore his gaze from the prisoners. Wasn't it enough to capture them? They didn't need to display them. A booming laugh shook the room; the candles on the far wall flickered and spit. Fasolt—a frost giant—stood in a cluster of brown fae women. A centaur in a vest of gray fur that looked as if it once belonged to a werewolf leaned against the giant's left side. On his right, a woman, clad only in blue feathers, sipped from an oversized cup of dandelion wine.

"—then I ripped off the wings of the little pixie and it crashed to the ground!" Fasolt let out another laugh. The women around him tittered and drew closer.

"I like nice *pixieses*," said a woman with scraggly brown hair and a nose that reached to her chin. "They makes a tasty treat."

The group giggled again. Aiden hurried past them; their conversation turning his stomach.

Someone ran a hand across his waist, and for a moment, the memory of the human girl flashed through his mind. He blinked. A dark-skinned young woman in a tight black dress leaned in and pressed her lips to his. Aiden jerked away. Pain, like pin pricks down the length of his spine, clawed at his magic. He couldn't afford to lose anything to her. Not tonight.

"What's wrong, Aiden?" Her voice was low and sultry.

"Not tonight, Mare." He ducked around her and continued toward the dais in the center of the room. Like him, Mare was a member of Oberon's special collection of uniquely-gifted soldiers, though she held none of the guilt which plagued his soul from their bloody missions.

She intercepted him. "You haven't come to visit me in so long. I promise I'll be kind."

Mare smiled, her pointed teeth glinting in the fairy-light. Only a short while ago, he had fallen for her charms and followed her back to her suite. There, he'd quickly learned she was just looking to feed off his limited energy. Aiden glared at her. If he could just get through this last part of the evening he could retire to the lower levels and collapse into his bed.

"Leave me be." Just being near her made the slow tingle of exhaustion creep deeper into his bones.

"You'll come to miss me, you know." She pecked him on the cheek and waltzed off into the crowd.

Aiden scowled, shaking off the remaining tingles of her magic. He crossed the room, stopping at the raised dais upon which sat three thrones — two were occupied. The would-be king and queen of Fairy, Oberon and Mab, looked out upon their revel. A pair of curved horns protruded garishly from beneath Oberon's chestnut hair. Mab stroked them, her moon-pale hand tracing a line from horn-tip to forehead. Behind them, standing with arms folded and chest puffed out, was Dek, the third rarity in Oberon's collection. His short, black fur flowed up from the neckline of his loose t-shirt to neatly coat his anubis head. Dek wouldn't have hesitated to attack that human girl. He was quite possibly the last of his kind — his parents murdered over a decade ago to decorate the home of some wealthy human.

Catching sight of Aiden, Dek jerked a nod and stepped down from the dais. His talents as their Majesties' truth seer would not be needed for Aiden's report. After all, his fairy blood prevented him from telling falsehoods.

Mab's golden braids tumbled over one shoulder as she turned to Aiden. He sucked in a breath and sank to one knee, dutifully keeping his gaze fixed on the ground. Mab stuck out her dainty, slippered foot and held it before his face. Suppressing the urge to cringe in disgust, Aiden leaned forward to kiss it. The strong glamour she always wore did little to sway Aiden who knew her to be pure troll. However, ten years with their majesties had taught him well of the perils of suggesting anything other than absolute adoration.

"Rise, my pet," Mab said in a voice as pure and clean as fresh-fallen snow. Her perfectly shaped pink lips curled in a way that accentuated her cold beauty. Lashes thick and black as ebony curtained her shimmering blue gaze. The only flaw in the queen's perfection was her nose, which had grown slightly bulbous and was fading into its original putrid green.

Aiden rose to his feet, face blank, suppressing his hatred of her degrading nickname.

"You were nearly late," Oberon's voice scraped out, gruff as bark. For all his wife's fae beauty, the horns he wore were the only remarkable thing about him. If Aiden had not seen Oberon use magic with his own eyes, he would have suspected the fae king of being human.

"Forgive me, my lord." He bowed low. Nearly late wasn't late—he hoped. Aiden rubbed his arm. Mab was fond of claiming quite literal pounds of flesh for the slightest infraction.

Oberon harrumphed, and Mab placed a hand on his. Her other hand, almost subconsciously, rose to cover her nose as the couple exchanged looks.

Aiden's body remained stiff as ice as he waited for one of them to speak.

Finally, Oberon sighed. "How goes your hunt?"

"More than thirty have joined us freely in the past two weeks, and the new location has yielded five recruits thus far." Aiden clasped his hands behind his back and stared at a spot on the wall just beyond the king's ear. In the past few months, the number of red fae to join the army had suspiciously surged. But the increase in followers had kept their Majesties happy, so he did not voice his concerns about these new followers being less than willing to lay down their lives for their cause. It wasn't worth risking his skin over.

"Good boy! And how many are trained?" Mab clasped her hands together.

"Over a hundred, my lady." Again, he was careful not to react, keeping his eyes down and his answers short.

"You have what you need to make another attempt then?" Oberon leaned forward. "We've yet to feel Summer's retaliation from your last failure."

Aiden's breath hitched; it was the question he'd been dreading. Careful to keep the fear from showing in his face, he answered. "Yes, my lord. The attempt is planned for two weeks from today."

Oberon nodded. "See to it you do not fail me again, or this time I will not be so lenient."

"Yes, my lord." After his last failure, he'd been forced to wear a pair of heated iron boots and dance before the entire court until he'd collapsed from exhaustion—Mab's idea. Even with his rapid fae healing, it had taken three days for his feet to recover enough to walk again. Now a cruel smile played about her lips. Aiden's legs trembled, fighting against the urge to take a step back.

"Let's get on with it, dear," Mab said to her husband. "I'd like to return to our festivities."

"Of course, you are right." Oberon helped Mab from her throne, and together they stepped off the dais, Aiden following behind.

They crunched through hallways coated in thin layers of everlasting frost. Portraits lined the walls, some of them draped in gray silk, others magically warped so their contents appeared dark and twisted. Occasionally, they would stop so Mab might admire her reflection in one of the shining pillars of ice lining the passageway—her nose growing ever fatter and greener as they passed. Aiden's stomach roiled and churned. After seven years of living with their majesties, he had yet to grow accustomed to these nightly rituals.

Oberon pushed open a door leading to a small study. Its only contents were a solitary desk and two plush, red velvet chairs. Mab swept into the room, her silvery gown fluttering out behind her as she sank into one of the chairs.

Mouth dry, Aiden leaned against the wall, trying to appear

bored while Oberon walked around a large wooden desk to a painting of a snow woman. He waved a hand over it, and the picture vanished, revealing a small silver door with a raised knob in the center. Turning the knob left, right, then left again, the door swung open. He reached in and pulled out a worn wooden box. Aiden's heart pounded as his eyes fixed on the small case. Magic flared around Oberon's hand as he pressed his fingers to the lock, and it melted into the wood.

Inside, wrapped in a velvet cloth, glimmered a slim, crystal wand. Aiden pressed his lips firmly together. Reluctantly, he stepped to the center of the room and sank to his knees.

Oberon's lined face was impassive as he walked slowly toward his kneeling subject. Aiden braced himself as the cool tip of the wand touched his forehead. Blue light shot through the wand and snaked up Oberon's arm.

Aiden squeezed his eyes shut. The wand's magic pushed its way inside him, slithering into his memories, his feelings, every part of him. It raked at his core magic. The mental wards he'd built up were torn to shreds as it dragged his power out into the crystal spike. Aiden grit his teeth. The wand's magic felt wrong, as it always did. It left no part of his being untouched. Energy flowed out of him until his bones screamed with pain.

Finally, Oberon withdrew it. Aiden collapsed forward onto his hands, wincing at the sharp agony shooting through his body. He panted and looked up. A shining blue light passed between Mab and Oberon. They gazed lovingly at each other, drinking in Aiden's magic from the wand. The green swelling in Mab's nose dissipated, and she was once more a flawless beauty. Oberon's horns grew large, branching into antlers draped with glittering crystals. The lines that had creased his face were gone. He now stood strong and fit, the image of a man in his early thirties.

"You are dismissed, pet." Mab waved a gold-ringed hand at Aiden.

"I expect to see plans for your next attempt soon." Oberon did not look at him, and Aiden didn't wait for him to say more.

He struggled to his feet and stumbled from the study. The

snickers of the guards and stares of the servants barely phased him as he thudded into his door and collapsed onto the bed in his private room. The old mattress with its black sheets and flattened pillows welcomed him to the place he had called home for the past seven years. Aiden rolled onto his back and stared up at the icicles hanging from the cavernous ceiling. He touched his lips, remembering the fresh-cream sweetness of the human girl's kiss. If not for the magical liquor, she probably would have treated him like all the others — only interested in power or too terrified to come near him.

He sighed. It was no use thinking of things that would never be. Another spell would cost yet more energy, but his muscles hurt too much to roll over. Aiden waved a hand and a book, hidden under his bed, flew up to land beside him. Its pages were warped and yellowed, its cover cracked.

Memories of his parents, and the brief years they'd spent together as a family, washed over him. He rubbed a hand over the silver band hanging on a chain around his neck — it had been his mother's. How different would his life be if they had never been taken from him? An image of their bodies burnt and twisted as the Summer king stepped over them flashed in his mind, and he shoved it back. Some day, perhaps soon, he'd avenge his parents. Now, Mare and Dek were the closest people he had to a family. They, at least, understood what it was like to have one's family ripped away and be forced to grow up under Oberon and Mab's brutal tutelage.

Aiden yawned and opened the book to where he left off. There was a diagram of a human machine called a submarine. His eyelids grew heavy as he traced a finger along the valves and pistons, incoherently muttering their names aloud. Before long the book was splayed across his chest. Tonight, his dreams were filled with levers and gears rather than the lives he'd taken or the destruction he'd yet to bring about.

CHAPTER 3

Freddie

Freddie's temples throbbed. The acid in her stomach pitched and turned to the rhythm of her heartbeat. An ache pulsed across her chest, now that her heart had finally slowed its frantic thumping.

She was never going to drink fae booze again. Hell, she might never drink *anything* alcoholic again.

It had taken a full day for her to sober up and another for her to stop vomiting. With Pelrin away, Raul spent the entire weekend fretting over her. Thank God, Raul had an Econ test today, or he might have followed her to class. She pinched the bridge of her nose — at least Raul was better than Pelrin. The thought of a Pelrin lecture in her current state made her head pound even more.

Freddie's oversized sunglasses dimmed the light filtering in through the classroom's dusty windows. She closed her eyes and pressed her cheek against the cool surface of the desk. The strong scent of whiteboard cleaner made her queasy, but there was nothing left to vomit up.

Pounding footsteps burst through the door and trooped through the rows of desks. Freddie cringed at the sound of screeching sneakers, sliding desks, and incessant chatter. She peeled her eyes open. An undine girl, her blue skin just barely visible beneath her heavy, beige foundation, slid past her to occupy the desk at the end of Freddie's row. Several human students filled in the row in front, while a group of banshee girls, their waist-length gray-black hair clouding out behind them, filled the last five seats at the back of the room.

A shrill scrape against the floor made her head jerk around as someone dragged their desk backward. A girl with a neat, red braid and an outfit made by Country-Clubs-R-Us settled herself in the desk next to Freddie's. *Her again.*

"Mallory," Freddie grumbled.

"Wynifred," she said.

The dark sunglasses hid Freddie's glare. Her full name was like something an old woman in a nursing home would have — not a high school student.

Two sets of footsteps sounded just outside the classroom door. It opened to reveal their teacher, Mr. Barker, a heavy, mustached human who hadn't noticed the 70s had passed. Beside him was a petite woman — made to look even shorter given Mr. Barker's six-foot stature. The woman leaned on a cane of a twisted red and gold wood and stared down the class with her narrow green eyes. Freddie quickly removed her sunglasses and shoved them into her bookbag.

"Professor Radel," she said in a hush.

Mallory tossed her braid over her shoulder. "I don't see what the big deal is," she said, but even she didn't raise her voice. "I bet her reporting class isn't even that hard. It's probably just a bunch of liberal extremists failing when they learn what unbiased journalism is."

Freddie's head ached too much to spit a retort to Mallory's stupid comment. The professor was famous for writing pieces that exposed the harsh discrimination against fae in this realm; Mallory probably hadn't read a single one.

"Mornin', dudes," Mr. Barker said.

There was a groan from the class that could have been interpreted as a "good morning".

"As you can see, I got this fancy prof with me today who's gonna lay down some real dope knowledge on you all."

Professor Radel turned to look at him and raised one eyebrow. "Thank you for that...interesting introduction, Mr. Barker." She continued to stare at him until he took the hint and retreated to one of the vacant first row desks. "At Mr. Barker's request, today I will be lecturing on what it takes to be a *real* journalist and how to identify media bias. Any questions?" Chuck Perrault, a fairy boy, in Freddie's row, raised a limp hand. Professor Radel drummed her fingers on the head of her cane. "Yes, there will be a test, and yes it will count toward your grade." Chuck put his hand down.

A yellow string dangled just over the whiteboard. The professor jumped and caught it, tugging down the ancient projector screen. She turned to scowl at the class, but no one dared laugh.

Striding over to Mr. Barker's desk, she opened her laptop and turned on the projector. The screen came alive with the image of a brunette journalist, flanked by a mousy-haired woman hiding behind an oversized pair of prescription lenses and a fat, balding man who looked as though he were slowly melting into a finely tailored suit.

Freddie instantly recognized both of them. The woman on the right was Karen Deschall, the assistant to the congresswoman from Freddie's parents' district. The man on the left was Richard Fallus, a deeply conservative candidate for the National Senate.

"I expect all of you to watch the anchor and the commentators to identify areas of media bias." She surveyed the class with the scrutiny of a general reviewing her troops before battle. "We will be having an *active* discussion afterward."

"Groovy, right class?" No one bothered replying to Mr. Barker.

Professor Radel started the clip.

"I'm telling you, Donna, they're not good people. They're crossing our border in droves, bringing in dangerous magic. We need our people in the capitol to shut it down. This has become an international problem," the melting man said.

The reporter nodded. "Thank you, Mr. Fallus. I don't think

anyone here disagrees with you. Something needs to be done." The reporter turned to the camera. "We cannot continue to let green and brown fae cross the borders en masse, undocumented and unchecked." She tilted her head to the side, a tactic Freddie had often seen her use to emphasize the seriousness of her words. "Let me hear from you Mrs. Deschall: what do you think should be done about this immigration crisis?"

"Well, Donna, I think we should treat it like what it is—a crisis," the aide replied in a whiny, unassuming voice—the polar opposite of Mr. Fallus's heavy boom. "These people are fleeing a war. We cannot condemn them to death by sending them back. These are not criminals and Dark Fae soldiers crossing the border. These are families. Women and children and—"

"No." Mr. Fallus held up a finger. "You see, this is the problem with you liberals. You let your bleeding hearts blind your judgment."

"Well, we have to—" Mrs. Deschall tried again.

"These are not good people, Karen." Mr. Fallus's neck folds rippled. "The children, you think they are so innocent? They have uncontrollable magic that can destroy entire cities and our way of life. It needs to be stopped."

"Please, Mr. Fallus, let Mrs. Deschall finish her statement," the reporter said.

"Thank you, Donna." Mrs. Deschall let out a small sigh. "As I was saying, we need a procedure put in place that these people can follow to come through as legal refugees."

"And bring the war to us? Great idea, Karen, great idea," Mr. Fallus said. "Look, I would love to help these people, I really would, but we have fae problems of our own. Lupinism is on the rise, and the vampires are taking over Wall Street, again. The last thing we need is more fae causing more problems."

The back and forth between the two pundits continued for the next twenty minutes. Freddie dug her nails into her thighs, carving moon-shaped marks into her skin. A desk over, Mallory bobbed her head enthusiastically, her eyes fixed to the screen.

There was a sharp click, and it went black. The projector

whirred as it powered down.

"Media bias exists whether we like it or not." Professor Radel rose from the teacher's desk. "As journalists, you will have to be able to tell both sides of the story." Her knee-length tartan skirt flared out behind her as she walked toward the rows of desks. "Who will start us off by identifying areas of media bias?"

Mallory waved her hand in the air. Freddie rolled her eyes and instantly regretted it as sharp pain shot through her forehead.

"Karen Deschall was blatantly ignoring the huge risk to all humans by inviting even more fae from across the border to live among us. As Mr. Fallus so wisely stated, it is no secret that we are plagued with fae problems of our own."

She shot a glance at the five banshee girls at the back of the class. Freddie could feel the prickle of their glares on her back as Mallory turned to face the professor.

"I'm afraid you are missing the point, Miss, uh —"

"Sheppard, Mallory Sheppard."

"Miss Sheppard, it is not our job to decide what people should think. We just tell the story and let them make up their own minds." The professor shook her head, allowing her bushy curls to cover her pointed ears.

"It's ok, Melody, I understand," Freddie sneered. "It's not like Fairy welcomed *our* refugees with open arms during World War II or The Middle Eastern Massacre. Oh, wait. Sorry. They did." She tilted her head toward Mallory and folded her hands primly on the desk — a challenge.

Those who had been in classes with the two of them over the past three years fell into a stiff silence. Freddie's hangover evaporated in the heat of her anger as her eyes fixed on Mallory.

"It's Mallory," the girl spat. "And those instances were different. Fae pose a very real threat to humans. We pose no danger to them."

"Sorry about that. I'm, *like*, so forgetful." Freddie forced her voice an octave higher and tossed her head, letting some of her black curls escape their pins. Around her, students suppressed snickers. "I just thought our iron bullets and nuclear weapons were a threat to them. My bad." She pouted. Quiet laughter moved through the classroom. Even Professor Radel appeared as though she were suppressing a smile.

Mallory rolled her eyes. "You know what I mean."

Freddie raised a brow. "I suppose I'm just one of those bleeding hearts who doesn't want to condemn thousands of people to be slaughtered." Around her, the laughter died down. Some of the fae students bowed their heads. "Not to mention what happens if the royals don't defeat the Dark Fae. Who's to say Oberon and Mab won't come after the Human Realm as well?"

"Oh, what would you know?!" Mallory jumped to her feet.

"A lot more than you it seems." Freddie stayed in her seat — arms folded.

"I suppose you would be soft on fae," Mallory said. "Let me guess, your fae boyfriend sneaks into your room each night to fill you in on the news? Oh wait, I forgot. He dumped you."

Ice spilled through Freddie's veins. "I dumped him," she said as though each word was a leaf to her pestle. Mallory knew nothing about the true reason she and Pelrin had split up. And Freddie had no intention of telling her about the joking question and his fairy inability to lie revealing him to be a cheating scum. "You need to stay out of my business, Misty."

Mallory's eye twitched. "It's pretty hard to miss the parade of fae boys you have wandering in and out of your room all night."

Freddie bit back a response to reconsider her words. She'd yet to do any of what Mallory was insinuating. Still...

"You should try getting some, Mal. It might help you to be a less uptight b—"

Professor Radel tapped her cane against the desk, and the class erupted into laughter. Mallory's face flushed scarlet. Freddie smirked.

"Although I'm sure you see personal attacks in the media, let's refrain from using them here, girls," Professor Radel warned.

"Yeah, chicks, that was *no bueno*," Mr. Barker said.

Professor Radel moved to block Mr. Barker from their line of sight. "Since you girls are such avid political commentators, I believe you will have no trouble writing an article on fae-human relations and getting it published by a reputable source before we all leave for the Thanksgiving holiday." Her heels clicked ominously on the linoleum as she picked up a stack of papers from the teacher's desk and handed a sheet to Freddie and Mallory each. "Mr. Barker, might I suggest making this a passing requirement?"

"That is a powerful idea, teach," Mr. Barker said.

Freddie skimmed the document in front of her. It was a scholarship contest from the *New Wall Inquirer*. Any high school senior who planned on studying journalism could earn a full ride to the school of their choice by getting an article published in the *Inquirer* or a paper of equal merit. Her heart rose; this was her chance. *But what if...*

"Mr. Barker, if we don't get our articles published, we'll still pass English, right?" Freddie might still graduate with one failed class, but Advanced English was a prerequisite for Professor Radel's Reporting and Writing next year, and they only offered the standard level of English during the summer. Retaking the class could mean spending an extra semester at the upper school...an extra semester her parents were not about to pay for.

"Sorry, dudettes. You gotta keep a cool head in the media, and you gotta keep a cool head in here."

"But that's not fair!" Mallory shrieked. "How are you even allowed to do this?"

"Life isn't fair, dear, but I'm the one with the tenure," the professor said as she handed out the scholarship announcements to the rest of the class. "Neither is media bias." She chuckled to herself as the bell rang one low, solemn tone. "I suppose that's time."

Freddie's hands shook as she held onto the paper. It would be nearly impossible to get an article published as a nobody high school student. She'd been trying for the past year. At least Mallory's parents would pay for her upper school tuition. An extra semester wouldn't doom *her* to crippling debt. Freddie ran a hand down her face. *Mom and Dad are going to murder me.*

Following the flow of students, she trekked out of the building and into the dreary courtyard. A trickle of students climbed onto the shuttle to the upper school, and Freddie raced to catch it. Leaping on board, she took a seat near the front and leaned her head against the window. As the shuttle pulled away, Freddie watched the red brick buildings slip past. How was she going to fix this mess?

Both New Wall's lower and upper school campuses were built by human and fae architects. The sharp lines and sturdy structures, favored by humans, and the smooth domes and gravity-defying towers, preferred by fae, blended into seamless designs. The gray sky made the red of the human structures and the gleaming blues and greens of the fae accents pop, reminding her of the surreal colors of Elessea, the capital of the Summer Realm. The memory clawed at her heart—there would be no more endless summer days spent strolling the palace grounds or kissing under the drooping palms. She and Pelrin were *not* getting back together.

Ten minutes later, the bus stopped, and Freddie stumbled off into something hard. "Sorry," she muttered—her gaze fixed to the ground.

"You okay, *compa?* I would have thought the effects of that drink would have worn off by now." Raul frowned.

"Raul, hey, sorry," she said. "I was just thinking."

"Mallory got under your skin again?" He shoved her playfully, but Freddie brushed him off.

They headed in the familiar direction of the upper school cafeteria. A group of weregirls passed them. Their eyes flashed yellow as they shot venomous glares at Freddie. Raul stepped in front of her and growled low.

Freddie caught a grumble of "she's not even old enough for him" and scoffed. As the running back of the university's football team, and a member of Alpha Beta Psi, Raul had no shortage of admirers—she was just not among them.

"You'd think they'd get it by now. Especially, after you and Freya went..." she trailed off. Raul's frame went rigid, his features tight. Freddie bit her lip. "Sorry."

"It's fine. Just tell me what happened with you and Mallory." But he no longer looked interested, as though her problems were a mere tool to distract him from thoughts of Freya.

"We got into a stupid argument," Freddie continued hesitantly. "And now we both have to get an article published by a 'reputable' source before Thanksgiving or we fail the class." She looked up at him. "I'm going to fail."

His shoulders relaxed, and he rested a hand on her shoulder. "That's harsh. I thought Mr. Barker was cool," he said, his voice still stiff.

"Yeah, me too."

"I'm sure you got this though. I mean, isn't it what you want to do?"

"I suppose, but it has to be in a big paper, like the *Inquirer*. Only real journalists can get published in something like that. If I had a really good story, I might have a chance, but..." She kicked a pinecone out of her path.

Raul didn't respond. His silence made Freddie glance up, and her stomach dropped. In front of the cafeteria was a poster of a spectacled girl with long, light brown hair. Her skin was pockmarked, and a heart-shaped locket with an embossed 'F' dangled from her neck. Above the photo were large block letters that read MISSING.

"No one has seen her in two weeks." Raul's hand slipped from Freddie's shoulder to clench into a trembling fist.

Freddie had seen Freya's picture on the news the other night. No one was connecting her to the disappearances at the other schools...yet. "Maybe the pre midterm stress got to her. She could be taking a break somewhere." Even as the words left her mouth, Freddie had trouble believing them. October had barely started, and midterms were weeks away.

"Look." Raul pointed to another poster on the bulletin board. A skinny boy with murky green eyes stared back at them.

"Daniel Brown? He must have recently gone missing. Did you know him?" Freddie studied the photo. He looked as though he could be in her year.

"No," Raul said. He squinted up at the poster. "It says he hasn't been seen since Friday." He grit his teeth and tore his eyes away. "This is bad. It's happening here now. Remember I told you about my cousin in San Antonio? There are even more people missing there. He had to leave school because everyone kept blaming and harassing him." Raul shook his head and moved toward the door. Freddie followed after him. "It's like it's been spreading north since June. The police, of course, are blaming us fae, but there's been no hard evidence, yet. It's only a matter of time before they get desperate enough to—"

"Of course! Why didn't I think of it before? This is perfect!" Freddie's eyes widened—the beginnings of an idea tingled in the back of her mind. She gripped his arm, bouncing on the balls of her feet.

"You alright?" He pulled her aside as a minotaur boy and a human tossed a football across their path.

Freddie rubbed her hands together. "But don't you see? That's my story. Biased police harass innocent fae while real killer goes free. If I could break it, find the real culprit instead, I'd be published for sure!" Her mind raced through potential headlines and outlets to target. Maybe she could even be on TV.

"Whoa! Who said anything about a killer?"

They swiped their ID cards and stepped into a large, glass-domed room. The greasy stench of melted cheese and old sausages wafted out to meet them. An onslaught of loud chatter and clattering trays forced the pair to halt their conversation.

Freddie marched over to the waffle maker and coated the iron with non-stick spray. The lower school cafeteria didn't have one of these beauties. It was well worth the shuttle trip up here to get her daily fix.

Raul drifted off to the deli counter to order his usual hoagie. Food in hand, they shuffled off to their table.

"Won't it be pretty dangerous, investigating those disappearances?" Raul asked. "I mean, no one has been found yet." He took a bite of the sandwich. Freddie stared, dumbfounded, as a quarter of it vanished into his mouth. She blinked and shook her head.

"Maybe." She shrugged. "I mean, if I could actually find out who's behind it before the other media outlets, it'd be worth it though."

He chewed thoughtfully. Swallowing hard, Raul took a long swig of Pepsi. "I don't like this idea, Fred. That's what the police are for." He belched.

"Of course, of course." She waved one hand while pouring syrup with the other. "I will be working with the police. They'll solve the case. I'll just be critiquing their process." *And giving them helpful nudges.*

He sighed and shook his head. "Just be careful, all right?"

Freddie beamed at him. "Aren't I always?"

CHAPTER 4

Aldon

CHAPTER 4

Aiden

A chill slithered down Aiden's spine as he marched through the tufts of brownish gray grass that covered the Tenger Plains. Clouds, pregnant with rain, blotted out the sun and filled the air with their damp scent. The only break in the seemingly endless gray expanse was a squat, yellow-domed building a short way off in the distance.

White patterns on its surface in the form of leaves, naked trees, and a horn-of-plenty marked it as a meditation hall for the people of the Autumn Realm. However, there were no people in sight, no birds cawed overhead, even the wind barely disturbed the gray grass. Black skeletal ruins covered in scattered ash marked where a small village once stood.

Aiden made his way through the abandoned town. Scents of burning wood and the screams of villagers flooded his senses, pushing his flames against his skin. He hurried across the barren stretch and yanked open the wooden door to the hall. It creaked softly on rusted hinges. The heavily-incensed room dulled the assault on his senses, filling him with a forced sense of calm. Still, memories from his last visit to this realm chewed at the back of his mind and settled in the pit of his stomach.

Something moved just out of his line of sight. Aiden walked toward the center of the room. The bamboo flooring moaned as he knelt and faced the star painted on the floor of the round chamber.

"If you show yourself now, I will consider letting you live." He sighed and looked down at his folded hands. The ripple of magic that usually preceded strong spells was absent—only the soft rustling of a small creature moving across the floor alerted him to another's presence.

"Forgive it, sir. It meant no offense." A creature no larger than two feet tall and covered from head to toe in dark brown hair bowed low.

"You're a domovoi," Aiden said. The words were choked out of him as he stared at the Autumn Realm creature. "You shouldn't be here," he said to himself. All the Autumn fae had been marched off to work with the other conquered in the Winter Realm. Somehow, this one must have escaped the recruitment force.

"Would it be able to get you some tea, sir?" The small creature trembled violently.

Aiden's jaw tightened. "No." He had already taken enough from these people. "My companions will be arriving soon, and they are not so accepting of your kind. I suggest you make yourself scarce."

"But sir, it is its duty to serve." The furry creature bowed again.

"Take my advice or leave it. It matters not to me." Aiden looked up, allowing the light to illuminate his eyes. The brown fae gasped.

"Y-you're the—" He pointed at Aiden's face, no doubt recognizing his rare flame-colored eyes.

"Yes, I am," Aiden said. "Now if you wish to live a long and relatively safe life, I suggest you leave."

The creature dashed through the door; it closed behind him with a loud smack. Aiden let out a breath and closed his eyes in an attempt to center his mind before the cursed meeting. The hairs on the back of his neck tingled as the memory of the girl crept back into his thoughts. *Why can't I get her out of my head?* It wasn't as though he'd never kissed anyone before. There were a couple women in their majesties' court with whom he had done much more than kiss. Like her, they had been beautiful, too.

He craned his neck up to the ceiling. Perhaps there had been something in that drink which made her linger like this.

Behind him, the door slammed open. Dek and a slender young woman with short-cropped blonde hair entered, arguing loudly. Aiden massaged his temples.

"You wouldn't know intelligence if it jumped right into one of your oversized ears!" The girl, Irina, spat on the ground just before the anubis's feet.

"What do you know about intelligence? You don't have to be clever to run around naked and howl at the moon!" A muscle in Dek's neck twitched. "Though I wouldn't mind watching."

"Why you—" She snarled, narrowing her ice-blue eyes. Her thick, black liner made her glare even fiercer.

Dek growled. His lips pulled back to reveal his sharp fangs, ears flicked back.

"Would you two mind stopping for a moment? Some of us have places to be after this." An auburn-haired vampire, his form frozen in that of a gangly teenager's, walked noiselessly across the floor. He swept into a graceful cross-legged position in front of Aiden. Irina turned her glare on him, but her growl softened.

Dek fell silent and took a seat next to Aiden. "Sorry," he grunted.

Aiden nodded at Dek then turned to the vampire. "I'm surprised you're here so early, Emerick. The sun's barely set."

"What can I say? I'm an early riser." He yawned, revealing his needle-sharp fangs.

At least Emerick was putting in effort this time. Since their last failed attempt, he and Irina had stepped up in their efforts to bring in new recruits. But Dek's job in training them had grown increasingly harder as the new red fae had such lackluster attitudes. Still, if Emerick put the same amount of determination into their current mission, maybe there was hope they'd succeed.

Oberon's threat still hung-over Aiden like a cloud of hornets; they needed a plan to steal the Summer king's crown, and fast.

"Figured out a plan yet?" Emerick jerked his chin at Aiden. Irina sunk next to Emerick and leaned in.

Aiden sucked in a breath. "That's what we're here to discuss. I'm not the only one who can—" He stopped. Wisps of black shadow raced along the walls and swirled in the center of the room to form the figure of a young woman—Mare. He rolled his eyes. "Thank you for joining us, Mare."

"Of course, darling." She winked at him. Her black leather jumpsuit clung to her body like paint. Aiden turned away as she made an exaggerated effort of bending over before taking a seat between him and Irina.

Aiden scooted away from her. Ever since they were children, Mare had been all over him, prodding and pulling at his energy.

Once everyone had fallen silent, all eyes turned to him. "Their Majesties' patience is running thin. The longer we take to get the crown, the more displeased they become."

"I'll say," Mare said. "They actually asked me to spy on you." She inched closer to Aiden. Her shadows pulled at his energy. "They wanted to know if you were getting soft-hearted toward these Summertons." She paused looking around the room. "I told them you would have to have a heart in order for it to soften." She laughed but no one joined in. "Oh, you fighting grunts are so blasé."

"Not all of us have the luxury of being one of their Majesties' special little pets," Irina said. "Emerick and I have only had a year to prove ourselves worthy of being in this little club."

Dek flexed his sizable biceps. "Our favor at court is dependent on actions, just like yours, Irina." His voice was harsh as though he were biting each word before setting it free.

"Besides, spying isn't all it's cracked up to be. Sometimes you have to get down and dirty to get the intel you need." Mare grinned. "Though I suppose that wouldn't bother you much."

Irina opened her mouth, but Aiden cut her off. "Our focus tonight needs to be on capturing the crown. Without it, we won't have a chance against the Summer fae."

He knew well the strength of the crown's magic, and would let the entire Dark Fae Army burn to ash before he gave up capturing it.

"Mare." Aiden moved away from her again, pressing close against Dek, who frowned. "What's the new security like?"

"Oh, it's dense." Her callous smirk sobered and she tossed her long black ponytail over her shoulder. "They moved the crown from the palace in Elessea to the fort in Shell Bay. The magic on the wards is the prince's — gold fae power. Practically impenetrable. Not to mention they have about fifty of their finest guarding the place."

Aiden traced the wood grain with his finger. The prince's wards would pose a problem. Even on their best days, none of his people could take on that pompous ass and walk away unscathed. And he didn't dare trust the actual stealing of the crown to any of them. What he needed was to split himself in two.

"Why don't you take on the prince, Aiden? We all can figure out how to get past the guards and steal the crown," Irina said. Her tone carried notes of suppressed smugness.

"Ah yes. An anubis, werewolf, and a vampire, will have no problem getting through the fifty magic-using guards. I'd rather take my chances in the Nightmare Plains than steal the crown with you lot." Mare clicked the toes of her high-heeled boots together. Irina sniffed.

"Weren't you born on the Nightmare Plains?" Aiden cast her a sidelong look.

"Yes. I know more than the rest of you about the horrors it holds." Her face grew solemn, and Aiden regretted asking. If Mare's past was anything like his, it was no wonder she rarely spoke of it — both the good and bad memories left bitter scars.

Emerick snickered. "We need to find a way to draw the prince away and drain his power." He rubbed his palm against his chin. "Although rumor has it the prince only uses magic to wend. He doesn't even use the most basic spells."

"Maybe the prince is a weakling. He probably had Mommy

and Daddy cast the wards. Doesn't know how to use his own magic." Dek's laugh rumbled up through his chest.

"He knows how to use magic." Aiden locked his jaw. "Mare, aren't power drains your specialty?" The wisps of her power that had been tugging at his energy drew back.

Mare lifted her chin. "Maybe I could make a dent, but that's a lot of magic, even for me." Aiden shot her a dark look. "Oh please, you're half dead anyways when I see you."

Emerick and Irina raised their eyebrows while Dek let out a choked snort. Aiden sighed. They were going around in circles. At this rate, it would be just like last time: a mad dash for the crown and hope they were strong enough to get through the wards. This time, they *had* to be smart. He did not want to know the meaning of Oberon's "less than lenient" punishment.

"We could draw him into a trap. Hold him while you get the crown," Irina said and looked around the room.

"And how exactly do you think the four of us could hold the Prince of Summer?" Dek's lips curled into a sneer.

"We could get help—" Irina began.

"No one is to know about this besides us," Aiden said. Irina shot a glare at him while the other three fell silent.

Finally, Mare let out a musical laugh and leaned back on her hands. "Well, he'd recognize me, but if we want to attract him, Aiden could do it. One look at those pretty blue flames, and the prince would come running. Gives me the tingles just thinking about it." She shivered.

"Keep it in your pants, Mare," Irina said.

Something in Mare's comment reminded Aiden of a passage he'd read once in one of his human magic books. "Humans have a way of conjuring artificial blue flames. If we could use them somehow..." He trailed off. "But we would still need more people to distract him. At least long enough for me to get inside and disable the wards."

Dek frowned. "We have some new recruits that might be up for causing a little havok, at least. Maybe Irina could lead a pack of weres." He flicked an ear, his frown deepening, then jerked his chin at Aiden. "If we made it look like you were attacking some important human place — I mean it won't be directed at the prince, but if he's hunting you and saving his precious humans... It could work, right?"

Aiden nodded slowly, the plan coming together in his head. "Mare, you could follow him — discreetly of course."

"You know that's not my style." Mare pulled her ponytail back over her shoulder and looked pointedly at Aiden.

"Aren't you supposed to be a spy?" Emerick licked his fang as he watched her fidget.

Mare glared back at him. "Fine. Follow him and do what?"

"Drain his energy," Aiden said. "Bit by bit, as he's fighting. It'll weaken the wards, and he'll think it's the battle. By the time he realizes he was chasing wisps, it will be too late." Aiden nearly smiled.

"You lure him out with a big, blue fire, then Mare can drain him. Once he's weak enough, Irina can distract the guards at the fort, I can meet her in the city with the recruits, and you can break in and steal the crown. It's foolproof!" Dek folded his arms, a look of triumph across his dog-like face. "Not a bad plan, eh 'Rina?"

She scoffed. "That has yet to be seen."

"We just need to find a place to set the fire that will get attention but is not too full of humans," Aiden said.

"Why not too full of humans?" Dek cocked his head to the side. The others stared at Aiden with similar expressions of confusion.

The idea of harming humans gnawed at something deep in the core of his being. He'd slipped; the others wouldn't understand or care about a few human deaths, and they would see his feelings as a sign of weakness. "We shouldn't spread ourselves too thin," he said hurriedly. "If the humans fight back."

Dek flexed. "I'd like to see them try. Besides, the more humans we attack, the more distracted the prince will be. We can keep him running all over the Human Realm while Mare drains him good."

"That's perfect!" Irina said. "Mare, you think you can suck him dry in a few days?"

Mare inspected her nails. "I'm not a vampire. No offense,

Emerick." He tensed. "I don't *suck* energy. And it will probably take at least a week for me to drain someone as powerful as the prince enough to make a dent in those wards."

Aiden ground his teeth. They could do a lot of damage to the humans in a week. But if Mare needed the time, he didn't have any other option.

"Mare's draining the prince, Dek and Irina are distracting the guards at the fort, and where exactly do I fit into all of this?" Emerick folded his arms and frowned at Aiden.

"You can help me take out the lodestones at Shell Bay. It'll make it easier for Dek and Irina to get the pack into the city." Aiden curled his fingers into fists. *What difference would a few more lives on his conscious make?* The prospect burrowed into his soul, adding to the festering pain and dread settling there whenever he thought of his murderous missions.

Emerick let his arms drop. "It'll be like a recruiting mission. Just you and me." He huffed a laugh. Irina shot him a meaningful look.

"Yes. We'll need to remove as many of their defenses as possible. Then, once the prince is drained, you and everyone but Mare can cause chaos in the city to distract the guards," Aiden said.

Around the room, everyone was grinning and laughing— excited over the prospect of terrorizing the human and fae innocents.

He clenched his teeth so hard his jaw ached. Experience had taught him that once the group decided on a plan—one that would work, no doubt—it was best not to argue. Especially not for the sake of humans. Not even Dek would back him up to save them. Mare would tell their Majesties, he'd be compelled to go through with it anyway, and they'd punish him for arguing.

Aiden pushed himself to his feet. "So be it."

CHAPTER 5

Freddie

During the weekdays, Easton was a quiet little town. Freddie walked past the charming storefronts lining Main Street. The ornate window displays held everything from unique—and in some cases magical—tattoos to the pig figurines the town was famous for. In the spring, tourists would pack into hotels and student-rented dorm rooms to attend the town's annual bacon festival. If there was one thing that brought both fae and humans together, it was bacon.

With the first kisses of chill in the air, The New Fae Library would likely have started selling their fresh apple cider. Freddie could practically taste it. However, as she rounded the last corner, a small crowd gathered in front of the building made her stop dead.

A white news van, with the channel five logo painted on its side, was half hidden among the group of people gathered around the café. Freddie sniffed the air. The last time a crowd had gathered here, it was because the local news was doing a feature on the best desserts in Easton. She hurried to the other side of the street, wondering if there would be free samples of the s'mores brownies or apple crumble like last time.

A middle-aged woman in a bright red sweater and black

pencil skirt stood in front of the café. She held a large microphone and stared into a camera.

"Cathleen Donovan here, for Channel Five News. As you can see, we have quite a crowd gathered in front of the New Fae Library. Everyone is clamoring for answers around what happened to poor Freya Park, a freshman upper schooler and the first student to go missing from the New Wall School." A look of practiced solemnity fell across her perfectly made-up features.

Freddie pushed her way to the front of the crowd to get a better view of the journalist. Most of the other people were more interested in the presence of a news van than the café. Several students, however, peered through the large glass window to the owner, an anxious looking dwarf woman, who stared back at the crowd.

"Just two weeks ago," the reporter went on, "the unfortunate Freya Park came here to get a pumpkin spice latte and was never seen again. There have been allegations that the owner, a brown fae woman, may have some connection to what happened to the girl."

Freddie frowned. This was almost as bad as watching that wrinkled candle, Richard Fallus, blab about the "fae threat." She slipped out her phone; on the off chance this reporter did uncover something interesting Freddie could revisit later. The reporter's hand shot out and gripped one of the passing students by the handle of his backpack. He stumbled, bewildered, and yanked out his earbuds.

"Tell me, young man, do you feel safe walking the streets of Easton with all these disappearances?"

"Look, lady, I'm just trying to get to class." He struggled to free himself from the reporter's grasp, but she held him firm.

"The students here at NWS are clearly traumatized by what is happening on their campus. They can barely even speak about it. If you have any information at all, please call the Easton Police Department at 555-258-7171. Now back to you, Trent." She scowled at the student and shoved him away. Her false sincerity slipped away as she stomped back to the van with mutters of "feel like I'm making up the news" and "there's nothing here." Freddie couldn't help but agree with her.

With the absence of the journalist, the crowd dispersed. Freddie slipped between the last lingering people toward the café. Maybe the owner really did know something about the disappearances or could at least point her in the right direction. The local news didn't seem to be any better informed than she was.

The bell jingled as she pushed open the door. Freddie breathed in the scents of fresh danishes and espresso. A woman with short, cropped, blond hair, and raccoon-black eyeliner leaned over the counter.

"I was just in here a week ago, and you had peanut butter scones, and now you tell me you don't have them?" The woman snarled. Her head snapped around as Freddie got in line behind her, cold blue eyes glaring before turning back to the counter.

"Look lady, we change our flavors every day. I don't even have peanut butter to make them if I wanted to—which I don't." Berta, the café's three-and-a-half-foot tall dwarf owner, put her hands on her hips.

"Filthy halfling, you should treat your customers better!"

"I don't need customers like you. Get out!" Berta pointed to the door.

The woman growled low. Her shoulder rammed into Freddie's as she marched out of the café—the little bell jingling madly.

"Hello, Berta. Sounds like you're having a day," Freddie said.

The dwarf woman jumped, nearly tumbling off her stool. "Uh—yes, hello dear. Sorry about that, first the reporter, then that crazy." She carefully stepped down from the stool. "An apple cider?"

"Yup." Freddie swung her backpack around to dig out her wallet. "It's weird all those disappearances though, huh?"

"That's one way of putting it," Berta grumbled as she heaved a jug of her homemade cider from the fridge and poured it into a pot on the stove. "It's not like that girl was dragged out of here. This was just the last place she was seen."

"Do you know where she actually disappeared from?"

"No idea." Berta sighed. Steam rose up from the cider as she stirred, filling the café-bookshop with a spicy sweetness that made Freddie's mouth water. "Somewhere between here and the football field is what I heard." She poured the hot cider into a cup and fitted the white lid on top.

Freddie stretched out her hands and bounced eagerly as Berta returned to the counter. "That reporter seemed to think you were involved somehow." She passed Berta her credit card, mentally subtracting the cost of the cider from her monthly food allotment.

Berta swiped it and shook her head. "They always blame us fae. I mean, I'm a brownie—what am I going to do?" She tugged on her braided beard. Freddie cringed at the use of the derogatory word for brown fae. "We left Fairy because of the greenies' oppression, only to get blamed left and right for everything here. The other boy vanished after visiting Stella's place, Charm City. They've been harassing her, too, and she only drinks animal blood—doesn't even buy from the hospital blood banks. Maybe Oberon and Mab have it right. It's time for a change." She wiped vigorously at the counter with a rag as though it could clear away the hurt of the past few weeks.

Freddie pressed the cider to her chest. Its warmth was comforting amidst the rather disturbing turn Berta's tirade was taking. Putting the hot liquid to her lips, Freddie resisted the urge to launch into a debate on why Oberon and Mab were bad news for fae and humans alike.

"So you didn't notice anything unusual that day?" she said.

"Like I told the police, there are so many people coming in and out of here every day I hardly notice the new faces," she said. "What is this anyway? An interrogation?"

Freddie shrugged. "You know me, Berta. Just curious."

"Well, you keep your big nose out of this, Freddie Jones." She waggled her stubby, ringed finger at Freddie before turning to clean the espresso machine. "It's not fae folk that are going missing. It's nosy humans like you."

"I'll be careful," Freddie said and took a step toward the door.

"Thanks for the cider. See you next time!"

She waved and left the café, stepping back into the crisp, fall air. The uneven pavement made the heels of Freddie's boots wobble as she headed back to her dorm. Berta had not been as helpful as Freddie hoped. Perhaps the other woman, Stella, noticed something Berta had not. Freddie made a note to stop by Charm City to find out.

❦

The rest of the week flew by in a flurry of homework, projects, and exams. A follow-up meeting with Mr. Barker proved useless, as he refused to budge on Profesor Radel's impossible assignment.

Freddie wasn't the only one drowning in class work; she'd spent way too much time fending off Raul's pleas for her to look over his essays for English. Freddie's other friend, Amanda, was able to take care of herself. Even if she did spend her days holed up in the upper school's science lab.

When class finally let out on Friday, Freddie darted to the shuttle and ran across the upper school campus to meet them for lunch. It felt like years since she'd seen anyone who wasn't in class with her. The bulletin board outside the cafeteria still had the posters of Freya and Daniel. At least no one had gone missing this week. Freddie's heart stuttered as she hurried past their frozen stares toward the waffle station. Neither she nor any of the news outlets had any leads on what happened to them. And if the police had found anything, they were tight lipped. Today, after school, she had to interview Stella. Maybe then Freddie could find *something*.

Waffle in hand, Freddie made her way over to their usual table. It wasn't long before Amanda skipped over with Raul trailing behind and set down her tray. Freddie curled her lip at its contents: a peanut butter and jelly sandwich, a handful of baby carrots, and an apple juice box.

"You eat like a toddler," Freddie said.

"Glass houses, Freddie," Amanda replied. "At least I eat more than just waffles. You really should vary your diet; you're going to get sick."

"Yeah, you two should be more like me," Raul said. "All the food groups in one adult-sized hoagie." He tore into the sandwich with a loud chomp. Amanda and Freddie exchanged looks and shook their heads.

"Movie night at my place tonight?" Freddie asked. Watching Raul eat made her queasy, but it was like a roadside accident — she couldn't look away.

He nodded emphatically.

After taking a sip of her juice box, Amanda said, "As long as Pelrin doesn't get to pick the movie again. I used to like *Titanic* before he made us watch it twenty times."

"I'm sick of it too, but you know it's a hint, right, Freddie?" Raul chuckled, and Freddie shot him a glare.

"Oh yeah, I got the message." She carved into her waffle, purposefully scraping the fork against the plate to make Raul flinch. He yelped and rolled back his upper lip, baring his fangs. "If watching the most popular romance movie ever made wasn't hint enough, all the elbowing and him constantly saying 'You see that? He's never letting go of her, never' really drove home the point."

Amanda shook her head. "Do we have to invite him?"

Raul nearly choked on his bite and took a sip of his Pepsi.

"I don't know. Ask your boyfriend. Jefferson can't keep anything from you-know-who. Besides, I thought they were going over battle plans." Freddie took another bite of her waffle and closed her eyes. Waffles were one spot of goodness that her post-break up blues could not, and would not, darken.

"Oh, come on, Fred. Pelrin can be a prick, but he's not some dark wizard," Raul said.

"He doesn't barge in on *you* when you say his name." She pointed her fork at Raul. He threw up his hands and sighed.

"I'll tell Jefferson when he wakes up tonight," Amanda said. "He won't have time to fly to Fairy and invite Pel — uh, you-know-who."

"Thanks, buddy." Freddie stole a baby carrot from Amanda's plate, swirled it in syrup, and popped it in her mouth. Each time

Pelrin wended in, Freddie's heart gave a familiar tug, and it took everything in her not to forgive him and go back to the way things were. But he didn't deserve forgiveness.

After lunch, Raul split from the others and headed to Alpha house to get in a few extra hours of studying. Amanda followed Freddie back to the lower school dorms. They took the long way, cutting down Main Street. Freya and Daniel's faces still nagged at the back of Freddie's mind—she needed to speak to Stella. There were only six weeks until Thanksgiving, and she didn't need her entire family knowing she failed English.

Charm City was situated at the far end of Main Street. Students often went there to purchase charmed gag gifts or other more kinky items. The outside of the gray stone building was flat without so much as a hint of decoration and the words "Townsend and Lee Attorneys at Law" printed in gold lettering on the door. A black, painted, wood railing led down a flight of steps; on it hung a large black and pink sign that read Charm City. Freddie flashed Amanda a mischievous grin.

"Freddie, you know I don't like these kinds of places," Amanda said. She took a step closer to her friend and tugged her away from the stairs.

"You can wait out here if you want. My grade, and future financial stability, depend on this." Freddie rested one hand on the railing and took the first step down.

Amanda bit her lip. "Fine. Let's do this. But I'm not doing it for you. My mom is friends with Freya's aunt. I want to help find her, too."

Freddie squeezed Amanda's hand as she pulled her down the remaining steps and pushed open the glass door. The inside was decorated as if a Halloween store and a sex shop had a baby. The walls were black with fake cobwebs stretched across the corners. A smoke machine blew a weak billowing mist along the floor, and a cage of fat, black rats sat on the counter. Amanda grasped Freddie's arm. Erotic books lined the shelves, some of their covers worn and cracked. Freddie moved toward the counter, passing an aisle filled with charmed, goth accessories: a choker hung with a blinking eyeball, a set of bickering vinyl keychains, and other items that made Freddie wish she had the money to splurge.

Amanda whimpered. "This place is so unnatural."

Freddie grinned. "So, you can date a vampire, but the occult is unnatural?"

"Science," Amanda said, "can explain things like how lupinism changes the blood and how vampire venom freezes certain cells. Red fae will eventually have the option of returning to their human selves because of science, not witchcraft."

Freddie rolled her eyes.

A woman with wavy black hair and bright orange lipstick drifted through the opalescent black-beaded curtain that separated the gift shop from the over-eighteen part of the store. "May I help you ladies find something?"

Amanda's grip tightened on Freddie's arm as the woman moved closer.

"Yes." Freddie cleared her throat to rid it of the nervous tremor. "We are looking for the owner, Stella."

"I am she." The woman swept over to the counter in a movement too graceful to be human. She leaned forward to uncage one of the rats, her too-tight black tank top squeezing her ginormous bosom. As she straightened, a lock of hair shifted to reveal the point of a tiny black horn. Freddie shook Amanda off and stepped closer.

"Hi. I'm Freddie, and this is my friend, Amanda." She held out her hand and had to fight the urge to flinch away from the woman's burning touch. "I'm writing an article on the disappearances for a class, and I was hoping you could share a bit of your experience with me."

The creamy white skin on the woman's forehead creased. "I have already answered multiple questions from the police and the media," she said. "I don't even drink human blood. Why would I kill the boy? I love men — and women." Freddie shifted under the woman's intense gaze. *Not helpful.*

She suppressed her frustration and tried a more sympathetic tactic. "People have been accusing you of killing him?" she asked —

eyes wide, feigning shock.

"Of course they have!" The rat let out a squeak as Stella threw an arm in the air. She lowered it and cooed over the tiny creature.

"People think because I'm a succubus I am some kind of man-killing machine." She settled herself on a stool and stroked the rat with two fingers. "They've already searched my home and my shop, twice."

"We're not blaming you," Freddie said. Amanda let out a breath that sounded suspiciously like 'speak for yourself.' Freddie stepped on her friend's foot, causing her to yelp. "I just want to know more about the boy who went missing."

"Daniel? Well, there's not much to tell. He was a regular, came in here all the time."

Freddie shoved down the judgment that attempted to push her lips into a smirk at the thought of doe-eyed Daniel being a regular. "What happened that day he disappeared? Anything out of the ordinary?"

In class, they had been taught to ask open ended questions when interviewing. Hopefully, it would encourage Stella to give her the answers she needed.

Stella glanced over her shoulder at the beaded curtain. "He was in here. Acting perfectly normal. Just came in, bought a book, and left." She patted the rat on the head and slipped it back into the cage.

"What book?" Amanda tilted her head to the side. Freddie blinked, startled by her friend's sudden interest.

Stella glanced at the beaded curtain and drummed her long nails on the wooden surface. *"Alchemists and Apothecaries* by Antonio Fulcanelli," she said. "Is that important?"

Amanda shrugged.

"Did anything else happen that day? Maybe not related to Daniel."

Stella shook her head. "The day was pretty normal. I mean, there were the regulars and the novelty shoppers. No one seemed particularly out of place: a group of lower schoolers tried to sneak into the back, a vampire thought he could buy blood here, and an old man was searching for a spell to conjure his dead wife's spirit."

Freddie nodded. Beside her, Amanda shuddered. There was no use in making Amanda suffer if there was nothing here. "Thanks for your time, Stella."

The succubus's lips parted, revealing perfectly white teeth. Amanda bolted for the stairs. Freddie followed, turning to give Stella an apologetic shrug.

Once they were back in the daylight, Amanda let out a breath. "Let's not do that again. That lady was a straight-up creep."

"She seemed perfectly normal to me. Since when did you start having a problem with red fae?" Freddie raised an eyebrow.

"I don't have a problem with fae," Amanda snapped. "I have a problem with creepy creeps who own creepy shops and have creepy pet rats!"

"The rat was your issue?"

"It was looking right at me!"

Freddie sighed and led the way back to the dorms. "Well, she wasn't really helpful anyways. I mean she knew as much as Berta. That Daniel kid just stopped in her store before he was never seen again."

"Well..." Amanda began and trailed off.

Freddie stopped. "What do you know?"

"Not that I'm saying we should go back there and question her. It's just when she told you about what happened the day Daniel disappeared, I'm like ninety-eight percent sure she was lying." Amanda cringed as though Freddie were about to drag her back into the shop.

"What? How do you know?"

"People always look up and to the left when they lie," she said. "You know, with what you want to do, it wouldn't hurt for you to take a class in neuroscience."

"Maybe... So what should I do next time I see her? Any science-y tips on how I can trip her up?"

"Just ask her about the book. She lied; I bet she'll have forgotten which one she said."

Freddie grinned back at her. "I knew there was a reason we

were besties!"

CHAPTER 6

Freddie

Freddie and Amanda trooped across the Bailey, the concrete courtyard between the two lower school dorms. Raul sat on one of the stone tables, his legs bouncing eagerly as he stared up at the waxing moon. He'd changed from the button-down and cargo shorts from earlier to some well-worn sweats.

"Where were you guys? I thought you came back here after lunch," he said. "I've been waiting."

"You should've texted," Amanda said. She pulled out her phone while Freddie dug in her bookbag for her fob and keys.

"Naw, my phone's dead." Raul shrugged. "But seriously, I was getting worried."

"We interviewed the owner of Charm City," Freddie said. She scanned the fob and led them upstairs.

Raul snickered. "You guys went to Charm City? I'd have liked to see that."

Amanda glared.

The RA, a fairy named Nyx, saluted as they passed.

"We'd never get away with this in my building," Amanda said, nudging Freddie in the side.

"How cute." Raul reached for Amanda's cheek, but she

slapped him away. "You lower-schoolers are coddled like babies."

"Careful, Raul. You're hanging in a *wittle* lower-schooler's room tonight. And she can still kick you out," Freddie said.

He threw up his hands. "All right, all right, I'm sorry."

They reached the end of the hall, and Amanda cursed. Freddie looked up to see her friend pointing at a large wooden cross tacked onto Mallory's door. *She* would *be that brazen*.

"I'll tell Jefferson to come through the window." Amanda pointed a finger at Freddie. "What did you do to her now?"

Freddie threw her hands up. "Nothing new, I swear! Just the fight last week." She opened the door to her cramped dorm. A solitary twin bed sat in the center of the room with a loveseat pushed against it, leaving just enough space for a small table and TV set.

"That Mallory is a piece of work." Raul pushed through the door and dove over the bed to the mini fridge, pulling out the six-pack of Pepsi he'd stashed there. "You know who else is a piece of work? That Charm City lady. She's hot, in like a kill-you-in-your-sleep kinda way."

"'Cause that's a way to be hot," Amanda muttered under her breath. She flopped backward onto Freddie's bed.

"Aw, come on, you know what I mean. My cousin, Marisol, hooked up with her once. Stella taught her how to use all those creepy spells and charms and stuff too. My aunt was fine with the relationship until she found out about the witchcraft. Practically disowned Marisol."

Freddie snorted. "I guess spells and stuff aren't really Catholic approved?"

Raul grinned. "We're Mexican. Being Catholic is practically a requirement. You can't go around spitting in the face of God and expect your family to be okay with it."

"What about Fairy magic? Isn't that all spells and stuff, too?" Amanda said.

Freddie knew where she was going with this. Amanda had been trying to kick Pelrin out of their group ever since he and Freddie broke up, but Jefferson was set against it, and Raul refused to take sides. Freddie rolled her eyes and busied herself making popcorn.

"Well, that's different," Raul said. "You can't change how you were born."

A soft tap tap sounded at the window. Amanda brushed a wisp of dark hair from her face and pushed herself off the bed to open it.

A tiny black bat fluttered in. It flitted around Amanda's head before hovering over the IKEA couch. With a woosh, a handsome boy, who looked as though he could be Raul's classmate, appeared, lounging on the blue cushions. Amanda shut the window and bounced over to him, planting a kiss lightly on his lips. Freddie averted her eyes, a sharp pang ringing through her heart.

"Did you eat?" Amanda wrapped her arms around Jefferson's pale neck. He let out a rumbling laugh.

"Yeah. I grabbed a bite on my way over." His red eyes flashed in the fluorescent dorm light.

"Hopefully no one we know." Raul took a long drink of his soda.

"Not trying to get arrested, doggy," Jefferson called over his shoulder. "You guys hear about the dude who got abducted last week?"

"Yeah, Freddie's doing a paper on it." Amanda turned and gave Raul a warning look.

"Be careful, Freddie," Jefferson said. "He's the second one to go missing. Just because you know Pelrin doesn't mean you're invincible."

Freddie's eyes widened at the mention of her ex's name. She pressed a finger to her lips, but it was too late. Before she had a chance to groan, the air rippled with magic, and a blinding light filled the room.

"Smells like a party," Pelrin said as he materialized in front of the TV. "How come I wasn't invited?"

"Pel! Glamour! Neighbors! Remember?" Freddie hissed.

The gold light faded, revealing a young man in his late teens. He wore a turquoise high-necked tunic and loose white pants with gold embroidery running down the sides. Brushing aside his long blond hair, he revealed a pair of glittering, gold wings laying flat against his back, signifying his status as a fairy royal — the Prince of Summer. Surveying Freddie with his cerulean eyes, he smiled.

"Did you miss me last week, Freddie?" Pelrin held his arms out as if to embrace her.

"Not at all." She deposited the fresh popcorn in a bowl and pushed past him to set it down on the cardboard box that served as a coffee table. "Haven't you heard of knocking?"

"If I knocked, you might not let me in."

"Damn right."

"Then I would have had to wend in here anyways." He looked to Raul, as always, to rally support. Raul ignored him, suddenly fascinated by the ingredients printed on his Pepsi can. Pelrin wrinkled his nose. "I'm just saving you a step, Freddie."

She glared at him and tossed Jefferson the remote. Raul moved over to the bed, and Freddie plopped down beside him, forcing Pelrin to share the couch with Jefferson and Amanda.

"So, what are we watching? *Titanic*?"

Raul launched himself at Pelrin before Jefferson could hand over the remote. Jefferson leaned over Amanda, shielding her from Raul's football player strength and Pelrin's beating wings.

"If I'm ever stuck on a door with you, I'll push you right off," Pelrin snarled, grasping one end of the remote.

"Don't worry, I'll jump if it means I never have to sit through this god-awful movie again," Raul barked back.

Freddie made a show of sighing and rolling onto her back. Pelrin noticed and momentarily allowed Raul full control over the remote.

"You like *Titanic*, don't you, Fred?" Pelrin turned to Freddie.

"I did before you made us watch it a hundred times."

He sighed. "Fine, you can pick the movie, Raul. But if I don't like it, we're changing it."

Freddie glared at Pelrin as Raul reclaimed his spot on the bed.

"So, what did you guys do last week while I was away?" Pelrin had twisted around to stare daggers at Raul, who ignored him as he scrolled through the movie library.

"Nothing." Freddie shrugged.

"We had a date night." Amanda nuzzled her face into Jefferson's arm while he ran his ivory fingers through her hair.

"*We had a date night*," Pelrin mimicked in a whiney, high-pitched imitation of Amanda. Jefferson leaned back to frown at him, but Pelrin focused his attention on Freddie. "Come on, Freddie, just because I can't lie doesn't mean I can't recognize one."

She sighed. "Raul and I just went to a club, nothing interesting."

Raul stiffened and shot her an alarmed look.

"What club?" Pelrin said, his voice light and casual, but Freddie knew there was more than mild curiosity brimming underneath. Raul watched him warily.

"None of your business, Pel," she said.

Pelrin turned to Raul. "Come on, Raul, friends don't keep secrets from friends," Pelrin sang. His eyes flicked to the TV. "Oh! Can we watch that?" He pointed eagerly at a thumbnail for *The Jersey Shore*.

Both Amanda and Freddie gave him judgmental stares. Jefferson smirked and shook his head.

"Come on, bro," Raul moaned. "We can't go from *Titanic* to *The Jersey Shore*. My eyes might start bleeding from all this trash. Besides, it's super old, like early 2000s."

"This," Pelrin said, leaning over Jefferson and Amanda, "is my favorite show, and we don't get TV in Fairy." He snatched the remote from Raul's hands, pausing before sitting back down to give Freddie a beaten-puppy stare.

They all sighed as Pelrin flipped through the episodes. Jefferson reached for a handful of popcorn. He popped a kernel into his mouth and pulled a face. Amanda rolled her eyes as he transferred his handful to her, forgetting that human food no longer suited his red fae tastes.

It was going to be a long night.

"Tell me what club you went to last Friday, and I'll give you back the remote." Pelrin dangled it just out of Raul's reach.

"We went to Illusion. Don't worry, nothing happened. I watched Freddie the whole time. Can I have the remote back now, please?" He whined like a dog begging for a treat.

Freddie tsked—breaking under the threat of watching *The Jersey Shore, weakling.* Pelrin's face hardened, his grip on the remote tightened and the plastic squealed, threatening to crack.

"You took her to a fae club? I suppose you let her drink there, too."

Freddie shot to her knees and gave Pelrin her darkest glare. "I am my own person, Pel! Neither you nor Raul can *let* me do anything. And yes, if you are so nosey, I did drink, and I made out with a hot guy who was *not* you!" She made a grab for the remote before Pelrin shattered it. His eyes flashed with fury.

Jefferson and Amanda cringed, sinking down into the couch as if they hoped to disappear beneath the cushions.

"Who was it?" Pelrin's voice was barely a whisper.

Freddie ignored the ripple of magic radiating off Pelrin. After over a year of dating the fairy prince, she knew better than to fear he would use magic to hurt her; he didn't use magic on anyone.

"Raul?" Pelrin asked. "Who did she make out with?"

Raul shook his head, his face nearly as white as Jefferson's.

"As if you know every fae in existence, Pel." Freddie rounded the bed so they stood mere inches apart. "Tan skin, dark hair, hot as hell, and these amazing amber eyes. Ring any bells?" She reveled in Pelrin's jealous fury. A tiny voice in her head egged her on, hissing, *yes, yes, hurt him like he hurt you!*

But Pelrin's face didn't crumble into a pained retreat as Freddie expected. Instead, his eyes flared the color of blue lightning as he glared at Raul.

"Please tell me she is not describing that Dark Fae dog, Aiden." Pelrin shook with fury.

Raul trembled. "Well, it was dark. You know, she probably didn't see him all that clearly, or him her. You know how clubs are and all—"

In one swift motion, Pelrin obliterated the cardboard coffee table and showered the small room with popcorn. Amanda shrieked, and Jefferson moved to block her from Pelrin's path. Freddie felt as though some slimy, clawed creature slithered down her back. This was more than a jealous rage.

"I told you about how dangerous he is, and you still let her — her — " he said, apparently struggling to find the words in his fury.

"Look, as soon as I saw her, I grabbed her and got out of there. I swear nothing happened." Raul was on his feet now, too, attempting to press himself into the corner between the wall and her nightstand.

"Wait, who is this Aiden anyways?" Freddie took in the expressions on Pelrin's, Raul's, and even Jefferson's faces.

"He is a murdering Dark Fae soldier. That's all you need to know," Pelrin said. "He's killed hundreds of my people, and all these disappearances are probably his doing too. He was probably at that club looking for his next victim."

"You don't know that for sure, Pel. He could have been there to have a good time, like us," Raul said.

"Aiden does not go out to simply have a good time. There is always a darker motive with him." Pelrin ran a hand through his golden hair.

"Well, I'm safe now, so there's no need to worry, right? I mean it's been a week." Freddie folded her arms across her chest to keep her hands from trembling.

"What did he do when you kissed him?" Pelrin spat.

Ice filled her gut. Freddie had to look away. She knew better than to drink fae liquor. Why did she have to be so stupid? "Nothing, he just stood there. I doubt it would have gone much further even if Raul hadn't pulled me away." She dared a glance at Raul, then Pelrin, hoping to see something reassuring in their faces. But when she looked to Jefferson, even his expression was grim.

"You should be fine." Pelrin let out a long breath. "It was dark. I've only brought you to court a few times. He wouldn't recognize you based on his spies' descriptions," he muttered, more to himself than to Freddie.

She and Raul exchanged worried glances.

"I have to go," Pelrin said. "I'll have someone stay with you

for the next few weeks, just to be safe. Raul, you watch her tonight."
Pelrin chewed his lower lip.

Fighting down the urge to argue with him about assigning her a guard, Freddie grit her teeth together. All of this was extreme, even when compared to Pelrin's usual dramatics. It'd been a week and she'd been fine.

"Sure, Pel," Raul said. "But do you really think it's that big of a deal? Nothing's happened yet. Wouldn't he have attacked already?"

"Yes. It is. I must go. Guard her well." Pelrin's gaze was stony as the air around him rippled. He turned and wended into nothingness.

"I should go after him," Jefferson said. He pushed himself to his feet. "Don't worry, Freddie. He's just being extra cautious. You'll probably be fine."

Freddie didn't like the way he said "probably." Jefferson walked over to the window in three fluid steps and opened it. He glanced outside before returning to Amanda, who was still sitting on the couch, white-faced.

"I'll see you tomorrow night," he murmured and kissed her forehead before whooshing into bat form and disappearing into the night.

Amanda, Freddie, and Raul all let out simultaneous breaths. Several minutes passed as guidos argued in the background. Freddie couldn't help her body from shaking. Pelrin was overreacting; she'd be fine. Finally, Raul broke the silence.

"I guess I'll start cleaning up." He started picking up bits of cardboard and popcorn.

Freddie and Amanda nodded dazedly and crawled to opposite ends of the room to clean the scattered mess. Freddie's hands shook as she carefully scooped up the tiny white puffs and tossed them into the trash. Pelrin had never gotten that angry around her before. Would that fae really come after her?

But it didn't matter. If Pelrin was right, and that guy she kissed really was behind the disappearances, she couldn't just stay away.

She had her lead and needed to find out more about him.

CHAPTER 7

Aiden

Aiden pressed his back against the brick wall as he waited for the students to filter out of the classroom. He'd already stolen a book recounting the history of the Human Realm and had spent the last several hours wending from monument to monument before settling on an ancient, damaged bell that was being carefully avoided by flocks of groaning schoolchildren. Once the sun set, and the children went home, it would be deserted. But its position in the center of the city made it the perfect target to enact their plan. The exhaustion of his efforts tugged on him like one of Mare's shadows, but he shook it off—there was work yet to be done.

A low and steady tone rang out from the building followed by sounds of chairs scraping, books slamming, and the noisy chatter of fleeing students. Aiden let out a breath as he watched the children rush out the doors. His own school days were hazy in his memory, as though he were recalling the life of someone else— someone with two loving parents, someone who didn't spend their days murdering without feeling.

He leapt onto the sill and crouched in the frame of the open window, his black uniform turning him into the shadow he felt like.

The schoolmaster was at his desk packing away papers; Aiden studied him as he silently eased himself into the room. Magic rippled around his body, blending it in with the long benches and strange lab equipment he'd watched the human children use. If he had a bit more time, he could wait until after the schoolmaster left and examine the materials more closely.

"Who's there?" the man called out. He got to his feet and looked around the classroom.

Aiden froze. The man must have fae blood if he could sense Aiden's glamour. Breathing slowly, Aiden watched the schoolmaster stare right through him. Finally, he went back to organizing his papers, making little marks on some of them. Aiden crept to the back of the classroom where a low shelf sat loaded with books.

Careful not to touch anything as he passed, his fingers itched to pick up one of the long glowing sticks in a basket labeled 'chemiluminescence.'

"I know you're there," the schoolmaster said. "I can feel your glamour."

Freezing frosts. Aiden clenched his teeth. This man was too sensitive, but the others needed to be able to create the blue fire while he and Emerick disabled the defenses in Shell Bay. Aiden reached out and grabbed a pencil resting on the edge of a nearby table. When the schoolmaster's eyes were busy scanning the other side of the room, Aiden tossed the pencil a little to the left of the man. He jumped. Aiden wended to the back shelf, knowing the man would feel the increased use of magic but hoping the pencil was enough to distract him.

"Did you really think that I wouldn't feel that?"

Aiden cursed. He bit his lip. *Perhaps.*

"Who are you? What are you doing in my classroom? Don't move."

"Just an urisk, sir," Aiden said in a high-pitched voice— imitating the invisible brown fae who snuck around old buildings doing household chores. He flexed his fingers and knelt to read through the books. There were so many. How was he supposed to find the one that could help him create a blue flame?

"An urisk? But my lab is already pretty clean, if I do say so myself. Besides, there are dangerous chemicals in here; your kind shouldn't be cleaning places like this."

Aiden swallowed. "Just wiping books, sir. I do it for the whole school, sir." He read through title after title meaning nothing to him — Biology, Global Tectonics, Chemistry, Physical Science. He scowled.

"Let me see you. I hate glamours. They creep me out. All this magic nonsense..."

"No, sir," Aiden said. He tried to think of a good excuse while narrowing down which of the books to take. "I — uh, it's against the rules." It was a safe bet that the one with the picture of the bird on the cover wouldn't help him, nor would the one with the picture of a mountain range.

"What rules?" The schoolmaster had stopped talking to the spot where Aiden had thrown the pencil and was walking back toward the table it had come from. "Surely the school doesn't employ such practices."

Heart pounding in his ears, Aiden looked up. The man was nearly at the back row of lab tables. Aiden pulled out the remaining two textbooks and held them close to his chest. The schoolmaster moved to snatch them away.

"Must go now, sir. More books to dust." Aiden wended. Cool air rushed against him as he reappeared in his room in the Winter Palace — the wards thankfully lowered.

Dropping his glamour, he let out a breath. Humans were much smarter than he gave them credit for. He collapsed onto his bed. The rumpled black comforter welcomed him into its warm folds. Aiden wrapped it around his shoulders and looked over the books. The first had a picture of a taxi and a lightning bolt on its cover. Eagerly, he flipped through the pages. Physical Science appeared to be a fascinating subject, but it contained none of the information he needed. Aiden set the book aside and promised himself he would return to it later when he had more time.

He picked up the second book and read the cover. *Chemistry:*

The Central Science. It had a strange pattern on the front, and the chapter names contained words he'd never heard. Dek would've told him this idea was stupid, that anything made by humans was weak and inferior. Still, Aiden skimmed the introduction. Matter, energy, and measurement—all the secrets to the human's magic, so simple—and yet, when woven together with creativity and nature, it could be so beautifully powerful. After a few minutes of skimming, he found a promising chapter on natural gas.

"Natural gas burns with a blue flame; however, most types of alcohol burn blue as well. With your parents' or teacher's help, let's try the following experiment."

A twinge shot through Aiden's heart as he read the last line, but he didn't have time to feel sorry for himself. He needed to find alcohol—and lots of it.

⁂

Creating the storm was simple.

Aiden stood across the street from the bell. It cowered in a glass building surrounded by an empty, green lawn as though it knew his plans. People walked along the edges of the green space, hurrying off to the bordering bars and restaurants—no one ventured near it. Above him in the orange sky, puffy clouds turned gray as he pulled them together.

The key to getting this spell to work properly was to substitute the water in the clouds for the alcohol pulled from the restaurants and let it loose at just the right moment. His "experiment" would be like the one in the book, only on a much larger scale.

A shadow flickered on the other side of the street. Aiden caught a glimpse of Irina's blonde hair as she stalked across the far end of the park. Somewhere, hidden in the shadows, Mare and Dek waited for his signal. When Emerick arrived, Aiden could release the liquid in the clouds, and the chaos would begin.

As soon as darkness fell, something moved at the edge of his vision. Aiden turned, and a pale figure stepped from the shadows on his left to stand alongside him.

"Is everything ready?" Emerick asked, his eyes steady on the building before them.

"As ready as it can be. Irina arrived a little while ago, and the others have been here for about an hour," Aiden said. "We have the difficult job, remember?"

Emerick chuckled. "You almost sound excited."

Aiden shot him a glare.

"Yeah, I know," Emerick said. "If everything goes according to plan tonight, why don't we meet up at Damun? We could have a drink."

Aiden huffed a laugh. "I doubt there is any drink at that vampire lounge that would interest me."

"You're right, sorry. Hey, plenty of red fae will be there, though. I'm sure it would be a good place to do some hunting."

"Why do you seek my company? You were content enough to leave me on my own the last time we failed," Aiden said under his breath.

Emerick cleared his throat. "It's like she said back at the meeting. Irina and I don't have the same protections the three of you have. It wasn't personal."

Aiden didn't respond, but the memory of their last failure sent ghostly tingles of pain down his legs to the soles of his feet.

Fingers numb from holding the spell, he glanced over his shoulder to Emerick. "Are you ready?"

The vampire nodded.

With a flick of his wrists, he released his hold on the clouds. Acrid scents of the blended liquors clogged the air as a torrent of alcohol pattered against the glass roof. Passersby had already begun to stop and stare at the foul-smelling shower raining over the bell. Reaching into his pocket, Aiden withdrew a pinch of blackish green powder — fairy wing dust. Their Majesties ground it from the wings of the fairy soldiers unfortunate enough to get captured. The thought of its origins sent sympathetic aches down his spine. But tonight he needed it; the dust allowed the user to travel between realms in the twinkle of a star, and Emerick couldn't wend.

From the shadows, Dek's hulking form emerged, a tiny lighter flame glowing from his clenched fist. He tossed it onto the side of the building. In an explosion of glass, the vibrant blue flames roared to life. Aiden tossed the dust into the air as the dizzying smoke and screams of the panicked humans faded, and he and Emerick blurred along with the landscape. When the scene cleared, they found themselves outside the limits of a brightly lit Fairy city.

The heat of Shell Bay pressed down through Aiden's black leather jerkin. Of all the realms in Fairy, he hated Summer the most. If tonight's mission was a success, they would have the crown in just one week. Then he could go about ensuring there was less of Summer to hate.

Emerick followed him into the town. People crowded the streets, and soca beats pounded through the air as the Summer fae paraded toward the beach. Aiden looked Emerick over; vampires were rare in Fairy. In Summer, where the days were long and the nights were significantly disproportionate, a vampire stuck out like a leprechaun among redcaps.

"Perhaps you could glamour me?" Emerick scanned the crowded streets. No one had noticed them, yet.

"I can't use my magic inside the city. The lodestones would pick it up; it's too unique."

Emerick sighed heavily, but Aiden ignored it. The streets were littered with debris from the passing parades. Part of a bright pink and green banner had been kicked into a crack in the road. Aiden walked over and fished it out. Grasping the filthy thing between thumb and forefinger, he passed it to Emerick.

"Put this around your head."

"You have got to be joking. My hair will get filthy."

"It will distract from your face. We're not getting captured tonight to save your vanity." Aiden narrowed his gaze, amber eyes flashing. Emerick nodded and wrapped the banner around his head like a brightly colored cloak.

The intense power of the Summer prince's magic protecting the city and shielding the fort pulsed around them. Three towers cast long shadows over the city, marking the hearts of its defenses. Every large city in Fairy had lodestone towers that, when activated, could block the use of magic within the borders and form a barrier around the set radius. When he made his move for the crown, Aiden didn't want to risk the towers neutralizing his magic.

He moved through the crowd toward the first tower. One of the guards appeared drunk, dancing with a couple of jaguar-women with patterned fur. The other was stiff and alert. Occasionally he would cast his companion a disgusted glare.

Aiden approached the tower from the left, while Emerick approached it from the right. Sticking close to the shadows, Aiden moved silently, waiting for Emerick to get into place so they could take out the guards.

"Hey, man. You're too pale," the drunk guard said.

One of the jaguar-women leaned forward and sniffed him. She wrinkled her nose. "What are you doing here?"

"I'm here to party, like everyone else," Emerick said.

Aiden watched the alert guard.

The man's stern face turned to Emerick, his eyes narrowed. "That is a good question. What is a vampire doing in Summer?" He shifted so his back was to the tower entrance.

Aiden took advantage of the distraction and slipped inside. It took what felt like ages to climb all those steps. Sweat clung to his brow, and the heat made his leather jerkin stifling. It would all be worth it, though, to see the look on the Summer Prince's face when Aiden stole the crown right from under his nose.

At the top of the tower, a chartreuse stone reflected the lights of the city, glimmering dimly in the twilight. The sounds of the carnival were muffled at this height. From his vantage, Aiden could see all of Shell Bay. The parade had made its way to the beach; party-goers set up bonfires that glowed like candle flames. Waves frothed white on the midnight ocean, marking the entrance to the Sea Realm. Aiden breathed in; the breeze blew up the scents of salt, curry, and sweet lavender, and his stomach growled. Turning his back to the view, he snatched the stone, placed it safely inside his chest pocket, and hurried back down the stairs.

Emerick and the serious guard were gone. Their Majesties would not be pleased if Aiden abandoned one of their inner-circle soldiers to the mercies of Summer. He cursed, walking through the dwindling crowd. There were still two more towers; Emerick could take care of himself for a few hours — Aiden hoped.

He set out for the next building. The guards policing the streets moved with the crowd flowing toward the beach. A jaguar-woman stood at the base of the second tower, her eyes scanning the crowd. Aiden looked around for anything he might use as a distraction. It would be best if his visit to Shell Bay was as quiet as possible.

Or perhaps not...

He shoved an obnoxiously drunk man in a brightly colored feathered headdress into a pinch-faced woman sipping nectar from an oversized orange flower. The drink sloshed, a bit of the sticky liquid spilling onto her front. She fluttered her butterfly-like wings and leapt into the air, scowling and cursing at the man below. Aiden ducked into the crowd, keeping his head down. Some of the man's friends spotted her as she alighted back onto the street. Aiden grinned as the friends of the drunk and those of the butterfly lunged for each other's throats. The man in the headdress bounced back and forth between the two sides, hurling punches at whoever was closest.

The guard at the base of the tower tensed, her black fur sticking up at the nape of her neck. She let out a loud yowl and dove in to break up the fight. Aiden moved quickly through the arch and jogged up the stairs. The sounds of the brawl faded as he climbed higher and higher.

This tower was much the same as the other one. It looked out over the city and beyond to the fort. The strength of the magic surrounding the great stone fortress buzzed in his bones. If they were going to get the crown out of there, the prince would have to fall for their distraction, and Mare would need to thoroughly drain him. Aiden's stomach twisted, and he bit the inside of his cheek. Maybe he should have stayed with the others and sent Mare to collect the stones.

The screech of an owl made him jump and jerk his head away from the fort. A woman dressed in a ragged gown of red and black stood before him. How had he not heard her approach? Aiden took several steps back and reflexively reached for the ring hanging at his chest.

"What is your purpose here, dark one?" she said, her voice low and heavy with rippling magic.

Dark one? That was new. "I'm just enjoying the view," Aiden said, his eyes flicking over to the stone.

No one but a gold fae should give off so much power. Any other fae who did would do best seal it away so as not to tempt power-hungry magic thieves. Aiden's heart beat rapidly as he looked for any hint of what manner of fae she might be, but the woman seemed unaware of the power leaking from her.

"You are threatening the protection of this city. I wish to know why."

Aiden clenched his fists to keep himself from flinching and wracked his brain to find a way around the directness of her question. "Revenge." His voice was practically a whisper. Against the Summer King for his parents, and the prince for everything else. He squared his shoulders; something about her aura made him unable to speak the fairy half-truths he'd come to rely on.

"No, that is not quite right." She moved closer. An unearthly chill wafted off her body. "There is much rage in you, but also much pain." Her hand stroked a path down Aiden's cheek. He shuddered.

"Don't," he said but made no move to halt her hand. The woman's power swept over him like mountain mists fleeing the dawn. She was no gold fae. Her power felt much deeper, older.

"You wish to be free, is that it?"

Aiden stared at her. How had she known? No one, except for perhaps Oberon and Mab, knew of his desire to rid himself of his bondage to their majesties. Who was this woman? What else did she know about him?

"Yes," Aiden croaked.

"What you seek to do here tonight will not help you to achieve the freedom you desire. You will fail if you continue to follow this path of revenge."

"We'll see." Aiden let out a shaky breath. His freedom was a hopeless desire anyway. It was getting late; he needed to capture the other lodestone and make it back into the Human Realm to check on the others.

"The path to freedom is hard and painful and is not without loss." She withdrew her hand and straightened. "I will not stop you tonight, but you have been warned: change your path." Her body shrank and twisted into the form of a screech owl, and she flew off into the darkness.

Her power faded several moments after she was gone. Aiden sagged against the wall. In all his travels across the seasonal realms, he'd never met anyone like her.

"There's a weird chill in here. Can you feel it?"

Aiden jerked. Emerick stood at the top of the stairs. His hair was ruffled and his clothes were torn in places, but he didn't appear injured. He was also grinning.

"Yeah," Aiden rasped, still trying to shake the woman's residual power from his bones.

"Was that you? Did you create that mess down there?" Emerick jerked his chin toward the edge of the tower.

Aiden stared at the city below. People swarmed like bees at a hive, their enraged shouts muffled by distance. He smirked.

"I knew it. The guards that were questioning me got pulled in. I managed to swipe this on my way over." Emerick held out a small yellow-green stone.

"Good," Aiden said. He walked over to the podium and snatched up the last glimmering lodestone. It had been freshly polished. With any luck, the Summertons wouldn't check the stones until the end of the next week. By then, Aiden and his people would have already worn down the prince and stolen the crown. He pocketed the stone and turned back to the vampire. "Let's go."

Emerick stood beside him as Aiden withdrew another pinch of the fairy wing powder and tossed it into the air. The strange woman's words still echoed in his head, but the prince deserved all that was coming after everything he'd done. *If I am doomed to fail so be it.* He might never get his freedom, but he would rather die getting his vengeance than live with the knowledge the prince was safe and happy.

CHAPTER 8

Freddie

I swear, Fred, if you wear those boots with that, we are no longer friends," Amanda said.

She sat cross-legged on the bed while Freddie picked out an outfit for the blind date she'd set her up on.

Freddie sighed, put down the boots, and returned to the closet. "What about these?" She held up a pair of chunky sandals. Amanda shook her head.

"What about these?" came a high, squeaky voice. From inside the closet, one of Freddie's old sneakers hopped forward.

Freddie stared down at the shoe as it plunked on the floor to reveal a six-inch-tall, green-skinned pixie—Pelrin's assigned guard. The irritating creature, also known as Ginnith, had nosed her way into all of Freddie's classes and free periods and was now threatening to join her on a date.

"Eww, Ginnith." Amanda fell onto her back and groaned at the ceiling. Her own skin-tight red dress had been paired with the black, red-soled stilettos that Jefferson had bought her for her birthday last year. Freddie pursed her lips; she knew which shoes would make Amanda happy.

"There is nothing wrong with these shoes," Ginnith said. "They are practical for climbing and running and fighting and —"

"She's going on a date, not basic training. Is that what you do on a date—run, climb, fight, or whatever?"

Ginnith's face turned from granny-smith green to candy-apple red. "Yes, if you must know. My kind hunt each other through the forest to prove they are adequate providers and defenders."

"You have a boyfriend then, Ginni?" Freddie grunted as she pulled a box from the top shelf.

"I do not have a boyfriend!" Ginnith's blush deepened to crimson, and her tiny wings buzzed madly. If Freddie didn't know it was impossible for green fae, she would have suspected the little pixie of lying.

"Right. Sure you don't." Amanda winked at her.

Ginnith bared her needle-like teeth.

"How about these?" Freddie opened the box and pulled out the pair of five-inch pumps. They were silver with straps that wove in an intricate design around the foot to connect at the ankle. At the toe was a glittering starburst that shone with the dust from real stars when they touched her skin, or so Pelrin had told her.

Amanda gasped. "Where did you get those?"

"They were the last gift Pelrin gave me," Freddie said, her nose wrinkling. She plopped onto the bed next to Amanda and slid her foot ungracefully into the shoe.

"Are you okay wearing them?" Amanda sat up and rested a hand on her friend's arm.

"I bet you miss him very much," Ginnith said. "With the war and everything, it's hard to be separated from those we love."

Freddie glared at her. "I don't love Pelrin, Ginnith. Did he tell you to do this? Try and convince me to take him back?"

Ginnith leapt into the air, furiously buzzing. "It is an honor for the prince to love you. You should be grateful he spares you any affection at all, human."

"Your prince is a man whore, Ginnith," Amanda said. "Maybe Freddie will give him another shot when he learns to keep it in his pants." She raked her fingers through her hair.

Freddie creased her brows and focused on sliding the other shoe onto her foot. They did pair well with her outfit.

"You humans know nothing!" Ginnith marched to the end of the bed.

"If you hate us so much, you can always go home," Freddie said. She got to her feet. It was her first time wearing these shoes since Pelrin. They had been too nice to throw away, and she couldn't bring herself to sell them. It would serve him right if tonight's date went well.

There was a soft tapping at the window. A black bat fluttered outside. The three girls rushed over and peered at the street below. Jefferson didn't bother to come inside but rather flittered back to his car. Ginnith stared at him until he resumed his usual form and ducked into the driver's side.

"That's the vampire who is friends with his highness..." she said aloud. "My prince told me you'd be safe with him. At least for one night, I think." She turned to stare thoughtfully at Freddie. "Yes, I will leave you with him. He knows to watch you."

"Okay. Bye, Ginni. Have fun wherever it is you're going. No rush to come back." Freddie waved at her absently while she and Amanda gathered wallets, keys, and phones into their clutches.

Ginnith heaved the window open a crack and turned to Freddie. "I will be back. Early. I would never let his highness down." Freddie sighed, her finger hovering on the light switch. "Until tomorrow, human." Ginnith jumped out the partially open window and flew into the night.

Flicking off the light, Freddie and Amanda hurried downstairs to meet Jefferson.

"I can't wait for you to meet Victor," Amanda said once they were in the car. "He's the sweetest guy. Right, babe?"

"Mhm." Jefferson kept his focus on the road as he pulled away from the curb.

This was not the first time Amanda had tried to set Freddie up on a blind date. Usually, it was some random guy she'd met in class, but this was the first time she was dragging Jefferson into it.

"Victor and Jefferson have been friends for... How many years is it?"

"We've known each other for seven years," Jefferson said. "I wouldn't really call us friends. Co-workers is the more appropriate term."

Amanda sighed. She gave Jefferson's arm a playful punch. "Ow! Why do you have to be so hard?"

He snickered. "You okay?"

"Fine. You can at least pretend you're happy for Freddie."

From the back seat, Freddie leaned forward. "That's alright, Jefferson. I know Pelrin's giving you a hard time about this."

"It's not that," Jefferson said. "I just feel for him. You should really consider —"

"He cheated on her!" Amanda folded her arms and turned away from him.

Freddie sighed. Even though he was a cheating piece of scum, maybe she should consider taking back Pelrin. Their break up was making her friends miserable. Raul felt obligated to babysit her, and Jefferson and Amanda were fighting. Even Pelrin — though it served him right — had been moping. Everyone would be happier if things could just go back to how they used to be.

Well, everyone but her.

"I know, but come on, Mandie, he's my friend. I have to defend him." Jefferson took his eyes off the road for a moment to nibble on Amanda's neck. Freddie couldn't help feeling, pitifully, like a third wheel. Amanda bit her lip and tried to brush him off. The car held unnervingly steady. "You know you'd do the same for Freddie." He kissed her cheek. Freddie looked away.

"Fine. Let's just not talk about this anymore." Amanda twisted in her seat to face Freddie. "You okay?"

"Peachy." Freddie leaned back and watched the shops and restaurants on Main Street fly by. Each day ticked closer to Thanksgiving, and with no leads in sight, she'd rather spend the evening researching than chatting up some rando. "What time do you think this will be over?"

Amanda sighed. "Come on, Fred. I promise he's not that bad."

"I need to work on my article. It's not him." *Not yet anyway.*

"Oh, well, Victor might know something, being a well-connected fae and all. Right babe?"

Jefferson paused, fingers halfway to the radio buttons. "Victor might know something about what?"

"The disappearances!" Amanda slapped a hand against one eye before gasping and flicking down the mirror to fix her makeup.

"Why would he know anything about—" Jefferson fell silent at a sharp look from Amanda. "I mean, he might know something."

Freddie rolled her eyes. She would just need to get through this night quickly. There had to be something in the backgrounds of the missing students she could follow to the culprit.

It wasn't long before they arrived at a sleek black, windowless building. In glowing, red letters above the entrance was the word, *Damun*. Jefferson pulled up to the front; his body blurred as he sped around the car to open the door for Amanda. She slid the seat forward and helped drag Freddie from the back.

A short man in a red jacket leaned against a podium in front of the lounge's entrance. He pushed himself upright and hobbled over to them. Freddie frowned, recognizing the same valet from Illusion. *This guy sure gets around.*

"Good evening, sir." The valet saluted Jefferson, but his eyes lingered on Freddie and Amanda.

Jefferson cleared his throat and threw his keys at the faun. The stunned valet scrambled to catch them. "Take good care of my baby," Jefferson said, nodding at his car.

"Sure thing, boss!" The faun gave Jefferson a cheeky grin and handed him a ticket. There was a screech of rubber on pavement, and Jefferson's silver Agera sped off into the dark. He stared mournfully after it.

"Your *baby* will be fine." Amanda patted his arm. Renting a modest coffin in one of the oldest cemeteries in town was apparently worth the ability to spend all his money on Amanda, his car, and the garage that housed it.

He relaxed, allowing Amanda to lead the way to a door carved into the building's glossy facade. A beefy bouncer stood guard, eyes glowing in the steady light from the street lamps. The stench of rotting meat rose up from his skin, making Freddie want to gag. *He must be an ogre.* After collecting their cover charge from Jefferson, the ogre stood aside. Damun didn't serve alcohol, so they didn't need to be twenty-one. Humans entered at their own risk.

The girls followed Jefferson down a flight of carpeted stairs into a cavernous space where colorful Moroccan lanterns spilled multi-colored stars across the medley of red fae that occupied the room.

Everywhere Freddie turned, vampires, and a few timid-looking humans, lay sprawled out on chaise lounges or clustered around low tables. They drank from an assortment of glasses all filled with the same thick, red liquid. Undead patrons danced in movements too smooth and too silent for them to be mistaken for anything but fae.

She swallowed and sucked in a deep breath. It was not that she had anything against vampires. Jefferson was one, and he was a really great guy. It was just that so many of them, in an enclosed space, triggered a primal instinct telling her to run. She focused on the music, the pulsing sounds of Romanian house mixes beating life into the eerie lounge.

Amanda moved through the crowd with a learned grace nearly putting her in the same class as the vampires. Jefferson's granite-hard body at Freddie's back ushered her forward. He was uncommonly tense and alert, no doubt following Pelrin's orders to guard her.

"Victor!" Amanda called and glided over to a man seated alone at a low table.

"Stay close," Jefferson murmured in Freddie's ear. "Remember, Victor is just an acquaintance. I don't know how much I can trust him yet."

Oh great. Freddie sank down on a cushion beside Amanda, wishing she had worn jeans or at least a longer dress.

Victor wasn't ugly; it was practically impossible to become a vampire and be homely. Something about the venom smoothed out wrinkles and corrected imperfections, making each person look like a china doll version of their human self.

But Victor also wasn't hot. He was just... a vampire.

He held his hand out to Freddie, and she shook it hesitantly.

"See? I told you he was cute," Amanda hissed in her ear.

Freddie winced. "Like a baby duck." Perhaps he had a really nice personality.

"Freddie, Victor works at Liberty Brothers. He and Jefferson are on the same floor. Isn't that nice?" She looked from Freddie to Victor; even he looked uncomfortable from Amanda's prodding.

"That's cool. What department are you in?" Freddie asked.

"I'm an analyst. I do data models. Are you interested in math?" Victor's boyish face lifted. Freddie's heart sank.

"Not really. I'm a writer," she said. "Hoping to be a journalist, you know."

"How interesting. I read articles. *The Wall Street Journal* and *The Financial Times* have good journalists."

Freddie nodded. She had read articles from those sites too but had found them unbearably dry.

"Freddie is working on an article right now." Amanda placed a hand on her shoulder, shoving her toward Victor. "It's about all these disappearances."

"Amanda mentioned you might know something about them?" Freddie inclined her head.

Victor's eyes widened, and he looked from Amanda to Jefferson. "Why would I —"

"It was a joke." Amanda pinched Freddie hard on the thigh. "Let's change the subject. Victor, did you know Freddie likes to sing? Victor used to be a singer, you know."

Freddie glared at her friend, rubbing the spot on her leg that was likely going to bruise.

"I sang in my church choir when I was a boy, but that was a long, long time ago." Victor gave an awkward laugh.

The problem with dating vampires was, although they appeared young, experience aged them. Victor could have been seventeen, but his Romanian accent and dusty yellow skin hinted at an age much, much older.

Freddie glared at Amanda, who shrugged. Pelrin, despite

76

being an immortal, had been only seventeen when they started dating—though he looked as though he could be a student at the upper-school.

"I just sing in the shower," Freddie said. "Amanda likes to exaggerate." Everyone except Amanda laughed.

Though, eventually, even she broke down, and her expression softened. "Why don't you two go dance?"

Victor rose gracefully and held out a hand to Freddie. She took it and let him tug her upright. Jefferson shot Amanda an irritated look, frowning as Victor waited for Freddie to stabilize herself in her spindly heels and take his hand.

Music rolled over them. The pounding beats and sensual rhythms were a perfect match for the graceful dance in which Victor led her, and Freddie lost herself to the music. She was pleasantly surprised when Victor spun and dipped her. His movements were not quite as grandfatherly as she'd expected. The song finished, and she smiled at him—he beamed.

Another vampire tapped Victor on the shoulder, and he jumped. It was odd to see a vampire jump. Their superhuman senses made it so they were rarely taken by surprise. Victor's eyes widened, and he took several steps back so the other guy could cut in.

The new vampire was impossibly beautiful. His slender, muscular body and thick auburn hair made him look as though he had stepped straight off a Milan runway. And there was something strangely familiar about him too as he stared deep into Freddie's eyes. A tingling numbness filled her body. The sounds of the music faded as he took her hand and led her to a darkened corner of the room. The world blurred such that all she could see was the vampire's glowing red eyes.

"You look lovely." He pressed himself against her. "And smell delicious."

He ran a hand down her side. Freddie's heart raced, and she let out a small breath. She tried to pull away and was horrified to find she couldn't. Her body was paralyzed. The vampire's eyebrows raised; she knew he could sense her panic.

Move Freddie. Kick him, hit him, run, do something. Her mind screamed, but her body would not obey. She swiveled her eyes to see if anyone else had noticed what he was doing to her, but she could only make out blurred figures and *him.*

"I'm going to enjoy this," the vampire said. His icy breath sent chills down her spine, but she couldn't even shiver. "Such a nice reward."

Freddie wanted to scream for help, but she could barely manage a whimper. The fuzziness faded as the vampire readjusted his grip on her. From the corner of her eye, she spotted Victor skitter away up the stairs. Her heart sank. She hadn't expected him to come charging in to rescue her, but at least he could have alerted Jefferson.

From her position in the shadows, she couldn't see either of her friends. No one was going to save her, and she was powerless to do it herself. Her humanity wasn't good enough for Pelrin, and now it would doom her to be lunch for this creep. Tears trickled down her face. A dark chuckle sounded in her ear. The vampire's cold lips pressed against her bare shoulder, inhaling her scent. She braced herself for the inevitable bite.

Just as cool fangs grazed her neck, someone grasped her hand. The vampire's spell shattered. She blinked, trying to shake the fuzziness from her vision as her savior pulled her close to their chest. She pushed away, trying to get her bearings but a harsh tug on her arm made her stumble forward. Before she was able to get a good look, they were running.

Freddie tumbled onto her hands and knees when they reached the first stair. The vampire shrank back into the crowd. *He was afraid of this person.* She tried to catch a good glimpse of their face. The back of a young man with dark hair was all she saw before he dragged her up the stairs.

They stepped out to the deserted front of the building. Cars raced by, and raucous noise rose up from the bulk of Main Street's bars two blocks away. Freddie placed her hands on her knees and took several deep breaths. Slowly, the fuzziness in her head faded.

They were alone, and the ogre and faun had disappeared to

places unknown. An icy tingle, that had nothing to do with the autumn weather, ran down her back. Who could be so terrifying that even a vampire—bold enough to bite someone in public—would back down with a single look? She straightened and ran a trembling hand down her neck. Nothing but smooth skin.

"Either you have a death wish, or you are very, very stupid." The dark-haired young man stepped into the light. He scowled, his bright amber eyes glowing in their bright fluorescent beams. Freddie's eyes widened as she choked on her breath. It was *him*.

CHAPTER 9

Freddie

Freddie gaped at the fae she'd kissed at Illusion. Her heart drummed so loudly it drowned out the raucous chatter of the distant bars.

"So which is it?" he said. "I would love to know."

"W-which is what?" Taking a stumbling step back, she closed her eyes and tried to recover her breath.

"Why are you throwing yourself at fae who can, and very possibly *want*, to kill you?" His amber eyes flamed as he stared her down. She shuddered. Ghostly shadows of the blue flames that had surrounded him the other night hovered around his arms.

Then it happened—the little voice in her head that told her to shut up and not say anything stupid packed a suitcase and left for vacation. *Fuck.* Freddie and her big stupid mouth were on their own.

"I'm not trying to get myself killed," she said, her voice shaking like a sundiva in Winter.

He stepped closer, and the tendrils of his flames ignited. "Then explain to me what you were doing down there, and last week."

"I was—" she began, pleading with her mind to come up with something smart. But there was no response from the little voice. "I was trying to get attention."

She regretted the words as soon as they'd left her mouth. Her heart, much like the first time they'd met, was pounding out of control. Though, this time, it was due to blinding fear and not magically-induced lust.

"Whose?" His eyes burned as he stared steadily at her.

The blue flames flared, licking at his chest and neck. Freddie's vision went hazy, and she let out a breath in a slow hiss.

"Yours?" The horror of her words hit her like a slap across the face. She was alone, in a dark and unfamiliar place, with a fae that scared even Pelrin. And she had just told him she wanted his attention. Were there no bounds to her stupidity?

"Mine?" The flames vanished, and he took a step back. "Why?" Something about the genuine curiosity, and probably the lack of flames, was comforting.

"You're hot." Her mouth was dry as she choked out the words. It had been the only thing she could think of. And she sure as hell wasn't going to tell him it was because she wanted to interrogate him about the missing students.

He smirked and looked down. "I see." Chuckling to himself, he met her gaze. His amber eyes bored into her skull. "Now that you have my attention, what do you intend to do with it?"

A million thoughts flooded her at once. She needed to keep him talking. If she could make it back inside the club, she could find Jefferson and Amanda and be safe. Freddie's eyes flicked down the street. She would never be able to outrun him long enough to reach the nearest bar — not in these shoes.

"Ask you..."

"Ask me what?" He leaned in.

He was trying to intimidate her, yet she couldn't help but notice his intoxicatingly floral scent. *What is wrong with me? Focus!* If she could get him to take a step back like he had before, perhaps that would give her enough time to sprint to the entrance. She needed to say something unexpected — but not crazy — to catch him off guard. Her throat ached, and her breath hitched in her chest.

"I wanted to ask you on a date." She waited, ready to run for it when he stepped back. A long minute passed, and he didn't move. *Crap.*

"You, a human, want to go on a date with me. Why?" His eyes narrowed. It was as though he were trying to determine how sane she was. Judging by his intense squint and his downturned mouth, she wasn't doing too well.

"I want to know where you're taking them all." Lightning shot through her veins, causing her legs to wobble, but she remained upright, staring into his amber gaze. She clenched her fists so hard that her freshly painted nails dug painfully into her skin.

"Taking who?"

"The girls." She bit back the urge to correct herself. Daniel and the students from the other schools hadn't all been girls.

To her surprise—and horror—he laughed. Not a cruel, calculating laugh, but a genuine chuckle. She nearly peed. "You want to know what I do with girls?"

Freddie ran her tongue across sandpaper lips and tasted waxy lipstick. "And boys too. Students, really." *Shut up, shut up.*

Freddie's heart froze as if it were about to give out. The fae boy stared at her blankly, waiting for her to finish her awkward ramblings. Getting attacked by a vampire, asking out the most dangerous fae in the seven realms, and surviving one of Amanda's blind dates—no heart was built for this much stress.

"I don't understand..."

"I just want a date," she said. If by some miracle she survived tonight, perhaps she could get some hard leads for her article.

He hesitated, something like uncertainty or suspicion darting across his face. "All right, one date. If it will keep you from reckless danger," he said. "What are the terms?"

"I will stop putting my life purposefully in danger if you take me on one normal *human* date. Happy?" She hoped the terms were clear and there were no alternate interpretations. Entering into an agreement with any fae was dangerous. Entering into an agreement with a Dark Fae soldier—who struck fear into the hearts of *vampires*—was probably about as safe as asking a shark to help you bandage an open wound.

He nodded. For a moment, she thought she saw a flicker of nervousness darken his inhumanly bright eyes, but then his expression smoothed. "Agreed."

She gave him a hesitant nod and turned to go back into the lounge. If she could just make it to Jefferson and Amanda...

"Wait!" he called after her. She stopped, suppressing a yell. "I promised to hold up my end of the deal. You must go home now," he said.

"But my friends—"

"Will be fine." He pointed to the more densely populated part of Main Street, two blocks down. "This way."

She glanced back longingly at the door, wishing that ogre bouncer would show up—or at least the faun. Following the fae boy down the street, she kept her senses alert to any sign he might betray her. At least they were headed toward people—she could always scream.

"Um, so, how do you summon one of those transport machines? I've seen other humans do it."

To both her relief and dismay, she recognized where they were. They stood on a corner of a brightly lit, and mildly crowded, strip of Main Street. Black Ubers and rattling orange taxis flowed up and down the street in search of drunken upper schoolers to overcharge. She sighed.

"You mean a taxi?" Judgement rang in her voice—her body could only hold onto the intense fear for so long.

"Yeah, whatever," he said.

She smirked at his reaction. Then she fixed her face into a more somber expression—he was dangerous. Wobbling in her too-tight heels, Freddie stepped over to the curb and held up her hand. Almost instantly a cab drifted over to them. She turned to look at her frightening savior. *What was his name again? Adam... Aldo... Adriane... Aiden!* He nodded. It was hard not to blush as he opened the door for her and she slid into the back seat. The faint scents of cigarettes and beer clung to the worn, cracked pleather.

"Good night," she said uncertainly. It was hard to believe he'd saved her and was now just letting her go. When Pelrin had called

Aiden dangerous, perhaps he'd been overreacting—it wouldn't be the first time.

Aiden still held the door open, running his tanned fingers over the handle and toying with the lock. Freddie cleared her throat. His eyes flicked up, and he shoved his hands behind his back, fixing his features into a neutral expression. Freddie's eyes narrowed. They stared at each other for a long moment.

The cabby grunted. "You coming too, lover boy? I don't got all night." He nodded at Aiden then turned to glare at Freddie. With her pallid face and trembling hands, he was probably worried she would puke.

Aiden frowned. She braced herself for a terrible display of his dark power, in retribution for the cabby's nickname.

Instead, he leaned in. "Go directly home." He hesitated before saying, "Good night." His lips twitched in a cautious attempt at a smile, and he gently shut the door.

The cabby harrumphed and gave her a wary look as he reset the meter. Freddie waved back at Aiden, and the cab pulled away, leaving him standing there—alone.

For several minutes, she allowed her fear and stress to flow out of her. She listened to the cars whizzing past. In the rearview mirror, the driver's continued worried looks irked her. She ignored him and took out her phone to find three new messages and two missed calls from Amanda.

[11:01 PM] Where are you??

[11:23 PM] Did you go home with Victor? You sloot!

Freddie smirked at her friend's euphemism for "slut."

[11:30 PM] Seriously we are planning on leaving now, just let me know if you're OK

The time displayed on the cabby's dash shone fifteen minutes to midnight. Amanda was going to kill her. Cowardice told Freddie it was best to text. She typed out the message, "I'm fine, at home," and pushed send. A heaviness settled over her as she leaned against the seat and closed her eyes, allowing her heartbeat to settle back into its usual rhythm. They were headed back to campus; he probably assumed she was a New Wall student.

She leaned forward. "Can you drop me off at the Bailey?"

"You're a lower schooler? Hanging out with a fae like that?" The cabby shuddered and turned down the street that led to the lower school dorms.

"I'm a senior," Freddie said. A sliver of haughtiness slipped into her voice.

"You kids are all the same. Think you're grown because Mommy and Daddy let you go off to school on your own. Haven't you heard about the disappearances?"

"What do you know about them?" She doubted the cabby had any more information than she did, but it didn't hurt to ask.

"Three students gone from this campus, and you kids strut around like it's a parade."

Freddie wrinkled her nose. "You mean two students. Two students have gone missing."

"I had a cop's wife in here the other day. She told me there was a third one, a girl. They're keeping it on the hush though, so don't go spouting off."

Like you just did? "Do you know the girl's name by any chance?" Exhaustion melted off her shoulders.

"Nah, just be careful out there." He stopped in front of the Bailey and Freddie sagged.

She swiped her card on the machine attached to the back of the passenger's seat. At least this expense came with some valuable information. Tomorrow, she could do some more digging, but tonight she needed sleep.

CHAPTER 10

Aiden

Aiden watched the taxi join the steady flow of traffic, wondering what in a pixie's left shoe he'd done. Why did he save her? What did he care if some human girl got herself killed by snooping around his kind? The memory of her lips against his gave him pause. He shook his head. And what in the seven realms was a "normal human date"?

Sticking to the shadows, Aiden walked down the street. The clock tower chimed eleven thirty, giving him time before he needed to return to Fairy. Time to do some research.

He wended.

A brightly lit bookstore sat opposite a cheery fountain. He'd once met some new recruits here and had made a note to come back if he ever got the chance. Though at this late hour, he'd assumed he'd need to break in, but the shop appeared to be open. Slipping a hand into his pocket, Aiden felt in vain for human money. Large stores like the one before him had scanners that could detect enchanted or false coins and bills. He had made that mistake once and had no intention of experiencing that embarrassment again.

Coins glimmered at the bottom of the fountain. Aiden would never understand why humans, who prized money so much, would simply throw it away. It wasn't like the nixies, who lived in these fountains, expected any offerings. He doubted whether they even knew what these coins were for.

Plunging an arm into the water, he winced at its cold bite. It soaked through the thin fabric of his linen tunic and pressed against the side of his jerkin. Silver coins, he knew, were more valuable than the coppers.

He fished for coins until he had a good handful and the chill of the water was more than he could bear. Shoving them into his pockets, he crossed the small square to the bookstore.

Aiden frowned. Bookstores were typically quiet places, but tonight he found himself wading through a sea of squealing human and fae girls. They eyed him critically, casually remarking his costume wasn't quite right. Some dressed like pixies, their skin painted green and their hair covered in sparkles. Plastic wings sprouted from the backs of those who didn't have wings of their own.

"Who are you supposed to be?" One of the false pixies separated herself from the group and blocked Aiden's path.

"What?" he said.

"You don't even have a wristband!" She glared at his dripping sleeve. He shrank back.

"All right, we have fifteen minutes to midnight. We are going to start another round of trivia, so please report to your stations to win some swag," a woman's melodic voice announced from the ceiling.

The girl's eyes lit up. She turned to her friends and squealed before stampeding off with the rest of the pixies. Aiden stumbled to the side, rocked by the movement of the crowd. A slender wilis clung to the information desk. She straightened her gray veil with her withered fingers. Her folded arm posture was so unlike the wilis he'd met in Fairy who'd flee like dandelion lace at the sight of him. Her eyes raked over his black leather armor.

"Can I help you, sir?" Her voice was light and wavery. "If you are here for the new *Silverlake* book, I'm sorry to say we're all sold out of wristbands."

Aiden swallowed; he could face down a hundred fairy

soldiers, but asking for a book at a human shop struck fear into his heart? *Pathetic.* Perhaps this was a bad idea. Perhaps he should try asking Dek what a normal date was like—though he tended to focus on more the intimate activities of courtship. Besides, he'd never keep Aiden's impending date a secret from their majesties. Especially if Dek knew she was human.

Aiden took a cautious step forward. "I, uh...I need a book about normal human dating."

"You wish to date a human?"

"So?" He folded his arms across his chest. His people had nearly been wiped out by ignorant fae who didn't think the realms were big enough for both human and fae-kind.

"I didn't mean any offense, sir. It's just that we have people who wish to study, um, human mating rituals, and then those who plan on actually dating a human."

Aiden bit his lip. Were human mating rituals really so different?

The wili cocked her head to the side. "I think we have just the thing."

She led him past a mob of squealing girls and into a section of books with blush-inducing covers. *She Comes First*—with a picture of a fruit that Aiden doubted he would ever be able to eat again without his mind filling with that awful innuendo—*The Sex Bible,* and other books about positions and techniques lined the walls. *Dek would love this section.* Perhaps human dating wasn't so different after all.

The wili stopped in front of a small section of shelf labeled "Dating." Aiden leaned in to get a better look at the titles.

"What stage is your relationship in?" The wili fluffed her veil, and Aiden wished he could read her expression.

"Stage?"

"Dating? Committed? Are you thinking of wifing her?"

"Wifing?"

"Wifing! Congratulations! Perhaps *Love Languages,* then?" She held up the book. "I'm not married, but I heard it really helps you understand each other."

Aiden flushed a deep scarlet. "Marriage? No. We just met."

"And you are already talking about wifing her?" The wili folded her arms across her chest. Aiden did not need to see beyond her veil to know she was judging him. "A word of advice: if you keep talking like that, you are going to creep her out." She pulled a black and yellow book off the shelf and handed it to him.

"It is now five minutes to midnight. Can we please have all booksellers to the front of the store?" the mysterious voice said.

A loud cheer went up. The wili patted him on the shoulder. "I am so sorry, sir. I have to go. If you are going to buy the book, I suggest you do it now, before *they* start lining up." She jerked her head at the mob of girls.

Aiden nodded and took the book she handed him. *Dating for Dummies.*

"Do you think I'm a fool?" Aiden asked. But she was gone.

He flipped through the book, embarrassed to find the advice rather informative. Midnight was fast approaching. If he wanted this book, he would need to be swift. Aiden wended to the counter and held the book out to a tired-looking human bookseller. The man was plump and balding, with a face covered in acne. He smirked when he read the title of Aiden's book.

"I would think with a face like yours you wouldn't have any trouble in this department." He picked up the book and scanned it. Yawning, he said, "I guess it takes all kinds. Do you have a membership with us?"

Aiden shook his head. His flames pricked beneath the surface of his arms.

"That'll be thirteen twenty-six."

Aiden dumped his handful of silver coins on the counter. The man sighed and counted them out.

"You only have seven dollars and seventy-five cents," he said.

Aiden clenched his fists. He would have to learn how this damned money system worked. Before he could snatch the book and wend away, the wili girl walked past and glanced over the human's shoulder.

"What's wrong, Frank?"

"He's short." The bookseller's voice dropped to a whisper. "You know how *they* are, no idea things cost real money."

The willi sighed. "Just use my discount, and I'll cover the rest. Trust me, he really needs this one."

The booksellers turned to Aiden and laughed. Blue sparks danced down his arms as he fought to keep the flames under control. Keeping his eyes fixed on the counter, Aiden muttered his thanks and snatched up the book.

He wended into the Winter Palace. The frost-covered hallways were deserted, save for the spare guard, as Aiden hurried toward the study and their waiting Majesties. Fixing his gaze on the ground, he tried to calm his racing thoughts.

What had he done? He shouldn't be frivolously dating humans when it could lead nowhere good.

"Is that for Mare?" Dek's rough bark snapped Aiden out of his worrying as the anubis sauntered out from the study.

Aiden looked at the book clutched in his hands, feeling a bright flush wash over his face. "No, this is…" He let the words die in his throat.

The anubis grinned. "If you need any tips, you know where I sleep." He winked before continuing down the passage.

Aiden shoved the book quickly into his jerkin before pushing open the door and stepping inside.

"There you are, pet," Mab's voice rang out, soft and pure. She looked up from her seat, her hands folded delicately in her lap. He crossed the room and bowed low. She stroked his cheek, her nails, ragged and torn, scraping against his skin. Swallowing his disgust, Aiden tried not to stare at her warty, green hands as he straightened. Across from her, leaning against the desk, Oberon folded his arms, his lips tight. The man's clothes were patterned in an intricate silver design that washed out his pale skin. It gleamed in a sickeningly familiar way as the chilly blue light reflected off it. A cold shiver ran through Aiden as Oberon approached, wand in hand. Aiden wondered which of their green fae prisoners had to sacrifice their blood for the king's fashion.

"Come now." The king's hand trembled, gesturing for Aiden

to kneel. Age spots trailed a path up Oberon's frail arm. Mab smiled, revealing her pearly teeth. By the king's tone, Aiden guessed word of the destruction in the Human Realm must have reached them. Their Majesties rarely showed anything kinder than mild disdain for him. "You have done well tonight. Perhaps you are deserving of a bit of a reward."

Mab laughed, patting her husband's arm. The millions of tiny, lavender dew drops that made up her gown slid against one another, creating a soft rustling, like the pattering of spring rain, as she moved. "After we have finished, of course."

CHAPTER 11

Freddie

Freddie kicked off her heels inside the lobby, the stardust on their tips fading to a dull crystal glitter as it did whenever they weren't touching her skin. Wincing, she carefully tiptoed up the three flights of stairs to her room. The lights were on, and the door was unlocked. She froze.

"Finally," Pelrin called from *her* couch. "I know Jefferson's friends can't possibly be that interesting." Freddie groaned and threw her heels under the bed. Of course, Pelrin would be here. "Fred, would you push start on the microwave for me?"

She didn't have the energy to argue, so she did as he asked. The microwave hummed to life as she made her way over to the couch. Propping her feet up on the new box she had found, she wiggled her toes. After a night of holding herself tense, tiny aches ran along her back and shoulders. She could feel Pelrin studying her, but she was determined to enjoy finally being back home.

"So, how was Victor?" Pelrin said as he examined his fingernails.

"Fine." Freddie doubted very much that Pelrin had come over just to ask her how her date was. There was always an angle with him. "How was your day, Pel?" She tugged her skirt down, wary of his intentions.

He sighed and ran a hand through his hair. "It's getting worse out there, you know? Ever since Autumn fell last year, it's been harder and harder to push them back."

Freddie sat up, surprised by the exhaustion and sincerity in his voice. "Are you all right?"

As usual, Pelrin was dressed in the finery that befitted a prince of Fairy. He appeared normal, save for the dark purple patches that hung beneath newly bloodshot eyes.

"I'm fine," he sighed. "I'm just spending more time in the war room than I'd like. My father wants me to lead the troops. I don't think I'll be around too much in the next few months."

Freddie's stomach dropped. *Isn't this what you wanted?*

But Pelrin shouldn't be fighting; he was a prince—he had soldiers to do that for him. She wanted him gone, but not in the middle of the war.

A soft popping noise distracted her, and the scent of butter filled the room. When she looked back at Pelrin, his face was unusually serious.

"But you can still defeat them, right, Pel?" Freddie fidgeted. "I mean, they only have control of Winter and Autumn. Isn't Summer the strongest?"

A wistful expression played across his features. "Perhaps if we had the Staff of Wind and Orb of Ice. Though, we should still be strong enough, especially with Spring..." He trailed off.

"The whats?" Freddie tried to remember if they had ever covered those Fairy artifacts in History. If they had, she couldn't recall.

"The Staff and the Orb are two of the four objects of power created and protected by the Seasonal Realms," he said. "The Staff of Wind was supposed to be guarded by Autumn. When wielded by gold fae, it has the power to summon forces of nature—tornadoes, hurricanes. You know. The Orb of Ice is the same but for Winter. It can conjure blizzards, massive freezes, that kind of thing."

She shuddered. "And Summer? And Spring?"

"We have the Crown of Flames under my protection. Its magic

is terribly powerful, and I have only used it once..." His brow creased, and his eyes glazed over as if recalling some terrible memory.

"And Spring?" she asked again.

The microwave beeped. Pelrin got up from the couch and walked over to it.

"Well, Spring is the big mystery. Nobody really knows what it is or if they lost it like the other realms." He sat back down on the couch with a steaming bag of popcorn. Freddie inhaled the buttery-salty steam as he pulled the bag open and waited for it to cool.

"But how could the other realms lose such powerful objects? Surely someone must know where they are."

Pelrin let out a cold "ha" and glared at the popcorn. "They are lost to the sands of time. We have some general information regarding all the objects in our library. My parents once tried searching for them years ago, but they couldn't find any." He shrugged and popped a kernel into his mouth.

"But there's still hope, right? Against the Dark Fae?" Freddie couldn't understand how he could sit here like this. If all the realms were going to hell, what was he doing here eating popcorn?

"Blizzards, Fred! I didn't mean to make you worry. Of course, there's hope." He hesitantly patted her knee. "The Crown of Flames is easily the most powerful of the four, and we haven't even used it yet." He laughed and reached for the remote. Freddie bit her lip, unsure if he was just laughing to put her at ease, or if the danger was much closer than she'd thought. "The problem we face now is their army has grown so much in the past year. All these young red fae crossing the border to join them are overwhelming my forces."

Freddie pulled her knees to her chest, shoving back images of hordes of vampires, werewolves, and other red fae ransacking Summer and torturing Pelrin.

"We'll beat them," he said and rubbed his chin thoughtfully. "I just don't want to kill that many people in the process. They are all fighting for what they believe in, even if it is misguided."

Freddie let out a breath. Part of the reason why she'd loved him so much was his willingness to listen to the brown fae's problems. He'd petitioned his parents several times on their behalf, but the king and queen of Summer believed the brown fae should be punished for their "rebellion." They even had some choice things to say about humans and red fae "staying where they belonged".

"Go change." Pelrin pointed to the closet. "I'll put a movie on."

Freddie hesitated, forcing herself to remember the pain she'd felt when she'd learned the truth about him and that fae girl. It was starting to feel too much like one of their old date nights. Just the two of them, snuggled on the couch, watching a movie, one thing leading to another, and...

Her face must have shown her unease because Pelrin said, "Just friends." Freddie almost relaxed, wanting more than anything to believe him. Pelrin held up his hands. "No *Titanic,* I promise."

Freddie nodded and slipped into the dark of her closet to grope around for a pair of sweats. She returned and sat on the small couch as far from Pelrin as she could get without falling off. He didn't seem to notice and started the movie.

Freddie recognized the intro theme to *Thumbelina.* It had been her favorite movie as a kid. For the first ten years of her life, she'd been madly in love with Prince Cornelius, which was why Pelrin had seemed like a dream come true—at first, anyway. Her eyes grew heavy as she recalled the way he'd pulled her from the sea two summers ago. It'd seemed like a fairy tale. But she was not like Thumbelina, marrying a fairy prince and getting her wings. Pelrin had decided a mere wingless human wasn't enough for him. She cradled her head on the slim arm of the couch. Perhaps in her version of the story, she would end up with the beetle instead of the prince.

"Blizzards," Pelrin yelled. "Just one damn night. Is that too much to ask?"

Freddie's eyes snapped open. She must have fallen asleep during the film. Groggily, she stared at him, her head throbbing. "What's wrong?"

He pointed at the TV with the remote. The movie had finished, and he was watching the news. Firefighters were putting out the remains of a large rectangular building—bright blue flames still flickered on one end. The bar at the bottom of the screen read: Fae attack on Liberty Bell. Freddie's stomach twisted. A reporter stood away from the building, clutching a microphone with both hands.

"Behind me is all that remains of the historic Liberty Bell," the reporter said. "Eyewitness reports state that a vampire man, a were woman, and an unidentified fae man started the fire and incited a fae riot in the surrounding area. Authorities are still tracking down those responsible, and several arrests have been made. Luckily, there were no serious casualties. However, residents of the New Wall area are advised to stay in their homes until the situation is under control. Now to Pat with the list of schools that will be closed tomorrow due to this tragedy."

Pelrin was on his feet. He gripped the remote so tightly that Freddie could see cracks webbing out from between his fingers.

"Pel—" She reached for the remote.

He threw it on the bed with a hard thump that made the batteries fall out. "Damn it! Why do they always try keeping these things from me? I have to go. They'll need my help. I really shouldn't be sparing any guards with the crown and all, but..." He gripped his hair.

"Wait, they're after your crown? Like, now?" Freddie sat up straighter.

"We've had one attempt. Nothing I couldn't handle." He frowned at the TV. The reporter was now doing a story about a rash of liquor store robberies—they were, of course, blaming fae, again. "Don't worry, Freddie. I'll handle it." He leaned toward her lips then stopped himself. Casting her a sorrowful glance, he wended away.

Freddie's knee bounced. Her head pounded with thoughts of Pelrin fighting. She got up from the couch and turned off the TV. He shouldn't be wasting his energy fighting fires. Humans were much more capable of handling their own problems than Pelrin gave them credit for. She chewed her bottom lip; Pelrin shouldn't be fighting the Dark Fae either. Dragging the comforter Pelrin must have spread over her back to the bed, she wrapped herself in it and stared out the window. She wanted Pelrin out of her life, yes, but not hurt or dead.

For several minutes, she tried falling asleep but eventually gave up and pulled out her laptop. Searching for student disappearances, she scrolled through article after article, hoping to find some scrap of a lead. Eventually, she came across the image of a memorial service in Maryland for the missing students. Amongst the mourners was a blonde girl who looked bored, her arms folded, her body slouched. Freddie yawned. She could have sworn she'd seen that girl before... Slumping onto her computer, she drifted into unconsciousness.

Sometime during her sleep-starved research, a puff of blue smoke appeared in front of her. Freddie put a hand to her head, not quite sure if she was awake or dreaming. From the smoke, a scrap of paper fluttered into her lap.

Written in neat, black script were the words "Friday, 5pm, North Tower."

She blinked a few times, each an attempt to make sure she had read the words correctly. Perhaps Aiden really did want to go on this date after all.

Now she would have to decide if *she* did.

CHAPTER 12

Freddie

When Freddie hurried into English, Mallory was standing, arms folded, over a girl whose beige foundation did little to hide her blue skin.

"It's people like you, Jaladri. Acting like you don't care when *your* people destroyed a national monument." Mallory leaned over the girl's desk.

Jaladri leaned back. "I didn't say I didn't care. All I said was I'm not apologizing for something I didn't do."

Freddie's eyes widened. Her feet moved across the room before her head caught up with them. "Did you seriously ask *her* to apologize for that crap at the Liberty Bell? Jaladri obviously wasn't there!"

"I asked all the fae to apologize. Their people brutalize us, and they say nothing, but every time there's an attack on a fae suddenly us humans are supposed to do something about it." Mallory turned to face Freddie.

"That's not fair." Jaladri shouted. "It was just some radicals."

"Besides, Margery, no one got hurt," Freddie said.

Before Mallory could respond, Mr. Barker puffed into the room, his face pink from running. "Sorry dudes, got distracted by some bomb grooves, ya dig?"

The class stared blankly back at him. Mr. Barker cleared his throat. "Right, uh, chic-as, take a seat-a so we can get started."

Freddie and Mallory stared daggers at each other as they took their usual places in the first and second rows. Jaladri shrank down in her desk as Mr. Barker instructed them to open their books to a chapter on poetry.

Freddie groaned – it wasn't even April yet. Beside her, Mallory began reading aloud in her annoying, nasally voice. Already, Freddie could feel herself nodding off.

Goodnight Fairies
By Marcus Bremen
Brownies hide beneath your bed
while greenies dance around your head,

Sleep and know red fae shan't bite
for golden ones shed watchful light

Blue fairy's shining; make a wish,
Now close your eyes and keep my kiss

"Hey, Freddie, can you lay down some words about this diddy?"

Freddie blinked and sat up straighter. Mr. Barker and Mallory both stared at her expectantly while the rest of the class was deeply engaged in various stages of boredom. Chuck Perrault's soft snores were just barely muffled by the giggling of the banshee girls snapping pictures of him. Freddie stared at the page, a nursery rhyme she'd heard at least a thousand times as a child.

"Uh, it's a political statement?" she said. With Mr. Barker, everything was a political statement against the so-called 'man'.

Mallory tisked. "It's just a poem meant to comfort children. It's the oldest poem mentioning all four types of fae." She blinked up at Mr. Barker, no doubt awaiting praise.

"That's right, *chicas*. 'A' plus for knowing your stuff," Mr. Barker said. "Now, Freddie, can you explain *how* this is a political statement?"

She swallowed. "Well, it paints red fae in a negative light for one." She read each line over again. "It looks like there is some sort of hierarchy here as well."

"Nice one!" Mr. Barker slammed his hand on the desk. Chuck fell sideways and hit the floor. His wings fluttered madly as he tried to right himself. "Bremen was a famous political commentator during the first inter-realm conference. It is widely believed this poem was meant to help the public understand the social hierarchy on the other side of the Fairy border."

"Mr. Barker?" Mallory waved her hand in the air, and Freddie massaged her temples. "This makes it seem like Bremen, or even the humans at that time, only feared red fae. When, in fact, we know the truth of the matter is all fae were viewed with fear in the early 1500s."

"That's a good point, Mal," Mr. Barker said.

"It's Mallory."

"Right. It could be viewed that the poet is trying to sway public opinion of fae so the conference would result in a peaceful relationship between the realms."

"Isn't that what happened?" Freddie didn't bother to raise her hand. "We have lived in peace with fae for generations. It was probably more than this one poem that changed public opinion."

"Actually, there was a lot of literature on both sides of the issue. There were those that wanted to keep persecuting fae and those that wanted to push for coexistence — which brings us to our assignment. You guys need to find a piece of literature that pushes for either persecution or coexistence. I'll need a five-page analysis on the biases, due by next Friday."

The class groaned. Mallory primly noted the assignment in her day planner. "Persecution is a bit of an exaggeration," she said under her breath.

"They were burned, Molly!" Freddie balled her hands into fists, crushing the paper. "Are you really that heartless?"

Mallory finished writing, her brown eyes widening innocently. "If the fae had just stayed in Fairy, they wouldn't have had to worry about being so-called persecuted."

"So, no diversity? Maybe all Black people should just go to Africa too, huh?" The words scraped at a hard, raw part of her. Not for the first time did she wonder if her passion for fae rights was just a facade to cover up her fear of her own brown skin.

"Well, actually—"

Freddie jumped out of her seat, the chair falling behind her. "Tell me, Michelle, what would we do with all the mixed race people?" Tears glistened in her eyes.

"Wow." Mallory tossed her braid over her shoulder. "And you wonder why we have such violence in our society," she said in a voice just barely audible.

Freddie's face flushed red. She opened her mouth to retort, when Mr. Barker cut her off.

"Whoa! Okay this is getting really out of hand, you two." Mr. Barker's laid-back attitude had dropped. A chill raced down Freddie's spine. "I can barely get through a class anymore without the two of you going at it. Maybe a detention or two will mellow you out."

"Mr. Barker, be reasonable," Mallory said. "You can see how she always instigates it."

"That's it. Mal, Fred—both of you, my office, Friday after school."

Freddie glowered at Mallory. Three years of a perfect record, now ruined. Fighting the urge to pick up her chair and hurl it at the bigoted red-head, she righted it and sat back down.

After the bell rang, Freddie was the first one out of the classroom, her ears still burning.

"What's a detention?" Ginnith wormed her way out of Freddie's backpack and fluttered in front of her.

A heaviness settled on Freddie as she sighed. "It's a punishment. We have to sit in total silence with Mr. Barker and each other. No phones. No laptops. Only homework on school issued computers."

Ginnith rubbed her chin. "We don't have any of those things in Fairy. I guess we have lots of detentions. Sitting in silence for an hour isn't that bad."

Freddie stared at her. How could you explain how awful detentions were to someone who lived without electricity? Ginnith's inability to comprehend detentions diffused her fury, leaving an emptiness in the pit of her stomach. Instead of bothering with an explanation, she shook her head and continued toward the lower-school cafeteria. It was Tuesday, which meant both Amanda and Raul had class, leaving Freddie on her own.

The images of Freya and the other boy, Daniel, watched her from the bulletin board. Freddie leaned in to examine the posters. Daniel had been in her grade. She frowned, trying to remember if she'd ever had a class with him. Skinny as a stick with thin-framed glasses magnifying his eyes, he looked like the type of boy who would keep to himself.

Freddie pulled out her phone and plugged his name into the search engine. The first thing that came up was a series of articles on his disappearance. She sighed and leaned against the side of the building.

"What are you doing?" Ginnith peered down to hover over the phone.

"Research. I want to find out more about that guy on the wall." Ginnith fluttered over to study the photo while Freddie scrolled through the results. She stopped when she saw a website titled *Curse of Ages* and tapped it. It was a profile for RodofWar12, aka Daniel Brown. Freddie rolled her eyes as she read through the last few posts.

"Any nymphs out there want to join the Rod on a chalice quest? I'll make it worth your while ;)" and "Hey, SexyNymph47, let's you and me go on a couple's quest."

She pulled the phone closer. There had been a response to that last one. Apparently, whoever SexyNymph47 was, they'd agreed to go on this quest and take their conversation to DMs. Freddie chewed her lower lip. The date on the message had been just a couple days before Daniel had gone missing. This could be a clue. Had the police found this?

"I doubt that human is going to be in that box of yours."

Ginnith fluttered into Freddie's face.

She brushed the pixie away. "Quiet, Ginni. I just thought of something."

Freddie searched through the lists of recent quests. One name kept appearing over and over again, RagingSword54. She shuddered. Couldn't these boys take their heads out of the gutter to think of better names? RagingSword's profile said his real name was Emmett Roe. Freddie let out a groan. Emmet had been the most obnoxious kid in her algebra class last year. Appetite gone, she walked a short ways down the path to find a bench, while searching her email for the class phone list.

"I thought we were going to eat." Ginnith plunked down next to Freddie on the edge of the bench, her little wings drooping behind her.

"I'm not hungry," Freddie said absently. She took a deep breath and began crafting a message to Emmett. If anyone knew what happened with Daniel and that SexyNymph, it would be him.

"But we haven't eaten since breakfast!" During Ginnith's first couple of days on guard duty, she had brought military rations with her from Fairy. After a week of picking off Freddie's plate, the pixie had decided that eating things like tacos, pizza, and ramen was much more suited to her tastes than the hard bread crumbs and jerky she'd brought with her.

"Here." Freddie plunged one hand into her backpack and shoved a half-crushed packet of Oreos at her. The pixie's eyes lit up as she tore apart the packaging with her razor sharp teeth.

[01:35 PM] Hey Emmett, it's Freddie from Algebra. Think you could help me with some Calc problems?

Freddie winced and pressed send.

[01:35 PM] At the dorm. Where r u?

Freddie hesitated. The cafeteria was too loud for an interview, but there was no way in hell she was inviting him up to her room.

[01:37 PM] Library. Do you have time now?

[01:37 PM] OMW!!

She turned her face away from the phone, cringing as though it were about to bite her. It would take him at least ten minutes to get from the Bailey to the library, and that was if he left right away. Ginnith perched on her shoulder, face covered in white smudges and black crumbs.

Freddie started across campus to the library. The New Wall Library was built in the skeleton of an old bank. Freddie passed beneath the looming white columns and into the cool dampened light of the building. Long wooden tables, paired with uncomfortable benches, filled the space where the lines once formed. Freddie took a seat midway between the circulation desk and the door. Miss Euryale, the school's ageless librarian, narrowed her eyes and patted her turban as Freddie hastily unpacked her things.

"What's this place?" Ginnith's voice rose above the accepted decibel. Miss Euryale looked up, and Freddie waved her hands frantically to shush the little pixie. Rumor had it that people who got on the librarian's bad side turned to stone. Freddie wasn't sure if this was true, but there was no reason to take risks.

"The library. Just keep your voice down. I don't want us to get kicked out."

Ginnith glared and marched into the shadows of Freddie's backpack.

Precisely seven minutes later, Emmett came panting into the library, his usually pallid face bright red and covered in sweat. As he searched the rows of benches, Freddie fought against every instinct in her body not to duck down and pretend to be invisible. He spotted her and strode down the row to take a seat beside her.

"So, Freddie, I was wondering how long it would be until you texted me." He hummed a stupid laugh.

"Hey, Emmett," Freddie said. She already wanted to punch him. "Before we get started, I wanted to say I saw your profile on *Curse of Ages*. You're pretty strong, aren't you?"

"You play?" Emmett looked at Freddie as though she'd just sprouted wings.

"I just started reading about it. I don't really know if I could keep up."

"I could totally teach you. You could come by my room, and

we could play together." He waggled his eyebrows at her.

Freddie swallowed down the urge to say something mean like, "only in your dreams, nerd" and instead said, "Wouldn't your roommate mind?"

Emmett ran a hand through his greasy brown hair. "I got a single this year. It could be just you and me. I could even score some of my mom's boss cookies."

Freddie fought a grimace. "I thought *Curse of Ages* was a group game. Don't you have friends that you play with?"

"Well, there was Dan... Daniel Brown... but he hasn't been around lately."

Bingo! "He's that missing guy, right? I'm so sorry. I didn't know you two were friends."

Emmett shrugged.

"Have the police been all over you?" Freddie did her best to sound more concerned than curious.

"Yeah, a bit. They swung by and asked me some questions, then left me alone. Just between you and me though, Dan's fine."

"What?" Freddie's false sympathy tone dropped.

"He met this chick in the game. They started DM'ing, one thing led to another, and he ran off with her. They're probably getting all hot and crazy right now. He'll be back."

"So you saw this girl, then?" How could Emmett think keeping this to himself was a good idea? Daniel's parents were probably sick with worry.

"Naw, Dan went to meet her that day they said he'd gone missing." Emmett hummed another smug laugh. "Guess he'll show them. I've been dying to tell someone, but I can't give Dan away. He deserves to have his fun, especially after Stella..."

Freddie blinked. "Stella, you mean that Charm City chick?"

"Yeah, Dan's pretty smooth with the ladies. Used to be a regular there if you know what I mean." Emmet winked.

No wonder Stella had lied about Daniel being at the shop. "So what, he went to see Stella and then went to see this SexyNymph girl?"

"Well...he texted me. Stella dumped him, so he met up with

the girl from the game. Didn't say anything after that."

"Emmett, it's been over a week. Don't you think something could have happened to him? That girl online could have been anyone!"

Emmett gave her a knowing smirk. Freddie grit her teeth and counted slowly in her head. "She sent him pics. And she was a legit fae babe, blonde hair, fuck-me blue eyes... He hit the jackpot." Emmett leaned closer. Freddie scooted back, nearly falling off the hard, wooden bench.

"I think you should tell the police, Emmett. This could be serious."

Emmett shrugged. "Let's not talk about Dan anymore. I mean, I saw you after that fairy douche dumped you. You were a wreck, but if you need a shoulder to cry on..." He leaned closer.

Heat flooded Freddie's body. She clenched her fists, breathing deeply through her nose as she tried to keep her voice calm. "I broke up with him. And I'm fine. I'm seeing someone else now." Her mind flitted to her impending date with Aiden. Could he have been SexyNymph47? It was easy enough to find girls' pictures online. Pelrin had said Aiden was behind the disappearances. Could he have been catfishing people and luring them into Fairy? If she decided to show for their date, maybe she could get the answer out of him.

"Yeah?" Emmett's voice was stiff. "He go here?"

"No, he's from Fairy." Freddie looked around. Only a few kids, noses buried in books, and Miss Euryale sat in the near-silent space. Freddie swallowed and glanced back at Emmett, who had a strange expression on his face.

"So you only date fae, huh?"

"Not exclusively. Just a coincidence, really."

"Maybe it's because you don't know what it's like being with a human man." He put a hand on Freddie's thigh and pulled himself closer.

In an instant, she had her gold flat in her hand and struck it across Emmett's face so hard it left a deep red shoe print on his cheek. Before he could cry out in pain, his eyes bulged and he slumped forward onto the table—a tiny arrow sticking from his neck.

Miss Euryale looked up. Her eyes flicked to Emmett's slumped form and the pixie that was striding across the table. Freddie clapped her hands together, silently pleading with the librarian. The corner of the woman's mouth quirked up, and she returned her focus to her books.

"Oh my God, Ginni, did you kill him?" Freddie hissed as the pixie yanked out the toothpick sized arrow buried in Emmett's neck.

"No, he's just sleeping. Want me to?" She hefted her sheath of arrows up, indicating the red-fletched poison ones.

"Uh, no, thanks. I was handling that though."

"Yeah, I saw. You did well, for a human." Ginnith sighed. "I was just bored." She jumped into the air as Freddie got to her feet.

Leaving Emmett to drool on the table, Freddie and the pixie hurried out of the library while she ran through what she had learned in her head. Daniel had met some girl he'd thought was a nymph and ran off to meet her. Then there was Freya—had she met someone online too? Raul had said they were going out; maybe he would know if she was a gamer. Then again, if all the missing students had been gamers, the FIDs, Fae Investigative Department, surely would have figured that out by now.

Freddie bit her lip. There was one more thing she had to look into. Aiden. Some red and brown fae in Fairy still ate humans; maybe he was kidnapping the students to feed to his army. She shuddered at the thought.

Friday, she would meet him and try to get the truth. It was a good thing North Tower was on campus. If something went wrong, she wanted to be well within screaming distance of campus security.

CHAPTER 13

Freddie

There was only one good thing about Freddie's detention: time to work on her poetry assignment. She had chosen to analyze *The Pied Piper of Hamlin*. The piper was most likely some type of fae, although she needed to do more digging to find out what kind. It demonstrated both sides of the argument by showing a fae who was both helpful and vengeful when he was wronged. The moral of the story: don't mess with people if you don't want to be messed with yourself. Though, she found it curious that one fae could lure away so many children... if she could just find out what kind he was, perhaps it could help her solve these disappearances. It wasn't too far a stretch to upgrade from a pipe to catfishing on the internet—things change in 500 years.

A little after four-thirty, Mr. Barker finally freed her and she hurried toward the shuttle stop. The North Tower was on the upper school campus, and she didn't have time to change. Perhaps that was for the best. She needed to focus on interviewing Aiden without tipping him off; she couldn't worry about tugging up or down a too-tight dress all night.

Ginnith buzzed beside her. "Where are you going?"

Freddie ground her teeth. "I already told you. Amanda,

Jefferson, and I are going to watch Raul's game." She'd told Amanda about the date the morning after she had received Aiden's message, referring to him as a "not-quite-friend" of Pelrin's. Amanda had been disappointed that things hadn't worked out with Victor, but Freddie hadn't mentioned how he'd abandoned her at the first sight of that other vampire. However, Amanda was eager to help her friend move on, and the game was the perfect cover story to ditch Ginnith.

Amanda leaned against the shuttle-stop post in a sparse crowd of lower schoolers, all decked out in blue and yellow — New Wall's colors. To make her lie more convincing, Freddie had worn a yellow sweater and blue jeans. Ginnith surveyed her critically. "The vampire and the werewolf will be watching you tonight?"

"Yup, they'll make sure I have food and water and sunlight. Everything I need to be safe and free from harm."

"Sunlight?" Ginnith's brow furrowed.

Freddie sighed. "Just an expression. Go have fun with your not-a-boyfriend or whatever." The shuttle pulled up to the curb and Freddie joined the crowd of students attempting to cram themselves through the tiny doors.

"Don't do anything stupid, human," Ginnith said and took off into the sky. Freddie waved after her.

When she returned her gaze to the shuttle, the doors were just about to close. She ran and jumped onto the bus. The shuttle driver narrowed her eyes as Freddie inched her way between the standing students to find Amanda. As she approached, Amanda moved her oversized purse so Freddie could sit.

"So, it worked?" Amanda grinned.

"I'm free," Freddie said. Her voice didn't hold the enthusiasm she'd hoped for. Aiden could be dangerous, after all — this wouldn't be as simple as interviewing Stella or Berta. There was still time to back out...

"It's so weird he's meeting you at North Tower, but I guess it's a central spot. Maybe he's prepared a romantic picnic with candles and —"

"Amanda, it's a first date. Besides, I don't even know how into me he is. Chill."

Amanda squealed and bounced in her seat. "Sorry, I'm just super excited for you. Even though... it'll probably end badly since he knows Pelrin, I'm proud of you for getting back out there."

Freddie rolled her eyes. Amanda had no idea how truly awfully this could end.

When they reached the upper school, Amanda followed the flow of the crowd toward the stadium while Freddie walked in the opposite direction toward North Tower. Its crystal windows glimmered in the bright autumn sunlight. Once she'd found the monument beautiful, but her impending date had transformed it into something sharp and menacing. She checked the time: five minutes to spare... maybe this was a bad idea.

"You're early."

Freddie jumped, nearly dropping her phone. She spun to face Aiden.

"You showed up," she said, trying to catch her breath.

"We had a bargain. I couldn't get out of this if I wanted to." He shrugged.

Freddie leaned to the side to search his back for any wing-shaped lumps beneath his Fairy-style black shirt and jerkin. They hugged tight against his body, hinting at nothing but the lean muscles beneath. Well, there were probably other fae besides fairies that couldn't lie or were bound to their word. Perhaps he was a freakishly tall elf, though his ears were only slightly pointed like Pelrin's. She considered the possibilities a moment longer.

"Do I appear strange to you?" Aiden stepped back.

Freddie blinked. She didn't realize she'd been staring for so long. "Uh—sorry, no. You look..." The first thing that came to mind was 'obviously from Fairy,' but she didn't dare insult him. "Nice." She bit her lip. Even Pelrin wore normal, human clothes when he was in public.

"I look the same as I did before," he said, then added, "You look different."

Freddie let out an awkward laugh. *For the article.* "Is that a bad thing?" Perhaps he was the type of guy who preferred girls in heels and skin-tight club dresses. If he was, then she was more than happy to disappoint.

Aiden's eyebrows shot up, disappearing beneath his wavy locks. He scrutinized her for a second time, eyes narrowed. "No, it's good. I mean you look nice. You have... nice teeth."

"Wow," Freddie said. She had to dig deep from her reservoir of fake sincerity. "You are really good at compliments."

He pushed back his shoulders, and his chest swelled slightly. *Good God.* Her stomach gurgled; nerves had prevented her from eating all day. Freddie cleared her throat to mask the sound.

"Shall we head up?" he said.

Freddie's stomach dropped into her boots. Had he somehow known heights were not her thing? Was he leading her into some sort of trap?

"Sure," she said, not daring to show weakness in front of him.

Her legs shook as she followed Aiden into the atrium of the stone building. It was just one foot in front of the other. "You're fine," she muttered to herself. It was only a one-hundred-foot tower with a possible fae serial killer.

Their footsteps echoed as they walked through the marble space. Freddie walked over to the elevator, then glanced back at Aiden. He stood a couple feet away with one foot on the stairs.

"So, not the elevator?" She pointed at the polished brass doors.

"The what?" He frowned. Her shoulders sagged. She would be sweating like an ice pixie in Summer by the time they got to the top of the tower.

"You're afraid," he said. Freddie walked shakily over to where he stood and took the lead up the stairs. At least if she fell he'd be there to cushion her.

"No, I'm not. I'm fine." Her voice broke.

Aiden smiled. Of course he would think her fear was funny; he probably reveled in the fear of his victims. Maybe this was a bad idea. Maybe he could sense her fear of heights and was feeding off it or using it to ripen her up to do God knows what. Images of Aiden laughing while he tortured the missing students flashed through her mind. Freya, Daniel, and the others appeared as shadows, screaming and covered in blood...

"If you're so afraid of me, why did you want to do this?"

Freddie jerked at the sound of his voice, slipping off the step and struggling to regain her footing. Her knuckles whitened as she gripped the railing, now slick with sweat, and turned to face him.

"I'm not afraid of you." Her voice rose an octave as she pulled herself up the next step.

"Then why are your legs shaking like that?"

"I'm cold." She closed her eyes and took another step, desperate to prove she wasn't afraid of him, or of the tower.

Her fake courage didn't help slow the beating of her heart or ease the churning in her stomach.

Aiden waved a hand. A warm breeze blew past her, causing her face and neck to tingle in its warmth. "Better?" he asked.

She stared at him. Pelrin had never used magic so casually. Freddie wasn't even sure he had the power to conjure warmth out of nothing.

"Y-yes, thank you." She returned her focus to rigidly climbing the stairs, keeping her knees locked so they wouldn't reveal her still very present fear.

They climbed in silence for several long minutes. Sweat beaded on her neck and trickled down her back as she reminded herself she should be interviewing him. She needed to relax the mood, so he'd reveal important information. The warm, magicked air had grown stifling, and a dull roaring swelled in her ears.

"Crazy about those missing people, huh?" Freddie said. Aiden paused on the step behind her.

"You must forgive my lack of knowledge regarding human news," he said. "Is that a significant problem here?"

Freddie's heart sank. He sounded so genuine. "Yeah, it's a pretty big deal. Some people say fae are behind it."

"It's possible."

They resumed climbing in awkward silence. Freddie wracked her brain to think up another angle of questioning.

"So, have you heard any good jokes?"

"What?" Freddie wheezed. Sweaty and disheveled, she

glanced over her shoulder. Up until now, Pelrin had been the most beautiful man she'd ever seen. Aiden, however, could give Pelrin a run for his money. His dark windswept hair and passive expression made it look as though they were going for a nice stroll rather than hiking up the tallest building in Easton.

Aiden huffed a laugh and waved his hand again. The warmth eased, and Freddie's grip on the railing relaxed. He was actually going out of his way to make her feel comfortable. *Like a normal guy, on a normal date.* Besides, if he wanted to kill her, he could have done it a hundred ways by now.

"Any good jokes?" Aiden said again.

Freddie scrunched up her face. What type of joke would someone from Fairy enjoy? A riddle, perhaps?

"What's green and has yellow wheels?" she said.

He slowed his pace as he mulled over the question. His face seemed to reflect his thoughts, brightening as he considered one idea and frowning as he discarded it.

"Is it one of those *taxis*, in those colors?" He pronounced the word 'taxis' slowly and deliberately, as if trying to impress her with his recollection of the word.

"Nope." She climbed several more steps. The windows were now so high that all she could see was the azure sky.

"A bicycle?"

Freddie raised her eyebrows, and Aiden's face lifted. "You know about bicycles?"

"We have them in Fairy, too." His expression fell, realizing he'd guessed wrong.

As they made their way up, he continued to throw out answers: everything from a garden cart to a green bird with wheels for feet. She replied 'nope' to each one, though Aiden didn't seem to tire from guessing wrong. Rather, each incorrect answer appeared to motivate him further.

Twenty minutes passed. The stairs let out into an open, circular observation room. Large arches framed the space, each in turn framing an iridescent crystal window. Several small podiums stood evenly placed around the room, each explaining the historical significance of the school, town, and tower. Beyond the windows, the sun was setting. Freddie sucked in a breath as she took it all in.

"What's the answer?" Aiden said. Defeat marred his handsome features.

Freddie bit her lip to keep from laughing. "The answer is..." She shook her head, pausing for dramatic effect. He just looked so sad. "Grass!"

Aiden frowned. "But grass doesn't have—"

"I lied about the wheels." She and Pelrin had played riddle games often. It'd been near impossible to stump him without lying.

"That was not a fair riddle." Aiden's frown deepened. "Though," he began slowly, "I suppose I should have thought of that. I have been around fairies for too long."

Freddie burst into laughter. She hadn't realized the additional layer of irony in the joke. Her laugh lasted longer and took on a hysterical note as her anxiety resurfaced.

Aiden didn't seem to notice—or, if he did, at least he didn't let it show. Walking over to one of the windows, he leaned against the bubble-like pane and gazed over the tiny homes and campus buildings below. Freddie took a deep breath and inched her way over to him. Her eyes remained fixed forward. Not daring to look down, she slid her feet across the ground until she was a hand's reach behind him. He turned to face her, his amber eyes glittering, as they reflected the brilliant sunset. She bit her lip, and he cocked his head to the side.

"You are still afraid," he said.

Freddie thought she caught a hint of sadness in his tone, but that would be ridiculous. "Not of you." This time she told the truth. His actions so far were not those of a killer, nor those of one who fed on fear. Pelrin was overreacting; there was no way Aiden could be the monster he'd described.

"If not me, then what?" He peered into the shadows around her as if expecting to see a spider, rat, or potentially something worse.

"I don't like heights." She flicked a glance at the stairs while he hid a smile behind his hand. "It's not funny!" Freddie glared at him and took a step back.

Aiden made to follow her. "You are afraid of heights but not of me?" He took another step closer, and his mischievous grin faded. "I suppose it is because you do not know who I am."

"I know who you are." She met his stare for a long moment before saying, "Aiden."

His brows shot up, and his eyes widened. "You know my name? But how?" His gaze intensified as he scrutinized her face. Freddie pursed her lips. A fae as powerful as Aiden could probably use her name to summon her right to him. It was probably best to keep it to herself. "You are human, right?" His voice was hesitant.

"I have fae friends." She shrugged and stepped away from him. This time he did not follow.

"Ah, the one who pulled you away that night? I guess I have met a few red fae who may have revealed it," he said. His brows creased. "And they approve of you going on a date with me?" Notes of sarcasm rang in his words.

A sly smile spread across Freddie's face. "No, they don't."

Aiden let out a breath, his brow still furrowed. Freddie wished she knew what he was thinking. A wall of silence passed between them. Several times he opened his mouth as if to say something but then thought better of it.

The feelings of doubt and fear that reflected back at her in Aiden's expressions would have never dared cross Pelrin's face.

She needed to break the tension and get the information she'd come for. "Why are we here?" If he were behind the disappearances, why on earth would he take her to North Tower? Anyone could pass by and see them.

"I am supposed to take you someplace I like," he said. She hadn't expected that. He moved closer to her.

"What do you like about being up here? Not that it's not beautiful."

"It reminds me of flying." He turned toward an arch that led onto the balcony. A breeze swept in, ruffling his hair as he stared out over the horizon.

"You can't fly?" She hadn't seen any hint of wings, but if his powers, love of riddles, and bargains didn't scream fairy, she didn't know what did. Was it possible he could have found a rare spell that could cast a glamour over his wings?

"No, I can't." A pained strain pulled at his voice, and his lips tightened into a grim line. "I don't have wings."

Not a fairy then.

"That's all right. I don't have wings either." The words left her mouth before she had a chance to think them through. Of course, she didn't have wings—she was human.

"Come out onto the balcony with me." He offered her his hand.

Freddie shook her head. "I'm not a fan of heights, remember?" She was about to move away again, but the saddened look on his face made her pause.

"I could help you," he said in a voice almost too quiet for her to hear.

She took his hand and stepped closer, breathing in his scent of lilac and sweet clover. It was so unlike the heavy summery scents that always rolled off Pelrin.

She mumbled a weak agreement, and they shuffled slowly toward the arch. Just before they stepped onto the balcony, Freddie's heart pounded and, without thinking, she tightened her grip on his hand. He jerked away as if she had touched him with lightning.

"How is it you show no fear in tempting vampires, but you cower before a balcony?" Aiden said.

"I don't know." It was somewhat comforting to know he hadn't seen her fear at the vampire lounge.

His eyes flicked to hers, asking wordless permission as he slid an arm around her waist. He took a small step forward, gently guiding her out into the open air. Wind whipped against her face, and she pressed herself into him, cringing as she dragged her feet across the ground.

"See, isn't this better than vampires?"

Freddie gasped as she stared out over all of Easton. The distant skyscrapers of New Wall City were no larger than Legos while the lights of the town glimmered like fireflies in the fading sun. A ribbon of gold, the Susquehanna River, cut through Easton, separating it from New Wall. The Delaware had already turned black from shadow.

For once, words escaped her as she leaned against him, watching the sky fade from orange to a soft pinkish-purple. She tilted her head up to see him staring at the far-off city and a hot blush raced up her neck, coloring her cheeks.

Her stomach, of course, chose this moment to let out a loud growl. Aiden looked down at her, the moment shattered. Freddie gave a nervous laugh.

"Can we go eat now?" she said. It was becoming harder and harder to believe he had anything to do with the disappearances. And if this was just a date, those typically involved food.

"Eat?" Aiden withdrew his hand from her waist to cross his arms in front of his chest.

"It's past dinnertime, and this is a date, right?" If she didn't get some food, and soon, she would get hangry, and this date would not end well.

"I had not planned on…" His hand moved to the pocket inside his jerkin then faltered. Freddie knew that expression well. She, too, had to scrounge for extra cash as she rationed out the money made from her summer job at the local paper. And unless you were a gold fae like Pelrin, human money didn't come easily to fae who didn't live on this side of the border.

"Come on. My treat." Freddie retreated into the safety of the observation room and marched over to the elevator. There would be no more of this stairs nonsense.

The elevator dinged, and she stepped inside. Aiden peered into the gold, wallpapered room. The mirror on the back wall reflected his startled expression. Aiden ran his hands along one side of the door and reached into the gap between. His arm snapped back when the doors jerked, trying to close. Eyes wide, he pressed himself against the railing at Freddie's side. She smirked. Doors closing, the elevator descended.

"So, burgers, tacos, or pasta?" she said, ignoring the whiteness of his knuckles against the brass.

"Dr. Joy says if you must eat, it should be fork food," he said. His eyes raced from the buttons to the doors, then up to the ceiling.

The monster in Freddie's stomach roared again; whoever this Dr. Joy was, she had great taste in food. "Pasta it is!"

The elevator dinged, and she strode out, Aiden wobbling behind her.

CHAPTER 14

Aiden

A iden let out a shaky breath—he would have to revisit that moving box later. For the time being, he was relieved to be in one piece and back on the ground.

This night was not going at all as he had planned. The book had specifically stated that food was not a required part of a first date. Perhaps she was doing this on purpose, so he would fail to fulfill his end of the bargain and... His shoulders slumped. The only consequence, for her, would be she could put herself in harm's way. And that didn't matter, or at least it shouldn't.

Somewhere in the distance came screams and the sounds of horns and drums. He glanced over at the girl, but she did not appear alarmed. Following her gaze in that direction, Aiden thought he caught the word "score." Could it be those noises were coming from some sort of human game?

A dull ache spread throughout his chest. It had been hounding him all evening—every time she had said something kind, she laughed or smiled, and now the memory of games. He hadn't played or even seen a game since he was a child, unless you counted the cruel and bloody sports their majesties enjoyed subjecting their prisoners to. Pitting him, Dek, and Mare against each other in mock battles, commanding the unlucky green fae to slaughter one another to survive.

A light breeze blew past, wafting heavy scents of garlic and butter from a brightly lit restaurant. Aiden grit his teeth. Of course, she would take him to a place of luxury, making him suffer while he watched her eat. He didn't dare taste the food for fear he wouldn't be able to readjust to his bland diet of bread, cheese, and the occasional fruit or dried meat.

"Look, I don't want to force you to be here," she said, turning on her heel to face him. "You already completed your end of the deal. That was a perfectly good, normal human date."

Another pain shot through him—this time sharp and jagged. "Do you not want me here?" The truth he'd been trying to ignore while they were up on the tower came crashing down now. She knew his name. Most likely, she knew the kinds of things he did. What decent human, or fae girl for that matter, would want to be around someone like him?

"You just looked so miserable." She jerked her chin at his slumped shoulders and bit her lip. "I don't want to obligate you to stay with me. I'll be all right on my own."

"I'm sorry. I'll try to look less miserable." If she was giving him a choice, he would stay. It would take Mare and the others a few more hours to wear the prince down enough for him to break through the wards and steal the crown anyway. Passing the time with her would be better than spending it alone. "I promise you, I will leave if I want to." This human girl could endure his company a bit longer.

Something in her expression appeared angry. He tried to mirror it, glowering back at her as they passed through the doors and into the restaurant. Music and noisy chatter filled the air while black and white clad waiters rushed about the dining chamber to tables filled with a mix of both human and fae patrons. Aiden's eyes flicked from side to side, watching their movements. He could probably rob a hundred fountains and still never possess enough coins to eat here.

Swallowing hard, he steeled himself against the heavenly aromas and followed the girl up to a podium. A cheery woman in a black and white uniform greeted them. The girl held up two fingers, and the woman nodded.

"Follow me, folks," she said.

The woman led them through the dining chamber. Platters heaped with food that Aiden had not even dared to dream of sat in front of casually chatting patrons. He watched them enviously as they shoveled down the food.

"Here you are. I hope a booth's okay." The greeter gestured at a small table with two padded seats.

The girl sat, and Aiden copied her. Handing them two menus covered in mouth-watering pictures of pasta and seafood, the woman assured them their bread and water would be coming soon and left.

Aiden set the menu on his lap, so he wouldn't be tempted. The book had mentioned that if you are eating on a date, you are supposed to make eye contact and mirror the other person's gestures to make them feel more comfortable. He sighed and watched the girl as she leaned back. He did the same. She folded her hands and twiddled her thumbs. He frowned at the restless movement but copied it nonetheless.

"What are you doing?" She pointed at his hands, still folded on the table.

"Making eye contact and mirroring your actions," he said, wondering if he should point too.

"Maybe you should stop. It's a bit creepy."

Aiden sat up. Either she was very bad at dating, or, more likely, he was doing something wrong. His fingers reached for the pages he had placed in his jerkin for reference, but stopped. *Don't be foolish.*

"I'm sorry." He stared down at the faux-wood table.

A waiter strode over to them and placed a bowl of fresh garlic bread and two glasses of ice water before them. Hot steam rose up from the knots, driving his nose mad with longing. Aiden's fingers curled, resisting the urge to tear into the bread—this was far from the soldier's rations style bread.

"Can I get you two anything besides water to drink?" The

waiter drummed his pen on a small black notebook. Aiden cast a glance at the girl. She was staring at him, a worried expression on her face.

"No," he said. The worried crease in her brow smoothed.

"I'm fine, too," she said. "Can we have a few more minutes? We're still deciding." The girl smiled at the waiter who nodded and walked off to another table.

Aiden let out a breath. He needed something to take his mind off the food around him. Just like he did with their Majesties, he picked a spot on the wall and stared past her while he tried to think of another tip from the book. Maybe this time he would get it right.

"Do you enjoy whale or spotted owl watching?"

She put the menu down and glanced behind her, then stared at him as if judging his sanity. "Maybe," she said hesitantly. He gave up on the spot, his gaze drawn back by her warm brown eyes. "I don't think I've ever seen a spotted owl, but I went whale watching once, on a school trip when I was little. It was cool, I guess. Do you like those things?"

Aiden searched her face, desperate to focus on something other than the fresh bread in front of him. "I have never watched either of those creatures." In all honesty, he wasn't too sure what a whale was.

"Why did you ask then?" She stared at him warily. Sweat beaded on his forehead as he focused on her and not the bread.

"Dr. Joy says it makes for good first date conversation." He swallowed. Admitting he needed the help of the book for fools had not been part of tonight's plan either.

"Who is Dr. Joy?"

He snatched the pages from inside his jerkin and threw them on the table. She leafed through them as though there might be something dangerous and alive inside. He gazed at her while she skimmed the first page.

When she got to the bottom, she laughed. Heat rose in Aiden's cheeks. Why did human dates have to be so difficult?

"Haven't you been on a date before?" Her words were choked between bursts of giggles.

"Yes." He thought of Mare and the other women at court. With them at least, he knew what he was getting. "Not with a human though."

Her laughter stopped abruptly. "Are human girls that different from fae?"

Aiden turned back to face her. "If you were fae, I would have laid you and left. There are no other expectations." He leaned forward and instantly regretted it. The scent of the bread hit him full on.

She crossed her legs. "Is that all you want? It doesn't sound like a very satisfying relationship."

"I don't have relationships," he said. At least he was trying to give her the date she'd requested. After all, she had already said that he'd met his end of their bargain.

Silence passed between them until she finally broke it. "So, what are you eating?" She pointed at the menu on his lap. "I think I'll go with the chicken alfredo."

"I'm not getting anything," he said. The bread's steam had died down, but the smell was still so alluring.

"Aren't you hungry?" She cocked her head to the side.

Aiden sighed. "Yes, I am hungry. But I do not want to grow accustomed to *this!*" He glared at the bread. It took everything in him to keep his flames from bursting out from under his skin.

"Oh." She pressed her back as far into the seat as it would go. If she hadn't feared him before, she certainly must now. "Can't you afford food in Fairy? I thought you were some powerful Dark Fae lord."

"Who told you that?" Was there really someone in Fairy so stupid they believed him a lord?

"My friend." She bit her lip.

He chuckled. "Well, your friend is wrong."

"You are not a powerful member of the Dark Fae Army?"

"I am not a lord," he said bitterly.

"But don't you serve Oberon and Mab? I mean, power is practically money in Fairy, isn't it?" Her voice wavered.

"You seem to know a lot about me. Tell me, who is your

123

friend?" He leaned in. Whoever this fae was, feeding a human so much information about him, they were playing a dangerous game.

She shook her head. "Answer my question first."

"All right," he said before inwardly cursing himself. It felt as though his blood had turned to lead. How could he have been so foolish? He knew better than to agree to things without knowing the terms.

"Why do you serve people who don't pay you enough to eat?"

The question struck him like a kick to the stomach. He had expected her to ask something different, something important that was bound to get him in trouble. Not something... personal.

Aiden grit his teeth. "I owe their majesties my life," he said. "And I suggest you don't go sharing that bit of information with your *friend*."

Tension settled between them, thick as mountain snow. For several minutes, they stared at each other in pregnant silence.

"Did you folks decide on what you're having for dinner?" The waiter was back. He leered at them, waggling his eyebrows.

"Um, yes." The girl's voice broke, and she cleared her throat. "I'll have the chicken alfredo, and he'll have the shrimp scampi. Right Ai—uh, dear?"

Aiden blinked. She had protected his name. Why did she keep showing him these kindnesses?

"You do like shrimp, don't you?" she said.

"I think I do, but—"

"Don't worry, it's a good choice. I've had it a few times." The waiter hummed a laugh. Aiden's mind was still stuck on how she'd purposefully not spoken his name to the man. He couldn't take his eyes off her.

"Let's go with that, then," she said.

"It's good, I promise." The waiter patted Aiden on the shoulder.

When they were alone again, Aiden turned to the girl. "I thought I told you I didn't want to get used to this type of food."

"Think of it as a special treat. Something to look forward to on date night."

Aiden blinked. Was this to be an ongoing thing between the two of them? Did she actually want to spend more time with him? If he was honest, he would have to admit this wasn't the worst thing he could be doing. Somewhere in Fairy, Mare, Dek, Irina, and Emerick were leading the prince on an energy draining leprechaun hunt. Eating a full meal — with *her* nonetheless — was just what he needed to get his strength up enough to get past those wards and steal the crown.

Aiden's eyes flicked back to the bread in the center of the table. Well, if it was going to go to waste, he might as well. He ripped off a piece and shoved it in his mouth, savoring the warmth and the flavors of garlic and butter blending together.

"Aiden?" Her soft voice pulled him out of his bread-induced euphoria. There was only one piece left, and his hands were covered in grease. "Tell me about something nice. Tell me about your favorite place in Fairy."

He took a large gulp of water. There were so few things that were nice about his life, least of all the places he went. "Why?" He wiped his hands on the tablecloth. Her face appeared genuine, no signs of the seductive prying that Mare's always had when she asked him a question about something... not terrible.

"I just want to know more about you. Isn't that what you are supposed to do on dates? Get to know each other?"

Aiden rubbed his forehead. Had the book mentioned that? It wouldn't hurt if he told her. It wasn't as though she was asking for information he needed to keep secret for their Majesties. "When I was a child," he said. His chest tightened at the memory; it had been such a long time since he had let himself think of that time before the Dark Fae. "There were caves near my home filled with light pixies. I used to explore them. It was like walking through the night sky."

"They sound beautiful."

"They were. And you? What is your favorite place in the Human Realm?"

She hesitated then asked, "Have you ever been to New Wall? It's only thirty minutes away by car."

Aiden shook his head. "I have not been to many places in your realm."

"It's a great city. People from all over the world—really all over the seven realms—built it. You can find pieces of their cultures in the buildings: restaurants, parks, everything. It's filled with stories waiting to be discovered." Her face went dreamy.

Aiden smiled. "Perhaps I will get the chance to explore it someday."

"We can go next week if you want..." She trailed off.

"You mean by taxi?" Aiden sat up straighter. He had always wanted to see the inside of one up close, but the etiquette surrounding those machines baffled him.

"I have a car. I mean, it's not a very nice car. Just an old Toyota." She shrugged.

"But it's still a *car*, and it goes? Like the others?"

"Yes, of course, it goes." She laughed. "As long as I remember to put gas in it."

Before he could ask her what gas was, two bowls of steaming pasta were placed in front of them. Aiden's nostrils flared as he breathed in lemon, cheese, and, best of all, garlic. This night far surpassed any with Mare or any other fae he'd been with. As soon as the waiter was out of hearing range, he launched into an avalanche of questions about the car between mouthfuls of hot pasta.

"Human magic is so incredible." He winced as he burned the roof of his mouth. The taste of the food was worth more than the pain of readjusting. Closing his eyes, he took a moment to savor a bite of shrimp.

"Human magic? You mean technology?" Her fork paused midway to her mouth.

He paused to slurp up a noodle. "The things you can do without magic are amazing."

"If you think cars are cool, wait until I show you my computer."

This ignited another series of questions that lasted throughout their meal. By the time they stepped back outside, the sky had turned a dull cobalt. The others would be just about ready for him.

"So, I'll see you next week? Same time?" She rocked back on her heels.

Aiden turned to face her. "Are you sure you want to do this again? With me?"

"Of course." She pushed him gently. He looked down at the place where her hands had been. "Have all of your dates been one-night-stands? I find it hard to believe that in all of Fairy there are no women that want more than just—you know."

"I have been with their Majesties since I was eleven. The women in their court are the only ones I have known. So far they've only wanted…" He smirked. "You know."

She led the way down the street. The noise from the game had died down and the streets were filled with people, but nobody paid much attention to them.

"How old are you now?" She spun in a circle beneath a streetlamp and walked backward.

Aiden's lips stretched into a thin line. "Eighteen, why?"

"That's so young!"

He flinched. Most people had that reaction when they found out his age. Nearly all the fae in their Majesties' court had a good century under their wings. His age had been yet another reason for them to treat him like their Majesties' stray dog. "How old are you?"

"Seventeen, but I'm a senior."

Aiden let out a chuckle. "Then I am your elder, and you have no business judging my youth."

She laughed, too. They walked until they reached an open space between two tall buildings.

"Meet me here next week?" She pointed her toes together, hands clasped behind her back.

"And I can see your car and how it works?"

"Yes, but no driving—my parents would literally kill me if it got into an accident."

Aiden nodded gravely. Her parents must be quite cruel, if they could make such threats against their child.

"I will be here at five in the evening next Friday if you will let me see how your car works."

"Aiden, it's a date, not a contract. You don't have to set terms."

He shrugged. "It's a habit, but I must go now. I'll see you next week." He gave a slight bow.

She moved closer; he could feel the heat of her body against his skin. Without warning, she wrapped her arms around him. He stiffened, but she didn't pull away.

"Good night," she said. The white light of the streetlamps reflected their silvery brilliance in her eyes.

"Good night," he said, leaning into her embrace. He moved an arm hesitantly, aiming to wrap it around her, but she pulled away before he could.

Cocking her head to the side, she waved and turned to enter one of the buildings. Aiden turned his back to her, smiling to himself. The week would move much faster now that he had next Friday to look forward to. Squaring his shoulders, he wended and braced himself for the task ahead. "I will be here at five in the evening next Friday if you will let me see how your car works."

"Aiden, it's a date, not a contract. You don't have to set terms."

He shrugged. "It's a habit, but I must go now. I'll see you next week." He gave a slight bow.

She moved closer; he could feel the heat of her body against his skin. Without warning, she wrapped her arms around him. He stiffened, but she didn't pull away.

"Good night," she said. The white light of the streetlamps reflected their silvery brilliance in her eyes.

"Good night," he said, leaning into her embrace. He moved an arm hesitantly, aiming to wrap it around her, but she pulled away before he could.

Cocking her head to the side, she waved and turned to enter one of the buildings. Aiden turned his back to her, smiling to himself. The week would move much faster now that he had next Friday to look forward to. Squaring his shoulders, he wended and braced himself for the task ahead.

CHAPTER 15

Aiden

Chaos enveloped Aiden as he took in the scene around him. From his position atop the northeastern lodestone tower, he could see all of the city and the fort beyond, but they blocked his view of the sea.

Shell Bay's wards had fallen. Dek, Irina, Emerick, and their red fae trainees were ransacking the city. Smoke billowed up from the jewel-colored buildings. Screams cut through the night as Irina and her makeshift pack tore into a panicked crowd at the base of the tower. On the hill opposite him, soldiers trickled down from the fort to help the terrified people.

Aiden wended. The carnage no longer turned his stomach as it had when he'd first begun serving their Majesties. But tonight, something, perhaps his time with the human girl, made him queasy staring down at the blood-streaked city. He knelt just outside the moonlit stone building; the real test would be if he could get inside. A howl sounded from the distance — Irina and her new packmates must have done something impressive. Rubbing his palms against the black leather of his pants, he counted the fort's guards. If he didn't work quickly, the royal soldiers would show up and overpower them. After that, it'd only be a matter of time before the prince arrived, and their Majesties would not take kindly to a second failure on his part. Aiden rubbed his forearm with a shaking hand. A tug at his magic made him grit his teeth.

"What is it, Mare?"

"Time to tackle these wards, huh?" Mare squatted beside him. Her dark skin made her near invisible in the blackness.

Aiden turned his head. What did she need all his magic for anyway?

"I've been running after that dolt all week. He's pretty tired, but I'm not sure it'll help much. He's like you; I can't hold too much of his power." Her tone held none of its usual sarcasm.

The corner of Aiden's mouth twitched at the semi-compliment. "As long as he's weaker. I might not even need to face him if all goes according to plan."

Mare nodded and moved closer to the stone building. She reached out a hand, and the air rippled around it, preventing her from moving closer. "All right, I think I can make a little dent, but it won't last long."

Aiden crept closer to her, staying just out of sight of the guards on the roof. Mare pressed her hand into a space no less than five feet away from the fortress's solid side. The air bent and twisted as she pushed, adding her other hand to absorb the magic. There was a soft pop like the sound of a soap bubble bursting as she ripped away a bit of the ward. Aiden slipped through just as the crack sealed itself up.

"Don't get yourself killed." Mare's words echoed through the invisible barrier. "We still need you to take down Spring."

Aiden glared in response. She tossed her black ponytail over her shoulder and disappeared into the shadows.

The fortress was a solid, stone rectangle that stretched nearly fifty feet high, but the height must be an illusion. Even the Summer Prince wasn't foolish enough to waste energy stretching his wards over a structure that large. The true bulk of the building, more likely, reached down into the base of the hill.

On the roof, the guards rotated position. Aiden pressed his back against the wall and inched his way along its side. He didn't dare wend into the fort directly, not knowing what he'd find there.

A cluster of six guards stood outside a small wooden door on the structure's side. The lack of gables and any fanciful architecture offered little cover. If he wanted to get past them, he would have to expend some magic. A cloud of blue smoke billowed out from around him, and he wafted it toward the guards standing around the door. One by one, they collapsed into a noisy heap. Aiden ran over to the door, used his flames to melt the lock, and slipped inside.

He winced as shouts — no doubt the guards on the roof roused by the clattering of their comrades — sounded behind him. They would be here soon. Working fast, he sealed the door with a ward of his own. It was weak and probably wouldn't hold long, but he hoped it would buy him some time.

The inside of the fortress was dark as ink. Blue flames lit on his arms, illuminating a small portion of the path before him. Ahead, the gentle lapping of waves echoed in the cavernous space. From deep in the blackness, rock tumbled off the path. Aiden dug his fingers into the damp wall, using it to guide him forward. He strained his ears for any sounds that might indicate the guards were closing in behind him, but there were none.

Something slithered across his foot, and he stopped. Increasing his flame, he crouched to inspect the ground. A thick snake made its way down the path in front of him. It turned and disappeared into the darkness. Aiden followed it, keeping low. Perhaps it could lead him to a place with more even footing.

As he followed the creature, it grew longer and larger in girth. Even though it drained him, he pushed more energy into his flames to study the slithering beast. His brow creased; even with the added light, all he could make out was the ever growing snake. The path was smoother now and had opened up into a large chamber. With a sound like rustling leaves, the snake lifted into the air. Aiden raised his flaming arm to follow it, and his heart stopped.

A deafening roar reverberated off the walls and shook the floor. The blue fire extinguished as Aiden flung his arms out on either side to keep from falling over. Instinct and years of training with their Majesties' army drove him to dodge. Wind ripped past him as he narrowly missed the swipe of what might have been an immense head. Hot, putrid breath rushed over him as he cringed against a crag of rock.

He reignited his flames. A large, scaly body and a hooded head with rows of teeth longer than he was tall was just barely visible in the pale blue light. It was still too dark to make out the full size of the cavern, but given the vast size of the beast, there were at least twenty feet between the floor and ceiling. The creature screeched, and its head lunged.

A small dagger in his boot was the only weapon he'd brought. His magic was more than powerful enough to defeat most of Fairy's monsters and was easier to carry. Though now, he longed for a sword.

The beast whipped its tail around, forcing Aiden to jump. Rocks tumbled from his left where the creature's tail slammed into the wall.

He slashed out with the blade, but it hit only air. Straining his senses, Aiden listened for the sounds of the creature's next attack. A blast of hot breath hit his back, causing him to topple out of range of the monster's teeth. He was back on his feet in seconds, ignoring the uncomfortable tickling in his left arm. Blue flame raced from his hands up his arms and shoulders. A head with large milky eyes surged forward. Aiden leapt and bore his dagger into the creature's slim, scaly neck. With a heavy wrench, he jerked his arm sideways. The beast let out a shrill scream before its head landed on the ground with a sickening squelch. The neck went limp, and Aiden dropped to the stone floor, panting and clutching his arm. Warm, silvery blood trickled between his fingers.

The beast's tail lifted and slammed him into the wall. He groaned, blinking the stars out of his eyes. Another deafening roar sounded, and Aiden increased the power of his flames. Three heads flew toward him from the darkness. The middle head was smaller than the others — growing steadily from the stump of the neck he'd just cut. Two of the heads slammed into the wall, and Aiden just barely made it out of the way.

"Freezing frosts." He rolled to his side. Of course the prince would leave a hydra in this darkened cavern. Even if he wended, he wouldn't be able to get past it in the dark without risking falling to his death.

There had to be a way to defeat this monster. In the slim radius of his blue light, no path forward revealed itself. The gigantic body of the creature filled most of the space, its tail and heads the only mobile parts.

Another head swooped past. He slashed at it with the dagger, his flames catching the stump of its neck. Aiden danced around the fallen head to avoid another attack. He braced himself for the return of the head he'd just cut, but it didn't come. One of the other heads swung forward. Again, Aiden leapt onto its back and stabbed at the slender neck until it was weak enough that one hard swipe took it clean off. The neck dropped from beneath him. Aiden flailed, grasping onto the remaining neck as the fallen head's pointed teeth grazed his back. The recently cut base hit the ground. But even as it touched the rocky floor, it was already rising again, minuscule jaws snapping from the bloody stump.

The head he clung to writhed. Aiden's heart drummed in his ears. He flung out a hand and shot a torrent of flame at the resurging neck. His blood-slick hands slipped, and he hit the ground with a painful thud. Darkness pressed in around him. Aiden's heart beat frantically as he relied on sound to predict the monster's next attack. There was a crash, and a second neck flopped down in front of him. He stared at the bit of roasted flesh in the dim light from his flames. The final head shrieked, and Aiden flung himself out of the way as the monster struck out. He shot another torrent of fire at it, but it shook it off.

Perhaps if he could get the last head off, his flames would make it stick. The tail whipped out, but this time he was ready for it. Dagger in hand, he flung himself onto the beast's tail and stabbed it, eliciting a loud roar. Aiden held fast as it wildly thrashed about. When the head finally made its move, he leapt out of the way before using the dagger to carve a path down the creature's neck. It let out another shrill cry, and Aiden blasted it with a jet of searing blue flames. The beast hit the ground, the weight of its crash raining sharp chunks of stalactites down around him.

He leaned against the wall. The slash on his arm throbbed. Gritting his teeth, Aiden closed his eyes; he would have to deal with it later. When all was quiet, he made his way cautiously around the monster's still body. A sliver of torchlight shone from the other side of an elf-sized crack in the wall. Aiden ducked and squeezed through into a high ceilinged room with long slabs of stone blocking his path at seemingly random intervals.

Of course there would be a maze; there was always a maze. He shook his head and pushed forward into the labyrinth. Several paces in, he came across a path that led to another doorway. He turned and walked toward it. A hard wall of nothing rebuffed him, and he stumbled backward. Aiden groped at the air in front of him. It had no give to it, solid, much like the wards that had surrounded the fortress before Mare drained the prince.

Aiden took a deep breath and felt for any holes or slips in the magic—nothing. There were no wards blocking the passage opposite the door. Taking note of the door's position, Aiden turned away from it and made his way down the other path.

It felt like an eternity before he came across another way forward. He turned and slammed into another wall of magic. *Freezing frosts.* There was nowhere but back the way he'd come. After another eternity of walking, he stared down the path that had the door at the end. This time he moved straight ahead, ignoring all the passages off to the left.

Finally, he came to a fork in the path. He reached out to the left. A hard wall.

Nodding, he turned down the right passage, then turned right again. His heartbeat picked up as he recognized the same place from before. At the end, he turned right and walked straight ahead through the opening. Smiling to himself, Aiden entered a small torchlit chamber.

The air hummed with a power that seemed to call to him—the crown was nearby. Two doors loomed opposite him, and two golden statues of Summer soldiers guarded each way forward.

Aiden hesitated, eyes flicking between the doors. Firelight glinted off the soldiers, making them appear almost as living beings. He picked a door and walked toward it. As he reached for the handle, a spear came down to block his path.

"One of us speaks only truths, the other only lies," the golden soldier beside him said in an oddly metallic voice. "One door leads to what you seek, the other leads to a terrible death. You have one chance to pick the right door, and one question you may ask."

Aiden tugged at his hair with his good arm. He knew this — every nursery school in Fairy taught this riddle. Stepping back, he scrutinized both guards. The answer was so simple; it always was. He tried to think, but the "grass" riddle kept popping into his head. That damned clever human girl could probably figure this out in a heartbeat.

"You wouldn't be able to give me a hint, would you?" He laughed and bit the end of his thumb.

"No," the guard said and stepped aside.

Aiden's eyes went wide. "No, no, no that wasn't my question. I take it back."

The guards didn't move. They stood frozen in the orange light. He walked over to the one that had tried to stop him before. "Hello?" He waved a hand in front of the gold face.

Nothing.

Aiden reached out to try the door again. How bad could the terrible death be, after all?

A thunderous crash boomed throughout the fortress as the wards fell. He threw his hands up against a blinding golden light.

"I knew you'd be here," the Summer Prince snarled.

Aiden lowered his arm and sneered. "You're looking well, Your Highness."

The prince's golden hair was tangled and caked with dirt. His face wore the smudges and scrapes of the past week's skirmishes — Mare had done well. "Go to hell, Aiden," the prince said. He leapt gracefully into the air and drew the sword hanging from his belt.

Aiden grit his teeth and shot a blast of blue flame at the prince.

The fairy easily dodged it. Gold flashed in the torchlight as the prince's blade sped toward Aiden. He wended out of the way. The prince skidded to a stop against the stone floor just as Aiden hurled another burst of flame at him. It parted on either side of the prince's weapon.

"What's wrong? Too good to use your magic on a lowly commoner?" Aiden dodged another of the prince's attacks. A sharp pain shot up from the wound in his arm, and he choked back a cry.

"Don't insult commoners. I won't waste my magic on a filthy dog like you." The prince's blade slashed forward and grazed Aiden's jerkin, cutting a shallow line across his side.

Before the prince could draw back, Aiden caught the fairy's shoulder with a jet of flame. He yelled and kicked off the wall to hover in the air.

"Your Highness is getting slow." Aiden made a mad dash for one of the doors and yanked it open. On the far side of the threshold, a ruby encrusted metal circlet rested on a podium, presumably guarded by the prince's wards. Sweat clung to the prince's brow, and dark circles hung beneath his eyes. Fights with Dek's trainee army and Mare had obviously worn him out. If Aiden could keep him fighting a little bit longer...

"Don't you dare!" The prince launched himself at Aiden, hitting him with a feeble wave of magic. Aiden grunted as he was pushed back. "I'll die before I let you touch what is mine." Energy in the room hummed as the prince summoned a spear of light and hurled it with palpable force. Aiden just managed to stumble out of the way. The spear shattered against the cave wall sending acorn-sized rocks raining down on them.

The prince slowed. With a sound like breaking glass, the wards around the crown split apart. Aiden wended over to it. The prince wended after him and fell to one knee. Pulling all his reserve energy, Aiden snatched the crown and wended out of the prince's reach.

"Too slow, Your Highness." Aiden wended again, this time leaving the prince, and Summer, behind.

CHAPTER 16

Freddie

On Saturday evening, Amanda burst through Freddie's door, her phone clasped tight in her hand. Raul followed her, wavering as he stumbled into the room. Freddie looked up from the textbooks splayed open on her bed.

"Did you see what's trending?" Amanda threw down her backpack and marched over to the bed.

"No, I've been studying. Did something happen?"

Amanda held out her phone, and Freddie's eyes widened. A girl with bright red hair stared unseeingly out of a photo. Her throat had been torn away. The caption above read MISSING STUDENT FOUND DEAD.

"They're going to be looking for weres, you know. Who else would rip someone's throat out?" Amanda asked. Freddie stared at Raul as he collapsed face down on the couch, his legs dangling over the side. Amanda shook her head as he let out a loud groan. "He didn't take the news too well."

There was a hard thump at the window. They jumped. A small black shape dipped and swerved, ready to make another attempt at entering the room. Amanda leapt over Freddie's books and thrust open the window. Jefferson soared in, crashed on top of Raul, and changed into his human form.

"Boys," Amanda grumbled as she helped them off of each other and into sitting positions. "Raul needed a drinking buddy, so his frat brothers sold Jefferson some blood beer."

"Hey, don't you judge us, Mnanda." Jefferson rested his head on Raul's shoulder. Freddie raised an eyebrow.

"Yeah, Banana!" Raul added. The two boys looked at each other for one drunken moment, then collapsed into hysterical laughter. Amanda frowned.

Freddie pulled out her phone to search for more information about the picture of the dead girl. There was something familiar about her green dress and the vines that twisted around her arms. Freddie's heart froze. She knew this girl. And worse, she recognized her outfit. Skimming the article, she searched for any hint of when the photo was taken. The girl's name was Vivica Planter. She'd been a sophomore at the upper school and missing since — damn — that same Friday.

"I'm gonna make some ramen for these two. It soaks up the alcohol," Amanda said.

Freddie nodded. Vivica had been with the vampire bartender from the night when she'd first kissed Aiden. Could he have done that to her? If this was tied to the other missing students, then that would mean this girl was the first fae — at least that she knew of — to go missing. She needed more information.

Freddie scrolled through the hashtags for promising leads. Amanda handed cups of ramen to Raul and Jefferson. Raul took his and tore into it with no thought for the salty steam that rose from the soup.

"Want me to make you some, Freddie?" Amanda pointed to the bubbling electric kettle.

Freddie shook her head. The post had come out just a few hours ago. She bit her lip. Had Vivica been dead for that long with no one noticing? The cabby's words about the third missing student echoed in her head. Why had she not tried to follow up on this earlier? By now, half the media outlets in the country would be flocking to Easton.

"Amanda, this blood tastes terrible." Jefferson set the cup down so hard on the table that it tore right through the cardboard. Freddie growled and dug her fingers into her curls.

"Just keep eating, Jefferson," Amanda said. She walked back over to the bed. "Don't worry, Fred. I'll get you another box."

Raul and Jefferson finished their ramen and passed out on the couch. Freddie put on some episodes of a trashy reality show but hardly paid attention. If the world at large was blaming were-people, Raul would be pretty high on the suspect list, especially given his past relationship with Freya and his presence at Illusion that night. She needed to know what the police knew.

When the third episode had ended, Freddie glanced at the microwave clock—past midnight. Amanda drooled into her pillow, and Freddie packed up her textbooks. Outside the door were the muffled noises of the other seniors celebrating the weekend. Jefferson stirred and rose gracefully from the couch. In a too-fast movement, he stood by the bed, gently tucking Amanda beneath the covers.

"Is it all right if she stays here?" Jefferson's voice was low and sober. "I can take her home, but she'd probably prefer to wake up with you."

"Yeah, that's fine." Freddie yawned and pointed at Raul's snoring lump on the couch. "You want to take him home?"

Jefferson grinned. "No thanks. I'd never get the stench of dog out of these clothes."

"Whatever." Freddie shrugged.

Jefferson had just reached the open window when a flash of golden light made him stop. When it faded, Pelrin, ragged and covered in dirt and blood, knelt on the floor, clutching his arm. Freddie and Jefferson rushed over to him. Raul snorted awake.

"My God, Pel, are you okay? What happened?" Freddie's hands hovered over the shoulder he clutched. The fabric of his crimson fighting-leathers had been burned away, revealing his raw, bleeding flesh.

"Dios, Pel!" Raul jumped up from the couch to give the injured fairy more room.

"They got it. My crown. We were spread too thin with all those red fae bastards." Pelrin's voice was rough as he spoke. Raul and Jefferson flinched. Freddie darted over to the mini fridge, grabbed a bottle of water, uncapped it, and rushed back to Pelrin. He winced as he took the bottle, but drank heavily—the cool liquid drawing lines in the filth as it trickled down his chin.

"What happened?" Amanda sat up.

Jefferson hurried over to her, murmuring quietly in her ear.

Freddie turned back to Pelrin. "What does this mean?"

Jefferson abruptly stopped muttering, and Raul paled. All eyes fell on Pelrin.

"I have no idea how we can defeat them now. There are so many more of them—every day more and more red fae surge over the border to join that damned dog." His hands clenched into fists. He cried out and wrapped an arm around his side, dropping the empty bottle on the floor.

"Are you going to be okay, Pel?" Freddie knelt beside his wounded arm. Silver blood was already staining her couch.

"I'll be fine. I'm fae, remember?" He stroked her cheek, his bottom lip quivering.

"We have to get the crown back," Jefferson said.

"What? How?" Amanda frowned. She was still sitting in bed, her eyes wide as she looked from Pelrin to Jefferson.

Pelrin's gaze fixed on the vampire. "There may be a way. Aiden has been surrounding himself with a lot of red fae ever since their first attempt. If you could blend in..."

"What does Aiden have to do with any of this?" Freddie jerked away from Pelrin. He glared at her.

"Your little make-out pal was the thief who stole my crown. He and those criminals have been wreaking havoc across all of Summer for the past week. And now this!"

"He's probably just following orders. It's Mab and Oberon who are to blame. Shouldn't they be your focus?"

"You speak of things you do not understand! He and his masters wish to enslave all of Fairy; he's no mere victim of circumstance." Pelrin sat up, his face twisted into a mask of pain, then leaned back against the couch, panting.

Raul nudged Freddie away from Pelrin, positioning himself between the two. Tears pooled in the corners of her eyes. Damn it, why did Pelrin always have to bring her to tears?

"Hey, Freddie. I-I'm sorry," Pelrin said. "It's just—if you had seen the devastation he's caused... entire villages wiped out, and he just stands there." Pelrin shook his head.

Raul sat on the arm of the couch.

"What can I do, Pel?" Jefferson said. "You want me to blend in with those red fae?" He crossed the small space to kneel next to Pelrin.

"Jefferson, you can't. It's too dangerous." Amanda kicked off the blankets and ran over to him, flinging her arms around his waist.

"I can give you a charm, so we can stay in contact," Pelrin said. "I just need you to find out where they keep my crown and maybe cause a distraction. My soldiers can do the actual fighting to get it back." Pelrin ran a hand down his face, smearing the dirt. The wound on his shoulder had already faded from an angry red to a deep pink. "It's dangerous, though. And if you are caught—"

"More dangerous than letting Mab and Oberon take control of Summer?" Jefferson folded his arms.

"I suppose you're right."

"Jefferson, you can't. You could die!" Amanda tightened her grip around his waist.

He gently pried her fingers away and rubbed her back. "I'll be fine, Amanda. Think of it as I'm going to make some new friends."

"That's not funny!" Tears slid down Amanda's cheeks.

Jefferson extended a hesitant hand. "I'll check in often. I promise."

Pelrin got to his feet. "You should be fine. Aiden doesn't know who you are. He has no reason to suspect you."

"When do we leave?" Jefferson rose, too. Amanda's sobs increased.

"Tonight," Pelrin said. "I want to get you briefed before sun-up."

"Let's go now, then." Jefferson offered a hand to Amanda.

She stared up at him, tears glittering in her eyes. Freddie couldn't help but feel a bit envious of her. Only a few months ago, she would have been like Amanda, clinging onto Pelrin as though she might never see him again. Now, there was no one she cared that deeply about.

Amanda rose to her toes and kissed Jefferson on the lips. "Be safe," she whispered.

Freddie caught Pelrin staring at her, and she averted her gaze.

"Anything I can do to help, Pel?" Raul rubbed his arm, his face creased.

"Take care of our girls." Pelrin smiled at Freddie. "I can't spare Ginnith anymore."

Freddie picked at the corner of her ruined coffee table. It was hard to believe that only a few hours ago, the boys had been drunk, and she and Amanda had been watching trashy reality TV.

"I won't be able to visit as often," Pelrin said. "Be careful, Freddie."

"You too, Pelrin, Jefferson." Freddie stood and nodded. She thought Pelrin's shoulders sagged slightly.

Again, Jefferson peeled Amanda off his body. He kissed her forehead, shrank into bat form, and whooshed out the window. Pelrin turned into a tiny golden ball of light and followed him. Freddie waved as they faded into the night, a strange emptiness consuming her.

The thought that it was tied to Pelrin made her skin crawl.

CHAPTER 17

Freddie

Freddie wiped crusted tear tracks from her cheeks. Amanda slept beside her, black hair clinging to her face. On the couch, a lump beneath a blanket marked Raul's splayed form.

Freddie eased herself out of bed. She and Pelrin were over — he shouldn't be able to make her cry like this anymore.

Nothing except the soft snores of her friends punctuated the early morning silence. She slipped out of the room in her flip-flops, towel slung over her shoulder and shower caddy in hand, and made her way to the bathroom at the end of the hall.

Under the hot water of the shower, she combed through her tangle of thick, black curls. How had she let her life get so complicated? The knot of feelings for Aiden and Pelrin throbbed in her gut. They were both terrible for her. Aiden, at least, she could shut out of her life, bail on the second date.

But she didn't want to. He was so... stupidly adorable. Freddie winced as she tugged out a particularly stubborn tangle. The urge to mope rather than focus on the disappearances and the looming assignment consumed her. Get your head in the game, Freddie. She stepped out of the shower and smoothed curl-enhancing goop through her thick locks.

Today, the love-torn lower-schooler would have to take a back seat to her inner journalist. Working her fingers through her hair, she smoothed it back into a high bun at the top of her head. She stared at her reflection in the mirror, frowning at the flat brownness of her eyes—not a hint of light behind them. Biting her lip, Freddie tilted her head side to side. She might not be fae, but she could still make a difference. And those missing students needed help. It was time she found out what the police knew.

Angry shouts carried down the hall. Freddie grabbed her things, racing back toward the voices. When she got back to her room, Amanda and Raul were standing nose to nose snarling at each other.

"See, I told you!" Amanda was already dressed. She pointed at Freddie with her toothbrush. "She went to wash her hair. She's stressed."

"Freddie, seriously, after that girl was found dead, you still go off and disappear like that? Anything could have happened to you!" Raul said.

Freddie put a hand on her hip. The other held the towel close to her chest. "Forgive me, Raul. Next time I go to the bathroom, I'll make sure to invite you along."

Raul's face flushed red. "Sorry, Fred. You know Pel; he really gets in my head."

"A little too much if you ask me." Freddie flipped through the clothes in her closet and tossed her red hoodie onto her bed. Amanda scurried off to the bathroom.

"So that girl from the article." Raul cleared his throat and turned his back to Freddie. "She's the same chick from Illusion, you know."

"I wasn't that drunk." She balanced on one leg as she struggled into a pair of jeans. "Do you think that guy she was making out with had anything to do with what happened to her?"

"I didn't see him, not that it matters. First with Freya, now her. There were tons of people at that club who saw us together. You know how the cops are—they're going to tie the two together and blame me."

Freddie turned around, zipping her hoodie up over a glittery, purple top. She touched her friend's shoulder. "Raul, you didn't do anything wrong. Besides, you're one person. There are hundreds of students who have gone missing from all over the country. They can't blame you."

"They'll say it's a pack thing. You've seen the news—you know how they are. Whenever a werewolf does something, it's like all weres are bad." He buried his face in his hands.

Freddie rubbed his back. "Stay here. Amanda and I will do some snooping at the police station. We'll let you know if we hear anything."

"No, I'm going back to the house. I have an accounting exam on Tuesday." Raul stood, ran his fingers through his hair, and crossed the room, pausing at the door. "Be careful, Fred. Pelrin's paranoid, but he's not wrong. His enemies could be after you. Call me if you need anything."

"I'll be fine, but thanks, Raul. You be careful, too." She waved.

Amanda passed Raul as she pushed through the door. "So, are we going for breakfast?" Her tone was forced. Red puffiness lingered around her eyes.

"You could call it that. There will probably be coffee and donuts." She nudged her, and Amanda's lips lifted in a smile, though it just barely reached her eyes.

"I'm game. Let's go." She sighed and followed Freddie down to the Bailey.

"Hey, Fred, what's the name of this place?" Amanda peered suspiciously out the window as she watched cafe after cafe go by.

Freddie winced and turned the car onto Main Street. "Um... It's just ahead. Don't worry."

"Uh huh. Not an answer."

"There it is." Freddie pointed as she pulled into a large lot packed with news vans. On the front of the building were the words Easton Police.

Amanda folded her arms but said nothing as she followed

Freddie inside. It was packed with people vying for the attention of the three uniformed officers behind the plexiglass counter. The usual reports ranged from "Mr. Tinkles has gotten stuck in the tree again and won't one of the nice-looking boys in blue come get him down" to "some idiot has teepeed my house and now they are sleeping on my roof."

Today, however, journalists and citizens alike clamored for more information about Vivica. Neither the papers nor any of the social media posts had called her out as fae, and given the buzz in the station, it appeared none of the citizens knew either.

Freddie dragged Amanda through the main entrance. "Please, Amanda, I need you in your usual character if this is going to work." Amanda rolled her eyes and burst into boisterous fake sobs. Freddie flashed her a grin. Patting Amanda's back, she twisted her expression into one of mock sympathy. "It's going to be okay," she said in a loud whisper. A couple journalists turned in their direction. "I'm sure she's just fine. We'll ask; don't worry."

"Hi there, Troy McCloud, Channel Seven. Did you guys know the victim, Vivica Planter?" A man in a crisp, blue button-down shoved a microphone in front of Amanda. Her sobs increased in volume.

"Have some compassion!" Freddie said and pushed the man aside.

Several other journalists closed in on them as they made their way to the guarded door that separated the lobby from the officers' workspaces. The officer on guard duty had her back pressed into the door, her arms spread wide on either side. The look on her face was a mixture of shock and horror, as though she were staring into the mouth of a fearsome beast.

"Excuse me, ma'am," Freddie said as she neared the officer. "We were wondering if we could get some information about our friend."

"What?" The woman leaned back, staring at the two girls as though they were rabid werewolves.

"She's not answering our texts, and we just wanted to know if she's okay. You know, with all that's happened." Freddie shrugged.

Amanda's sobs intensified.

"This is about the Planter girl?" The woman gazed uncertainly at Amanda.

"Her roommate is a friend of ours. We haven't heard from her in two days. She won't even answer the door."

The officer frowned. Freddie blinked, letting her own eyes get a bit teary. "Well, all right. The second door on your right is Sergeant Colon's. He'll help you out. I really hope she's not missing, too. This is really getting out of hand."

"Oh my goodness, thank you so much," Freddie said, letting a whine slip into her voice.

'Out of hand' was a severe understatement. In Easton, the police were trained to either see obnoxious school kids or senile old ladies. Murder was a concept that went far over their heads.

"Are you sure this is a good idea?" Amanda whispered as they slipped into a room filled with frantic policemen. Freddie couldn't help but notice there wasn't a single fae among them.

"Not really," Freddie said. She nodded toward the second door on the right, and Amanda resumed her sobbing. Freddie knocked.

"I already told you, I'm not doing any more intervi—" A potbellied man with an impressive mustache yanked open the door. "Well, how did you two get back here?"

Amanda looked up at him with tear-filled eyes and sniffed. "Our friend. Won't answer. Dead." She hiccupped and began crying again.

Freddie patted her on the back. "The lady in the front said you might be able to tell us if our friend was all right. She was Viv's roommate." Freddie hoped calling her 'Viv' wasn't pushing the familiarity envelope. She'd already studied Vivica's profile on the school's roommate finder site. Vivica lived off campus, and she wasn't searching for a roommate, hopefully because she already had one.

"Well, she shouldn't have done that."

Amanda let out a high-pitched whimper. Freddie and the sergeant winced.

"But I suppose we can take a look. No details, mind you. Just going to make sure she's not missing too."

The girls followed him into his office. It was small and dark, the only light coming from a small lamp on his desk. "Guess I'd better open the window in here now that it's daytime." Sergeant Colon chuckled. Amanda and Freddie did not.

He shuffled through the piles of folders spread out across his desk. Some of them were marked with a red dot. The name "Freya Park" was printed on one of the marked folders. Freddie nudged Amanda, who coughed.

"Can she have some water?" Freddie stared imploringly at the sergeant. Amanda coughed harder. "Or coffee, if you have it."

The sergeant sighed and squeezed himself back around the desk. Freddie glared at Amanda. "Don't, uh, touch anything. I'll be right back," he said.

"We won't," Freddie said.

As soon as the man shut the door, she pulled out her phone. Snapping a picture of the desk, she opened the Freya folder and photographed its contents.

"Freddie, is this legal?" Amanda hissed.

"I'm going to be a journalism major, not pre-law. How should I know?"

She sifted through the folders, taking as many photos as she could. Finally, she located a dotted one labeled "Vivica Planter" and took several more photos of the contents.

"He's coming," Amanda said.

Quickly, Freddie rearranged the file back to the way he'd had it, turning around just as Sergeant Colon entered the room. She bent over Amanda's chair and blinked up at the sergeant, who held a styrofoam cup that smelled wonderfully of coffee. His eyes narrowed.

"Oh, thanks so much!" Freddie relieved him of the cup and handed it to Amanda.

"Not a problem, ladies. One sec." The man flipped through the folders and found Vivica's. Freddie sat back down. "Yes, we interviewed her roommate, Erica Flores. Says the officers were over there yesterday. Does that help?"

"She's okay?" Amanda leaned forward, placing a trembling hand on the desk.

"As of yesterday at three in the afternoon."

"That's a relief," Freddie said. "She's probably just hiding. We should go over there and bring her something nice."

Sergeant Colon nodded. "You girls be careful. So far the roommate's not a suspect, but you never know."

"Thank you, sir," Amanda said. After picking up her coffee, she followed Freddie out of the room.

Once they made it back to the car, Freddie scrolled through the pictures on her phone. Locating Vivica's folder, she zoomed in on the address and punched it into her GPS.

"You know, some friends have brunch on Sunday mornings," Amanda said.

"I know. Thank God we're not that boring." Freddie grinned at her. "Let's go see our good friend Erica." She laughed and slid into the driver's seat. They took off down the tree-lined street, back toward the upper-school.

Erica lived off campus in a brownstone in the historical part of Easton, not especially far from the police station. On the way, Freddie stopped and made Amanda get some cupcakes, calling them lip-looseners. Amanda put up little resistance, as neither of them had eaten breakfast, even though now it was past lunchtime.

They parked and walked down the shady street, leaves crunching beneath their feet. Stairs, on the side of a three-story brownstone led to the first floor apartment. Only the handle was visible, the rest of the door hidden behind a thick curtain of ivy.

"Erica?" she called. Ripping the ivy aside, she pressed her ear to the door. There was a faint rustling coming from the other side. "Erica, it's Freddie. I know you're home."

Beside her, Amanda mouthed, "You know her?"

Freddie shook her head. "We have cupcakes."

The door opened a crack. They jumped back. A girl with long brown hair and a floral headband poked her head out of the door. "I don't know you." She looked down at the bright pink box in

Amanda's hands. "Are they vegan?"

"I think the key lime is," Freddie said cheerily. "Are you Erica?"

The girl's eyes narrowed. "Yes. Why? What do you want?" Her tone was wary. The door opened a fraction of a centimeter more.

"We just wanted to check on you. Make sure you're okay. You know, after Vivica…" Amanda said and trailed off. "Can we come in?"

"All right." Erica's eyes flicked back to the cupcakes. "Just for a bit. I've been getting interrogated by police and journalists all week. No one's brought me cupcakes, though." Her lips twitched into what might have been a smile, if not for the way it fell back down into a somber frown seconds later.

The inside of the brownstone was more greenhouse than apartment. Potted plants of all varieties lined the floor while creeping vines hung from pots that dangled from the ceiling. The air smelled of damp earth. Freddie felt the moisture frizzing her bun.

"You sure like plants," Amanda said as they tiptoed their way to the kitchen where the plant population retreated to reveal a white-speckled linoleum countertop.

"I guess so." Erica ducked down, allowing her dark hair to curtain her face. Freddie couldn't help but notice the way the vines on the floor pulled away from Erica as they passed.

Tendrils stretched down from the ceiling to wrap themselves around Erica's fingers, but she expertly moved them away. Amanda placed the cupcake box on the counter, and Freddie gestured at the key lime. Erica bit into it, her eyes closed as she chewed.

"So, Erica, I've been thinking—since the news broke, that is— I just really want…" Freddie blinked up at the light, her eyes tearing up. "I really just want to say goodbye to Vivica. As a friend, you know?"

Erica folded her arms across her chest. Swallowing her mouthful, she pursed her frosting-dotted lips.

"I was wondering... do you mind if I get a look at Vivica's room?" Freddie could feel Amanda's incredulous glare on her neck but ignored it. The police had probably already been through it, but there may be a clue they'd missed.

"How did you know Viv? I don't think she ever mentioned you." Erica took another bite of cupcake, her eyes narrowed on Freddie.

"We met at Illusion. She was dancing with me and one of my friends but ended up turning her attentions to some other guy before we left." Freddie wiped away a tear with the back of her hand. "I wish we had more time to get to know each other. Outside the club, you know."

Erica nodded "All right. But you can't stay long. The police keep barging in, and there's always reporters snooping about. It's like, can't she get a little peace!" Amanda nodded as Erica led them through a leafy hallway. "So, is your friend a red fae?"

"He's a —" Freddie stopped and decided to play it safe, or at least safer. "Yeah, he is." There was a small, but very vocal, faction of green fae who believed red fae were monsters. These kinds of fae sided with people like Richard Fallus, voting for him even though he preached about kicking them out of the Human Realm.

"She's had a thing for red fae ever since we moved here. I think they made her feel dangerous, powerful, you know?"

Freddie bobbed her head. "The police think it was a were who killed Vivica."

"It wasn't a were," Erica said, finishing off her cupcake. "They just want to tie her death to the disappearances. Their suspect is a were, so that must be how she was killed. Some police force." She pushed open a door rimmed with pale pink roses and stood aside.

Vivica's room reminded Freddie of the kind of place a girl in a fairytale would sleep. Twigs twisted in a double arch to form a canopy dripping with living ivy above the bed. The dresser and desk looked as if they had grown from the floor. Painted on the walls in a rainbow of colors were various types of plants and flowers, each labeled in neat black writing.

"This is really cute," Freddie said as she stepped into the room, scanning the photos lining the dresser and the papers neatly stacked on the desk.

"I tidied it up after the police left. They mostly rummaged through the papers on the desk and took fingerprints, but I didn't want Viv's parents to see it looking all messy."

"That's really sweet of you," Amanda said. She followed Freddie into the room and leaned against the desk.

"So, you don't think she's tied to the other missing students?" Freddie moved her fingers along the dresser, studying each of the photos intently.

"I told the police that, but they said to let them do the detective work."

"Is there anyone you suspect? She never mentioned any enemies to me."

Erica let her hair fall over her face, turning back to the door.

Freddie sighed and noted a picture of a middle-aged woman with loose, reddish gray hair. Beside her was a short man with a thick, curling beard and ram's horns sprouting from his forehead. They must have been Vivica's parents. Another frame held a photo of Vivica and Erica. They were making silly faces, their cheeks smeared with blue and yellow paint.

Freddie pressed her lips into a thin line as she studied the fragments of Vivica's life. It wasn't fair she'd been ripped away from it. Her story deserved to be told and her killer brought to justice. There was also a small frame that was face down, most likely knocked over during the search.

Erica wiped the frosting and crumbs from her mouth. Avoiding Freddie's gaze, she let her hair fall forward, casting her face into shadow.

Freddie turned back to the dresser, lifting the tiny, fallen frame. "Oh, this is... what's his name, Viv told me about him." Freddie squinted at the photo of a young boy. It was heavily wrinkled with large Xs scratched over the boy's eyes. Freddie could barely make out anything else about him. But she recognized the condition of the photo; she had a similar one of Pelrin.

"Dion?" Erica said hesitantly. "She told you about him?"

"Um, yeah, not much though. They were friends and had some kinda falling out." Like her, Vivica must have cared about this boy enough to keep his photo around.

Erica scowled. "He's not her friend. He's some jerk from Fairy. I told the police all this, but they didn't seem to think it was really important. I guess they didn't think someone would go through all the hassle to come here from Fairy just to murder Viv. I mean, we're from Summer, so it's pretty safe back home, but still..."

Freddie cocked her head to the side. "But if he were able to get over here, would he have wanted to hurt Vivica?"

Erica bit her lip. "Maybe. I mean you have to understand, back in Fairy, where we're from, everyone is super traditional. Like all nymphs must marry only satyrs and can't even kiss a boy before marriage — that sort of thing. Our parents all participated in that 'safe education' program. That's how we got to come here."

"You've been here since lower school?" Freddie's fingers itched to break out her phone and take notes, but Erica would probably clam up if she did.

The nymph fiddled with the cupcake wrapper. "Yeah. You see, there was this guy — a satyr guy — who was super popular at our school in Fairy. All the girls wanted to be his 'chosen.' Technically, you are allowed to choose or be chosen at thirteen, but most people wait until they are at least eighteen or twenty. But this guy, Dion, he chose Vivica as soon as they were both of age."

"You mean she was married?"

"No, just promised, like engaged. She was really happy at first; they would sneak off and do all sorts of romantic stuff together, even kiss. At some point, though, things got bad. He started being really mean to her.

"I knew something was wrong: she was jittery all the time and forgetful. She hardly ever spoke in class and wouldn't even talk to me. It wasn't until we started going to school here that I found out he was threatening her — telling her she was ruined from kissing him, and he could do whatever he liked to her because she was a whore." Erica's fingers clenched into fists. "When we got the opportunity to go to the Human Realm, I asked Vivica if she would go with me. I was kinda surprised when she said yes, but Dion was livid. I know we were only kids, but our people take the choosing seriously. I just know he found a way to get to her." Erica shuddered, ripping the cupcake wrapper to shreds.

"Hey, it's okay. That guy sounds like a real douche," Freddie said as she patted Erica on the arm. "If you told the police, I'm sure they are investigating him." However, Freddie had seen nothing about it in Vivica's file.

"You guys should probably go," Erica said. She sniffled and rose to her feet.

Amanda let out a stiff breath. "Let us know if you need anything. We're here for you."

Freddie smiled at Erica, and she and Amanda picked their way through the maze of plants and left. Once back outside, Freddie turned to her friend.

"At least now we have a lead," she said.

Amanda nodded. Her eyes were bloodshot, and she slouched in a very un-Amanda-like way as they walked to the car.

"I mean, that guy doesn't seem like he would have much of a motive to hurt the other students, but it's more than what we had." Freddie bit her lip.

Maybe satyrs had some sort of magic that let them change shape. He could be the sexy nymph girl that Daniel was talking to. And Freya... well there could be some connection there.

Amanda slouched against the car and sighed. Freddie's chest ached for her friend, wishing there was something she could do to bring Jefferson back. But the only thing to do now was to go back to her room and compile her notes. She needed to find out what a satyr was.

CHAPTER 18

Aiden

The tiled city of Kesh shone ivory against the red sands of Rydah, the northernmost province of Summer. Flat-topped mountains rimmed the horizon, casting deep shadows that crept toward the city. Aiden's muscles cramped as he crouched in the shadows. It had been nearly four hours since their arrival, but he needed to make sure everything ran smoothly.

The guards changed shifts every two hours. He counted slightly over a hundred standing watch over the wall and estimated there were double that number patrolling the city. With the crown gone, Summer had increased its defenses in Luching, the southern province bordering Autumn. It had taken a significant portion of the fairy wing powder to transport a full legion of the Dark Fae Army here. But if they were able to capture Kesh, their Majesties would forgive his heavy-handed use of the rare substance.

Aiden licked his lips and wended to the shadows beneath the city wall, wincing as he straightened out of his crouch. Dek was already there, a deep, red cloak wrapped around his head and shoulders. How is he not sweating?

"Took your time," Dek said, his eyes fixed on the city gates. The new recruits were still some miles back with the other soldiers, amongst the shadows of the mountains. When the sun set, Aiden would send them a signal to advance.

He sighed. "I had to make sure the guard shifts were regular. We don't need any surprises." Aiden rolled his shoulders, shaking out the small aches. "If Rydah falls, Summer's armies will be forced to divide to protect the rest of the northern lands. They'll be spread too thin, and without the crown, we'll crush them." Aiden clenched his hands. His heartbeat thrummed in his ears the way it did whenever he pictured the demise of Summer. Its king dead, and the prince on his knees before him, begging for mercy.

Dek coughed. "What's got you so excited? You were practically a wailing woman when we took Autumn."

"I just—" Aiden's lips tightened into a thin line. "I just hate Summer."

"You're from here?" Dek's tone softened.

Aiden turned to him. The anubis no longer watched the city gate but stared at him—a melange of pity and understanding in his dark eyes.

"I've spent some time here." Aiden moved closer to the gates as the shadows shifted with the setting sun.

Dek nodded. "They'll be nothing but a smudge on the earth when we're through."

Aiden's stomach did a strange flip. Dek probably wished the same for the Human Realm for slaughtering his parents and displaying them like trophies. The words of the woman in Shell Bay came back to him: Change your path.

He shook his head. Now was not the time to feel guilty; besides, it was not as though this path was one of his choosing.

"I need to rid the city of as much protection as possible," Aiden said, his words congested with suppressed emotion. "Go back to the others, and watch for my signal."

Dek jerked his chin up. A slight smile flitted across his face before he bounded off into the red desert.

Blue-skinned djinn, green-skinned marids, and feathered garudas paced through the streets, armed with a collection of homemade weapons. Aiden bowed his head, the hood of his cloak obscuring his eyes from the view of the city guard. Nagas dressed in plain brown shifts and headscarves slithered about, serving water and food to those patrolling the city. He passed a naga man herding a group of slithering children down an alley, toward a mud structure pressed between the white-walled homes of the city's green fae residents.

Above him, a flock of garuda archers soared in broken formation around the perimeter. He waited, sagging against the immense steps of a vast building. Several beggars, all brown fae from what he could tell, huddled along the steps. Aiden wrapped his cloak tighter hoping he could blend in.

Another flock of garudas passed. There were four in the group, like before. As the sun sank lower, he counted five more groups of four. Taking them out would be a challenge, but if he could make it to one of the lodestone towers or the city wall, their arrows would be no match for his flames.

A harsh cry snapped Aiden's attention from his analysis of the militia. A naga woman cowered before a heavily jeweled marid. "Clumsy, khadima! You've drenched me." The marid glared at her. Aiden was too far away to hear the woman's response, but she trembled, her lips moving rapidly. "Let's see how you like being wet." The marid raised both of his hands. The woman screamed as the air around her rippled and grew misty. When the mist faded, the naga struggled for breath in an airborne bubble of water, her tail thrashing furiously.

Aiden grit his teeth. This was exactly why brown fae were racing to join Mab and Oberon. Though their Majesties had shown little compassion for their kind, they at least spoke of an end to the green and gold fae tyranny.

When the woman's movements slowed, the bubble burst, and she fell gasping on the ivory-tiled street. A few of the other green fae stared down at her with expressions of disinterest and disgust. After several moments of agonized coughing, a naga man helped her right herself and guided her down a side street. Aiden let out a breath. He'd nearly left the cover of the steps to help her himself. He couldn't afford slip-ups like that, not when there was so much counting on his success.

The sun dipped below the ridge. Shadows spread across the sands like spilled wine, creeping over the city walls and reaching for the first of the five pillars. Aiden sucked in the heavily spiced air and crept into the shadow of one of the buildings. Dusk would fall soon. And the red fae, which made up the majority of his army, would be strongest at night.

He followed the flow of the city patrol as the other beggars scattered. Likely, there was some nonsense curfew for the brown fae in this region. Passing beneath the shadow of the white tower of Rha, Aiden broke away from the city patrol and drifted toward the tower. It was the smallest of the five pillars and had the weakest defenses — so said Mare, anyway. But taking out even one lodestone could change the tide of battle in their favor.

Inside was quiet as a spirit's footsteps. Stairs spiraled for nearly a hundred feet above him. Black marble walls lit in intervals with flickering oil lamps made the shadows dance in the semi-darkness. He looked up, running a hand through his hair. How much easier this all would be if the tower had a moving box like the one in the Human Realm. The memory of the human girl huffing and puffing as they climbed that tower sent a warm tingle across his cheeks. She would be even more loathe if she were forced to climb a Keshian tower. Aiden let the thought linger in his mind as he made his way up.

Though he was tense and ready, no guard met him. Perhaps they were out helping the others stand watch on the wall. Still, even the Keshians didn't seem so foolish as to leave a lodestone tower unguarded, especially now. Strange shadows stretched across the wall, elongated by the shifting light in the lanterns. Occasionally he would pause, thinking he heard something slide across the onyx walls. But when he listened, there were only the noises from the militia outside, muffled by the thick stone.

Aiden relaxed his shoulders; the end was just a few levels up. A hissing scream sounded from above and an anansi leapt from the ceiling, eight legs splayed and a dagger in her hand. Aiden sprang aside but caught the tip of her blade down his shoulder. She skittered up the side of the wall opposite the stairs, her black eyes glinting in the lamplight. Her lean torso was covered by a tight-fitting black vest, the uniform of the Keshian guard.

Aiden cursed himself. How could he be so foolish as to walk right into her trap? He should have never let his guard down.

She launched herself at him again. Aiden dodged. Instinct told him to draw on his flames. But now all of Summer was on alert for his unique brand of magic—if he used his power, especially this close to the lodestone, the entire city would be alerted to his presence.

"Turn back, little thief." The anansi-woman hissed. Green acid shot from her mouth and hit the far wall, a shadow's breath away from Aiden's head. It sizzled and smoked, leaving a dark groove in the black stone.

Aiden took comfort in the fact the guardswoman didn't seem to recognize him. She'd called him a thief. Hopefully, she would try to deal with him herself rather than alert the others to his presence.

"Lodestones can be ransomed at a premium in a time like this," he said, careful not to lose her in the shadows.

"Filth," she spat and sprang again.

Aiden drew his sword—this time he'd come fully prepared to battle monsters. Its moonstone hilt burned with an inner flame as it reflected the light of the setting sun. Something flickered in the corner of his eye. He slashed out and hit only air. Spinning around, he searched for the tower guard. Blistering heat!

She had disappeared, and he did not have time to hunt her down. Knowing she was likely waiting to spring on him again, he raced up the stairs—sword unsheathed. When he reached the top of the tower, the guard still hadn't attacked. Aiden's stomach churned with an uneasy sense of foreboding. He pressed himself against the wall and listened. Only silence.

A sharp tingle ran down his spine, and he tensed. Tightening his grip on the sword, he searched the ceiling for any flicker of movement.

The spider people were at home in the darkness, usually keeping to Fairy's thickest forests and jungles. It was rumored they had been banished from the Human Realm hundreds of years ago.

But the unrest in Summer and the other Seasonal realms had likely driven these unique red fae from their territories to choose a side in the war.

Pale, green light glimmered ahead as the last dying rays of the sun reflected off the tower's lodestone. Aiden's breath hitched as he picked up his pace. It had taken longer than he'd thought to get here. It was now dark enough for most of the red fae in his army to hunt through the streets without fear of the scorching rays of the sun. Grab the stone and give the signal.

The open room reminded him of the tower he'd visited with the human girl. The eight pillars holding up the pointed roof cast long, black shadows that fanned out to frame the pale green gem. Something nagged at the back of his mind, a prickling pain. He ignored it. Tonight, he couldn't lose focus.

Reaching down, he grabbed a dagger from his boot and hurled it at the stone. It bounced off harmlessly and clattered onto the floor—not even a basic ward surrounded it. This was too easy. His eyes flicked around the room again; no sign of the anansi.

Aiden inched closer, not daring to use his magic to shed light onto the space. He strained his senses through the strange silence, but it only made his head pound. Taking a deep breath, Aiden walked across the tower to the yellow-green gem. He reached a hand out to it and stopped.

The stone was within his reach, but something prevented his arm from moving forward. Aiden struggled, his legs drew together against his will, and his arms clamped down to his sides. Near-invisible strands laced around the room. Light danced off them as they held him tight as wire.

"Well, well, well," a cool voice hissed from above. "It looks like I caught a little thief." The anansi glided down from the ceiling on a thread. "Have you no respect?" She hung before Aiden, smiling broadly, revealing her thick fangs.

Aiden swallowed, his eyes fixed on her spindly legs. "I am just doing my job, mistress." Staring at the ground, he hoped his golden eyes would not give him away. He could burn free the threads easily, but he still needed to rid the tower of its lodestone. If he could just gain a little movement, he could use his sword to cut the threads and free himself without magic.

"Your job?" She let out a snickering hiss. "Do your masters not care about how desperately the people of Kesh need this to protect themselves against the Dark Fae?" The irony of her statement might have struck him as funny if not for the throbbing pain lancing through his skull.

Aiden scrunched his face, unable to find words through the blaze of pain.

"Hurts, does it, my little greenie?" She scuttled aside. Where before a pale, green stone rested on top of the pillar, now it held a shiny, black rock. The anansi reached into the front of her uniform and pulled out the true lodestone and smiled.

"Freezing frosts," Aiden muttered under his breath.

How could he have been so stupid? He should have seen through the glamour. Curse that damned spider for making him believe a chunk of iron was really a lodestone. The pain in his head intensified as the glamour melted away, but he wasn't yet desperate enough to risk tripping the alarms by conjuring his flames. Summoning all his strength, Aiden strained his arms to break through the anansi's threads and failed to tear even one. His sword dropped to the ground with a clatter and he moaned.

"I don't think anyone would be upset if I ate you. It has been decades since I've tasted living flesh."

The anansi's strands tightened, lifting him off the ground and slowly rotating him sideways. His heart beat a staccato rhythm. As he spun, the thin strands took on a silvery sheen, and he could now see where they bound his hips, ankles, and wrists. The spider woman's hands on his body made him cringe.

There was no way out of this without summoning his magic — but if he did put it to work and failed to secure even one lodestone, his army might be defeated. Aiden did not want to think of what Mab would do to him if that ever happened. Not now that they had the crown and Summer was supposedly weaker.

The anansi's acidic breath on his neck stung his bare skin as tiny droplets of her venom dripped from her lips. He closed his eyes and took a deep breath. With the iron so close, he needed to concentrate to conjure his flames.

A sharp scream pierced the air, and the anansi fell back. Aiden's eyes snapped open. Something cut through one of the strands with a loud twang, and he dropped several feet until he hung mere inches above the ground, flailing his arms. A man with flashing red eyes grinned at him then raced out of sight toward the anansi's screams. Below Aiden lay a double-jointed, black leg.

"You shall pay for that, vampire," the anansi shrieked. Righting herself, she used her threads to fly toward the vampire, but she was no match for his speed.

The vampire and the anansi danced about the chamber, lunging, dodging, and attacking in movements blurred by their immense speed. It seemed the newcomer was trying to exhaust her. As Aiden tried to wriggle himself free, the spider-woman sprang from the thread that held him, causing the world to spin. Wishing he hadn't thrown his dagger, he curled up to examine the threads that bound him. They were strong as steel chains but thin as hair.

Aiden swung like a pendulum, watching the battling pair with growing frustration. The anansi hissed and spit streams of acid as she leapt from one side of the tower to the other. Aiden's eyes widened as the acid sizzled in dark steaming puddles—perhaps that was something he could use. He moved his hips and arms back and forth until the thread holding him began to swing. The anansi shot another jet of acid, and Aiden swung hard toward it. The acid ate through the spider thread. He fell, hitting the floor hard and rolled onto his stomach, his legs and arms still bound together.

"Nice move!" The vampire sped past him. This red fae wasn't one of his.

Another piercing scream shook the tower. Blue blood gleamed on the vampire's fingers as he stood above another six jointed leg. Aiden dodged the anasi's flailing body and rolled over to his dagger. He sawed through the threads holding his ankles, all the while rolling sporadically, trying to avoid the anansi's acid.

The lump of iron had fallen to the ground. Aiden crawled over to one of the severed spider legs to prod the metallic rock. A deep ache spread through his bones, but he ignored it, nudging the iron to the edge of the tower. It fell into the indigo haze that was the city below.

The limping scuttle of the crippled anansi scraped against the smooth stone. Aiden spun and let loose a jet of bright blue flames. She didn't have time to scream before the flames engulfed her, lodestone and all.

"Whoa, watch it!" The vampire flung his arms in front of his face. "You nearly toasted me."

Aiden looked at him, and then walked to the edge of the tower. It was too late to collect any more stones. The noise of their battle had probably alerted any nearby guards. He shot another jet of flame into the sky, signaling Dek. Now, his army would be on their way across the Rydah sands. It wouldn't be wise to linger; already, boots clamored on the onyx steps, no doubt summoned by the anansi's screams. The militia below would have seen the flames, and would know exactly who waited for them.

"Who are you?" Aiden faced the vampire. Around the city, gold light flickered from the tops of the other pillars. The wards were up, but they were weak, wavering without the strength of the fifth stone.

"Jefferson, of Thonis." The vampire swept into a bow.

Aiden folded his arms. The war cries of the green fae guards rose up from the wall as the encroaching footsteps thundered away. His army must have just reached the city.

Aiden's eyes flicked back to Jefferson. "What business does a subworlder from Summer have with the Dark Fae Army?"

"I've a restless spirit, and I tire of being trapped underground. I long to walk beneath the stars and feast on the blood of the living. Your army provides a good sport." He licked a fang. "So how about it?"

Aiden frowned. "Sportsmen do not make loyal soldiers. I have no reason to trust you, and I have no use for those I cannot trust." Blue flames surged down his arms. It would be a shame to kill this man. He was a skilled fighter, which was more than could be said for most of the new recruits. But there was no chance he would give some stranger the opportunity to stab him in the back. Aiden intended to live long enough to see how the human girl's car worked.

"I did just save your life." The vampire stepped back, knees bent, glancing over the side of the tower. "Is this how you repay all those who save you?"

Aiden flinched, letting the flames fade. "My life was not in peril," he snarled. "And I will not hesitate to kill you the moment I suspect you might betray me."

"I won't betray you." The vampire's face held no hint of the jovial humor that had marked it before. Perhaps it was over cautious to think he was a spy or traitor. More and more red fae joined the army each day, and this one at least seemed enthusiastic.

Aiden nodded. "Go join the other grunts if you wish to prove yourself. There is still more work to do here."

Retrieving his sword from the floor, he wended to the city's wall. If the vampire survived the battle, he could train with the other new recruits and be Dek's problem.

Aiden focused on the roiling battle around him. A boom sounded from the other side of the city. One of the lodestone towers crashed to the ground and burst into orange flame. This battle would be over quickly, probably before midnight. The people of Kesh hid behind their elemental magic and were no match for the savage violence of five thousand hungry red and brown fae. Aiden let loose a jet of flame. It engulfed several archers on the wall. Many of those near him ran or dove out of his path to their deaths — terrified of his flames.

He walked the perimeter, crisping anyone foolish enough to stand before him. Several marids banded together, levitating a torrent of water in a pathetic attempt to drown him. Aiden raised a hand, the water turning to steam. Cringing at their screams as the boiling mists seared their flesh, he swallowed back bile. Only a few more hours, it would be over, and their Majesties would be pleased when the city fell.

And tomorrow night he would see her. For a few blessed hours, he would be able to pretend this part of his life didn't exist.

CHAPTER 19

Freddie

Freddie patted her jeans: phone, wallet, keys—good. Thoughts of Pelrin and Jefferson in battle against Aiden nagged at the back of her mind. Could he really kill hundreds of innocent people and feel nothing? That didn't seem like the human-magic-obsessed fae she'd been out with the other night. She shut the door behind her and whirled into Mallory.

"Watch it, weirdo," Mallory said and straightened the unusually short hem of her pink miniskirt.

"Going out tonight, Maureen?" Freddie didn't wait for her response and headed down the hallway.

Mallory trailed her. "I was invited to the Alpha house party, weren't you?" Mallory looked scathingly over Freddie's red jacket and jeans—obviously not a house party outfit. It wasn't that Freddie hadn't been invited. Raul had invited her and Amanda weeks ago; she'd just forgotten it was tonight.

"I'll take that as a 'no.' Don't feel bad though. It was a very exclusive guest list." Mallory strode past Freddie, shoving her into the hard, metal railing as she made her way to the bottom of the stairs.

Freddie rubbed her side. "So I guess you're crashing then," she grumbled.

Whipping out her phone, Freddie sent a quick text to Amanda and Raul, letting them know she was skipping the party. When Amanda replied with a sad face, Freddie messaged she was behind on her article, but that wasn't necessarily true. She'd already compiled her notes on Vivica, Daniel, and Freya. Somehow, they were all connected, or at least Daniel and Freya were... maybe. Maybe, like Daniel, they were all lured away. But none of her research had shown any evidence that Freya or Vivica had any online relationships. A Post-it with the word satyr scribbled on it was stuck to her laptop as a reminder to look it up. Maybe there was some instinctual evidence for Vivica's ex to kidnap the other students.

The clacking of Mallory's heels on the concrete dragged Freddie out of her puzzling. It was as if each footfall uttered a smug "haha." They both signed out at the front desk and entered the atrium between the doors in the lobby. It was filled with scantily clad girls who'd convinced themselves the upper-school parties were worth waiting in the freezing Bailey to catch a ride from a trolling frat boy.

"You could always wait here," Mallory said. "Some Alpha might take pity on you."

"Actually, I was invited, Martha." Freddie put one hand on her hip, the other on the glass door to the outside. "But I can't go. I have a date, but you wouldn't know anything about those."

Mallory growled as they stepped out into the windy night. She stormed off towards the street where a line of cars waited to pick up the lower-school partygoers.

"Have fun tonight, Mark," Freddie called.

Mallory shrieked and tripped, one of her shoes flying off behind her. Hurriedly, she retrieved it and raced off to the cars. Freddie smirked and leaned against one of the stone tables sprinkled throughout the Bailey. Winter's bite nipped at her cheeks and arms. She tugged at the sides of her red leather jacket and checked her phone.

He was late. A nasty voice in the back of her mind said he was probably busy murdering innocents and kidnapping her classmates, but she ignored it. He'd told her about the life debt, but still… did Oberon and Mab really order him to murder civilians?

She shivered again, wondering if it was due to the cold weather or the disturbing turn her thoughts had taken. The student parking lot was just beyond the Bailey. Freddie looked to her car, parked in the closest row. It was too cold to wait out here for him all night. She scampered across the courtyard and slid into the car, cranking up the heat. The minutes ticked by slowly as she watched the spot where she was supposed to meet Aiden. She'd started to doze when someone tapped at the window.

Aiden, dressed in his usual black, stared past her to the rest of the car. "Hello, uhh—" He paused. Freddie nearly filled in the blank, then stopped. She still wasn't sure how much she could trust Aiden, especially not after Pelrin…

"Hi, Aiden," she called through the window. "You're a bit late."

He tensed. "You did say it was not a contract."

She shrugged and got out of the car. "It's fine."

"Your car is very beautiful." He stepped away from her to examine the back bumper.

Freddie's lip twitched as she bit back a smile. If only he could see a car like Jefferson's Agera—the shock might kill him. That is, if Jefferson and Pelrin didn't get to him first. "It's ten years old," Freddie said. "It's hardly beautiful anymore."

Aiden tapped on one of the brake lights, his face mere centimeters away from it as he traced his fingers along the surface. "It looks as though there might be an opening here." He pointed at the crack that outlined the trunk.

"Yeah, there is. Stand back." Freddie ducked into the car and popped the trunk.

Aiden gasped. When she rounded the car to stand beside him, he was half inside, examining the space where the trunk opened up to the backseat. "This isn't very secure. Anyone who has seen how this works could easily open it. I could fix it for you."

Freddie laughed. "Anyone breaking into my car is going to be disappointed. I wouldn't be surprised if they left money rather than steal anything." The contents of her trunk included an old fuzzy blanket, a car jack that was rusted beyond use, and a few pairs of shoes that hadn't quite made the journey from her parent's house to her dorm room. "Do you want to see the front?"

Aiden brightened and leapt out of the trunk. Freddie slammed it shut and followed him around to the hood. Dead bugs and an assortment of other grossness had accumulated on the front bumper—Freddie, and her wallet, were firm believers in rain washing. She popped the hood.

"Is that the distributor?" He pointed at a frightening object with a mass of cords sticking out from it.

"Maybe." Freddie leaned in. "To be honest, I don't really know what most of this stuff is." Perhaps he could come along when she got her next inspection or oil change. No, Freddie, he's a killer. This is a bad idea. She bit her lip and stepped away from him.

"Do I frighten you?" Aiden tore his gaze from the engine to meet her eyes.

She forced herself to not look away. "Should I be frightened? You kill people, don't you?" Perhaps being this direct was a bad idea, but the words were already out there, and she needed to know.

His hands clenched into fists. "It's a war, and I'm indebted to their Majesties. I have to kill people." Aiden turned away. "I understand if you've changed your mind. If you want to end—if you want me to leave."

Freddie hesitated. Letting him leave was probably the safest option, but it wasn't his fault he was forced to kill people. She cringed, watching his shoulders slump, his head bowed. "I'm sorry," she said. "I don't want you to go."

He looked up, his eyes scrutinizing her face. "Are you sure?"

Freddie forced a smile. "I'll tell you when I want you to leave." She closed the hood and slid into the driver's side. "Come on, let's go." She patted the seat next to her.

Aiden stared at it, his expression seemingly torn between excitement and agonized apprehension. The seconds inched by in stiff silence until, finally, he sat.

Freddie started the engine, and Aiden jerked. The look of shock on his face with each new bit of unexpected "human magic" sent shivers of delight down her spine.

"Buckle up!" She pointed to the seat belt on his side, then buckled her own. "New Wall has this great restaurant I want you to try."

Aiden studied the gray strap as if it were made of some fine silk before he clicked it into place. Freddie shook her head and backed out of her space.

The car rattled a bit as she drove it across the parking lot, the sound was oddly comforting, though she knew it shouldn't be. Aiden's hand moved to grab hers — as if by reflex — but he stopped just short of touching her. Heat prickled in her cheeks, but she ignored it as she pulled onto the busy road.

"So, how was your week?" Freddie swallowed, nearly choking on the last word. No doubt he'd been busy hiding the crown. What if he told her where it was? Would she betray him to Pelrin?

"It was not terrible. Why?"

"I was just asking. You don't have to tell me if you don't want to. Did you do anything fun?" The lights and boisterous sounds of Easton on a Friday night gave way to the moonlight reflecting off the Schuylkill and the deep quiet as they drove along the highway.

"Besides kill people, you mean?"

Freddie shrank back. "Killing people is fun?"

"No. It's just something I must do." Aiden stared out the window, the streetlights catching in his glowing eyes as they passed. After a long while, he said, "I did do something I'd been wanting to do for a long time. So, it wasn't a terrible week."

"Oh yeah? What?" Freddie let out a breath, relieved they'd finally made it back to what passed for normal conversation for them.

He shook his head. "Why don't I tell you a riddle instead?"

"All right."

"Two soldiers are guarding a treasure, and there are two doors, one leads to death, the other leads to the treasure. One guard always tells the truth, the other always lies. You may ask one question to find the right door."

Freddie glanced over at him. His expression was still solemn. This was a riddle Pelrin had told her once, and she had discovered a fatal flaw in the telling. "The two doors are in front of me, and I need to pick the right one?"

"Yes. It is a difficult riddle. Don't worry if you cannot figure it out."

"Do I have to ask the guards a question?"

Aiden raised a brow. "You can solve it without?"

"Well, I mean, I know the difference between right and left."

"But—" Aiden muttered his way back through the riddle. "You are not wrong, but I don't think—" He put a hand to his head. "Of course, they were supposed to say 'correct.'"

"It's all right, you are not the first person to make that mistake." She laughed.

"You are truly clever." He studied her. "Are you sure you weren't raised in Fairy?"

Freddie laughed louder. "Pretty sure."

They continued onwards, past several regatta houses outlined in brilliant white lights. The lights of New Wall came into view. A tickling sensation crawled across Freddie's neck. Aiden's eyes were still on her.

"What?" She touched the sides of her face, wondering if there was something clinging to it.

"I'm trying to figure out what you want."

"What do you mean?" There were a lot of things she wanted: to pass English, to find out who was really behind the disappearances, for Pelrin and Jefferson to be safe, to date a guy that wasn't destined for disaster. All things just out of her reach.

"This is the second time we have been..." He hesitated. "Together. You haven't asked me for anything. No one wants to be around me without wanting something. Perhaps I can save you some time?"

Freddie's heart cracked. "I don't know. I guess I just want this to go well, maybe." She cringed, then plunged ahead. "I want a normal relationship. I know it's not really possible with us, but something close to that might be nice, don't you think?" He didn't answer. The silence clawed at her as the minutes ticked by. She nearly missed the exit for New Wall. Aiden gripped the armrest as she swerved.

"What's so wrong with normal?" she said. "What do you want?" The question came out angrier than she'd intended. Slamming her foot on the brakes, Freddie breathed in a slow breath as the car trembled behind a long line of cars stopped at a red light.

"No one has ever asked me what I want." He stared up at the skyscrapers as though he longed to join their glowing lights.

"Well, I am. Aiden, what do you want?" Freddie dared to take her eyes off the road for a moment to meet his. For the first time since she'd known him, he smiled.

"I want someone who asks me what I want."

Her cheeks turned bright red, and her fingers tightened on the steering wheel. He couldn't have possibly meant he wanted her. As they moved through the city, she stole the occasional glance at him, but his eyes were fixed on the scenery. By the time they pulled into a crowded gravel lot, her heart beat so quickly she feared it might bruise her chest. They got out of the car. Aiden gawked at the red and gold gilded buildings around them.

"Hey." Freddie cleared her throat to bring her voice back down to its normal octave. "You need to stop that, or we'll get mugged."

"I am more than capable of handling any assailant foolish enough to try and harm us." He continued to stare up at the buildings.

Right, he's killed people. "Still, probably best to avoid those kinds of situations."

Aiden sighed. "I suppose you're right."

Freddie grabbed his arm and pulled him down the street. At first, he flinched at her touch but relaxed as they continued to walk arm-in-arm. Hesitantly, she slipped her fingers between his and was met with a gentle squeeze. She swallowed hard, her heart thumping faster.

They stopped in front of a shabby-looking building with a

faded green awning. Brightly colored gift shops on either side only enhanced the plain facade. Above the door were the words "Dim Sum" printed in both English and Chinese. Freddie pulled open the door, and Aiden followed her inside.

Bright shades of gold and green greeted them as they entered the restaurant. Shining bronze lions guarded an intricately carved jade arch beyond which lay an open dining room decorated in red and gold.

"Hello, honey!" The owner, a woman called Longmu, said to Freddie from the hostess stand. Her bright green eyes glowed as they raked over Aiden. "New boyfriend?"

Freddie's cheeks warmed.

"If I could only be so lucky," Aiden said. He flicked a glance over to Freddie, whose entire face was flaming.

Longmu nodded approvingly and led them through the restaurant to a table against the back wall. Freddie sat, and after taking a steadying breath, did her best to distract Longmu from asking questions regarding her complicated relationship with Aiden.

"How are your boys doing?" she said. "Still in Fairy?"

Across from her, Aiden tensed, his gaze fixed on the beaming woman.

She didn't seem to notice. "They are so big now, you should see them! Big as houses, all five of them."

"I hope the war isn't impacting them too badly," Freddie said.

"Oh no, the Seasonal Realms hardly affect us in the Air Realm. Earth people problems." She laughed. "Are you getting the usual?" Longmu patted Freddie's shoulder affectionately.

"Yes! And can he get a shot of baijiu?" The woman flashed Freddie a conspiratorial grin and winked before shuffling off to the bar.

Aiden leaned forward. "You know people in the Air Realm?" He raised his eyebrows as though impressed.

"Well, only Longmu and her sons. Have you ever been there?"

Aiden shook his head. "I have been to all of the Seasonal Realms, but never to Sea or Air." That nagging voice that told her

Aiden was a killer resurfaced. With all the conquering he did, she supposed it made sense that he was well-traveled. "What was that thing you ordered? She gave you a look..."

"Don't you trust me?" Freddie batted her eyelashes. Though it would serve her right if he said "no." After all, she didn't even trust him with her name.

"I suppose if you wished to poison me, you could have attempted it already." His eyes narrowed.

Longmu returned and set a small goblet filled with clear liquid before Aiden. He frowned and waved a hand over it. The air rippled, but nothing happened. So maybe he didn't completely trust her. Freddie's lips tightened; she hadn't expected to feel hurt by his lack of trust.

"You drink it all at once," Longmu said, gesturing to tip back the shot.

Aiden did so. His face scrunched up. Blue flames flared along his arms, and he shook his head. "That was horrible."

Freddie and Longmu burst out laughing. It was like letting go of a deep breath, and the strange pain that had crossed her heart with his spell eased. Longmu brushed away the flames with a flick of her wrist. "First time trying baijiu?" She patted him on the back and conjured up two glasses of water.

Aiden gulped his down. "Do humans really enjoy that stuff?"

"Oh yes, some too much." Longmu's eyes trailed wistfully off to the bar. "I have to go back up front. Your food is coming." She rubbed Freddie's shoulder and left them alone.

Silence settled between them for a moment.

"Why did you do that to me?" Aiden ran a finger around the rim of the glass.

"I'm sorry, I thought you might want to loosen up a bit. And I like teasing you. Does it bother you?"

"No." Through the fabric of his shirt, he fiddled with something that hung around his neck. "I like it when you laugh, even if it is at me."

Heat rose in Freddie's cheeks again. "You can tease me, too. I'm very teasable."

Aiden seemed to take this to heart. Throughout their meal, he had a very hard time teasing her. He tried confusing her with riddles—though he was terrible at them, especially for a fae. He ordered her a random drink from the menu, but when Freddie tasted it, she found it was non-alcoholic and very good. He even asked one of the waitresses for help. This backfired as the waitress only remarked on how adorable he was. Freddie nearly fell off her seat laughing. By the end of the meal, Aiden had thoroughly failed to tease her, but at least he'd made her laugh.

They waved goodbye to Longmu as they stepped out onto the busy sidewalk, shouts and pumping bass radiating around them.

"I'm not good at teasing," he said, his shoulder slumped as they walked side-by-side back to the car.

"I'm sure you'd be better at it if we were in Fairy. I have the advantage here." Freddie leaned into his side. Aiden stopped, nearly sending her sprawling.

"I hope we never meet in Fairy. It would not be good for either of us."

Freddie gulped. The idea of meeting Aiden with Oberon and Mab or on the battlefield were not prospects she'd like to fantasize about. She scanned the street, trying to find something to lighten the mood. Across the street was a blue, neon sign that read "Karaoke."

"I have an idea. Come on!" She dragged Aiden toward it.

He scanned the building, his eyes narrowing on the bulky werewolf guarding the door. "What's this?"

"It's a, uh—" Freddie tried to think of a Fairy equivalent to a karaoke bar. "It's a place where you can sing and dance. It's fun, like a party." The only not fun part was she would have to pay for it, and her "fun budget" was already pitifully low.

"It's like a revel?"

"Yes!" She had been to a few revels with Pelrin at the Summer palace. The karaoke bar wouldn't be half as elegant as those.

Aiden let out a breath. "It has been a long time since I last reveled," he said. "Their Majesties rarely invite the likes of me to celebrate the changing of the seasons."

"Well, you can celebrate with me then. Tonight. Right now." Outwardly she smiled, but inwardly she groaned as she doomed herself to another week of ramen. It would be worth it, though, if only to encourage another smile out of him.

They stepped up to the bouncer. Freddie's gaze flicked to the wristbands in the man's right hand. Aiden followed her stare and stopped as the bouncer shoved his other hand out in front of them.

"You eighteen or twenty-one?" He jerked his chin at Freddie.

She shrank back. Something cold and biting rippled through the air.

"Does it matter?" Aiden's voice was cool. His eyes burned with a terrifying light.

While an oppressive fear gripped her heart, the bouncer seemed to be getting the full effect of Aiden's spell. He shook his head and cowered away, holding out two neon-orange bands with a trembling hand. Freddie snatched them from the man's grasp and let Aiden guide her inside. The spell dropped, and she gulped in air.

Pulsing beats and a cacophony of noise roared over them. Freddie blinked, her eyes adjusting to the bar's darkened interior. The main source of light came from the multi-colored strobe lights over the occupied stage on the opposite side of the overcrowded bar.

"What the hell was that?" She shrieked over the sounds of three drunken boys shouting out the words to NSYNC's "Bye Bye Bye." Crowds of people gathered around them, bouncing along with the dated song.

"He wasn't going to let us in." Aiden frowned and took a step back.

"What? Can you read minds now?" The thought made Freddie's dinner consider reversing course.

"No, but I can read body language. Didn't you want to come here?"

"Yes, but you can't just go around magicking people because they won't do what you want."

"Why not?"

175

"It's rude, for one." She paused as someone bounced past screaming, "bye bye bye." "And it's illegal." Despite her irritation, she couldn't help the electric shiver that shot through her body when the bouncer had backed away from them. Pelrin had never been so bold.

"I'm sorry," Aiden said. "I'm not familiar with all the human laws. Next time, I'll use other means to resolve the situation." Freddie didn't like the sound of "other means" but dropped the issue.

The boys left the stage as the song ended, making way for a woman who warbled out Celine Dion's "My Heart Will Go On." Freddie groaned and leaned over the bar to order two shots. This time she ordered something sweet, like Fairy wine, to appeal to Aiden's tastes and her need to get buzzed. The last thing she needed was to think about Pelrin right now. The bartender eyed her wristband with suspicion but accepted Freddie's cash and handed over the two drinks. She passed one to Aiden.

"The music here is strange." He lifted the shot. Green light from its contents shone jewel bright in the dark bar. "Do you think me so foolish as to fall for the same jest twice?"

"These are different. They'll make the music better." She grinned and tipped one back.

Aiden sniffed the liquid and frowned. "As you wish." He gulped it down. His expression slowly straightened. "This one was not as bad. What's it called?"

"Jello shot." Freddie inched toward the end of the bar and pulled over a large binder. She held it up and turned back to Aiden. "Shall I sing for you, m'lord?" She said, mocking the formal Fairy speech.

Aiden swayed. "You shall, dear maid." He laughed and waved a hand. "Go on, entertain your lord."

She hefted open the book and flipped through its massive song list. Her fingers slid down the laminated pages; oldies, rock, pop... Smiling to herself, Freddie landed on a top forties love song, more about sex than love. The DJ nodded when she told him her selection and put her name into his computer. Freddie's heart raced as she walked back to Aiden. He was easy to find. While he wasn't the only fae in the bar, there were significantly fewer glowing eyes than she'd seen at Illusion.

"You were right." His voice held a slight slur. She frowned, spotting two more empty shot glasses on the bar beside him. "These really do make the music better."

Freddie pursed her lips, not wanting to ask how he'd paid for them. "Let's go dance."

She pulled him through the throng of bodies jumping and swaying to the poorly replicated renditions of popular songs. Aiden spun, twirled, and dipped her so fast she thought she was going to be sick. Grateful when it was her turn to sing, she took the microphone with sweaty hands. Her gaze flicked to Aiden, who stared back at her expectantly—perhaps she should've chosen a tamer song. The music started, and Freddie bobbed along to the intro. The first few words came out shakily, but she truly did love this song. Aiden's eyes widened as she reached the first innuendo and the bar's other drunken patrons cheered. Her heartbeat picked up as she belted out the lyrics while Aiden bounced along in the crowd.

When she returned, he raised an eyebrow. "That was some song."

Freddie shrugged and pulled him into another dance. Grateful for her jeans and comfortable boots, hours slipped by unnoticed in the haze of music and laughter as they danced. Soon, however, Aiden's wild dancing gained more control. The effects of human alcohol didn't last as long on fae. When the overhead lights came on several songs later, they were forced to follow the crowd out into the street.

Freddie untied her jacket from her waist and slipped it back over her shoulders. Around them, black ubers and yellow taxis loaded up with women clutching their heels in their hands and men whooping and stumbling into the cars. Aiden reached a hand around her waist, and then pulled it back as if struck by lightning.

"What's wrong?" Freddie asked.

He shook his head. "I let myself get carried away tonight," he said, more to himself than to her. "How close is it to midnight?" He tilted his head up to the cloudy sky.

"Midnight? It's at least past two." Freddie yawned as she dug in her purse for her phone.

"Two?" he rasped.

Freddie looked up. Aiden's usually tawny skin turned a ghostly white. She scanned the crowd, trying to find the source of his horror.

"What's wrong?" Her heartbeat picked up. His eyes were wide, staring straight ahead.

"I-I must go." He took off down the street, Freddie jogging after him.

"Aiden, what is it?"

"Please, I'm late. I must go." He pointed at the car as though it were the last lifeboat and they were on the Titanic. They made their way across the gravel lot. Freddie dragged her keys out of her purse and fumbled with the lock. "Be safe while I'm gone." A pained calm settled across his features.

"Same time next week?" Her hands shook as she tried to turn the key. He placed a hand over hers to steady it.

"I will do my best to see you—" His voice hitched. "Soon."

Freddie opened the door and turned to face Aiden. "Are you coming?"

He shook his head and stepped away. The air around him rippled, and he vanished. Freddie's eyes widened, the breath sucked out of her. Only gold fae had the power to wend. Aiden couldn't possibly be royalty, could he? She would have seen his wings. Even Pelrin couldn't cast a glamour strong enough to hide his.

Freddie dropped into the car. Fingers fumbling, she swiped at her phone. The answer was surely somewhere on the internet.

Her hand stiffened. She had twelve missed calls and eight text messages—all from Amanda. Heart pumping, Freddie scrolled through them until she reached the last one.

[2:03 AM] Mallory called the cops. They're taking Raul in for questioning. CALL ME BACK!!!!!

CHAPTER 20

Aiden

The icy bite of the wind scarcely phased Aiden as he stumbled across the barren tundra. Deaf to the moans and howls of the winter fae foolish or desperate enough to be out at night, he forced himself across the slick bridge to the glittering palace beyond.

Triglav merely stepped aside to allow Aiden inside, the night's wind bitter enough to tame even his sour spirit. Aiden shook the snow from his hair. His footsteps echoed against the frost-covered walls as he made his way through the silent hallways. The brown and red fae courtiers, along with their green fae slaves, were abed. No one save for the occasional troll-faced guard passed him by.

Late. For the first time in five years, he'd failed to be on time for their Majesties' ritual. Heart racing, Aiden clenched his hands into fists to stop them from shaking. Mab's violet eyes, glittering in cruel excitement, flashed to the forefront of his mind.

"There you are!" Mare hurried out from a frost-coated passage. Her wispy nightgown twisted and stretched in the shifting light of the candlelit sconces. "Do you have any idea what time it is?"

Aiden halted. His stomach dropped. Explaining himself to Mare was the last thing he needed right now. "I know the hour," he said, hoping if he kept his answers brief and uninteresting she'd leave him alone.

"Then where have you been? They're pissed, you know that? Dek has been running all over Summer looking for you, and I've been searching the palace." She folded her arms and blocked his path.

Aiden stared desperately over her head to the hall beyond, but she wouldn't budge. "Why is Dek in Summer?"

"To find you, idiot!" Mare threw her hands in the air. "Maybe he doesn't want to spend the next week helping you hobble around the palace like last time."

Aiden cringed. Phantom pains from Mab's last punishment clawed up through the soles of his feet to his knees. "Are they waiting for me?"

Mare nodded. "I couldn't convince them otherwise." She sighed, stepping aside. Aiden brushed past her, but she fell in step alongside him. "You're really not cut out for this kind of work."

Aiden shook his head. "It's not as if I asked for this."

"I know. Sometimes I wish..." But she didn't finish.

They stopped in front of a plain door. Light from beneath, broken by shifting shadows, told them Mab and Oberon were still inside.

"Good luck." Mare patted him on the back then vanished, the wisping shadows of her gown swallowing her and dissipating into nothingness.

Aiden's stomach turned over. He reached for the handle, but his hand faltered as the neon orange wristband slipped from the cover of his sleeve. Hastily he ripped it off and shoved it into his pocket. Taking a deep breath, Aiden pushed open the door.

Mab looked up from where she knelt beside the red plush armchair. Her violet eyes narrowed in on him as he approached. Oberon gripped the chair's arms, his face worn and haggard. His trembling hand stroked the deep golden waves of Mab's hair.

"Where have you been?" The queen's voice cut through the air like shards of ice.

Aiden flinched. "I was in the city, your Majesty." He bowed

low. "I apologize. I lost track of time." Aiden made sure to carefully word his answers. He dared not give away the girl. If their Majesties ordered him to harm her, or worse... He wouldn't be able to live with himself.

"You were hunting? How many did you bring us?" Mab rose to her feet. Her silver gown swept the ground like mercury.

"None tonight, my lady." He braced himself.

"You lazy dog!" She slapped him hard across the cheek. Aiden turned his face, his eyes squeezed shut. The sting of her blow burned on his skin as he waited for the inevitable.

"My dear," Oberon said. His voice was weak, like that of a fae far older than he appeared. Aiden dropped his head, resisting the urge to look up and study the man's face. "The wand."

The furious tension slipped from Mab's body as she drifted back toward her husband. "Of course."

Aiden sank mechanically to his knees and Oberon touched the wand to his head. Again, the magic invaded him, ripping power away from his core. This time it felt hungrier, the pain more violent, as it raked its way through his body. Aiden's jaw fell agape. His scream was torn away by the intensity. Black spots clustered before him, and the world fell away. Just before blissful oblivion could claim him, Oberon jerked the wand away. Aiden gasped, leaning forward on one arm, the other clutching at his chest.

An urgent knock sounded at the door.

"Who is it?" Oberon marched to the door, the weak waver in his voice gone.

"Just me, your Majesty," a cheerful voice called from the other side.

Oberon wrenched open the door. Jefferson strode into the room, and Aiden's eyebrows shot up. *Is this vampire insane? What in the seven realms is he doing here?*

"Who are you, and what do you want?" Oberon stepped back from the door and folded his arms. Jefferson beamed at him, then bowed to Mab.

"I came to tell you it wasn't his fault, your Majesties."

Aiden stared at Jefferson, his mouth open.

"Wasn't *whose* fault?" Mab's voice had resumed its bell-like tone.

"Aiden's." Jefferson jerked his chin over at him. "It was mine. I distracted him."

"You are the reason he's late with his report?" Oberon asked, disbelief clung to his every word.

"You know how it is. You start talking and drinking, next thing you know time has slipped away from you." Jefferson shrugged.

"He doesn't drink." Mab smiled at Jefferson, then looked to Aiden. "Isn't that right, pet?"

Aiden grit his teeth. How he loathed her nickname. "I did drink tonight," he replied. It was lucky he had, otherwise the vampire's lie could have led to more questions, ones he couldn't safely answer.

"Alcohol?" Oberon shifted his gaze from the vampire to Aiden.

"Yes," Aiden said.

Their Majesties exchanged looks.

"Usually the punishment for late reports is a half pound of flesh," Mab said. Aiden shuddered as echoes of the wand's agony reverberated through his bones. He rocked back onto his knees. "However, since both of you are to blame, I will be kind and split it between you. A quarter pound from each."

Aiden paled and stared up at Jefferson. The vampire's smile slipped. His Adam's apple bobbed as he took a step back, staring at Mab with an expression of horror. Oberon waved a hand, and two bewildered guardsmen appeared in the middle of the room.

"Your Majesties," a troll-guard snorted through his pig's snout.

They bowed, and the one who'd spoken cast a wary glance at Aiden. The other tucked a hand behind his back, wiping it vigorously on his uniform. Aiden thought he caught a glimpse of something blackish-green clinging to the guard's fingers. Perhaps he'd been rolling dwarf-moss. Mab had been known to lash out on those carrying its bitter scent.

"Have these two await me in the dungeon." Mab gestured at Aiden and Jefferson. "I'll be along shortly."

Aiden rose shakily to his feet. Jefferson caught him as he nearly lost his footing. Hands now clean, the second guard hobbled forward on cloven hooves and prodded Aiden with the butt of his spear. Aiden glared back at him and stumbled. Jefferson caught his arm again as they made their way slowly out of the study and down the empty passageway.

They headed down a long flight of stairs to the dungeons far beneath the palace. The pig-faced guard led the way, followed by Jefferson. The other brought up the rear, spear tip pressed into Aiden's back.

The endless dripping of water filled the dungeons as a cool breeze wafted over them. Aiden was well acquainted with this part of the palace. Whenever he wasn't sent here to endure one of Mab's cruel punishments, his duties in extracting information from the prisoners often brought him to this dark place. A shiver ran through him, and he yelped, nearly falling down the steps.

"Watch it, dog," the guard, who still held his spear against Aiden's back, spat.

Aiden didn't reply and continued to follow Jefferson into the gloom.

They entered a wide passage lit by a slithering green light. Its movement made the shadows on the floor shift sickeningly. Tiny barred windows were set in each of the doors that lined the grim hallway, holding the few prisoners the Dark Fae bothered to keep alive.

Aiden didn't look at the cells. He concentrated on being as sure-footed as possible in his weakened state. They came to a dark path bisecting the green passage—the light had yet to slither into its blackness. A row of iron-barred cells lined the walls. Aiden's palms scraped against the hard, stone ground as the guard pushed him into one of the cells. Jefferson was placed in the one beside his.

"See you later, *pet*." The hoofed guard sneered and followed his comrade up the stairs. If he had just one more ounce of strength, Aiden would have committed the guard's face to memory and remind the goat-man the dangers of provoking the truly powerful.

He pushed himself onto his hands and knees and crawled to the wall, as far from the bars as possible. Twisting into a sitting position, he wrapped his arms around his knees and tried to block out the bone-aching pulse of the iron.

"Hey, so they aren't really going to take a quarter pound of flesh from us, right?" The vampire leaned against the bars facing Aiden. His position was that of boredom, but the muscles in his arms were tense, braced against the ground.

"What you did back there was very stupid." Aiden's voice was flat. He didn't even have the strength to rebuke the low-level soldier properly.

"You're not very good with 'thank yous,' are you?" Jefferson said.

Aiden did not reply. He felt no need to thank the vampire for attempting to cover for him. He'd failed. Besides, the entire concept of "thanking" was so *human*. Where had the vampire said he was from? Whatever his motive, Aiden doubted it was driven out of any sense of friendship or camaraderie.

"So, where were you really? Visiting your girl? Guy?"

Aiden tensed, hoping the dark hid the alarm on his face. "My life is none of your business."

Jefferson sighed and stretched against the bars. "You won't make any friends keeping yourself closed off like that. You work hard; you deserve some time to yourself. I wanted to show you I meant what I said. I won't betray you."

Aiden cast a glance over at the vampire. Before he could respond, Mab's silvery form wended before the bars. She smiled broadly, revealing her perfect, pearlescent teeth. Aiden's grip around his knees tightened.

"You are first, my little jester." She pointed to Jefferson.

The vampire backed away, pushing himself to his feet in one fluid motion. He looked at Aiden, his face was awash with newborn dread. Aiden swallowed a mouth full of bile as he met the vampire's gaze.

"I'll be back for you, pet." Mab tossed her golden hair. With one perfectly tipped finger, she beckoned, and Jefferson followed her down the dark corridor.

A sick, crawling feeling crept through Aiden's stomach. He waited in the dark for several long moments before the first sounds echoed throughout the dungeon. Pressing his forehead to his knees, Aiden tried to block out the vampire's screams as Mab claimed her first quarter pound of flesh.

CHAPTER 21

Freddie

Freddie pressed the wrong buttons three times before she finally managed to call Amanda. *Please pick up, please pick up.* The car came to life with its usual rattle as she pulled out of the lot, her knee bouncing the phone on her lap.

"Jesus! Freddie, where have you been?" Amanda said.

Freddie winced. "I just got your message. Are you guys okay?"

"We're okay. Raul's still with the police, but they haven't officially arrested him. Where are you?"

"Just driving back from the city. I can be there in twenty."

"Great. Raul's car is back at the house, so we're not going anywhere."

Freddie pressed harder on the gas, glad the highway was practically deserted. Moonlight followed her like a milky bright snake as she whipped past the river. When the orange lights of Easton came into view, she slowed. Her heart thumped wildly. With his fae blood, connections to Freya and Vivica, and whatever happened with Mallory, Raul was as good as guilty in the eyes of the police. And she was nowhere closer to finding the real culprit than they were.

Freddie shot into the first parking space she found and ran into the station, searching frantically for her friends.

Sitting on a blue plastic chair, Amanda looked up from her phone. "Thank God, Freddie. Raul's paranoia was starting to get to me."

"Where's Raul? Is he okay?"

"He's been back there for hours." She jerked her chin at the door leading to the offices.

As if on cue, it opened. A tired-looking Raul followed by two members of the Fae Investigative Department, a man and woman in crisp black suits, entered the room. A chill ran down Freddie's spine—Raul was in big trouble.

"Don't leave town, Mr. Lupez," the male FID said.

"How can I? You took my car." Raul glared back at the man.

"Evidence."

"If you think of anything else, make sure to give us a call." The woman nudged him forward.

Freddie and Amanda got to their feet.

"Thanks for waiting, guys," he muttered.

"Of course." Amanda slid her phone into the back pocket of her jeans and wrapped Raul in a one-armed hug. Freddie fidgeted, torn between feeling horribly guilty and utterly useless.

They followed Raul to Freddie's car. He stopped in front of it, allowing Freddie to dash around the front and unlock the doors. Once everyone was buckled in, they took off down the street at a snail's pace.

"Are you all right?" Freddie glanced at Raul, hunched against the passenger's side window. "Come on, Raul. Are you okay?"

"Fine."

Biting her lip, Freddie continued down the dark streets to the Alpha Phi house. The only creatures out this late were Easton's gangs of stray cats and the occasional vampire couple. When they arrived, Raul got out of the car and slammed the door behind him. Freddie frowned in brief concern for her car but followed after him in silence.

The home of the Alphas was an old Victorian mansion. Its lawn was littered with broken beer bottles, ribbons of toilet paper, and red solo cups. Freddie and Amanda followed Raul up to the house. The overpowering scents of sweat, alcohol, and vomit greeted them as they entered the near-silent building. Upper-school girls lay in a heap with upper-school boys, creating a cacophony of snores atop the frat's well-loved sofas.

Footsteps came down the stairs. Three Alphas in various stages of sobriety blocked Raul's path.

"Brother Raul, we have a problem." The soberest of the boys stood with arms folded. "Kidnapping breaches our Alpha code of conduct."

"You can't really believe I would do that," Raul said.

"It's unfortunately not what we —" He nudged the chubby boy on his left who slumped against his shoulder. The boy snorted to attention. "School policy states if you're under police investigation you can't live in the house."

"Come on, Trent. Please, I just want to go to bed."

"Look, I'm sorry, man. We already had the head of housing give us a letter. You need to be out tonight. I promise, as soon as they realize it wasn't you, you can move right back into your old room."

Freddie pursed her lips. When Jacob Garrison, a human Kappa Sig, had been accused of sexual assault, the school had given him three weeks to find other housing.

"What, you're not going to give it away? Afraid I've marked my territory?"

Trent blanched, his brown eyes widening. "You didn't..."

"Just let me get my stuff." Raul pushed past Trent.

Freddie and Amanda stepped over the chubby boy who'd fallen onto the stairs. Amanda not-so-accidentally stepped on the boy's arm with the toe of her shoe as they headed up. Once upstairs, they navigated around empty solo cups and questionable puddles toward Raul's room.

It was as neat and put-together as the rest of the house was in disarray. Amanda was the first to step inside. Raul and Freddie followed her. Dragging a suitcase out of the closet, she whipped around the room with fae-like speed, packing all of Raul's belongings. He sank onto the bed, and Freddie sat beside him.

"I didn't ask to be this way." There was a slight tremor in his voice that made Freddie's heart squeeze.

"What do you mean?"

"I didn't ask to turn into a wolf every full moon. Don't you think I would stop if I could?" He looked at her as if her response would either save or condemn him.

"Of course, Raul. You shouldn't be ashamed of who you are. The wolf is part of you."

"I wish it wasn't. Mallory just screamed I was trying to kidnap her, and I got hauled off. If I was human, do you think they would do that?"

Amanda halted in her packing to exchange looks with Freddie.

"Come on, Raul. You're staying with me while they sort all of this out," Freddie said. "My RA won't mind."

"It's fine. I can stay with my parents." He sighed and flopped on the bed.

"Raul, your parents live in New Wall, and you don't have a car, remember?" Amanda had finished packing. She handed Raul his suitcase and hefted his backpack onto her back. "I'd let you stay with me, but I have roommates. Freddie has a single. It's perfect."

It was nearly four in the morning by the time the three of them trooped down the hallway to Freddie's room. Mallory's door was shut, the cross hung perfectly in its center. Freddie ripped it down, barely stopping herself from snapping it in half. Her troubles weren't with God; they were with Mallory, and she would pay for this.

⚘

Throughout the week, Freddie resisted the urge to strangle her neighbor. When her second Friday detention rolled around, Mr. Barker cautiously put her and Mallory on opposite sides of the room to reduce the risk of any incidents. They'd kept their fighting in class to dark glowers and intricately woven doublespeak. The

silent tension between them caused the rest of the class, including
Mr. Barker, to speak in hushed tones and avoid walking too close
to them. Now, Freddie settled herself in front of one of the school
computers and began working on the poetry assignment.

*Satyr: a brown fae with the torso, arms, and head of a human male
and the horns, ears, legs, and tail of a goat. They are known for their
hypnotic flute melodies, love of alcohol, and lustful nature towards
nymphs.*

Freddie copied this down into her English notebook. The pied
piper of Hamelin could have been a satyr. Vivica's ex was one too.
Freddie chewed her bottom lip and studied the curved horns in the
picture on her laptop. It could explain how the students vanished
without a trace if the satyr used his flute to hypnotize them. But one
satyr wasn't enough to kidnap hundreds of students, at least not all
over the country. How could he have ripped out Vivica's throat? It
was something... but there were so many holes.

When Mr. Barker dismissed them, Freddie headed off to the
upper-school cafeteria to meet Amanda and Raul. A girl dressed in
a bumble bee costume ran past her, and Freddie groaned. She'd
been so worried about her friends and Aiden that she'd completely
forgotten about Halloween. The one time of year when she could
dress as a fairy and feel worthy of Pelrin — but not this year.

The cafeteria was packed with students in costume. Some of
the fae upper schoolers were dressed as human professionals:
firemen, nurses, and the like. Freddie shook her head.

She sat with Amanda and Raul. Her appetite had been slim
over the past week, but Raul helped out by borrowing her car and
bringing food home from his parent's restaurant. Still, she'd felt too
sick to eat. There'd been no word from Pelrin or Jefferson since
they'd left, and hoping to hear something from Aiden was like
hoping for a snow day in June.

"Guys, this is terrible," Raul said, breaking their miserable
silence. "I know everything's shit right now, but we can't just be
mopey all the time."

Amanda glared at him. These days her eyes were permanently
rimmed in red. Looking at her made Freddie's stomach twist. If

Jefferson was killed, and Aiden was to blame, what would she do? It'd been a week, and she hadn't heard a word from him... and the way he'd left so suddenly... She hoped he was all right.

"Would you rather us fake smiles, Raul?" Freddie traced her finger along the table's faux wood grain.

"It's Halloween. Let's go out for a little distraction. Want to meet after class to go costume shopping?"

Freddie and Amanda said nothing. After a few insistent nudges, the girls gave sullen nods.

When class let out, they dutifully piled into Freddie's Toyota and drove to the Halloween store. It was pitifully picked over—a victim of being too close to the New Wall School.

Amanda shuddered as they stepped inside. "I hate Halloween," she moaned. "Why does everything have to be so scary?"

"This isn't scary." Raul held up a bikini claiming to be a snowman costume.

"You're right. That's just plain terrifying." Freddie scanned the wall.

"I'm not sure we can wear any of this out tonight." Amanda frowned at a bag that contained three leaves connected by bits of string. It was supposed to be an Eve costume.

"Hey, guys, look at this!" Raul held a Batman costume reverently to his chest. Freddie rolled her eyes. "Come on, it's *Batman*. You two could go as some sexy villains." He gestured at some of the girls' costumes around it.

"I think not," Freddie said.

"Some of us would like to make it back in one piece tonight." Amanda eyed the villain costumes with disapproval.

They resorted to searching a large bin, labeled "odds and ends," which ultimately proved far more fruitful. Amanda found a floral print dress and gogo boots. She declared she would pair them with her heart-shaped sunglasses and go as a hippie. Freddie found a knee-length blue cloak, a pair of false wings, and a star-tipped wand.

"I can be the blue fairy, like from Pinocchio or Cinderella!" she said, wrapping the cloak around her shoulders.

Raul gave an exaggerated sigh. "You guys didn't want to try on anything a bit more..." His eyes drifted over to the skimpy costumes.

Freddie and Amanda turned their sharpest glares on him. "No," they said in unison.

Raul grinned and held up his hands. "Just a suggestion."

The line for the valet at Illusion was four cars deep, so Freddie parked at the back of the crowded lot. She stared at the feather-winged backs of two blondes dressed in yellow and red body-hugging mini dresses with matching cones on their heads. Raul nudged her and grinned. At least he was feeling better. Amanda gripped Freddie's hand as they waited in line. Raul had paid to get their IDs glamoured to indicate they were eighteen — security had increased since Vivica's body was found. Even the fairy who'd glamoured them flat out refused to do twenty-one.

They inched closer. Freddie watched as the minotaur argued with a vampire over the authenticity of his ID, and the faun valet looked ragged as he raced back and forth to park the cars.

It took forever to get into the club, but once inside, it was just as Freddie remembered — if a little more crowded.

Raul patted Freddie on the shoulder. "You guys go dance. I'm going to chat with ketchup and mustard over there." He pointed at the two fairy girls.

"Good luck," Amanda said.

"He'll need it," Freddie added. They laughed and hit the dance floor.

Amanda was more reserved in her movements, awkwardly side-stepping any attempt at grinding. Freddie danced with everyone, girl, guy, creep, normie, it didn't matter — anything to keep her mind off of everything that might be happening to her friends in Fairy.

"Need to pee?" Amanda shouted after they had danced long enough for Freddie's feet to start aching.

"Okay," she shouted back.

The line for the ladies' room was nearly as long as the line to enter the club. Freddie was grateful she didn't have to go too badly. The girl in front of them, dressed as Snow White, didn't look to be as lucky. Freddie was about to mention this to Amanda but paused at the shock on her friend's face.

"What's wrong?"

"Jefferson," Amanda said and pointed to the VIP section.

Sure enough, Jefferson, his pale form menacing in all black, stood beside a fae with the head of an Egyptian god. They made a blood-curdling pair, but that was not what made Freddie's face burn red-hot. Just beyond them, seated on one of the white sofas was Aiden, a pretty vampire girl beside him.

Freddie marched toward the door. She needed to leave, now. Her thoughts and emotions battled in her head as she moved through the crowd, not bothering to check if Amanda was following her or if Raul noticed them leaving.

How could he? Pelrin was right; Aiden was awful; he was on a date. Why was she never good enough? Tears clouded her vision as she stalked through the club. She would write an article exposing his every secret. The FIDs would hunt him down and… and…

Something gold flashed in the corner of her eye. Glancing back at Aiden, and his date, she saw the vampire girl drinking greedily from a large, blood filled goblet, a gold locket hanging from her neck. Freddie's first thought was the girl must be young. Vampires older than a decade rarely drank so heavily, at least not in public. But there was something else about the girl that held her attention. The locket, her face. She'd seen it in photographs over a hundred times as she studied the missing students.

Freya Park.

Freya's glasses were gone. Her skin had been cleared up by the vampire venom, and her hair now curled perfectly around her face. She looked like a girl from a k-pop video, a far cry from the mousy student she'd been.

Freddie gasped, and Aiden turned his head to her. The club was a blur of moving shadows. She wanted to run, get as far away from this club, and *him*, as possible. He was with Freya. If that wasn't hard evidence he was behind all of this, she didn't know what was. Freddie smeared blue eyeshadow across her face as she wiped away her tears. She was probably his next victim. He was enchanting her to...

It didn't matter. Exposing him would require more evidence. She wouldn't lower herself to the Mallory's level, accusing people with only hunches. Perhaps she could get him to confess.

Freddie stumbled as she reached the stairs to the outside and leaned against a pillar. Amanda hadn't followed her. Taking a deep breath, Freddie pressed herself into the small space between the pillar and the wall.

"What are you doing here? It's dangerous." Aiden appeared in front of her, filling up the remaining space between her and the wall.

"There are other humans here," Freddie said. She gestured at a cluster of ninja turtles, two of whose eyes did not glow when the light fell on them.

"Those humans did not make me a promise they wouldn't put their lives in needless danger," he hissed. "I followed through with my part."

"No one forced you to keep going out with me. Besides, what should I care for promises when you're out here with other girls? Other girls *you* kidnapped. And turned into what? A vampire?" If she was going to expose him, she might as well confront him, maybe surprise a confession out of him.

Aiden looked at Freya. He rubbed his chest, moving something beneath his shirt. "I'm not—surely you know that I can't... Look, I'm being watched. Please go home. I'll explain later."

"I'd love to hear it." Freddie tried to wriggle her way out the other side of the pillar. Rage and hurt swirled in her chest, constricting her lungs. She needed fresh air. Aiden tugged at something hanging from around his neck.

"Please, I can't stay any longer. Just—" He bit his lip and peered around the side of the pillar. The vampire girl guzzled down her second goblet of blood. Jefferson and the other fae now actively searched the dance floor.

Freddie looked up at Aiden, her heart pounding at the thought of being caught by the jackal-headed fae. Aiden was staring at something cupped in his bandaged hand. She frowned, even when Pelrin had been hurt in his attempt to protect the crown, he hadn't needed a bandage. "What happened to your—?"

He cut her off. "Take this." Aiden pressed something small and hard into her palm. "It will keep you safe. I must go now. I'm so sorry." His brow creased, and he peered over her shoulder again. "You look very nice."

Freddie lifted a hand to slap him, but he'd vanished, reappearing as he strode through the crowd. On the dance floor, the Egyptian god-like fae clapped a hand on his back. Freddie counted to ten before she let herself leave the safety of the pillar and jog up the stairs and out of the club.

Outside, in the fresh air, she slumped against the wall. There was no line. The only people around were the bouncer leaning against one of the heat lamps and one of the ninja turtles smoking a little ways off. Likely, the valet was off joyriding, as he was nowhere in sight. Freddie looked down at what Aiden had given her—a tarnished, silver ring. It glinted dully in the blue porch light.

She slipped it on and tried to determine if there were carvings on the side or if it was truly as battered as it felt. What had he meant when he said it would keep her safe? Was it charmed to ward off vampires or something? The ninja turtle dropped the cigarette and wandered drunkenly down the street. Freddie scowled and walked over to stomp it out.

The door to the club burst open, revealing Amanda, followed by Raul.

"There you are, Freddie. We were so worried." Amanda wrapped her in a tight hug.

"Let's go. It's not safe in there with *him*," Raul said. Freddie knew better than to think "him" referred to any of the drunk turtles.

"At least we know Jefferson is all right," Amanda said.

Raul took the keys and drove them back to the dorm. Freddie curled in the passenger's seat, watching the costumed students parade down Main Street; it was only a little before one. The ring Aiden had given her was still on her finger. Frowning, she took it

off and tossed it into her purse.

CHAPTER 22

Freddie

Freddie's nerves were strung tighter than an anansi's web. Her tiny dorm room had been taken over by Raul and Amanda, who didn't want to study alone after seeing Jefferson with Aiden. With Thanksgiving less than a month away, Freddie's teachers had decided to increase their number of assignments. Neither Pelrin nor Jefferson had contacted them since that night, and Aiden's ring constantly burned in her hoodie's pocket, where she'd hidden it away. Freddie hadn't put it on—that would mean she forgave him and that they were *something*—but she kept it close, just in case.

When Mallory announced she'd submitted her article on the so-called 'werewolf threat' for publication during class on Wednesday, it took all of Freddie's willpower to keep from stabbing the conceited little prep with her pen. She settled for carving a line of black ink on the underside of the desk. If she didn't care about hard facts and truth, she could have submitted her article, too.

That evening, when she got home—her stomach boiling with anger, guilt, and nerves—Freddie slammed shut the door to her room. Amanda and Raul looked up from their respective spots on the floor and couch.

"Everything okay?" Raul asked. He moved aside on the couch so Freddie could sit. She opted instead for the bed.

"Fine," she yelled into her pillows.

Hot tears stung her face. In that moment, she could break; she could cry and scream. For just one moment, she would let herself feel, and then she would be fine. A hand rubbed circles on her back as Freddie cried harder into the pillow. She should be the one comforting Amanda, but instead, she had let herself catch feelings for the enemy. Jefferson could be hurt or dead, and she had been going on dates with his potential murderer.

"Want me to make you some ramen, Fred?" Amanda gestured to the microwave on top of the mini-fridge.

Freddie nodded as her friend's weight lifted from the bed. Taking a steadying breath, she lifted her head. She needed to get through tonight, and then the day would be over. She was okay.

Amanda shrieked as a bright gold light filled the room. Its rippling pulse did little to lift Freddie's mood, but she wiped furiously at the tears. Blinking dully, she waited as the light around Pelrin faded. He looked just as tired as before, but this time he was dressed in the red leather uniform of the Summer soldiers.

"Hi Freddie, guys," he said and sank down on the couch beside Raul.

"Pelrin, you're all right. How's Jefferson?" Amanda rushed over to him while Freddie wriggled to the edge of the bed. Her emotions were too muddled to be close to Pelrin right now.

"Fine, but you already know that," Pelrin said. "He told me he saw you guys the other night." Pelrin's voice sounded too tired to yell, but it was making a valiant effort.

"Sorry, Pel. I just thought the girls needed a night out," Raul said.

Pelrin nodded. "I warned you about letting them go to fae places."

"Sorry, but they're not prisoners. You can't keep them locked in here forever."

"Why are you here, Pelrin?" Freddie folded her arms and stopped herself from reminding him, for the millionth time, that she didn't need his permission to live her life. Amanda wanted to know about Jefferson's progress, and so did she. If only to find out more about Aiden.

"I just came by to give you an update, like I promised." Pelrin rubbed a hand down his face and stared up at the ceiling as though trying to count the pockmarks in the plaster.

"What's the plan? When will Jefferson be back?" Amanda perched on the edge of the couch and rested her elbows on her knee.

Pelrin turned to her. "Your boyfriend is amazing. It's only been two weeks, and he's already made it into that filthy dog's inner circle."

Freddie's hands curled into fists. Her last encounter with Aiden pressed down on her already-stressed mind.

Pelrin's eyes flicked around the room, his incredulous expression crumpled into one of pained confusion as his gaze settled on a pile of Raul's laundry. "Freddie, are you and Raul..." He trailed off.

"I got kicked out of the house. Freddie's letting me crash here. That *puta* next door told the police I was behind all the disappearances."

Pelrin harrumphed. "Want me to take care of her?"

"Are you insane, Pel? That would only make things worse!" Freddie jumped up from the bed and rounded the couch. "We need to find out who's really behind this. It's the only way to clear Raul's name."

Pelrin got to his feet. "We already know who's behind this! It's *him*. It's always *him*." He glared down at Freddie. She put her hands on her hips and returned his glare. "And I forbid you from nosing around that worthless dog for those stupid classes you take, Fred."

"You what?" A silence fell across the room — cold and still as death. "My classes are important to me. I am not one of your soldiers you can just order around."

"Like it or not, you remain under my protection and will do as I say!"

"I didn't ask to be under your protection. Why can't you just stay out of my life!"

"Freddie." Amanda placed a hand on her arm, but Freddie shook her off.

"I'm doing this for your own good, because I care about you." Pelrin's voice was strained.

"Did you care about me when you slept with that girl, Pelrin?" Her chest ached as she fought the tears threatening to pour down her cheeks. "Get out. I'm not yours to protect anymore."

Pelrin crumpled as if Freddie, or more likely someone much stronger than her, had dealt him a heavy blow to the stomach. She fought the urge to cringe away from the pain that marred his handsome features.

"I was going to tell you I will be going into battle this week against *him*." His voice quavered, and his jaw locked. "I wanted to say goodbye before I left. Just in case."

Freddie turned her back to him. Her shoulders shook with silent sobs. Magic rippled against her back, but she fought the urge to turn around. When the air went still, Pelrin was gone.

❦

The remainder of the week passed in a church-like silence. Freddie was a mess of emotions. Whenever Amanda or Raul spoke to her, it was as though they feared she was about to explode. Pain pounded on her temples and raked across her chest. She felt like a ghost, going through the motions of living without truly existing. On Friday evening, Freddie sat cross-legged on her bed, staring blankly at her Calc book. With no new clues, progress on her article had ground to a standstill. Despite Pelrin's rantings, she couldn't shake the sight of Aiden and Freya together at Illusion. If he was her culprit, it would be nearly impossible to track him down and find any shard of hard evidence.

Someone banged on the door, and Freddie twisted toward it. They banged again. Amanda looked up from her seat on the floor. Raul had his Economics homework splayed out across the couch. It drooled down onto Amanda's Psychology book. They exchanged looks, and then glanced up at Freddie. She sighed and rose to answer it. It couldn't be Pelrin; he never bothered with knocking. Whoever it was had started to bang again when Freddie yanked open the door and stared up into the faces of the two FID officers from the police station.

"Is Raul Lupez here?" The female officer pushed her way into the room. Freddie took a startled step back. Nerves buzzed throughout her body like a swarm of angry pixies. *Are they allowed to just barge in here?*

"What do you want with me?" Raul closed his book and slowly got to his feet.

The FID held up her badge. Amanda looked from Freddie to Raul, her eyes wide as she rose shakily. "Raul Lupez, please keep your hands where I can see them."

"What is this? What's happening? You can't just come in here." Freddie's voice cracked. She wanted to scream as her heart and stomach jumped in unison.

The female FID sniffed. "We're the law, sweetie."

Amanda got to her feet. Her hands shook as her gaze shifted between Raul and the FIDs.

"Three other girls have been reported missing after that party we picked him up from, and another boy missing from Illusion the week following. Witnesses said he was seen there. I'd be much more careful about who I let in my room if I were you, Miss." The male FID slipped Freddie his card.

"Raul Lupez, you are under arrest for conspiracy to kidnap. We are taking you down to the station to be questioned. Any attempts at retaliation will be viewed as resisting arrest. Do you understand?"

"I—I don't understand. I didn't do anything. I didn't kidnap anyone." Raul shook. Amanda cried silent tears. All Freddie could do was hold the FID's card tight in her hand.

"We'll read you your rights at the station before you're questioned. Come on." The woman escorted Raul out of the room, hands cuffed in front of him.

"If you think of anything that might help our investigation, give me a call," the man said, gesturing at the card in Freddie's hand. "Don't worry. We won't let him hurt you for turning him over."

Freddie blinked. "I didn't—" She choked and bit her lip.

Raul gave her half a smile. The female FID shoved him hard, and he stumbled forward. Words failed her as Freddie watched the FIDs pull Raul down the hall. Across from her, Mallory stood in her doorway watching, a smug smile stretched across her over-glossed lips. Hatred washed over Freddie. She needed to get away from here before she did something she'd regret.

"I'm going to follow them to the station," Amanda said. Her purse was already slung over her shoulders.

"I think I'm going to go home." Freddie's voice was weak. All of her friends were suffering, and there was nothing she could do. "I'll find a way to get him out of this. He didn't do anything wrong."

Amanda hugged her. "I know. Just don't do anything stupid, Fred. Please." She cast a scathing look over her shoulder at Mallory. The redhead let out a shrill giggle and turned back into her room.

Freddie nodded, her body still shaking.

Once Amanda was gone, she packed a bag, making sure to include every clue she had gathered thus far. Nothing else was important right now. She needed to tackle one problem at a time. And finding out who the true kidnapper was, well, that was the kind of work real journalists did. If she wanted to be like them, it was time to start practicing.

Nearly two hours later, she pulled into the driveway of her parents' two-story colonial. The porch light was on, and her mom waved to her from the front window. Freddie wondered how her mother seemed to know whenever she was coming home, even when she didn't call ahead. She got out of the car and raced to the front door.

The fragrance of pumpkin spice candles rolled out to greet her as her mom wrapped her in a tight hug. Freddie let a few tears leak onto the green velvet bathrobe her mom had worn for as long as she could remember.

"Judy, you're smothering her." Freddie's dad sat in an

armchair near the unlit fireplace. A book entitled *The Pilgrimage* rested in his lap as he waved to his daughter.

"Really, Earl? Wyn likes my hugs. Don't you, dear?"

Freddie smiled. Only her family was permitted to call her "Wyn." To everyone else, she was Freddie — or, in the case of her close friends, Fred. "They're fine, Mom."

"You should have called first. Are you hungry? I'll fix you a plate." Judy Jones ushered her daughter inside, planting kisses on her brow between questions.

Freddie nodded, eager for a taste of something other than waffles or ramen. She followed her mom into the kitchen. Pristine white cabinets gleamed from all angles of the open space. Copper-bottom pots and pans, all meticulously clean, dangled over a white, granite island. Freddie sighed, dropping onto one of the stools before it.

"Your father and I were so worried with all those disappearances on campus. You're being safe, aren't you?" Her mother's eyes narrowed.

"Aren't I always?"

"Don't try to fool me, Wynifred Jones. I'm your mother." She eyed Freddie as she bustled off to the fridge and loaded up a plate with leftover rice and chili.

Freddie's stomach growled. "I'm investigating it for English. If I get my article published, I could get a scholarship to the upper school."

Her mother sighed as she shoved the plate into the microwave. "As nice as that sounds, snooping around this mystery is too dangerous, even for you."

"But, Mom —"

"I've been following this story too. Look at this." She dug into one of the drawers built into the island and took out a freezer bag filled with newspaper clippings.

"Oh, Mom. You really need a better hobby," Freddie said.

From the living room, her father chuckled. Her mom dumped out the clippings and began sorting through them.

"I know you've always had a special interest in fae — especially since that nasty fairy—but they can be really dangerous. Right, dear?" She raised her voice to carry to the living room.

Freddie's dad didn't look up but called back all the same. "Listen to your mother."

Freddie scowled. "I just need to find something that connects all the victims together." The microwave dinged, and her mom retrieved the plate of steaming chili, setting it in front of her. Freddie tore into the comfort food as though she hadn't eaten in days.

"You want to know what all these kids had in common?" She pointed at the picture on top of the stack of articles. It was of a boy in a green and white striped polo, and the caption read: Eric Peterson. *He must be the most recent victim.* Freddie glanced at the date as she swallowed another mouthful of chili.

"What do they all have in common, Mom?"

"An unhealthy interest in fae. Just like you, Wyn." She yanked the plate away before Freddie could lick up the last few grains of rice. "You be careful; that's who they're targeting."

Freddie rolled her eyes. "Sure thing, Mom. Hey, can I take these articles with me?"

"Of course, just don't stay up too late. I'll need your help getting the house ready for company tomorrow."

Freddie rolled her eyes and gathered the clippings back into the bag. She then made her way up the stairs to her bedroom at the opposite end of a long hallway from her parents' room.

Her walls were painted a rose pink and decorated with awards and certificates from various essay competitions. A dark wood bureau was pushed against the wall beneath a window that overlooked the backyard. On its surface were several photos from Freddie's time at New Wall. There was the homecoming dance from last year where she and Amanda waved at the camera. The figure that stood beside Freddie had been neatly removed. Like all the other pictures with Pelrin, she'd dissected them, and then burned his image along with the fairy-made homecoming dress he had given her. Only the shoes from junior prom had been spared Freddie's fiery wrath.

Next to the bureau was a desk littered with bright pink office supplies. A whiteboard hung on the wall above it. After setting the articles down, Freddie tore off bits of Scotch tape and placed the articles on the board in chronological order. She wrote the dates of the disappearances beneath each of the articles: seven people in the span of two months. Her mother had highlighted words in each of the articles, too. They seemed to be tied to the location of where the victims had gone missing, but occasionally they would point to any fae interactions they'd had.

One of the more recent articles had a picture of three girls. The words highlighted were "mixed fae fraternity." Freddie frowned; those must be the girls that went missing after Raul's party. She jotted down all the evidence she had gathered from her investigations as well. Beneath Daniel's article she wrote, "went to meet SexyNymph47," and under Vivica's article she wrote "possible violent satyr." Perhaps there was something to her mom's comment that all the victims had an *unhealthy* interest in fae. Each one of them had disappeared after visiting a place frequented by fae. Charm City, The New Fae Library, Raul's frat, Illusion—all these couldn't be a coincidence.

She drew a makeshift map to try to determine a pattern and ended up with a misshapen scribble. Frowning, she put down the marker and read through the last of the articles. Eric Peterson, according to his friends, was last seen on his way to have a smoke while at Illusion on Halloween night. He was wearing a Donatello Ninja Turtle costume.

Freddie's heart raced; she had seen a turtle that night. Racking her brain, she feverishly jotted down all she could remember about spotting him. Focused on her discovery, she nearly didn't feel the ripple of magic behind her.

Pelrin knocked on the side of her desk. "Hey, I hope I'm not interrupting."

Freddie clenched her fists, took a deep breath, and turned to face Pelrin. "I'm working on my article. How did you know I was here?"

"I checked your dorm first. It was a guess." He sank to one

knee. "Freddie, I'm sorry. I know this school of yours is important to you, but I just want you to be safe. Will you forgive me?"

She glared at him but let the image of Pelrin begging sink in. Finally, she nodded, and he got back to his feet. "Did you have an update on Jefferson or something, Pel?" Freddie leaned against the desk.

Pelrin moved closer to her. "Yes. Well, not really. I just came to tell you..." He paused and took her hand gently in his. She let him hold it, unsure why she wasn't immediately pulling away. "Curses, Freddie, I'm such an idiot. I am so sorry for all I've done to you." His lips grazed her fingertips. She sucked in a breath and pulled back her hand. The ring Aiden had given her pulsed treacherously against her leg.

"Have you been drinking?" Freddie sniffed the air. "What's wrong with you, Pel?"

He smiled and let out a soft laugh before dropping both his hands to his sides. "I came to tell you goodbye."

"Goodbye? Pel, what's happening? Where are you going?" She instantly hated herself for making it sound as though she wanted him to stick around. Purple bruise-like patches colored the space beneath his eyes, and the sharp angles that had carved their way across their cheeks marked the change from the prince she knew to the tired man before her.

"Tonight's the night. I didn't want to worry the others. Either our plan goes well, and we get the crown back, or we die trying." Pelrin's lips were set in a grim line.

Her stomach dropped. He was going to face off against Aiden tonight. There was no way this would end well. One of them was bound to get hurt—or, more likely, worse.

"But it's your soldiers that are going to do all the fighting, right? I mean, you and Jefferson will be fine."

"It's war, Freddie. You never know what might happen. I just wanted to make sure to tell you goodbye before I go and give you a real apology." He pulled her into a tight hug.

Aiden's ring in her pocket pressed into her skin as Pelrin held her. Freddie squeezed her eyes shut to prevent the tears threatening to pour out. Even though he was annoying and overprotective and a cheater, she didn't want him dead or injured.

"Please be careful, Pel. We need you guys back here for movie night." Her voice cracked.

"I'll see what I can do." He grinned, though the smile didn't quite meet his eyes. "When I get back, I want to talk. About us."

A sharp tingle ran down her spine. "Pel—"

"Just talk. I know I was awful to you, Fred. I promise I'll be better."

"Just be safe, Pelrin."

He bent down to kiss her forehead, a lock of his long blond hair escaped its tie to brush across her cheek. The scent of ripe peaches rolled off his body as he pulled away. "Goodbye, Freddie." He bowed and wended into nothingness.

CHAPTER 23

Aiden

Y ou are asking for trouble," Dek said.

"I haven't done anything." Aiden rubbed the spot on his chest where his mother's ring once hung. Now, it kept the human girl safe. She would be able to use it more than he could anyway.

"You've been brooding for over a week now. Don't think their Majesties won't notice. They'll think you're ungrateful." Dek leaned across the jasper table, his arms folded. "Where were you that night? I hardly believe you were out with Jefferson."

Aiden curled his lip. "Their Majesties need not fear for my loyalty. And I haven't been brooding."

Dek scoffed. Before he could respond, Irina entered followed by a too-eager Jefferson, and they took seats beside each other. Irina sat opposite Dek, casting him a look Aiden couldn't quite identify.

"We're not finished, Aiden," Dek muttered under his breath. "I don't want to see you like that again."

Aiden nodded. He would have to find some way of avoiding that conversation. Dek would never understand about her. The girl had been furious with him—he'd ruined everything, but perhaps it was for the best.

He could try to send her a message and apologize. But then

what? If she forgave him, if they spent more time together, their Majesties or, worse, Summer, could discover their connection. Aiden drummed his fingers on the smooth surface. There was still a chance someone knew about them and was waiting for the opportune moment to strike. Either way, he should send her a message. But for now, he was trapped.

Aiden scanned the table. Emerick had been sent off to hold the newly-conquered city of Kesh while Aiden was forced to remain at the palace with Irina, Dek, and Mab's newest favorite, Jefferson. That damned vampire never left his side. It was as though he believed getting skinned together somehow meant they were friends.

They were not.

Aiden rubbed his neck. The constant tug on his magic from Mare's shadows only served to intensify his bone aching exhaustion. But at least he had the crown. One of his strongest wards protected it; any Summer fae the prince sent to steal it back would have to get past the protections surrounding Mab and Oberon's palace before they could even attempt to dismantle his spell. Aiden glared at the golden circlet through the ripples of his magic. Perhaps, when Summer was nothing but ash, maybe then he could visit the human girl again. Soon.

He turned his gaze from the crown to Dek on his left, who was giving a report on their new recruits. Across from him, Irina clicked her nails against the spotted, black surface of the table. Her tongue toyed with the tip of her fang as she stared at the ceiling. Occasionally, Dek would flick a furtive glance at her as though willing her to pay attention. Aiden shifted, lingering aches from their Majesties' magic drain pulsed throughout his body. The energy it would take to scold Irina for ignoring Dek's intel did not exist within him.

"Some, not all, but a growing number of the new recruits are being a bit problematic," Dek said. "They don't act willing to partake in our missions. Some even resist killing. It's disgusting." He curled his lip and folded his bulky arms.

"Why do they agree to join if they do not wish to kill?" Aiden looked to Irina. She turned her icy gaze from the ceiling to stare daggers back at him. "Surely they know this is a war."

"It sounds to me as though they don't have the proper motivation." Irina sneered.

Dek glared at her, a muscle in his neck twitching at her implication. Aiden doubted that laziness would prevent them from killing, but he couldn't deny the strangeness of their recruits' behavior.

"They are well motivated. Some of them, mostly red fae, have asked to return to the Human Realm. Perhaps you need to do better screening. Make sure they are truly willing before they join," Dek said.

Irina and Emerick had been handling most of the recent recruiting missions. However, there were still those, like Jefferson, who'd sought him out—even if they hadn't been so bold. But those the others introduced him to appeared willing enough.

"My recruits are always eager. It would be impossible to hand them off to you kicking and screaming." Irina scoffed and flicked a hand through her short, blonde hair. "Tell me, Dek. What are you doing to demotivate them?"

Dek bared his teeth, and Irina did the same. From the corner of his eye, Aiden caught Jefferson smirk as he watched the exchange. A twinge of pain lanced through his chest, but Aiden couldn't tell if it was his exhaustion, Mare's roaming shadows, or the vampire's dubious "otherness" that wore on him.

"Perhaps we should take a closer look at the recruits," Aiden said.

Irina went rigid. "Do not let his laziness sway you. There is nothing wrong with them."

"No reason to get so upset, Rina," Dek said. He moved back to his seat and folded his hands. "He needs to see firsthand what trash you're bringing in."

Aiden massaged his temples. This needed to be fixed before word got back to their Majesties.

"You obviously just don't know how to control them." Irina's eyes flashed.

"Filthy bitch!" Dek barked.

"Watch your tone, jackal!"

The two leapt to their feet, and Jefferson waggled his eyebrows at Aiden. Irina snapped her fangs at Dek. He snarled and leaned across the table. Aiden sighed and buried his head in his hands. The door burst open, causing Irina and Dek to freeze.

"What's going on in here?" Mare stood in the doorway, one hand on her hip. "I can hear you from all the way down the hall."

She strode into the room, torchlight reflecting off her shiny fighting leathers. Her hair was pulled back into a braid that swished back and forth at her waist. Aiden pulled away as Mare leaned across the table, her bosom much too close to his face for comfort. She scraped away at even more of his energy.

"Mare's right. You two are getting out of hand," he said. This meeting needed to end before she tried to drain him any further. Passing out in front of all of them would do nothing to gain their confidence.

"I will hear no more of this. You do as you choose!" Irina pushed past Mare and stormed out of the room, slamming the door behind her.

"Well, that was something." Jefferson cleared his throat.

Dek sat and growled low.

"What have you come for, Mare?" Aiden asked.

"I wanted to check in with you, Aiden." She tried to nudge his arm aside to sit in his lap. When she failed, she settled for Irina's seat on his right. "Rumor has it the Summer Prince will make an attempt to get his crown back soon." She gestured at the circlet in the center of the table. The wards were solid and immovable as mountain stone as she prodded them.

"A rumor from who? Are you able to give me anything useful, or are you just here to gossip?"

"Darling, you wound me. Of course, I've brought you useful information. Perhaps you might wish to make a trade." She cocked her head to the side and pouted her lips. Dek snickered but abruptly stopped when Aiden shot him a dark look.

"Perhaps I should tell their Majesties you are withholding

information."

"No need to be so mean. I'll tell. One of my people reported the prince has managed to get a spy quite close to you."

Everyone in the room shifted uncomfortably.

"Did your spies give you any clue as to who?" Aiden's head pounded.

"They have not penetrated so deep into the court that they know details. Knowing the prince, he would have sent someone close to him and tried to put an undetectable glamour on them."

Aiden pressed his palms against his eyes and mentally ran through the Summer fae who'd recently joined the army. His thoughts immediately flicked to Jefferson, but he was just a red fae. The Summer Prince would never lower himself to consort with a vampire. Aiden rubbed his chest again. He made a mental note to have Irina review the new recruits for anyone who smelled of Summer. If the crown was recaptured, Mab would want more than a mere half-pound of his flesh.

"Thank you, Mare. I have a theory. I'll look into it." Aiden looked around the room. No one spoke. Perhaps he would have time to at least write the human girl an apology note before he fell asleep. "Jefferson, if you have nothing to report we can—"

"Actually, sir, I do have some news." The vampire held up a slender hand. Beside him, Dek groaned.

"Go on," Aiden said.

"Three days ago, while I was on survey duty, I discovered a weakness in our defenses on the border between Autumn and Summer."

Aiden sat up straighter. "What weakness?"

"By the hanging gardens, in Luching. The flota plants there give off an essence that weakens the wards around the city. Summer troops could easily break them."

Aiden looked to Dek. "What do you know of these plants? Anything?" Jefferson had been paired with the anubis for survey duty while Aiden had worked on the crown's wards.

"Yes. It's a small opening though. Didn't think it much of a threat." Dek frowned at Jefferson.

There would not be time to write out the note if he set out to destroy the plants now. However, it was better taken care of now, then to wait until their Majesties found out.

"Let's go then."

"Tonight?" Dek and Mare asked.

"Yes." Aiden sighed and rose from his chair.

He waved his hand. A black wood box appeared in front of him. Inside was a blackish-green, sparkling powder—fairy wing dust. Just looking at it made him want to vomit. With trembling fingers, he took a small pinch and sprinkled it into his pocket before taking another pinch and holding it between his thumb and forefinger. Dek walked around the table to stand behind Aiden. Both Jefferson and Mare rose to their feet.

"All of us then?" Jefferson asked and prodded the dust with his finger.

Aiden jerked it away and waved his free hand. The box and its vile contents vanished. With a flick of his wrist, he threw the powder into the air. The room lurched. For a moment, the world turned black. Several seconds passed before the blackness faded, and the lights and colors of Luching came into focus.

The sickly-sweet scent of lilies hung in the humid jungle air. Pearly white flowers dangled from vines overhead like the hands of the dead reaching out from the abyss. Aiden stalked forward, turning away from the vines to concentrate on the path ahead. Bioluminescent fungi glowed on the ground and clung to tree trunks, turning the jungle an eerie blue.

"Show me the break," Aiden said.

Jefferson led the group through the understory. A wall of bamboo shoots enclosed the border between the two realms. Just ahead, a vine clung to the wall spotted with red flowers. Mare drifted silently by Aiden's side as he squinted at the plant in the darkness. He scanned the path ahead for any indication Summer spies had gotten through.

The air changed. Power rippled through the darkness, and Aiden held up a hand. Dek and Mare stopped.

"What's wrong?" Jefferson turned around.

Everything went silent. Even the birds and jungle creatures quieted as though they too were listening.

Then, Mare shrieked. A vine, thick as Aiden's arm, whipped down from a tree and tossed her into the brush. The tree, nearly a hundred feet tall, ripped its roots up from the ground and shook its branches, showering the group with bugs and leaves. Dek snarled and launched himself at it, fangs out.

Blue fire shot down Aiden's arms. He had squared his shoulders to face the tree when a blast of white fire surged in his direction. Aiden ducked just in time. The flames hit the tree, which roared with rage as it was singed.

A sundiva hovered just above the bamboo wall, her great feathered wings spread behind her. Several other green fae emerged from the bushes. A squadron of pixies launched a volley of arrows at him. Aiden's flames flared up, devouring their tiny poison-sticks.

Freezing frosts. Jefferson dodged attacks from the ent as a herd of unicorns burst from the trees, their sharpened horns shining deadly in the glow-light. They charged the vampire and he ran, narrowly avoiding the tip of one of their horns.

Aiden let loose a wave of flame, and several pixies shrieked as their comrades turned to dust. Dek cried out. Aiden spun around to see him bounce off a branch and hit the forest floor. The anubis rolled out of the way before the ent's roots could crush him. They needed to switch—Dek could easily handle pixies and outrun the sundiva, while the ent needed to be dealt with by fire.

Aiden dodged another blaze from the flaming woman. She leapt from her place on the wall and ran across the jungle floor— her wings wouldn't lend her an advantage here.

"Dek, to me," Aiden shouted as another blast of white-hot flame skimmed the side of his leg.

The ent roared again. Shadows raced through its branches, tangling them, making its vines useless. Mare's slim form was silhouetted against the moon as she moved through the ent's limbs, drawing out its energy.

The pixies buzzed around Aiden's face, their needle teeth

bared. Before they could bite, Dek was upon them. He snatched them out of the air so quickly they barely had a chance to scream before he bit off their heads and spat them onto the ground.

Aiden turned his attention to the sundiva. Sweat ran down his face and neck. Sharp aches shot down his limbs as he pushed far beyond the limits of his power.

"Hold still, little dog," the sundiva said as she drew closer.

Aiden let his flames go out, letting her come to him. If he continued to use his magic like this, he risked draining himself completely. He needed to tire her out before striking his next blow. She shot another jet of flames at him. He dodged, drawing her closer to Mare and the ent. Nearby, Jefferson ducked behind a cluster of bushes. At least Mab wouldn't punish him for letting her new favorite soldier get killed.

"We have to get out of here." Mare was at his side, her shadows pushing the sundiva back. "There are too many of them. We're not prepared."

Aiden grunted. "Get Dek."

"Give me the fairy dust. I don't have the strength to run through the shadows."

As if to prove it, the sundiva's flames shot through Mare's shadow shield. Aiden threw up a wobbly ward to reinforce it while one of the ent's vines broke free and slammed them into a tree.

Gritting his teeth, Aiden sat up and gathered Mare into his arms. She bled from a cut on her head, and in the low light, it was impossible to tell how serious it was.

"Please, Aiden. We have to get out of here," she said again. Her voice cracked as they got to their feet, using each other for support.

He was about to give her the dust when he saw Jefferson, a few feet away, narrowly miss one of the sundiva's blasts. The ent had a branch raised, ready to stake the vampire. Aiden wended into its path and shot a jet of flames so hot the ent, and several of the surrounding trees crumbled to ash. They crumbled to ash, leaving a steaming hole the size of a full-grown giant in the forest clearing. Aiden lost his balance and fell to his hands and knees, panting.

"You saved me." Jefferson stared back as though Aiden had kissed him, rather than merely roasted their common enemy. The vampire stooped shakily and helped Aiden to his feet, the stunned expression unfaded.

Aiden winced as he straightened. Before he could respond, an inhuman scream echoed throughout the forest. He turned.

Dek ran toward them, his back ablaze. The sundiva was not far behind, laughing. No. Empathetic pain shot through Aiden's spine as he ran toward Dek. The anubis's face was contorted in unintelligible agony. Arms spread, Aiden knocked Dek to the ground to smother the flames. Before he could effectively put them out, the sundiva shrieked, letting loose another blast of fire. This time it was not as strong as her previous ones. Thank the sweet rain, she is starting to tire.

Aiden took off into the deepest parts of the brush. The sundiva followed him, away from the others. The twigs and low-hanging vines tore at her wings, causing her to shriek and curse as she ran. After what felt like a mile, the sounds of the sundiva's crashing fell silent. Aiden looked back, his eyes searching the trees for a shadow with her shape — but there was none. Nausea plunged through his gut. He ran. The others were weak, defenseless. Their Majesties would make him wish for death if he lost them all.

He burst into the clearing. Jefferson was shouting at Mare, but there was thankfully no sign of the sundiva.

"You can't just leave us here." Jefferson marched toward her.

"This will not be my grave, blood-sucker." Shadows gathered around her, growing darker and darker.

"Stop!" Aiden held out his hand and pushed himself toward her.

If the creature came back, he would need her help to defend Dek and Jefferson. The shadows dissolved into the night, Mare with them. He cursed. She'd lied to him, and he'd nearly fallen for it. Holding back, betraying her comrades, betraying Dek, just to conserve some energy. She would be hurting for a few weeks until her body recovered enough to draw magic from others again. But she would be fine.

Dek, on the other hand…

Aiden reached the others, dropping to his knees beside Dek while keeping his senses alert for the sundiva. Dek's breathing was ragged, and his muzzle was wrinkled in pain. He lay on his side, his back a bloody mess. Hands trembling, blue light flickering along his palms, Aiden tried to conjure the power to heal Dek, but his power was pitifully low. Please, Dek. Come on. Jefferson took several steps closer to them. Aiden dug in his pocket for the fairy dust and held it out to the vampire.

"Here. Take him and go." Jefferson stared at the dust as Aiden sprinkled it in his hand. "There are healers in the palace. Tell them — tell them I'll give them whatever they want."

"No, don't." Dek lifted a trembling hand to clamp limply around Aiden's wrist. "I'm not — could you tell Irina that she's not so bad?" His voice held the all-too-familiar rattle of death.

"You hate Irina, Dek." Aiden's hands shook. Dek's red blood coated them like a gory pair of gloves.

"Funny thing about hate. You hold onto it for one person long enough it starts to feel like a part of you is missing when they're gone."

"Stop talking, Dek," Aiden said. "Jefferson can take you back to the palace." He couldn't tell the anubis he would be fine when he knew death already had a clammy hand around Dek's throat.

"You know what else feels like that?"

Aiden swallowed hard. The last person he expected to get love advice from was Dek. The same Dek who'd screwed his way through nearly all the women in their Majesty's court. Who'd told Aiden everything he wanted, and didn't want, to know about lovemaking, but never just love.

Aiden looked imploringly at Jefferson. "Take him back. See if you can find Irina before…"

"It's too late," Jefferson said softly.

Aiden looked down. Dek stared up at the canopy, slivers of moonlight shining through the trees to reflect in his glassy eyes.

"No." Aiden struggled to push the word through his tightening throat. "He's just resting. If you go now…"

Fire, hot and intense, blazed before them. Jefferson leapt back, and Aiden jumped to his feet, blocking the blast with his own flames. Wings torn and ruined, the sundiva lurched toward him. Aiden stared back at the place where he'd stood seconds before. Dek's body was now just a pile of ash. Jefferson backed toward the bamboo wall. That cursed red-spotted vine still clung to it, leaving the way open for more Summerton vermin to slink through.

Aiden crouched, waiting for her to get closer — she wouldn't risk throwing another blast. Silver blood leaked from the myriad of cuts across her body, and patches of her skin were burned black where his flames had grazed her. She staggered forward. Aiden waited. When the sundiva was about a meter away, she raised her hands to summon her fire — but Aiden beat her to it. His blue flames swallowed her whole; she perished with one final scream.

Aiden panted. He turned to Jefferson just as the vampire disappeared in a cloud of fairy dust. Freezing frosts. It would have been nice to save what little strength he had left to get back to the palace.

Aiden took a deep breath and braced himself for another sharp pain as he prepared to wend. Despair and exhaustion weighed heavy on his shoulders as he pushed thoughts of Dek aside. There was nothing to be done now. Like both of their parents, he was gone, and Aiden was on his own, again.

An arrow whizzed past his cheek. Aiden's stomach turned over as he searched the trees for its source. The Summer Prince in all his rotten, golden glory strode toward him.

"I believe you have something that belongs to me, dog."

Aiden glared. He was nowhere near strong enough to fight off the prince now. He needed to regroup. His heart thudded as he watched the gold fae approach, mind racing to come up with a plan.

"Don't worry, I'll get it back." The prince smirked.

Aiden ignored him, focusing on gathering together all the shreds of magic he had left to wend. The prince waved a hand, dispersing Aiden's magic. "You really are weak. A spell like that wouldn't have worked on you last time, would it?"

Aiden slowly straightened. If the swamp rat was going to kill him, he planned to go down fighting.

"You can't run from me." The prince drew his sword. It shimmered with gold fae magic. "Time to face me, one-on-one."

Aiden pushed back his sweat-soaked hair. He braced himself, preparing to run. If he could lose the prince in the trees, it might buy him enough time to gather the strength to wend.

The prince swung his blade. Aiden threw himself out of the sword's path. Gold light flashed as the blade came down, nearly severing his arm. With a grunt, Aiden took off into the brush. If the trees had worked to tear the sundiva's wings, perhaps the same trick would work to tire the prince. One small ounce of revenge before he—

"Running away? You move like a mortal." Snapping branches and the rustling of leaves told Aiden the prince was catching up quick. "Blizzards! You couldn't have chosen a better path." The prince's crashing stopped. Aiden hoped it was because his wing was caught on something.

He kept running. If he could find cover, if he could hide…

An intense pain shot through his back and down his arm. Aiden cried out and fell to his knees. He twisted his neck around to see a red-fletched arrow sticking from his shoulder. Freezing frosts.

"I've been waiting years to finally cut you down, dog." The prince wended over to him, his blade raised over his head.

Aiden closed his eyes. He wished he had the strength to wend, but he could barely stay upright. Pain clouded his mind as the world swam before him. He thought of Dek and his dying declaration of love for Irina. At least Jefferson would be able to deliver the message to her. Aiden would die, and there was no one to tell the human girl of his feelings.

CHAPTER 24

Freddie

The familiar ripple pulled Freddie from sleep. Her eyes snapped open. Her heart raced. Was Pelrin back? So soon? There was a thud—she sat up. Fumbling in the darkness, she cursed as her plastic Ikea lamp tumbled off the side of the nightstand. She ran her fingers up the cord and found the switch. A soft golden glow illuminated the room. Freddie squinted as her eyes adjusted to the light.

"Pel, are you all—" She gasped. The figure huddled in the center of the room was not Pelrin.

Aiden crouched on his hands and knees, a red-fletched arrow sticking out of his back. Silvery blood leaked out of the wound trailing down his side. Freddie threw back the covers and dangled her legs off the bedside. Arms trembling and teeth gritted, he looked up at her. She sucked in a breath, momentarily paralyzed by his blood-soaked chest and the splatting of tiny silver droplets on the hardwood. His arm gave out. He grunted and collapsed onto his side.

Freddie launched herself off the bed and rushed to him, but Aiden lay still.

"Oh my God! Are you—? Can I—? What can I do?" Her fingers hovered over the arrow. It looked as though it had struck the lower part of his shoulder blade. From what she remembered from Health, Freddie was about seventy percent sure it hadn't hit anything vital. But the hospitals near her parents' house didn't treat fae. With their fast healing abilities, most fae rarely needed emergency medical care. The specialty facilities for their serious injuries and illnesses were all in the city, and Aiden didn't look as though he'd last that long.

She bit her lip and grabbed the shaft to pull it free. Aiden groaned and shook his head. He moved his arm, face contorted in agonized concentration. Blood-slicked fingers gripped her hand and motioned for her to push rather than pull the arrow. Freddie's stomach twisted as she examined him. There was red mingled with the silver on Aiden's hands. *Could it be human?* She pushed the thoughts of the missing students from her mind. They *would* talk about this later.

"Aiden, we are trying to get the arrow out, not keep it in," she whispered, but he tugged it forward. "Okay, okay, let me just look it up first." She scrambled over to her nightstand, wiped her hands on her pajama pants, and yanked her phone from its charger.

"How do you heal an arrow wound?" she asked the search engine. After tapping the first result, she skimmed the page. It talked of using a potion. She frowned when she saw the source. Of course, *Curse of Ages* — though in their defense, the average person probably didn't have to treat real arrow wounds. She went back. The next page looked promising. It was a review based on an account by a Civil War doctor. He recommended pushing the arrow all the way through and breaking off the tip to prevent the creation of a larger hole by pulling it out the back.

Freddie took a deep breath. What if he died? His skin was already so ashen. She gripped the arrow shaft. "Aiden, this will probably hurt, okay?"

He didn't answer. His mouth was open. He stared straight ahead at nothing.

"Here it goes." She pushed hard, disturbed at the strength it took to force the arrow out the other side. It wasn't like how it was in movies — a quick push that tears through the clothing. Pushing it through his muscular arm took effort and an agonizingly long time. His body trembled beneath her hands. When it finally got through to the other side, Aiden cried out. Freddie's eyes flew wide.

"Wynifred Jones, turn down the volume on your laptop!" her mom yelled from down the hallway.

Freddie froze. Aiden lay still, unconscious but breathing. "O-okay, Mom," she said and returned her attention to the bleeding fae.

His shirt blocked the tip of the arrow from view. Freddie uselessly shook her hands—she would have to cut open the front. After retrieving the pink Fiskars from her desk, it took everything she had to keep from gagging as she cut across his linen shirt, attempting to make some room for the arrowhead.

She cursed. The tip remained hidden beneath his jerkin. She cut that away too, leaving him shirtless and covered in blood. Balling up what was left of the black tunic, Freddie dabbed at Aiden's chest around the tri-blade tip. Grimacing, she snapped it off and pulled the shaft out of his back with a sickening squelch. The metallic scent of blood filled her nose. Freddie stared hard at the silver covering her hands and clothes and shuddered.

"Aiden," Freddie hissed. His eyelids had drooped closed. "What do I do now?"

His breathing was shallow. A hollowness pierced through Freddie's heart. He couldn't die, not here, not like this. She rubbed the blood off her hands and picked up her phone to figure out what she needed to do next. There had to be a way to stop the bleeding.

She checked her phone again. The Civil War doctor had applied pressure to the injury; he also noted many of his patients hadn't survived. *Well that's just great!* Freddie pushed herself onto her feet. Aiden rolled onto his stomach. If Health class had taught her anything, it was that she needed to disinfect the wound, then she could make a tourniquet. She could do that. She hurried off to the linen closet before returning with a brown bottle of hydrogen peroxide, some gauze, and heavy bandages from the first aid kit. She emptied the bottle over Aiden's wound and watched as tiny bubbles fizzled on the edges of the hole. Peroxide and blood seeped into the hardwood, creating a silver stain around his body. The bleeding slowed as she pressed the gauze to his chest and then wrapped the bandages around it to hold the gauze in place. Aiden didn't move, still unconscious.

"Now what?" she said. Freddie hoped she wasn't imagining it as Aiden's chest rose and fell with increased regularity. "You're going to be fine. See? I fixed you."

She hurried to the bathroom to dampen a cloth so she could clean the blood from his body. Flexing her trembling hands under the warm water of the sink, Freddie wondered if Pelrin was injured too. Had he wended to the fae healers in the Summer Palace? Surely Aiden had healers that could patch him up better than she could. A nagging thought in the back of her mind reminded her Aiden had barely been able to afford decent food. How could he afford a fae healer?

Once she rinsed the blood off her hands, she redid the thick french braid that had come partially undone while she slept. The momentary distraction calmed her enough to return to her room with a clear head and a Tupperware container full of water. Aiden appeared to be sleeping. His breathing had definitely picked up to a regular rhythm. She wiped the blood from his wound, then ran the cloth down his hands. Would he feel better now that his skin was free of that horrible stuff?

She sat back on her heels. The least she could do was make him more comfortable. Freddie dragged the pillows and comforter from her bed. She gently tucked the pillows under his head, turning his face to the side, and wrapped the blanket around his shoulders.

He shivered. Freddie jumped. When he didn't wake and his chest continued to rise and fall, she relaxed and retreated to her bed. Curling up with a pink microfiber blanket, Freddie fell asleep.

It was still dark outside when she woke again. The soft light from her lamp filled the room. Aiden moaned. Freddie hurried over to him and touched his cheek. Heat radiated from his forehead, and she bit her lip. Fae weren't supposed to get fevers, were they? In the past three years she'd known them, neither Pelrin, Jefferson, nor Raul had ever had so much as a cold. There was Motrin in the linen closet, and Freddie rushed down the hall to fetch the bottle. When she returned, she measured out the orange liquid into the cap and pressed it to Aiden's lips.

"Come on, wake up," she said running her free hand down his cheek.

Aiden's brow wrinkled. His amber eyes fluttered open. "What?"

She hushed him. "It's just medicine — it's okay."

Aiden's lips parted slightly, and she gently tipped the contents into his mouth. When his Adam's apple bobbed, she sighed. He gave a wheezing cough, then settled back against the pillows.

Freddie leaned closer and stroked his hair. He smelled like sweat and blood, but also the subtle hints of lilac and the sky just before it rained. While he lay there, it was hard to imagine him as the monster everyone told her he was.

Throughout the night, every one of Aiden's slight rustles or coughs roused Freddie. Her heart thudded each time she glanced over to see him curled up on the floor, wrapped in her floral comforter. When the first rays of the sun peeked through her window, Freddie gave up on getting any sleep and tiptoed to the bathroom to shower and dress. Aiden was still asleep when she returned. The comforter had slipped off his shoulders to reveal his bare back. The color had returned to his skin. The blood had crusted and was flaking off into the blanket.

A dark patch of something stuck out from beneath a crust of silver. Freddie frowned and knelt beside him to get a better look. A bit of leaf or something must have plastered itself to his skin. She reached out to peel it away, but it twitched when she touched it. After brushing away the silvery flakes, Freddie's eyes widened as she revealed a charred, blue wing stub — its twin only a few inches away.

Impossible. Most fairies had clear or green wings. Some, in rare cases like Pelrin's, had gold. Blue was the color that only fairies in storybooks had: the benevolent, all-knowing, the "good fairies". They didn't exist. They couldn't.

Aiden moaned and rolled over to face her. Freddie backed

away, her heart pounding like a rabbit facing off against a fox. His eyes opened and they stared at each other in frozen silence. Then Aiden touched his chest and reached back. His expression mirrored Freddie's with a wide-eyed horror of his own.

"I won't tell," Freddie said. Who would believe her?

Aiden just stared back.

"I thought blue fae didn't exist. But your wings..."

Aiden looked around, running a hand through his hair. "How—? Where is this?"

Freddie let out a shaky breath. "We're at my house. I mean, my parents' house."

"In the Human Realm?"

"Of course."

Aiden let out a breath and sagged against the pillows. "Thank the Seasons."

"What happened to your wings? How are they blue? Who are you really?"

Aiden turned to her and shook his head. "I'm still trying to remember last night, and you already know who I am."

Freddie frowned. She wanted answers. But she forced herself to be patient. "You were in pretty bad shape when I patched you up. I didn't even know fae could get sick. Are you feeling better?"

Aiden nodded. "We can if we are super low on magic. Could you spare me some water?"

"Sure." Freddie got up from her crouch. "I'll be right back."

She left the room and raced down the stairs to fetch the glass. How had he found her? Pelrin only had the power to wend to places he'd been before. Was Aiden truly that powerful, even when he was admittedly super low on magic?

She returned to find Aiden sitting upright, examining the remains of his shirt and jerkin. Freddie bit her lip as she moved to stand beside him.

"Sorry about those. You were bleeding, and I needed to bandage your chest."

Aiden looked down at the bandage. "You saw, then?" He reached for the water and gulped it down.

Freddie gave him half a smile. "Your wings? Yes, but I thought blue fae weren't real."

"Just rare," Aiden said. He put the empty glass aside and looked up at her. "I would appreciate you keeping my secret. There are not many who know, and it would cause more problems for me if word got out." Freddie nodded. While breaking a story about a living blue fairy could be huge for her, the consequence of incurring the wrath of those on both sides of the war was enough to keep her mouth shut. "You saved my life last night. I must have thought I was going to die."

"You did lose a lot of blood. I wasn't too sure you would make it through."

He hesitated, as if thinking hard, then said, "Thank you."

"Uh, sure. That's very human of you." Pelrin had never said so much as please. She never understood why human manners were viewed so negatively in Fairy. "I couldn't just let you die on my floor." She looked down and kicked the bloody rag and the arrow under her bed. Her mom would kill her if she found a cloth soaked with fairy blood in the wash. She'd have to dispose of it and her bloody pajamas elsewhere. "Besides, I'd totally miss out on that explanation you promised me." She quirked an eyebrow and cast him a sidelong, sarcastic look. "You know, from the other night?"

"It wasn't a date." Aiden's voice was rough. Freddie opened her mouth to tell him she was joking, but closed it again. "I was being watched. I really did want to talk to you, but if their Majesties found out…" He trailed off.

Freddie could draw her own conclusions as to what would happen in that case. "Why were you with her?" If Aiden was behind all the missing people, would she be able to expose him? She needed more than his word as proof. Didn't she?

"The vampire girl was asking to join the army."

"She what!"

"You do know that many of the Dark Fae Army are, in fact, red fae from the Human Realm."

Freddie shook her head. That was impossible. Students couldn't be leaving the mixed schools in droves to fight against the

Seasonal Realms. Why would they leave their comfortable lives here to venture into war-torn Fairy? "But why?"

Aiden shrugged, then winced, cradling his shoulder with his good arm. "I'm not sure, I've never asked. Usually, if they are willing and able, I let them join and send them off to training. Do human armies work differently?"

Freddie was about to respond when her phone rang. She marched over to it and picked it up. "Yes, Mom, I'm awake." Freddie paused to listen to her mom rattle on about how she always got up and "played on her computer" rather than get a head start on cleaning. "I'll be right down." Freddie turned to Aiden.

"Would you like me to leave?" He gathered up the remains of his shirt and got to his feet.

"No. I mean, my mom wants me to help her clean for company tonight, and I've got homework. You're welcome to stay."

A smile spread across Aiden's face. "Then I will stay."

He unwrapped the bandage around his arm. Freddie watched him. How was she supposed to explain to her mom the shirtless injured fairy in her room was staying for dinner? Aiden licked his thumb and motioned as though he were wiping the blood away from the arrow hole. When he moved his hand there was nothing but smooth flesh remaining.

Freddie's eyes widened. "Too bad you can't do that to your shirt," she said.

Aiden shook out the bits of fabric, and a ripple echoed around them. When he held it up to her, his shirt and jerkin were whole. He put them on.

"I stand corrected. That blue fae magic is some powerful stuff."

"I believe most fairies have the power to mend a shirt," Aiden said.

"Yes, well." Freddie wasn't sure what to say. Pelrin rarely used magic and she wasn't entirely sure what he was capable of. "You couldn't change it by any chance? My parents are a bit... conservative."

Aiden examined his clothes. "How do you wish me to dress?"

Freddie thought hard on how to describe a button-down and

jeans in a way he could understand and replicate. Her gaze flitted around the room and fell on a row of old Cosmopolitan magazines at the bottom of her bookshelf. She grabbed a November issue and flipped through it. An ad for a department store featured a couple. The man was dressed in dark wash denim with a powder blue button down and a navy sweater. Freddie passed the magazine to Aiden. The air around him rippled, and the black uniform faded into the same clothing the model wore. Aiden looked much like a model himself, with his handsome features and somehow perfectly sleep-tossed hair. Freddie caught herself blushing and turned away.

"Now if you could meet me at the front door in say, five minutes? My mom might have a heart attack if she saw you coming out of my room. And maybe keep your hair over your ears."

Aiden raised a brow, but bowed. "As you wish." The air rippled and he was gone.

She hurried down the stairs and skidded into the kitchen. Wordlessly, her mom held out a bowl of oatmeal and a spoon. Pointing forcefully to one of the kitchen island stools, she gave Freddie a fierce look. The oatmeal was cold and semi-solid. Freddie prodded it with her spoon, but her mom's expression kept her from complaining. Her stomach squirmed as she strained her ears for the doorbell. She nearly choked on her mouthful when a knock sounded at the door.

Freddie's mom turned slowly from her cookbook to narrow her eyes at her daughter. "Are we expecting anybody, Wyn?" She didn't wait for a response before padding off to the door. Freddie trailed after her, wishing she had a plan to explain Aiden's arrival. *Guess I'll have to wing it.*

"Well, you never know who might drop by." Her voice pitched.

Putting one hand on the doorknob and the other on her hip, her mother looked over at her husband. Freddie's dad lifted his gaze from his Bible. A man of few words and even fewer expressions, her dad's face barely betrayed his curiosity. Her mom yanked the door open. Aiden stood on the doorstep as handsome as ever in his fresh-off-the-pages-of-a-magazine fashion. She frowned from Aiden to Freddie expectantly.

"Um, Mom, this is Aiden. Aiden, this is my mom." From behind her, Freddie could hear her father rise from his seat. "Mom, Aiden is the guy I've been, um, dating."

Her mother's gaze scoured him as if trying to delve into the depths of his soul. Freddie swallowed. "Nice to meet you, Aiden. We've heard so little about you." She turned her glare on Freddie.

"Likewise, it is a pleasure to meet you, my lady." Aiden inclined his head in a slight bow.

Freddie burst out in fake laughter. "So funny, Aiden. You are so funny." Aiden looked at her, clearly confused. "Mom, isn't Aiden so funny?"

Her mother didn't respond, though her unamused expression spoke volumes.

"What is it this time? A troll?" Freddie's dad came up behind her mother and rested an arm on his wife's shoulder.

Aiden stiffened. "There have been trolls here?"

"Everyone is just being so funny today." Freddie reached out and tugged Aiden inside by the sleeve of his sweater. "No, we've never had trolls here."

Her father shrugged. "No trolls. Only the odd vampire, werewolf, and fairy... so far." He winked at his daughter and chuckled. "I'm waiting for the day she brings home a leprechaun, then we're talking gold!"

Aiden's lips twitched into a hesitant smile. Freddie could tell her father's reassurances hadn't put him entirely at ease. "You have a lovely home," he said.

Freddie's mom smiled. "Thank you, dear. I was just about to make some *garlic* scrambled eggs and toast. Would you like some?" She looked meaningfully at her husband as if to say, "*this* is how you root out a fae." Aiden's eyes flicked to Freddie.

"I want some. All you made me was that oatmeal," Freddie said.

Her mom tsked and strode back into the kitchen. Aiden fell into step beside Freddie as they followed her mom.

"So, Aiden, have you come to help Wyn with her chores?" One by one, Freddie's mother cracked the eggs, never taking her eyes off him.

"I would be delighted to help *Wyn* with her chores." A triumphant grin spread across his face. It was strange to hear someone other than a blood relative call her Wyn, but she supposed she could let it slide—just this once.

CHAPTER 25

Freddie

Aiden graciously accepted a pile of steaming eggs and toast from Freddies' mom. Freddie glared at the plate and prodded the slimy lump that was her oatmeal. Her mom handed Aiden a fork and watched him intently. He moved slow, lifting the eggs to his lips under the woman's watchful gaze. Tense silence surrounded them as Aiden put the eggs into his mouth and chewed. When he didn't burst into grotesque hives, Freddie's mom let out a breath and returned to the stove.

No longer the object of her watchful eye, Aiden shoveled down the eggs, only pausing for a brief moment to take a bite of toast.

"My, my, you are really wolfing it down," Freddie's mom said, stroking her thick braid. She gave Freddie a look that said, if he's not a vampire, then he must be a werewolf.

Aiden stopped and stared mournfully at the bite of food that remained. "My apologies. I didn't get a chance to eat yesterday. I did not mean to be so rude, it's just so good."

What he had said on their first date—about not wanting to get used to the cheapy Italian food—echoed in Freddie's mind. How could Oberon and Mab think letting their most powerful weapon go hungry was a good idea? Especially not on the eve of a battle.

"Oh. You don't need to be sorry. There's plenty if you want more." Her cheeks flushed a bright pink, and she turned around to pore over her cookbook.

"I want some," Freddie said.

Her mom shot her a look. "You have oatmeal."

Aiden offered her the remains of his eggs, but she shook her head. Freddie passed him her oatmeal, which he enthusiastically devoured as well. She wrinkled her nose. When both the plate and bowl were empty, Freddie's mom bit her lip and scrutinized Aiden's face.

"You have such lovely eyes, Aiden. I bet you're the only one in your family who has eyes like that."

Freddie rolled her own eyes. Once vampire and werewolf were ruled out, changeling was her last resort—at least his ears were well hidden. Not in a million years would her mother guess what Aiden truly was. He looked down and rubbed at his chest.

"Actually, I believe my mother had the same eye color as me."

Freddie frowned. "Had?"

"She died when I was young," he said.

Freddie placed a hand on his arm, and he stared at it, not moving.

"Oh, you poor thing. You'll have to forgive my husband for prodding me to ask you all these questions." From the living room, Freddie's dad let out an unamused 'ha.' "We've just been so protective of our Wyn, ever since that nasty fairy broke her heart."

Freddie's cheeks heated. "That's it, Mom. You're done. We are not talking about this anymore."

Her mom flashed an innocent smile but retreated back to her cookbook. Aiden leaned close to Freddie. A shiver ran through her as the heat of his breath tingled against her neck. "Do you exclusively date fairies, or is this a happy coincidence?"

She tensed, running through ways to explain away Pelrin. Her dad saved her from answering. "You there," he said.

"Sir?" Aiden whirled off the stool to face him, his back stiff.

"We'll work on the yard while the girls work in the house, got that?"

"I'm going back to working on my article, Dad," Freddie said.

Her mom put her hands on her hips and scowled. "I still don't like this, Wyn. At least clean your room while you're up there."

Because her room needed to be clean for company. She opened her mouth to protest, but then thought better of it. Raul had been arrested, and as much as she wanted to spend time with Aiden and her parents, she needed this time away from everything to go over the clues. There had to be something, something she was missing. Aiden cast her a look that somehow perfectly captured his mix of fear and excitement.

Freddie waved him off as her dad led the way to the garage. She trooped back upstairs, taking the steps two at a time. Sitting in front of her computer, she stared up at the whiteboard. All the victims had been to a fae place before they disappeared. Well, she'd been to plenty of fae places, and no one had ever tried to kidnap her. She drummed her fingers on the keyboard. There was nothing else, but there had to be.

Vivica stared at her from the black and white newspaper clipping. Had that guy, Dion, really killed her because she wasn't into him? Freddie searched for Vivica's name with Dion's. She should have tried to get the guy's last name out of Erica. She sighed, after scrolling through endless results on Celine Dion and Vivica Fox. Somehow Freddie found herself on that strange part of YouTube.

Head resting on her hand, Freddie watched video after video of cats falling off things in supposedly hilarious ways, fainting goats, and a super strange video on a fainting faun. There was a knock on the door.

Freddie jumped. "Come in."

Aiden pushed the door open. He balanced a plate and a glass in one hand. "Your mother sent me with these. Have you been up here all day?" He set down half a sandwich and glass of cold cider on the desk.

The clock on her computer told her it was 4:30PM. "Thanks. Sorry about my parents. I hope they haven't been too bad." Leaving Aiden with her dad was probably not one of her best ideas. Though at least her dad wouldn't pester him with questions, trying to root out what type of fae he was.

"Your father let me mow the lawn," Aiden said with a giddiness in his voice she'd only heard when he'd been under the influence of four shots.

"He did?" Freddie stood and looked out the window. Irregular patterns were carved into the uneven grass.

"Well, just the back. I wanted to see how the mower worked, and I fear I was rather distracted." Aiden looked down.

Freddie patted him on the shoulder. "Next time." She turned her gaze wistfully back to the whiteboard and took a bite of the sandwich.

"Why do you have these?" Aiden pointed at the pictures.

"They are for a class I'm taking. All of them are missing students from my school. I almost forgot you know one of them." She pointed at the photo of Freya. Perhaps her running off to join the Dark Fae was a fluke. It didn't make sense.

"Missing? She freely came to join us." He squinted and stepped closer. "She looks human in this image."

"She was human when she went missing. Are you saying you didn't turn her into a vampire?"

Aiden chuckled as he examined the other pictures. "I can do a lot of magic, but that is a gift reserved only for your red fae." He tapped the photo of Daniel. "He also joined. A werewolf right?"

"No," Freddie said. "He's human. They're all human. Or at least, they were." They all were except for Vivica... how did she fit into all of this? Freddie skimmed through her notes.

Aiden rubbed his chin. "That might explain why we are having issues with some of the new recruits. But who would do this? And why?"

"Someone who wants the Dark Fae to win," Freddie said.

Aiden shook his head. "Perhaps someone who is naive to how much effort goes into training entirely green recruits. Or someone who doesn't care how many deaths it takes to win."

Freddie stared hard at the board, her mind turning over the possibilities. If someone was taking people for the Dark Fae, it'd make sense they were targeting people who acted as though they wanted to be fae. "If you were kidnapping people for your army, where would you strike next?"

Aiden jerked away from her. "I don't take those who are unwilling."

"I know, I know." Freddie read through each of the descriptions again. The last two places had been parties, and both Freya and Daniel had been in relationships with fae. Even Vivica had been all over that vampire at the bar, even though she wasn't human. "It's someplace where fae hook up with humans." She chewed her lip. Vivica was dead, and her body hadn't been found in some obscure place. Maybe she wasn't involved in all of this.

"Hook up?"

"Um…" She tore her eyes from the whiteboard to look at Aiden. He was examining the photographs. "A place where fae and humans have the opportunity to" —she cleared her throat— "get close. Relationship-wise." A pang hit her as she thought of her own not-quite relationship with him.

"Some of my people mentioned a place called Fade." Aiden said. The inflection in his voice made it sound as though he were unsure. "I'd planned on recruiting there next."

Freddie typed the name into her computer and frowned. She tried again with the words 'Easton club' attached to it. The results came back for a club called 'Faed,' and she scribbled down the address. "This is perfect! If I leave now, I'll have time to change and go tonight."

"Isn't this dangerous?"

"My friend is going to take the blame if I don't do something." Freddie hastily packed her things back into her backpack. "Besides, someone needs to stop this. Two hundred students, like me, have gone missing all over the country. People have a right to know the truth; this war is impacting everyone!"

Aiden pressed his lips together. "I'd hoped it wasn't impacting this realm at all, but I fear you may be right. What you're doing, it's very —"

Freddie stiffened. "What? Dangerous? Stupid? Certain death?

Go on tell me, I've heard them all." She didn't need another person like Pelrin trying to talk her out of her dream job.

Aiden smiled and met her glare. "I was going to say brave."

"Oh." Freddie looked down as heat flooded her cheeks. Pelrin would not have said 'brave.' It would be dangerous, but the truth was worth the risk. People needed to understand the hardships the fae across the border faced. Providing aid was all well and good, but if no one empathized with the cause or the people it impacted, one might as well be shoveling water out of a bucket with a thimble.

Aiden stared down at her hands. "Where is the ring I gave you?"

"I still have it." With everything that'd happened that morning, she'd forgotten to put it in her pocket. Freddie hurried to retrieve it from her nightstand. "Do you want it back?" She held it out to him.

"Do you not like it?" Aiden reached out and cradled it in his palm.

"I do. I was just... mad at you." She hadn't been half as mad at him as she had been at herself for making the same mistake again: falling for a fae despite knowing she could never be enough. "It's not your fault. We never said we were exclusive."

He stepped forward and placed the ring in her hand, closing his fist over hers. "Wyn, I want nothing more than to give you the normal relationship you said you wanted." Something in Aiden's eyes was pleading.

A coil constricted around her heart. "Then how come you flinch when I touch you? You haven't even tried to kiss me." She moved closer to him, but he pulled away. "Am I that repulsive to you?" Freddie braced herself for his response.

Aiden's Adam's apple bobbed. "I don't deserve... I can't want you," he said. His voice was laced with strained notes of pain.

"What's wrong with wanting someone?"

Before he could answer, her phone rang. "Yes, Mom. We'll be right down." She put the phone down. "My parents have company. My mom wants us to say hi." Freddie didn't doubt her mom also wanted to make sure she didn't leave the two of them alone for too long in the bedroom.

Sighing at the remnants of their shattered moment, Freddie shoved the silver band into her pocket and led Aiden down the stairs. In the living room, her parents greeted a balding man who was melting into a white turtleneck. Beside him stood a woman who looked as though she were staring directly into a powerful fan. Freddie froze. No, not here. Not in my house.

"What's wrong?" Aiden placed a hand on her shoulder.

Freddie looked up at him. "You'll see."

"Oh good. Rich, this is our daughter, Wynifred, and her friend, Aiden." Her father hadn't called Pelrin her boyfriend either. Apparently, he wasn't breaking with this tradition anytime soon. "She just came down from New Wall last night."

"New Wall, huh?" Mr. Fallus said. "That's a mixed school, isn't it?"

"Good education though," her dad said. She had never thought of her parents as being anti-fae but her father's tone sounded almost embarrassed by the fact she went to a mixed school. Freddie's jaw tightened.

Would she have gone to an all-human private school if her family were richer?

"If you say so, Earl." Mr. Fallus laughed. The woman tittered on his arm. Freddie walked down the remaining steps. "This is my wife, Minge."

Freddie smirked.

"Nice to meet you," the squinting woman said. Her voice sounded as though she were trying to whisper while imitating a toddler. The result was rather unsettling.

An awkward silence passed between them. Freddie had no intention of lying and saying it was nice to meet them, and the human pleasantries were probably lost on Aiden.

"That's a lovely dress, Minge," Freddie's mom said, and cleared her throat. She shot her daughter a warning look.

"Thank you, Judy. It's a Valentino. I can put you in touch with my stylist if you want one." Minge's face stretched into what Freddie assumed she considered a smile. Her mom looked away.

Never in a million years would her family be able to afford a Valentino, especially not one custom-made.

Freddie folded her arms. Mr. Fallus turned his gaze on Aiden, his eyes narrowed. "Earl, I'm honestly surprised you're okay with this. No offense," he said.

Freddie grit her teeth, glaring daggers at the candle-man. She looked to Aiden. Aiden's eyes scrutinized every sagging wrinkle on Mr. Fallus's face.

"Oh, Rich. No, I—" Her dad turned from his house guest to Aiden. "He's not what you think he is."

"Changeling?" Mr. Fallus said. "They look like us, but then you see their eyes. Scary."

Aiden blinked. Freddie put her hand on his arm. It wouldn't do for Mr. Fallus to become a martyr for his sick cause.

"You're awful quiet, Wynifred," Minge said.

Freddie's mom winced. "So, Minge, where did you say you were from?"

Minge ignored her. "If he were my boyfriend, I would say something. That is, if he truly wasn't fae."

"Oh, don't read too much into my silence, Minge. I was brought up to believe it's rude to talk about someone as if they aren't in the room."

Minge let out a tiny squeak and looked meaningfully at her husband. Mr. Fallus's face changed, oozing into one of contentment. "You're right, Wynifred. I'm sorry. See, I said it; my opponent thinks I can't." This brought a round of laughter from the adults. "It was Aiden, right?" Aiden nodded. "Probably have some fae blood in you somewhere, am I right?"

"Probably," Aiden repeated.

Definitely, Freddie thought.

"Have you two been following the election?" Mr. Fallus's neck wobbled.

"I have," Freddie said. Aiden shook his head.

"They have really been villainizing me. Now you know me, you can tell all your little friends that I'm not that bad, right?"

"It's true," Minge added. "The media has been so unfair to

him. They're always turning his words against him and reporting on things that are just not true. It makes me so mad."

Freddie glowered. She'd hoped to grab something to snack on as she drove back to campus. But now, her appetite was long forgotten. Mr. Fallus patted his wife's hand. "I hate to see her upset. When we win in a couple weeks though, Earl, all this will change, huh?"

Freddie's eyes flicked to her father.

"Looking forward to it, Rich. I can't thank you enough."

"It's your campaign strategy that is going to give us the win. Stroke of genius working that Liberty Bell angle. Still can't believe those damn fae destroyed it."

"Dad, you're managing his campaign?" It was as though someone had shoved a white-hot poker down her throat. The world seemed to turn on its head.

"Just the media side. His real campaign manager contracted the agency."

"Then I fired him when I saw what a good job your daddy was doing." Mr. Fallus's too-small mouth strained to accommodate the grin that stretched across it.

Blood pulsed in Freddie's ears. "Dad, he's racist!"

"Now you see what harm the media is doing. The kids think I'm this racist, bad guy. I can assure you I'm the least racist person you will ever meet."

Freddie's face burned, her vision blurred, and she fought to keep her voice from cracking. Why did she always sound so pitiful when she was angry? "You called werewolves a plague on society. You support sending over three hundred thousand refugees back to Fairy. You said you want to look into how native red fae really are to the Human Realm. How is any of that not racist?"

Mr. Fallus frowned and looked at her dad. Freddie's parents watched the exchange with expressions of horror. "Earl, I came here for a nice dinner, not to discuss policies with some kid. Are you going to let her talk to me like that?"

"What's wrong, Dick? Can't hold your own with a layabout student?"

Freddie shoved her arm into her backpack strap and marched toward the door. Her dad frowned, his brow knitted together. But there was a thoughtful look in his eyes as though he were trying to find the right words.

Before her dad could tell her off, she said, "I'll be at school if you need me." Freddie pushed past the Falluses and marched outside. Aiden hurried after her, giving a short bow to her parents.

"Can you believe he's actually supporting that—that—" Freddie shrieked and slammed the door behind Aiden. "I work so hard so I can be a journalist and show the truth about what's going on in Fairy. So people can see the pain and destruction on these people's faces and want to help them. To have my own parents..." She grit her teeth and pounded her fists against the driver's side door.

"Do they really send them back? The people who come here from Fairy?" Aiden moved cautiously toward her.

"In some countries, like South Africa, France, and China, they do. Other countries, like Britain and Mexico, are talking about doing it as well. They say the refugees are a drain on their resources. It's like they're not even people."

Aiden laced his fingers and stared down at them. "I didn't know they were sent back. What you want to do, help them by telling their stories, it's very admirable."

"Aiden," she said.

He stared at her as if he were trying to memorize every little freckle on her face. "I must go before it gets too late. I will miss you, Wyn."

Thoughts of Pelrin and the crown came rushing back, threatening to rip her heart in half. "I'll miss you too," she said, blinking back tears. She needed to focus.

Aiden looked away. "Wear the ring. It will keep you safe."

Freddie dug it out of her pocket and slipped it on her ring finger. "You be safe too. I'm not a doctor, and I can't make any promises for healing you next time." She couldn't bring herself to say goodbye.

He chuckled, low and soft. Without a word, he wended,

leaving Freddie to investigate on her own.

CHAPTER 26

Freddie

In many ways Faed was like Illusion, full of glamour-less fae dancing wildly to the pulsing beats of the music. All the same, Freddie gripped Amanda's hand; Illusion had been filled with mostly red and green fae, whereas Faed catered toward the brown fae crowd. Long-bearded red caps watched them as they moved past the bar — blood dripping from their dangling hats. Goblins beat their leathery wings, and centaurs stomped to the pounding of the fae drums.

"Remind me, Freddie, what your plan is here." Amanda's eyes were wide as she looked about the club. Even the scattered red fae had a more sinister look to them.

Freddie swallowed, recalling the odd look the valet had given her. Perhaps he knew this was not a place where humans were welcome. "We look around, find the kidnapper, and call the police."

"Right, I was just hoping it would sound less terrible the second time. How are we supposed to find a kidnapper in a place like this?"

"I didn't say it was a good plan!" Freddie chewed her lip. She needed to do something. With all those clues, she couldn't just sit at home and hope something would happen to fill in the final piece of the puzzle. "We are looking for a vampire or werewolf. Probably both." Someone must have changed those students into red fae. She hesitated. "Maybe a satyr too… I have a theory…"

Amanda let go of Freddie's hand and took a deep breath. "Okay. Let's meet back at the exit in one hour. I don't want to spend all night here. It's creepy."

"It's not that bad," Freddie said, more to herself than Amanda. She searched the dance floor for some non-glowing eyes. There were very few. "See you in an hour."

They set their phones and took off for opposite ends of the club.

Faed was hidden in an old office building on a small corporate campus. From the outside, it was sterile and drab like every other building in the complex. Inside, however, Spanish moss hung from the ceilings, a light mist blew across the floor, and the live band appeared to be sitting among the branches of a fallen tree.

"Hey, girl. Can I, like, creep on you or something?" Freddie whirled around. A goblin grinned down at her. His long nose dangled just below his lower lip, gray eyes gleaming in the semi-dark.

Suck up your courage, Fred. This is for Raul.

"Hope you can keep up," she said.

She twisted her arms and stomped her feet to the fae rhythms. Beside her, the goblin flapped his wings. As they danced, Freddie scanned the crowd. There was a group of were-girls. One of them looked a few years older than the others, but they were probably all together and more interested in dancing than kidnapping. It didn't look as though there were any vampires though.

Perhaps Amanda was right; this was a bad plan. One of her curls broke free of its bobby pin and tumbled into her face. She paused to fix it.

"You okay, babe?" The goblin yelled over the din.

"Just tired. Maybe we can sit down?"

He guided her over to a couple of mossy tree stumps. Freddie kept her senses alert for a suspect. Amanda was by the bar, chatting up one of the bartenders. Freddie couldn't make out his face, but from behind, his icy pale skin hinted at a vampire. Leave it to Amanda to find the only one in this place.

"Not too many humans out tonight, huh?" She sat on her hands to protect the bottom of her red-hooded romper from the bark.

"They all got scared by the kidnappings. It's just what we need right now, more bad press on fae, ya know?"

Freddie nodded. "Can't imagine who would be stupid enough to pull something like this. It makes everyone look bad."

The goblin nodded, causing his floppy ears to waggle on the sides of his face. "Probably those fae purists. They come 'round the factory all the time trying to recruit us. Spouting their 'superior beings' nonsense. Keep that stuff in Fairy, ya know?"

She considered this. But if they were anti-human, wouldn't they want people who were already fae to join the army? The alarm on her phone went off. Freddie looked up at the goblin and shrugged.

"Sorry, it's my friend," she said holding up the phone, pretending to answer. "I gotta go." This had been a complete waste of time, and Raul needed her to find something meaningful, and fast. She couldn't spend all night at a club. Maybe she could snoop around the crime scene at Illusion.

"Can I at least get your number, babe?"

"Oh, you'll see me around." Freddie winked and darted off into the crowd.

Amanda stood by the door, tapping the toe of her beige red-soles. It was probably a good thing they hadn't found the kidnapper. Amanda had many skills, but Freddie had a hard time picturing her running in those shoes.

"Got anything good?"

Amanda shook her head. "No one knew anything. Let's get out of here."

Freddie dug in her purse for her valet slip as they trooped outside. Cold wind tickled her back as she stood on the curb, waiting for the valet to return. It had seemed like such a good idea in her head. Go to the club, find the culprit, and clear Raul's name.

But she was just one girl, and if the FIDs couldn't find out who was behind all of this, how in the seven realms was she supposed to? Her hands shook as she fiddled with the ring Aiden gave her. Everything was going to hell, and there was nothing she could do about it.

Freddie shivered. "Amanda do you have my —?" Amanda was heading toward a different office complex. "Hey, friend, where are you going?" When Amanda didn't react, an icy sensation slithered down Freddie's back and settled uncomfortably in her stomach. She squeezed her phone. "Amanda!"

Amanda continued walking. Freddie followed her to a silent building, a 'For Lease' sign posted in its front. Amanda pushed open the door and to Freddie's surprise, it was unlocked. They went inside. "Amanda, this is not funny. If you don't stop this, I'm calling the police."

Her heart thudded. Could this be how the victims had been lured away? Freddie strained her senses. She could just make out a faint flute melody.

"This is your last warning. Stop this, or I'm calling 911."

Amanda continued to follow the music. It was getting louder. They tread silently across the coarse carpet and through open spaces once home to cubicles but now decorated with scattered papers and broken office furniture. Freddie dialed 911 and prayed they would come fast. Amanda opened a door that led to a windowless room. Freddie followed her.

"911, what is your emergency?"

"Hi, I—" Something knocked the phone out of her hand. Freddie knelt to pick it up and shrieked as fur and something solid and fluttering collided with her face. Frantically, she waved her hands. The music stopped, and the flapping creature halted its attack. Freddie felt around again, landing on something soft and fleshy.

"F-Freddie is that you?" Amanda's voice trembled above her.

"Yeah. We should get out of here."

A high-pitched laugh echoed through the darkness above them. "Leaving so soon, ladies? But you just got here." The light came on.

Freddie cringed, momentarily blind in the brightness. When her eyes adjusted, she stared up at the valet. "What?" It was all she could think to say.

Amanda helped Freddie out of her crouch. "Listen, goat-man, it's been a long night. We have our slip. Just cut it with the games, and fetch the car."

"I'd watch how you speak to me, human," he snarled.

Freddie put a hand to her head. This wasn't possible. How could a little faun be behind all of this? He looked more like the type to welcome her to Narnia than a guy who lured hundreds of kids into an evil army. "But you're just a faun."

"Satyr, not faun. There's a difference." He pointed to the horns curling beneath his bushy, brown hair.

So that was a satyr. Freddie's eyes roved over him. His horns were much smaller than the ones in the picture she'd seen.

"Right. Well, not one that evolution thought to make apparent." He must have used his flute to control the people he captured. She glanced down at Aiden's ring. Was that why it hadn't worked on her? "Come on, Amanda. Let's leave before this faun — I mean satyr — gets really angry. He might do a jig or whatever it is they do." Her voice quivered as she tried to sound confident. The memory of Vivica's ripped-out throat pushed its way to the front of her mind. If this was the same guy, they needed to get out of here fast.

The satyr glowered at them. "You are not welcome to leave."

"Watch us," Freddie said and turned on her heel. It was all she could do to keep her knees from shaking. With a tight grip on Amanda, she towed her friend out of the room.

"Stupid girls," the faun said. "My filthy, greenie ex tried to leave too. We put a stop to her, didn't we, Emerick?"

So it's the same satyr.

There was a whoosh as a small black shape flittered down from the ceiling and materialized into a vampire. His upper lip curled back, revealing his needle-sharp fangs. Both Freddie's and Amanda's eyes widened.

"You!" Freddie pointed.

It was the bartender from Illusion. And now that she had a good look at him, wasn't he also the vampire who tried to eat her at Damun? Aiden wasn't here to save her this time.

"So good to see you again, sweetheart." The auburn-haired vampire grinned and took a step toward them.

Amanda gripped Freddie's arm. "Please tell me this is part of the plan," she whispered.

Freddie shook her head. "What do you want with us?" All the pieces were falling into place: Vivica's death, the humans transformed into red fae... but why?

"I just want to make your dreams come true," the satyr said.

They turned slowly to face him. "What makes you think being trapped in a crummy office building with the two of you is part of my dreams?" Freddie spun Aiden's ring with her thumb. If it was supposed to do something to protect her, now would be a great time for it to kick in.

He chuckled. "I've watched you two, not just tonight, but at Illusion and Damun. You love fae, want to be around us, want to become one of us."

Amanda bit her lip.

Freddie nudged her. "Perfectly happy as humans, actually. Thanks for the offer though."

Amanda opened her mouth as if to say something, but Freddie pinched her, and she shut it.

"Just because we have friends who are fae doesn't mean we want to be one of them. Let us go."

"Oh, don't be like that." He pushed himself away from the wall and walked around the table to them. "I'll even give you a choice: vampire or werewolf."

Freddie turned. Just beyond the vampire blocking their path, a blonde werewolf woman with strangely familiar ice-blue eyes leered at them from the doorframe.

"Still not interested." Freddie's voice wavered as she spoke. If it ended up being a choice between becoming a red fae and death, she would gladly become a red fae. But she hoped it didn't come to that.

"Brave talk for a tasty morsel like you," the werewolf said. Freddie glared at her. "Full moon's coming. You'll change your mind."

"Irina, stop." The satyr massaged his temple and waved a hand. "Put them with the other one. They just need some time. I can't have them kicking and screaming when we turn them over."

The vampire placed an icy hand on Freddie's shoulder and steered her through the door. The were-girl guided Amanda. Freddie moved, testing the vampire's grip—it wasn't too strong. She reached down slowly and grasped Amanda's hand. They came to a fork in the corridors.

Freddie bolted left, hoping to make her way back to the door they'd come in by. The hallway was wide but littered with broken office chairs and scattered bits of trash. Amanda screamed as she stumbled in her heels. The vampire moved to block their path before they even made it five feet. He exhaled into Amanda's face. She collapsed. Freddie suppressed a gasp, reaching down to her friend.

The vampire tried to do the same to her, but nothing happened. He frowned. Before he could call for the werewolf, Freddie imitated Amanda and collapsed beside her. It would be better to try an escape again once the fae had their guard down. The vampire hesitated. For one heart-stopping moment, she feared he might suspect she was faking, but then he tossed both Freddie and Amanda over his shoulders and headed back down the hallway.

"Are they out?" The satyr fell into step beside his cohorts.

"Yes, I can bite them both right now and save ourselves the trouble when they wake up."

"No, Emerick," the satyr said. "I want to coax them some more. They need to be at least somewhat loyal to me if my flute is to continue working on them."

"Won't Aiden coax them enough before he sends them off to Dek?" The werewolf's last word came out choked. She cleared her throat. "To training, that is."

Freddie forced herself not to tense at the mention of Aiden's name.

"Aiden is a fool and will hopefully be out of the picture soon." The satyr laughed. "Their Majesties were not at all pleased with him last night. If he's still alive, he'll wish the Summer prince had killed him."

Freddie's heart raced. Aiden had said he was going to return to them, but he hadn't seemed concerned or scared — or had he? He was valuable to them; they wouldn't kill him, but the idea of him being hurt...

It was all she could do to lay limp over the vampire's shoulder and remind herself Raul and Amanda were counting on her. She needed to find a way out of this for them. Then she could worry about Aiden.

"You really think their Majesties will let you take his place, Dion? You can't even stand the sight of blood." The vampire, Emerick, chuckled.

The satyr growled. "Red blood. Filthy, greenie blood, silver blood, doesn't bother me. Besides, it will be the three of us. I will be the brains, and you two, as always, can handle the messy stuff."

There was a huff that sounded as though it'd come from the werewolf-girl, Irina. "Watch your tone, goat, or we might just make you part of the messy stuff."

"Please. Without me, Aiden would have never fallen into disfavor with their Majesties. Don't forget who crossed the border to tip off the Summer fae before the first attempt on the crown. It is time to remind them their pet is just a tool, not a general."

"In that case," Irina said, "Emerick and I need to leave soon. We are supposed to be holding a city, and we, at least, need to stay in their Majesties' good graces."

"Give me two hours. When the spell wears off, I'll talk to each of them one-on-one. The boy is about ready to crack."

They stopped.

"Are you sure you want to leave them here? Unchained?" The werewolf said.

"They're out. Not going anywhere. Stop worrying, Irina." The vampire dumped the girls onto the hard carpet. He nudged

Amanda with his foot, but she remained asleep.

Freddie forced herself to keep her eyes closed. A chain rustled against the carpet from somewhere in the room, and someone — not one of the three fae — moaned. Her nerves tingled as she waited for three sets of footsteps to fade down the hall. When they finally did, she let out a slow hissing breath. She opened her eyes a crack.

They were in one of the office's all-glass conference rooms. Light poured in from the streetlamps outside. If she listened really hard, she thought she could hear sirens, but that was likely wishful thinking.

Opening her eyes fully, she scanned the open space for red exit signs. Of course, there were none in sight. Listening again for hints of her captors, Freddie crawled to the glass wall and peered out.

"Y-you're not asleep?" A boy in a ragged Ninja Turtle costume stared at her. His leg was chained to the desk. He'd turned the shell part of his costume around and hugged it to his chest.

"I was faking it," Freddie said. "Now be quiet. I'm going to find a way to get us out of here."

Across from their room was an evacuation map. Freddie squinted through the darkness to make out the directions to the nearest exit.

"There's no way out. Didn't you see they're fae? We're just humans. We can't beat them," the boy said.

"Shut up, will you?" Freddie snapped. "Maybe you've given up, but I haven't." She located the exit, then hurried back to Amanda. "Wake up, bud." Freddie shook her friend gently — no response. "Amanda, I have bacon." Freddie peeled back her friend's eyelids.

Amanda moaned but didn't wake.

"Sorry, friend," Freddie whispered. She slapped Amanda hard across the face.

Reflexively, Amanda's fist came up and slammed hard into Freddie's boob. She gasped and rolled to the side.

"The hell, Fred?" Amanda said.

Freddie pressed a finger to her lips as she blinked back tears of pain. Sitting up, she massaged her chest. Amanda's eyes widened as reality crept back into her expression.

"I found a way out. We just need to make it down one hallway and up a few steps. We got this." Freddie smiled at her then turned to face the turtle boy.

"They'll be mad when they catch us. They'll hurt us. Trust me; I've tried," he whined.

Freddie crawled over to him. Prying one of the bobby pins out of her hair, she wriggled it into the lock and felt around for the lever. Luckily, their captors didn't use anything more complicated than the basic locks that were sold at every hardware store, or they'd be toast.

"Why do you know how to do that?" Amanda said. Her tone was teasing and unsurprised.

"I forgot my key a lot in middle school." Freddie took out another pin and maneuvered it through the lock until there was a satisfying click. The chain fell limply on either side of the boy's ankle. He stared at it in horror. "Can you walk?" Freddie held a hand out to him.

He shook his head. "I'm staying. They're not t-too bad. Besides, I don't want them to be mad at me again."

Amanda rolled her eyes. "Don't you think they'll be even more mad if they see us gone and you just sitting here, free? They may even think you helped us." Amanda took off her precious red-soles and handed one to Freddie, making a stabbing gesture. If the situation wasn't so grim, she would have laughed. "To be honest, I don't really care if you come with us or stay, but you better make up your mind fast."

The boy got shakily to his feet, and Amanda helped him get his balance. Freddie stood and led the way out of the conference room.

The door to the conference room didn't lock. It opened silently as the three tiptoed through. Two doors down, a light shone from an open office. The vampire and the werewolf were arguing, something about the were-girl's traitorous infatuation with an anubis. Freddie pressed herself against the wall, hoping to hear some scrap of information about Aiden. Amanda tugged her wrists and pointed urgently in the opposite direction. Ahead of them, the exit sign glowed like a welcoming beacon.

Freddie swallowed her fear and ignored the frantic pounding of her heart as they neared. She stepped aside to let Amanda and the turtle go first. With Amanda shoeless and the boy limping from being chained to a desk for so long, she was easily the fastest runner of the group. After placing her trembling hands on the door, Amanda pushed it open. A piercing wail rang throughout the building.

"Run," Freddie screamed.

Tugging the turtle boy along, they bolted for the short flight of stairs just beyond the door. Before they had even made it halfway up, the door they had just come through burst open. The werewolf and the vampire crouched in the entrance below them, fae eyes gleaming in the dark. Curse their inhuman speed.

"Nice try," Emerick growled.

Amanda continued to drag the boy up the stairs while Freddie stood frozen in front of the two red fae. She needed to do something; Amanda needed time to get away. She shouldn't have even been here in the first place. Freddie held up the bobby pin she'd used to pick the lock. The rounded plastic end had come off, revealing the sharp metal underneath. Before she could think herself out of it, she slashed the pin across her hand. The cut was deep, and she was unable to tear her eyes away from the swelling blood.

The werewolf shoved Freddie down the small stairwell as she stalked toward Amanda and the turtle. Freddie smeared the blood that now ran freely down her palm against the metal railing, and the vampire's eyes became like a shark's during a feeding frenzy — black and soulless.

Freddie screamed. The vampire ran past her to lap up the blood. She took off down the hall, Amanda's shoe clutched tight in her good hand. With the other, she smeared blood on any and every surface she could find.

A disabled rolly chair blocked her path. The heel of Freddie's boot caught it, and she fell. The broken plastic on the edge of the chair cut into her leg, and sharp pain shot through her ankle, followed by a tingling numbness. Crashing through the office just a few steps behind her, the vampire closed in. Freddie pushed herself to her feet, her adrenaline carrying her farther and faster than she'd ever run before. Racing up a carpeted staircase, she left a trail of blood behind her. A chilly numbness spread out on the cuts on her hand and knee. Exhaustion weighed heavily on her body. If she could just sit down, just for a moment...

Despite the darkness, every detail of her surroundings was clear and sharp. Somewhere on the floor below, the vampire crashed through the office debris. The world swayed, and the pain returned, pulsing and strong, to her ankle. Why had she run upstairs? Now she was trapped and needed to find a place to hide. Yanking open a solid door at the end of the hall, she peered into a dark office. It looked to be as good a place as any. Freddie ran into the room, closing the door behind her.

White dots flashed before her. She moved to the opposite wall and slid down it, wrapping her blood-smeared arm around her knees. Had Amanda made it out okay?

Probably not. That werewolf had been fast, and Amanda wasn't wearing shoes. I killed her. The thought swirled in Freddie's head, making her feel dense and heavy. Aiden was probably facing a fate worse than death about now if the conversation she'd overheard was true. Raul was in jail, Pelrin was probably injured or worse, and Jefferson... well, there was probably no hope for him either. The tears came fast and hot. How had everything gone so wrong? Freddie clutched Amanda's shoe tight to her chest.

With an ear-splitting crash, the door exploded off its hinges. Wood dust rained down on the blood-crazed vampire. His black eyes fell on her. Freddie pushed herself farther into the corner. She blinked, and he was in front of her, fangs bared.

The last of her survival instincts kicked in. Without thinking she raised her arm and rammed the heel of Amanda's shoe into the vampire's neck.

For a moment, he grinned. Freddie cowered at his maniacal laugh. Then his eyes widened. He wrenched the shoe from his skin and stared at it in disbelief.

From the doorway, someone shouted at him. "What's wrong with you? Bite her already."

The vampire screamed, the noise radiating in Freddie's bones. A light glowed from inside him, brighter and brighter. He stumbled back to the center of the room. His flesh blackened and peeled away from his bones. With a crack like a tree snapping in half, the vampire collapsed into ashes. Freddie stared, open-mouthed, at the gray pile.

"You cursed human, what have you done?" the satyr shouted. Freddie blinked at him. He stared at her, pointing a trembling finger at her still-bleeding hand and leg. Her eyelids grew heavy as she struggled to focus on the satyr. Arms shaking, she crawled over to him, only half aware of what she was doing. He'd destroyed everything. So many families broken. So many innocents blamed. So many students, just like her, were gone, perhaps even dead, because of him. The satyr took a step back and gagged.

"You're covered in it. Get away from me."

"Don't like blood, goat-man?" she rasped. That stupid prank video of the fainting faun flicked into her mind.

Moving her good leg under her, she launched herself at the satyr. White-hot pain shot through her as they hit the ground. Something in the corner of her vision flashed gold, then everything went black.

CHAPTER 27

Aiden

Aiden's stop at the Winter Palace had been brief and painful. With Dek dead, Mare injured, and Jefferson inexplicably gone, their Majesties were livid.

And he was to blame.

In punishment, Oberon drained his power so thoroughly Aiden hadn't even woken when Mab claimed her half-pound of flesh. As soon as he'd regained consciousness, they'd sent him, still bleeding, to assist Emerick and Irina in putting down an uprising in Kesh. Even with a bandaged arm and Emerick and Irina missing, it had only taken a day to subdue the rebels. Their Majesties had ordered Aiden to remain in the city until Emerick and Irina had a firm grasp on the city. No doubt they didn't want to risk losing more of their inner circle.

Aiden had seen neither of them since he arrived. And now that the uprising had been settled and Mab's punishment all but faded, Irina and Emerick's absence gnawed at him like a swarm of beetle pixies. One of his soldiers had told him Irina had taken the news about Dek hard. She'd gone off on her own, and Emerick went to find her. But that had been days ago. Now they had rounded up the Keshians, and those that had survived the brutality of the attack were to be slaves in the mines beneath the Winter Palace.

Aiden walked through the quiet city. Wards, conjured by their few green fae soldiers, wavered like desert heat on the walls, preventing anyone from magically entering or leaving Kesh. There were only two gates, and they were both heavily guarded by groups of brown and red fae soldiers. A cluster of Keshians sat in the center of the square in chains. Their gaze on him sent tingles down his neck as he walked to the guards' outpost. A troll, sweating profusely through a black leather uniform, nodded.

"'Bout time you showed up," he said.

Aiden didn't react to the troll's slight. The Dark Fae, especially the trolls, knew their Majesties would not tolerate him harming members of their army. The only people who feared him were those on the opposite side of the war.

"Did the slaves try to break their chains again?" Aiden jerked his chin over at the people sitting in the square.

"No, they're fine. If we can get them out, that is. Something worse is on the horizon. Come see." The guard led him over to the lodestone tower, which was now being used as a lookout post. Aiden sighed as a goblin flapped toward a perch at the top.

He jogged up the steps behind the sweating soldier. "What am I supposed to be looking at?"

"Trouble."

Aiden stopped running. If the troll wasn't going to tell him, he might as well wend to the top and see for himself. The goblin, crouched on the tower ledge, nearly lost his footing as Aiden appeared beside him.

"What am I meant to see?" He looked out toward the red sand desert.

Small shapes wavered in a glimmering line in the distance. The goblin handed him a spyglass, and Aiden took it and peered through. At the base of the northern mountains was a line of moving shadows. He could just make out the glint of wings and steel as they moved toward Kesh.

Blazing heat! Summer was going on the offensive. The prince must have thought Aiden had died during their last battle and now believed Kesh would be easy to reclaim.

A smile quirked the edge of Aiden's lips. "Let them come."

He was eager to see how the prince fared in a true fight. With his full strength, it would be easy to crush that snub-nosed fairy and drag his corpse before their Majesties. He would take the prince from the Summer King as his parents had been stolen from him. Dek would be avenged.

The goblin cast him a wary stare. "You think we have enough soldiers to defeat them?"

"I can take them out. They will fall like willis in the wind." Aiden wended to the base of the tower.

The prince's army would reach the city within the hour, and in the daylight, he couldn't use the vampires in his force. He needed to find Irina to get the troops ready.

Forty-five minutes walking through the city's desolate taverns and Dark Fae posts and there was no sign of the werewolf. Aiden stared up at the sky—at least Emerick would be waking up soon. He wended back to the top of the tower. The red uniforms of the Summer soldiers were now clearly visible without the spyglass. Aiden turned his gaze to the Dark Fae within the perimeter. The centaurs among them stomped restlessly before the gates while winged goblin archers perched on top the wall. Everything was eerily calm.

The Summer soldiers halted before the main gate. Their faces, like those of the Dark Fae, were stoic as they stared up at the city. A horn bellowed from somewhere amongst the Summer ranks. Aiden tensed. On both sides of the heavily-warded barrier, archers raised their bows. An arrow thwished from the ground and struck one of the goblins in the wing.

For one breathless moment, nothing happened. Then the space between the two armies blackened as arrows burst between them. Flashes of green light flared and swirled around the walls as the Summer fairies pounded against the wards with their spells.

Aiden's brow creased. The wards would not hold long under such a barrage. He'd have thought the prince would vary the makeup of his soldiers, not wanting to risk too many powerful magic users in a battle like this—he must be confident in his victory.

Aiden wended to the wall, ducking out of arrow fire. He found a break in the line where one of his archers had fallen and let loose a blast of blue flames. A cluster of Summer's green fae archers fell, and a rousing cheer rang out around him.

He grit his teeth; they only cared because he'd saved their worthless hides.

Moving down the narrow walkway, he sent out more and more bursts of flames. The arrows from Summer died down. At this rate, the battle would be over before the gates had even been breached.

An arrow whizzed past him, grazing his shoulder – a minor wound. Aiden wended to the ground where his centaurs stood. He licked his thumb and ran it down the cut. If the prince made an appearance, Aiden wanted nothing slowing him down.

A loud crack sounded from the other side of the city. The earth shook as the wards around the wall broke. His chest tightened, and he wended to the back gate. Already his fighters were hacking away at the Summer soldiers with finely-crafted steel blades, clubs, and claws. Ducking through their ranks, he shot smaller bursts of flame, careful not to take out his own as he moved.

The sun set. Where in the four seasons are Emmerick and Irina? And Jefferson, for that matter? It had been days since he'd seen Mab's favorite "jester," too. He could use the help from someone more skilled than the half-trained grunts that were falling by the dozen to the Summer fairies.

Swirls of red and blue flashed around him as he shot more jets of fire at the soldiers. Sweat beaded on his brow and stung his eyes, making it difficult to see. A boom from far off told him the other gate had fallen.

Green dust rained down from above, choking the air. Aiden gasped. The soldiers around him had already fallen to their knees. He threw up a ward, pushing back the green powder, and squinted up. Above him, two green fairies had their arms outstretched, their palms glowing. Aiden wended to the roof of a nearby building. A carefully aimed blast of fire took out the two fairies' wings, and they tumbled to the ground to be trampled by his centaur's hooves.

Aiden winced at the sounds of their shrill screams rising over the noise of the battle. How many had he killed? Hundreds? Thousands? When he was younger, he thought the worst part was seeing the faces of the dead when he closed his eyes. But now it was so much worse; he couldn't even remember their faces. That was how he knew he was a monster.

He wended to check the front gate. Vampires darted at blurred speeds between fairies, their eyes glowing red in the light of the fae magic. Blue fire swirled around Aiden as he took out any fairy that showed the tiniest glimmer of green magic. Trolls with their spiked clubs beat the fairies the goblins shot from the air. Warm, silvery blood spattered over Aiden's face; its metallic tang tainted his lips as he trooped through the chaos. The smell of blood copulating with the scents of smoking flesh turned his stomach, but he was well used to the sensation.

Another crack of magic echoed across the city. His pulse pounded wildly in his ears as he searched for the source. The guard post exploded in a shower of hissing orange flames. Blue, red, and green-skinned Keshians ran in all directions from its remains.

Freezing frosts! With the slaves free, the Dark Fae would be fighting the enemy on all sides. Aiden wended to the gathering force of Keshians. A stinging whip of flame struck him, knocking him to the ground. His blue fire flared around him, ready to push back another attack. Aiden got to his feet in time to see five ifrits combining forces to launch a jet of pale orange flame. With ease, he shot back a torrent of his own flames. The red-skinned fae howled as the blue fire swallowed their burning whip and them along with it.

Bodies fell around him, the ground scorched black and steaming. Aiden leaned against a ruined building to catch his breath. The Summer soldiers fell back. Silhouettes of goblins and fairies wrestled in midair against the purple sky. More often than not, it was the figures with translucent wings that tumbled to the ground to be swallowed up by the waiting shadows.

Fire, red and blistering hot, roared toward him. Aiden threw up his hands, blocking it with his flames, but he could barely make it budge. Wending out of its path, Aiden shot a blast of blue in the direction from which the fire had come.

"So, you didn't die after all." The Summer prince snarled from behind another torrent of red flame.

Aiden blinked. The prince never had this kind of power before. "It takes a lot more than the likes of you to kill me," Aiden said.

He wended behind the prince. Again, their power met in an explosion of red and blue. Something gold glinted around the prince's head, and Aiden's heart stopped. Icy dread spilled down his back as he recognized the Crown of Flames.

But it wasn't possible. His wards could only have been down for a few hours that night. There were so many other protections around the palace; it would be impossible for someone to get in.

"I see you've noticed my new accessory, dog," the prince spat.

Aiden let out blast of flame and wended, narrowly missing another of the prince's fiery attacks. "It's a fair copy." His voice quavered as the crown's magic called to him.

The prince laughed. "Can't even recognize the real thing? Your judgment's slipping. My spy was able to get in and easily steal back my crown." Flames grazed past Aiden's thigh as he threw himself out of their path. Mare had been right about the spy. "You let my vampire friend get real close. Didn't you?"

Aiden let loose a strong blast of blue. Another roar sounded as it collided with the prince's. He knew that vampire couldn't be trusted. Curse Mab and her terrible judgment for forcing him to keep Jefferson close.

Aiden gritted his teeth. Screams of centaurs as they were struck down by fairy magic and the heavy thud of goblins' leathery wings as they hit the ground echoed around him.

A horn sounded from somewhere far off. The prince jerked his head in that direction. Without a word, he wended. Aiden gasped, desperate to force air back into his lungs, and wended to the only remaining tower. The bloodied bodies of a goblin and fairy lay precariously balanced on the tower's ledge. In the darkness, Aiden could make out the shapes of brown and red fae soldiers fleeing the city.

He gripped his hair; this couldn't be happening. He couldn't lose the city and the crown too. The thought of what Mab would do to him when she found out made him retch over the side of the tower. He grasped the ledge with trembling hands. The prince's red flames flared up on the northeastern edge of the city where a cluster of goblins tumbled from the sky.

"Looks like you really blackened this one," a weak voice said from behind him.

Aiden spun around. Mare, wan and thin, leaned against the archway. "What do you want?"

"Their Majesties want you back at the palace as soon as the battle is over. So right about now." She folded her arms. Her eyes narrowed as if trying to look threatening, but instead only made her appear more tired.

Needle-like tendrils crawled up Aiden's back. They must have found out about the crown. He tightened his grip on the railing to keep his fingers from trembling. "Help me, please. Don't let me lose this city."

Mare tilted her head, pressing her lips into a thin line. "You think you're the only one they make suffer? I scrounge energy for them every day until I'm fit to burst, but I didn't go sobbing to Dek when they're vexed with me."

"If you hate it so much, why don't you leave?" Aiden's voice was low and quiet, dripping with all the despair and hatred for their Majesties he'd built up over the years.

"I want to see Summer fall. I want to see all the realms fall." Her eyes glimmered in the lights from the blazing city below. She moved closer to him. "I thought you understood that. Dek did..."

"Dek is dead." Aiden turned from her. He'd wanted to see Summer fall too, but it wasn't worth his freedom — there were other things he wanted more now. Aiden faced Mare. "What do they need with all of that power?"

"It's none of my business." Her expression softened, and she met his hard stare. "But I do need your energy more than you do. If I don't give them enough—"

His knuckles turned white on the railing. "More than me? Do

you have any idea what they do to me when they are not parading my punishments to the entire court?" Aiden shook his head. "My magic is mine."

"You have nothing." Her voice was empty as a dried well. "You're just their pet."

Aiden swallowed. His lips tightened. "Tell them I'll be there when the battle's over."

Mare scoffed. "I'm not your messenger, dog. You nearly got me killed in that jungle. Be there within the hour. They're expecting you." Shadows, thick and black, wrapped around her.

Aiden held out a hand. "Mare, wait! I need more time—" But she was gone. He turned his gaze back to the city.

Dek was dead, Mare was injured, Emerick and Irina were missing, and Jefferson was a traitor; all the blame for this loss would fall on him. There was nothing to do now and no hope the city could be saved. He and the prince were evenly matched at best. If he stayed, he may defeat the prince only to fall to one of the Summer soldiers. But he didn't dare return to the Winter Palace, not yet.

He wended, wishing to see the star-dusted lakes and snow-kissed peaks of Spring. It had been so long since he'd been there, and once their Majesties discovered his failure, he wasn't sure how many more chances he'd get. Mid-wend, his body jerked. Deep power, older than the magic that pulsed in the prince's crown, pulled him back and deposited him before a pure white wall that reached up into the clouds. A sharp ache ran through his chest as he placed one hand on the wall's pearly surface. The wards on it were strong, created long ago by his ancestors, no doubt. He could no longer pass through; Wyn had his ring. It was for the best though. His parents would have been ashamed of the person he'd become. The Summer king's laugh echoed in his ears, a ghost of a memory of the boy he'd been watching the fearsome fae stride over his parent's bodies toward him. Aiden covered his ears to block out the past.

A naked tree sat beside the wall. Perched on one of its branches, an owl screeched. Its voice was so loud it thundered in his head, forcing him to his knees. Aiden cringed, wincing at the power radiating from the creature.

"This path of revenge will never lead you to freedom, Dark One." The owl leapt. Its white spattered wings gleamed like stars as it flew into the growing dark.

Aiden turned his face away. That woman had been right — he'd lost so much already. The blood and dirt that coated his hands left an ugly smudge against the clean, white exterior of the wall as he pounded his fists against it. At least he had her. But would Wyn even want to see him? He had practically told her she could expect nothing from him the last time they'd spoken. Perhaps her friends, whoever they were, had finally poisoned her against him. They were right; she deserved better than someone like him in her life. He clenched his fists, shoving down the pain tearing at his heart.

There wouldn't be time to visit her before he was supposed to return. It would be selfish to go to her now anyway. Even if she let him in, what was he to say? That he was afraid, and he wanted to spend a few moments pretending he was someone else? How pathetic.

Overhead, the sky rumbled. He looked up. From somewhere on the other side of the massive white structure came the rustle of leaves. The rain was close — he could smell it. Aiden leaned against the wall, slid down, and closed his eyes.

The first drips of rain pattered against his forehead. He breathed in deep as they gathered in speed and intensity, praying they would wash him away. Their Majesties would be beyond vexed if he didn't return to them now. The rain came down in sheets, drenching his body and sticking his hair to his face.

He needed something good, even if it was just pretend. Aiden's knee bounced. Did he dare visit her? Did he dare defy them? Smoothing back his hair, he tried to rub away the blood from his face and hands. She didn't need to see that.

Wyn had once said she knew exactly who he was, but that couldn't possibly be true. How could someone so good care about someone who destroyed the lives of thousands? Slowly, he pushed himself to his feet.

Taking a deep breath, he took one last look at the border to his home. The smudge from his hand was gone, washed away by the rain. Perhaps he couldn't stay away forever, but tonight he would go see her. Their Majesties could wait, at least for a few hours.

CHAPTER 28

Freddie

Freddie blinked up at the dull, fluorescent light shining above her bed. Vague memories of waking several times earlier pulsed dully in the back of her mind—trying to remember hurt. The air had a stale, sterile smell. An IV trailed up from the bend in her arm to a bag of clear fluid. There was a line of six black stitches on her hand, a gauze bandage around her knee, and a brace on her ankle. She wiggled her foot and winced at the dull ache that radiated from beneath the brace. Goosebumps broke out across her arms, and she was suddenly all too aware of the thin blanket and hospital gown that covered her.

Beside the bed, slumped over the arm of an uncomfortable-looking sofa was Pelrin. His wings were neatly folded, and his golden hair fell in a sloppy mess across his face. Ginnith lay curled up atop the sofa's back. Freddie blinked, trying to remember why they were there, and, more importantly, why she was here. Memories flickered through her mind like nixies in a pond, flashes of clarity just out of reach.

On the table beside her bed was her laptop. With considerable difficulty, she managed to turn on the computer, wincing as pain shot through her hand. Her inbox was filled with messages. Almost all were from her mom, reminding Freddie to call her as soon as she found a phone and saying she loved her very much. Freddie smiled. The one message from her dad stated that he'd restocked her popcorn and replaced her waffle mix with a gluten-free version. She wanted to roll her eyes, but the pounding in her head reminded her not to. Even if she was too out of it to remember their visit this time, at least she would see them over Thanksgiving break. Which was in... Crap! Next week!

Changing tabs, Freddie clicked on a document titled "My Article." She skimmed it. Yikes, this is bad. Did I write this?

"You're not going to try and write again, are you?" Ginnith alighted beside Freddie on the under-stuffed pillow. She yawned and rubbed her eyes.

"I really wrote this?" Freddie frowned as she read over the line, "The vampire went poof because of the shoe."

"Amanda said not to give you the computer, but you were mad, and His Highness gave in."

"How long have I been here?" The clock on her PC told her it was near five in the morning.

"Three days. The human healer said it was shock that kept you out of it for so long."

Freddie bit her lip. She still needed to edit whatever this hot mess was and at least try to get it published.

"Amanda said not to let you stress out about this," Ginnith said.

Freddie's eyes widened. "Amanda! I forgot. Is she okay? Is she here? What happened?"

Ginnith scrunched her brows together. "Amanda also said not to let you freak out about that."

"If she's saying all this, I'm guessing she's fine." Freddie's eyes narrowed. "Tell me, Ginni, what happened?" On the sofa, Pelrin snorted in his sleep.

"Well, she's okay. She said she was going to come back after class." Freddie let out a breath and sank back onto the pillow. "His Highness got worried that night when we arrived at your room and you and everyone else were gone. He went to all these fae clubs because he said you liked places like that." Ginnith narrowed her eyes in an accusatory glare. Freddie shrugged and instantly regretted the way it made her stiff muscles ache. "When we saw the police lights outside of that last one, he asked what was going on. Then we saw Amanda wrapped in a blanket. There was also this snarling werewolf in the back of one of the police cars."

"The police came? But I lost my phone before I could tell them where I was." Freddie closed her eyes, trying to think back to exactly what she'd said to them. When she was little, she'd been told the police came even if you hung up on them, but she'd never thought to look into how they found you.

"Do I look like an expert on your human police?" the pixie snapped. "Amanda said you lured a vampire away so that she could escape. Is that true?"

"I think so," Freddie said. Everything that happened that night was such a blur.

"Well, that was stupid." Freddie and Ginnith both turned to see Pelrin sitting up on the sofa. "You should've staked him before you bled all over the place."

Freddie frowned at him and looked back at Ginnith. "What about the other kid? There was another kid with us, right?"

"He's fine. They brought him here with you. He complained a lot," she said.

"So he's better?" Freddie made to lift her hand to her head, but cringed against the pain. "How —"

"How are you feeling?" Pelrin combed his fingers through his hair and walked over to Freddie. "Humans really shouldn't go provoking vampires."

"Thanks, Pel. I'll keep that in mind for the next time Amanda and I are being chased by a crazed one," Freddie said. "What I don't get is how I got here. I vaguely remember stabbing the vampire with a... a shoe?" That couldn't be right. How could a shoe kill a vampire? "But there was someone else there, too. A faun?"

Pelrin grinned. "I took care of that little bugger. Though he was totally passed out when I got there. You must have tackled him pretty hard. But no one hurts my Freddie and gets away with it." He stroked her hair.

"You killed him?"

"No, I dropped him off with those police. Traded him for Raul. Don't worry Freddie; everyone's fine." He kissed her forehead.

Something about this was wrong. "Did Jefferson make it back okay?"

Pelrin nodded. "A few scrapes and a close call, but he's fine. He's home sleeping. Everything is fine. I've got to go check on a few things back home. Will you be all right if I leave you here?" He glanced out the window. The sun had yet to rise, but a lighter blue on the horizon hinted at its approach.

"I'll just work on my article," Freddie said.

He saluted her and Ginnith before wending away.

It took her two hours to get her article in a condition she was satisfied with. The headline now read "War in Fairy Hits the Human Realm—Over 200 Students Lost." It had taken her a few tries to get it to a point where it didn't sound like she was blaming the incompetent Easton police department or the biased FIDs, but Ginnith proved to be a very critical editor. If her finished product didn't make people think what was happening in Fairy was relevant, she didn't know what would.

She emailed it to Professor Radel, copying Mr. Barker. Though... it probably wasn't good enough to get published. She sighed. No doubt in the three days that passed hundreds of journalists had already covered this story.

By lunchtime, Freddie felt like a genie trapped in a lamp. She needed to get out of bed before she went crazy. The IV had drained, and she had to pee. Ginnith went to fetch a nurse. Several minutes later, a plump human woman in floral scrubs strolled casually into the room.

"You're feeling better?" Her tone indicated she really didn't care if Freddie was or not. Easton's hospital had been set up primarily for student use. The nurses were numb to the many injuries as a result of reckless, often alcohol-induced, behavior.

"Yeah, I feel fine. Can I go now?"

The nurse picked up the chart and flipped through it. "Okay, let me just get the doctor for your release papers. Doesn't look like there's anything too wrong with you." She narrowed her eyes, skimming down her clipboard. "Don't go thinking you're a hero just because some gold fae prince stopped you from getting taken." She gave Freddie a look as though it was somehow inconveniencing her life by having the audacity to take up a hospital bed.

It took an hour for the doctor to come and give her the final release papers and another hour for Freddie to shower in the awkward hospital bathroom, dress in the clothes Ginnith said Amanda had left for her, and find a shuttle to take her back to campus. Her ankle still hurt, but Freddie could put a little weight on it. She pulled the red hood of her jacket over her head as she limped off to English class. Ginnith sat in Freddie's backpack, empty but for the laptop Pelrin had brought for her.

English had started a little over ten minutes ago, but she figured being in the hospital was a pretty good excuse for being late. She tried to slip quietly into the back of the class, but Professor Radel was making another guest appearance, and her hawk-like radar spotted Freddie like a white rabbit on a golf course. Freddie braced herself for a telling-off, but instead, Professor Radel set aside her cane and clapped.

"This, class, is what a hard-working journalist looks like after she's made the front page." The rest of the class, save for Mallory, broke out into applause. Freddie looked around, bewildered.

"I don't understand. What front page? I just turned in my article this morning," Freddie said. Mallory glowered at her.

"Supernova, chica!" Mr. Barker said, slapping Freddie on the back. She winced. "Those sick lines you sent over this morning were so good that Bunny here sent them to the Inquirer."

"It passed through proofing and fact-checking this afternoon and is slated for the front page in the evening edition." Professor Radel didn't smile, but the slight twitch of her lip indicated that if she could, she would. Freddie opened and closed her mouth. "Of course, you were not the first to break this story, Miss Jones. However, the others who covered it were not able to piece together the dots so intricately to form the entire picture as you did. Your investigation was admirable, even if you did get a bit reckless at the end."

"Oh." Was all Freddie could think to say. She sat in her usual seat behind Mallory. How had everything gone from falling apart to put back together so neatly?

"I got my article published too, Professor," Mallory said and waved her hand in the air.

"Did you? I don't believe you submitted it to me first." Professor Radel turned to Mr. Barker who shrugged. "Well, show us, then."

Mallory pulled up a page on her laptop. "Here." She turned her computer around. Professor Radel leaned down to skim over the article. Freddie watched as the professor's expression turned from mild curiosity to red fury.

"Mallory, I believe the terms of this assignment were that you must get your article published in a reputable place. This is a tabloid." The woman straightened, and her fingers tightened around the head of her cane. "The article itself has no solid evidence and is at best an opinion piece."

Mallory crossed her arms. "But that's not fair. Are we just supposed to believe Freddie confronted the kidnappers? She could have made everything up. Where's the proof?"

"The proof has been gathered by the police and fact-checkers all morning, which is what happens at real publishers."

"Mine could have been fact-checked too," Mallory said. Her voice was a high-pitched whine.

"Miss Sheppard, the article beneath yours is titled, 'The President is a Were-ape: How He Keeps His Secret.' As incredible as it would be to have our first fae president, he is unfortunately still only human."

"He hasn't presented a birth certificate!" Mallory got to her feet. Her face was red, and her knuckles were white as they gripped the front of her desk.

"Enough, Miss Sheppard. I'll give you two weeks to write a real article and get it published. My office hours, of course, are open to you."

Mallory shrieked. She slammed her computer shut, threw it in her bag, and stormed out of the room. Freddie hid a smug grin as she watched Mallory go. Some of her other classmates burst into not-so-discreet giggles as the girl's footsteps faded down the hall.

After class, Professor Radel pulled Freddie aside. "The Inquirer also has offered you a paid internship. Usually, this is an opportunity reserved only for juniors in the upper school. You should be proud."

"They have? That's incredible! What would I have to do?"

"Five high-quality articles per semester. It's a pretty big ask, but I would be willing to coach you. Nothing goes to the Inquirer without going through me first, understand?"

"Yes, thank you!" Freddie's fingers trembled with anticipation.

She couldn't wait to tell her parents. Perhaps her father would even tell Mr. Fallus to shove it now that he didn't have to worry about her expenses for next year — though probably not. She should feel as though she could drift up to the Air Realm, yet something weighed her down.

"Impressive work, Miss Jones. We'll make a real journalist out of you yet."

The remainder of Freddie's classes were not nearly as exciting. Mostly her teachers piled on study packets for midterms — she groaned as she flipped through the Calc packet. Ginnith bounced on her shoulder as she walked back to her dorm. It felt so strange how things had snapped back to normal, but still, there was something aching in the hollow of her chest. As wonderful as everything was, it was as though something was missing.

"Oh my God, Freddie. Tell me you did not go to class," Amanda yelled from across the Bailey. She charged, a flattened cardboard box flapping awkwardly at her side, her eyes narrowing in an accusatory glare.

"I was bored," Freddie said and backed away.

"You need to be in bed. Your Mom's been calling me like every five minutes to make sure you rest. Ginnith, I thought I told you not to let her worry about things like class. She just got out of the hospital."

"I didn't!" Ginnith leapt off Freddie's shoulder to buzz in front of Amanda. "She was worried about not going to class, so we went."

"Amanda, are you making Ginnith babysit me now too?" Freddie sighed.

Amanda laughed. "You could use a babysitter with the trouble you get into, Freddie Jones."

"You were there, too," she said, pointing an accusatory finger at her friend. "Besides, next time we'll be better prepared."

"Haha. Oh, Fred. There will be no 'we' next time." Amanda walked toward the dorm, Freddie following alongside her. She turned the silver band on her finger, her stomach twisting along with the ring.

"Oh, come on, that was a fun adventure." Freddie's logical mind told her she was being sarcastic, though her inner journalist — the little part of her brain that would snoop into anything to find out the truth — was serious.

Freddie and Amanda said goodbye to Ginnith just outside the door. Apparently, she had business to attend to in Fairy but would be back soon to check-in.

When the girls got to Freddie's room, Amanda told her everything that happened after they separated. Amanda too had made good use of her shoe by throwing it at the werewolf's legs and tripping her up. It had given her and the turtle-boy just enough time to make a mad dash for the police, who'd arrived in force outside the club.

"That was good thinking, dialing 911. They said they were able to trace your phone to the general vicinity, but couldn't tell which building we were in," Amanda said.

Freddie bit her lip. On a normal day, being without her phone would have driven her mad. It was probably still somewhere in that office building or buried in some evidence locker at the police station. Today, however, she was distracted by the pain in her chest — she pushed it away with all the other nagging thoughts of Aiden. "I'm just glad you were able to get away okay. What about turtle-dude?"

"He cried like a baby when the police turned up. They took him to the hospital with you, but his parents had him transferred to a specialty facility in New Wall." Amanda shrugged. "Rich people."

When Amanda finished her story, Freddie told hers. Amanda listened with rapt attention, occasionally letting out little gasps when Freddie would say something like "there was blood everywhere" or "I could practically smell the vampire."

"One thing I still don't understand, though, is how I managed to kill a vampire with a shoe. I mean, doesn't it have to be wood?" Freddie tried to replay the scene in her head.

Amanda grinned. "Those shoes were the Louboutins Jefferson got me. The heels are made of wood."

"Cute and deadly?" Freddie laughed.

Amanda placed a hand beneath her chin. "That's me!"

By the time they'd finished their stories, it was dark. A knock at the door sent confused looks flitting across their faces. Before Amanda could fully open the door Pelrin pushed his way inside, followed by Jefferson and Raul.

"Surprise! We got Chinese!" Raul said as he bounded over to the couch.

"See, Freddie? I knocked, just like you wanted." Pelrin stuck out his chest.

"Now if you could only wait until I invited you in, you'd be positively respectful." Freddie stretched out her hands for the box of lo mein Raul had begun opening.

Jefferson took a seat on the couch beside Amanda. He looked as though he was trying very hard not to be sick so close to the garlicky food. Raul jumped up from the sofa to wrap Freddie in a tight hug. She yelped as he rocked her back, causing pain to shoot through her hand, knee, and ankle.

"So sorry, Fred. I owe you big time for what you did for me. I doubt I can ever repay you," he said. He bounced over to the new cardboard coffee table and handed her a fork. Pelrin sat beside Freddie on the bed.

"Chinese food and waffles, Raul. That's all I ask." Freddie dug into the noodles, eating as though she hadn't seen food in weeks. The taste brought back the memory of her last date with Aiden. She shoved more food into her mouth. It wouldn't help anyone to dwell on thoughts of him...

"Isn't anyone going to ask me how I got my crown back?" Pelrin said. He dunked a dumpling in sauce and popped it in his mouth.

"You mean how we got it back, Pel?" Jefferson laughed as Pelrin frantically fanned the steam pouring out of his mouth.

"Tell us, Jefferson," Amanda said. Freddie and Raul twisted to face him.

"Well, let's see. When I saw you all at the club, I was really worried we were going to lose. Things were not going well, and I think Aiden suspected me." Jefferson rubbed his shoulder, his brow creased as if remembering something painful.

Freddie stiffened. The hollow place in her chest throbbed, and she took several more bites, hoping to make it stop. "The crown was under some serious wards—his wards. I think they might have even been stronger than yours, Pel."

"Whoa now, let's not get carried away. My wards are plenty strong. Summer hasn't fallen yet, has it?"

"No one is saying you're weak, Pelrin," Freddie said.

Amanda leaned in close to Jefferson. "What was he like, this Aiden? Was he scary and cruel? Did he hurt you?"

"He was..." Jefferson paused.

Freddie held her breath, not sure if she wanted to hear the answer. Aiden had pretty much told her he would never see her again, yet something begged for her friends to like him. If they did, there could be some sliver of hope that things between her and Aiden might be okay... maybe.

"He wasn't like the others. He didn't try to be scary or cruel. Though a few of them weren't half bad." Jefferson glanced over at Pelrin and cleared his throat. "I'm just saying, there was one time he even saved my life. Good thing I'm not a fairy, huh? Don't want to serve him forever." Everyone laughed. Freddie tried to keep her cheery expression from slipping.

"So, he was normal?" Amanda cocked her head to the side.

"He was just serious all the time. I don't think he could laugh if his life depended on it. And believe me, I tried."

Sadness twinged Freddie's heart. She put down the lo mein and inched away from Pelrin.

"I heard he's doing the dirty with both Mab and Oberon. Poor guy's probably too exhausted to laugh." Pelrin snickered while Jefferson and Raul gave hesitant smiles.

"That's gross, Pel. Really uncalled for," Freddie said. Amanda nodded.

"Sorry, I was just trying to lighten the mood. And he deserves it."

The words she'd overheard in the abandoned office came back to her. They'd said Oberon and Mab would make him wish Pelrin had killed him. What did they plan to do? What had they already done?

"After weeks of watching and analyzing, Pel and I finally came up with a plan to lure him away from the crown and break down his wards."

"Let me tell this part!" Pelrin cut in. Jefferson rolled his eyes. "You see, Jefferson lured him to this forest on the border of Summer and Autumn. I was practically alone, and he had his army to protect him."

Raul's eyes grew wide as he leaned over Freddie to stare at Pelrin.

"Pelrin had me and two of his best fighters," Jefferson said in an unamused tone. "Aiden also had two fighters. They were more than evenly matched."

"Fine, whatever. You're ruining my story."

"Just keeping you honest, Pel." Jefferson shook his head.

"Anyways, he took out my fighters, but not before they were able to take out his. That's when I pounced. We fought an epic battle in that forest, him with his magic and me with my blade. When I finally wore him down enough to fire an arrow, he wended away like a coward. A full day passed before anyone saw him. More than enough time to steal the crown, get Jefferson back over the border, and gather my army to reconquer the cities he took."

Freddie's stomach clenched with guilt. Aiden had wended to her; it'd been Pelrin who had shot him. If he had died that night... She closed her eyes, not wanting to think of what she would do if Pelrin had killed Aiden.

"I say let's go out and celebrate! How about it, Fred?" Pelrin took her hand gently in his and turned the intensity of his crystal blue gaze on her.

Freddie shook her head. "I'm really tired. You go out. Have fun."

"I won't take no for an answer." Pelrin tugged her arm, trying to pull her off the bed. Freddie cried out and pointed to her leg. "I'm so sorry, Freddie. I forgot."

"Freddie needs her rest, guys. She just got out of the hospital." Amanda got off the couch and moved to inspect Freddie's stitches. "Stay here and relax. Do you want me to keep you company?"

"Thanks, Amanda, but I'm okay. I think I just need some sleep."

Pelrin's shoulders sagged as he walked over to the couch and placed a hand on Raul's shoulder. Jefferson rose to stand beside them. "Don't look so glum, boys. We can go out on the weekend when Freddie's feeling better. The girls have homework and midterms coming up anyway, so let's have a boys' night."

"Don't you have finals, Raul?" Freddie asked.

Raul grinned sheepishly. "Yeah, in like two weeks. I have plenty of time to study later."

Amanda rolled her eyes. "You boys have fun."

"Are you going to be all right if I go out with them tonight?" Pelrin took a step toward Freddie.

"Pel, we're just friends," she said. It felt as though she were speaking around something hard in her throat. "You are free to do whatever you like. Don't worry about me. I'm moving on."

Pelrin's gaze turned stoney. "I'll win you back, Freddie. I promise I'll find a way."

Freddie cringed.

"I know what I did was terrible, and I can't ever say sorry

enough but… Please, don't shut me out of your life. Let me earn my second chance."

"We are just friends, Pel," Freddie repeated. Her chest tightened as she said it. "That's all I want." What she really wanted was for Pelrin to have never cheated on her in the first place. Then she wouldn't feel so torn about letting him go. But it was the right thing to do. Even if she couldn't have Aiden, clinging on to Pelrin would only hold her back from becoming a journalist.

His eyes danced as he looked up at her. "That's good enough, for now."

The three boys trooped out of the room. Raul waved to her as they left. Amanda gave her a quick hug, grabbed her purse, and followed after them.

When Freddie was alone, she changed into her comfy sweats and curled into a ball on her bed. The stitches on her hand throbbed in painful beats, keeping time with the rhythm of her heart. Could Aiden be facing a fate worse than death right now? She was supposed to be happy; her friends had won. It wasn't like Aiden was her boyfriend. They'd only been on two dates, three if you counted his surprise visit to her parents' house. Pain tugged at her chest at the thought of how he came to her when he thought he was going to die. The notion sent chills down her spine.

Freddie laid on her bed for an hour until a soft knock on the door pulled her out of the tumultuous crap storm her brain had been brewing. When she didn't immediately answer, the knock sounded again. So it isn't Pelrin. She unfurled herself, limped over to the door, and opened it.

"Aiden," she gasped.

Aiden stood in the doorway; his black hair was plastered to his face, and his Dark Fae uniform clung tight against his body. Freddie's eyes widened, lips slightly parted, as he dripped on the floor. All day she'd fought back the fear he was somewhere hurt or dead, believing she'd never see him again. Aiden stared back at her, as if he were stranded on a deserted island and she was the first fresh water he'd seen in days.

CHAPTER 29

Aiden

Now that he stood before her, all the things Aiden had planned to say fled his mind. He drank her in: the way her curls tumbled about haphazardly to frame her heart-shaped face, the amazingly human scent of food and clean linen that rolled off her, and the breathiness in her voice as she gasped his name. There was nothing cold or hateful in her brown eyes. Nothing that told him to stay away.

"Aiden," she said again.

He swallowed and took a step closer. She closed the remaining distance between them. For one perfect moment, they stood so close the heat of her body seeped through the thick, wet leather of his uniform. His gaze trailed to her lips. Her hand reached up to cup his cheek and, with fervent need, he pulled her to him.

Aiden sucked in a slow, desperate breath. This was nothing like the tense awkwardness of their first kiss. She wrapped an arm around his neck, pulling him inside. He held her close, savoring the feeling of her body against his. Somehow, they'd switched places. She pushed him back, running her hands through his hair, down his back. And their lips always together, his tongue flicking along her lower lip and grazing her teeth. He stumbled against something hard and toppled backward onto the bed, her crashing on top of him. They broke apart panting, a pained grimace painting her lips.

"What's wrong?" He searched her face for any hint of something he'd done. Perhaps he'd misread her actions, that she didn't truly want him here.

Wincing, she leaned back and pointed at her leg. "I'm a little busted up. I forgot, for a moment, but now…" Wyn stifled a cry as she lifted her booted leg onto the bed.

"Let me help." Aiden dropped to one knee and undid the bandage at her knee. Three black stitches had been sewn into her skin, binding her injury together. He grimaced. *Was this what constituted for human healing?* He pressed his lips to her wound. For a moment, the skin around the stitches glowed blue against the surrounding brown. When the color faded, the black thread fell to the floor.

Wyn gasped. "That's incredible." She hastily removed her boot. A choked cry escaped her lips as her foot came free.

Again, he kissed her and she held out her palm for another kiss. "Better?"

"Much. Thank you." Wyn ran a hand through Aiden's thick, black hair. He closed his eyes and tipped his head back. This was more than he could have hoped for.

"Wyn," he breathed.

She rolled to the side and sat upright beside him. "Yes?"

Aiden shook his head. "I just wanted to say it, your name. Wyn," he said again.

"Aiden," she said.

A smile spread across his lips, and he let several seconds pass, his mind replaying the sound of his name on her tongue. Finally, he sighed and sat up. Their Majesties would be furious. He needed to return. But how much more vexed could they be if he stayed for a little while longer? Say, until midnight? With the thrill of his defiance blazing in his chest, he slowly met her eyes.

"What happened to you?"

"Oh, you know, me and vampires." She shrugged and flashed a grin at him.

He smiled hesitantly. Perhaps this was one of her jests. If any vampire dared attack her, he'd hunt them down and... Silver flashed on her finger. His mother's ring winked at him, pulling him away from his violent thoughts. At least for tonight, he could pretend everything was all right, that this normal could last.

Aiden opened his mouth to speak, then closed it. The minutes ticked by in thick silence as he tried to think of the perfect thing to say. "I have ruined your bed," he said at last. *What in the seven realms was that supposed to mean?* Aiden cursed himself. He had dreamed of spending this time alone with her, and now *that* was the only thing he could think of.

"I have some extra sweats if you want to change," she said, eyeing his wet clothes. "I'm not sure if my sweatshirt will fit you though."

"I—" Aiden stopped.

He was about to say he didn't need to change, that he had more than enough power to dry his own. But their Majesties would be able to find him faster if he kept using his magic.

Besides, it wouldn't be the same. They wouldn't smell like her. He could be human, just for tonight.

"Thank you," he said, choking out the awkward, human phrase.

Wyn raised an eyebrow. She rose from the bed and walked over to the closet, wobbling on her newly healed ankle. Aiden wandered the small room. He prodded the flimsy box she used for a table, wishing he could give her something better. She turned around, clutching something soft and gray in her hands.

"They're mine," Wyn said, pressing the bundle into his outstretched arms. "I got the wrong size and never got around to returning them."

"They're perfect." He bowed his head and hugged the clothing close to his chest. Tonight, he would give her normal, and then he would go and face whatever hand fate dealt him.

"You're not leaving soon, are you?" Her voice cracked as she spoke.

Aiden swallowed hard. The pain in her voice stung like a pixie bite. It surprised him how much it hurt. "I don't want to leave," he said.

Her lips tightened; she could see through his fairy lies. Aiden examined the soft gray pants. They were just like the ones she wore, with the letters "N" and "W" printed in yellow and blue on the hip. Wyn turned her back to him as he shed his sopping leathers and changed into the comfortable pants. He stripped off his shirt and jerkin too; there was no need to hide his wings from her.

When he'd finished, she turned back around. "My God, you're beautiful."

Aiden's wing stubs fluttered. He flicked his eyes to the glowing clock in the corner. They had two whole hours of normal. Wyn wrapped an arm around his neck. He bowed his head to breathe in her scent, sliding his other hand around her waist. Heat rose up from his stomach as she placed slow deliberate kisses along his jaw, tracing her way back to his lips.

Somehow, he lost his fingers in her curls. A low groan stirred in his throat. Her arms were around his neck, then down his back, stroking the oh so sensitive part of his body where wings met flesh. He kissed her back, hard, trying to communicate his complicated tangle of fear and desire into her lips. He hadn't realized they'd moved across the room until she fell back against the bed, and their lips parted.

"Seasons, Wyn," he gasped. He fell sideways to land beside her, his heartbeat humming in his ears.

Wyn's eyes darted from his face downward. Aiden moved closer, but she placed a hand on his chest.

"I'm not—" Her fingers curled against his skin, and there was a look of timid fear in her eyes he'd never seen before. It was a far cry from the fear she'd shown on their first date, her expression hinting at something deeper. "Not tonight, okay?"

He pulled back. Swallowing hard, he looked away and sat up, gripping the edge of the bed. "Do you wish for me to go?"

"No." The strained note in her voice made him turn back around. She'd pulled her knees to her chest and stared down at her bare feet. "Stay?"

Aiden stared at her, his lips pursed together. The fear in her eyes intensified. He sucked in a breath and bowed his head, letting it out slowly. Wyn placed a hand on his knee. He stared at it for a long moment.

"I'm sorry," she whispered.

Aiden shook his head. "Don't be." He met her gaze, hating that look on her face. Leaning forward, he cupped her face and kissed the corner of her mouth. She let out a breath, and her lips quirked ever so slightly upward.

"Don't go back," she said. "Please."

"I must. If I don't, they will send soldiers after me."

She sat up and moved to lean against the wall. He joined her, cramming himself into the small remaining space. They were so close, touching with nothing but the soft fabric of their clothing between them. "You are stronger than anyone they could send, right? Couldn't you just fight them off?"

"And when Mab or Oberon themselves show up to reclaim me?"

He clenched his fists. He was their Majesties' most powerful weapon—they'd never come close to defeating Summer without him. The elation from the kiss faded as the cold reality of his servitude slammed back into him. Weariness settled on his shoulders. He could never have anything with Wyn. His life wasn't his own to share, no matter how much he might want to. Would it be like this for the next six-hundred-odd years? Never letting himself feel for fear of it ripping him apart? Aiden buried his head in his hands. Wyn's body pressed into his side, her head resting on his shoulder. He should go. They would be furious with him for ignoring their order.

"Would you like to hear the tale of how I fought off a vampire with a hairpin and a shoe?"

Aiden lifted his head. "You are serious?"

"Oh yes." She nodded solemnly. "It's going to be in the paper and everything."

He slid down the wall until he lay flat on the bed, staring up at the ceiling. A little bit longer wouldn't make too much of a difference. "Tell me your tale then, dear maid."

CHAPTER 30

Freddie

Freddie woke, wishing she had listened all those times her mother had lectured her on the need for curtains. Sunlight blinded her as it streamed in through the dorm window. She felt around to pull the blanket over her head, but her hand met warm flesh. Someone stirred. Freddie squinted, allowing her eyes to adjust to the bright light. Aiden, shirtless and gorgeous, lay next to her, his face relaxed in peaceful sleep. She sucked in a breath. He smelled of tulips and fresh grass even first thing in the morning. A tendril of black hair fell across his face, and she lifted a hand to brush it away.

Aiden's hand shot up to grip her wrist in an iron-like hold. She yelped as his fae strength pressed into her brittle, human bones. He opened his eyes and instantly loosened his grip, pulling her wrist close to kiss it. Freddie closed her eyes, letting the sunlight wash over her face, the pain fading beneath his lips. Last night had been perfect, almost normal. They had fallen asleep after she told him how she'd tracked down the kidnapper and staked the vampire with Amanda's heel. Aiden had been awed and praised her bravery, while Pelrin had just said she'd been stupid.

Now, Aiden yawned. Stretching, he sat up. Freddie tried to comb her fingers through the tangled mess that was her hair but gave up. This was going to take more than fingers to undo. She inched her hand toward Aiden's, wanting to trace its outline on her bed, but he withdrew it suddenly.

She looked up. The color drained from Aiden's face as he stared out the window, the soft light of dawn only making him appear even more ashen.

"I must go," he said and leapt to his feet.

"Is everything all right?" She knew he had to return, but surely it would take them at least a few days to find him. He could stay a little longer. Couldn't he?

Aiden searched the room, gathering up his shirt and jerkin. He shoved them on and squeezed into his shrunken leather pants. "I should have been back hours ago."

Freddie's heart pounded in her ears. She walked around the bed to where he stood in front of the couch. "They're not going to kill you, right? Promise me."

He kissed her, a mere brush of his lips against hers.

A roaring rose in Freddie's ears, drowning out all other sounds but his voice. "That wasn't an answer. Please, Aiden, promise me."

He looked at her, golden eyes filled with sorrow. "You know I can't do that."

"What can I do then? There has to be a spell or something that will get you out of this."

He ran a calloused hand down her cheek. "There is nothing you can do for me." He pressed his forehead against hers. Warm tears trickled down Freddie's cheeks. "I will have to face what's coming." He sucked in a breath. Freddie gripped the front of his shirt with both hands. "I'm not sure if I can come back, but… " His voice trembled.

Freddie grit her teeth. Something inside her chest snapped, and she turned her head away.

"Aiden, I'm not going to wait for you." Every word felt as though she were carving it out of her heart. Telling the stories of those beyond the wall, that was what was important. She couldn't spend her life searching for a way to break Aiden's curse, no matter how much she might want to.

"Don't," he said. "I would not ask you to live your life for me. Besides, someone has to help those whom I condemn."

Freddie looked up. Her mouth opened and shut. He remembered her passion, her career. Finally, the words came to her. "I'll miss you. Please come back… If you can."

"I promise." Aiden bent to kiss her one last time. Freddie tried to press her tangle of incomprehensible feelings out through her lips so he would understand.

He pulled away. "Be safe, Wyn. Try not to do too much vampire fighting." His lopsided smile didn't quite meet his eyes.

"Goodbye, Aiden. Be safe." She took a step back, swallowing down the dull pain in the back of her throat.

Aiden bowed and wended away, leaving a hollow emptiness in his wake.

Freddie walked back over to her bed and pulled her knees to her chest. She'd gotten everything she'd wanted; her friends were happy, she had a shot at becoming a real journalist, and Aiden had given her a normal relationship, at least for one night. It would hurt for a while. It had hurt after Pelrin too, but she would get past this.

Freddie's phone buzzed. Amanda wanted to come over and study. Warmth fluttered in her chest. With her internship, she could write tons of articles on how the war impacted the Human Realm. As a writer for the *Inquirer*, people would actually take notice, maybe even try to get involved.

And when it was over, when the war had ended, and the dust settled… maybe there was a sliver of hope that everything would be okay for her and Aiden.

Maybe they could try again.

Ann Dayleview

Ann Dayleview writes fantasy novels which aim to transport the reader to worlds unlike any other. She reads any young adult and middle grade fantasy novel she can get her hands on. Her writing is often inspired by the wild assortment of music she listens to. Everything from classical to pop and beyond!

In addition to writing, Ann loves spending time with her two dogs, baking all the sweet things, and bringing awareness about taking care of your mental health. She lives in Pennsylvania with her ever-rotating collection of books she lugs from place to place.

Visit her online:

www.anndayleview.com

Social: @anndayleview

Glossary

Fairy – The land separated from the Human Realm by invisible borders accessible in specific locations in the Human Realm. Fairy is the homeland of the green, brown, and gold fae.

The Dark Fae Army (Dark Fae) – These rebel forces led by Mab and Oberon who've crowned themselves Queen and King of the brown fae. They seek to overthrow the gold fae rulers of the Seasonal Realms.

The Seasonal Realms – Summer, Winter, Autumn, and Spring are the four Seasonal Realms that make up Fairy.

The Sea Realm – The Sea Realm encompasses all of the magic of the oceans. It expands between Fairy and the Human Realm.

The Air Realm – Similar to the Sea Realm, the Air Realm encompasses everything in the sky. It is also said to be home to dragons.

The Human Realm – This is home to the humans and red fae. It borders Fairy and polices the crossing locations.

Blue Fae – The mythical and most powerful of all the fae. They are marked by their blue wings and have been known to grant the wishes of humans.

Gold Fae – Rulers of Fairy, the gold fae are incredibly powerful. They are marked by their gold wings.

Green Fae – These are magic-using natives of Fairy. Some examples include genies, fairies, and leprechauns.

Brown Fae – Non-magic-using natives of Fairy. Some examples include dwarves, goblins, and fauns.

Red Fae – These are closely related to humans but are supernatural in nature. Some examples include vampires, werewolves, and banshees.

Sundiva – A type of green fae who have immense power over fire. They have large feathered wings and are rumored to have lava instead of blood.

Drekavac – Derived from Slavic mythology, these brown fae are humanoid with disproportionally large, bald heads and are thought to be the souls of dead children.

Undine – These green fae are derived from the writings of Paracelsus. Also known as water nymphs, undines call the Sea Realm home.

Mare – Derived from Germanic folklore, this green fae is traditionally a creature who rides on people's chests and brings them nightmares.

Anansi – These rare red fae live in Fairy. They are half spider and half human and are said to feed on "flesh".

Satyr – A bipedal green fae with the torso of a human and the lower half of a goat. They also have large ram's horns and pointed ears. Satyrs can use their magic flute to compel people to follow them.

Faun – These are brown fae, similar to satyrs, but with much smaller horns and no magical abilities.

Minotaur – Inspired by Greek mythology, these brown fae have the head of a bull and the body of a human.

Garuda – Inspired by Hindu mythology these brown fae are native to the Air Realm and have a mix of human and eagle features.

Naga – Inspired by Hindu mythology, these brown fae have the tale of a snake and the torso and head of a human.

Marid – Inspired by Islamic mythology, these green fae are humanoid with blue skin and power over water.

Anubis – Inspired by the Egyptian god, these rare red fae have the heads of jackals and the bodies of humans. They give off an energy preventing people from lying in their presence.

Wili- Inspired by Russian folklore, these red fae are veiled, graceful women. They are spirits with a reputation for dragging philandering men to watery graves.

Ifrits – Inspired by Islamic folklore, these green fae have power over fire, though often not as powerful as sundivas.

CPSIA information can be obtained
at www.ICGtesting.com
Printed in the USA
LVHW040918210421
685101LV00006B/673

9 781736 370513